T. WRECKS

MURDER IN THE
GEOLOGY DEPARTMENT

A PROFESSOR CANDREW NOR MYSTERY BY
Colin Barker

To David and Cheryl
— hope you enjoy it

T. Wrecks - Murder In The Geology Department
Copyright © 2017 by Colin Barker

Book Design by Molly Bradbury

First Printing: 2017
First Edition: 2017

ISBN-13: 978-1542550567
ISBN-10: 1542550564

Acknowledgements

No book is written in isolation and I have benefited from the comments and help of many people. Early motivation came from Chris Liner, Teresa Miller, Gill Bockmeulen, and Lynn Stegner. I especially appreciated the help and encouragement of my local writing group that included Marigay Grana, Bruce Moss, Charlie Romney Brown, Tori Shepard, Joan Baker, and Margaret Mooney. I thank them all.

My wife Yvonne patiently put up with my hours at the computer. And the book was written under the watchful eyes of my dog Chile.

Prologue

Gavin had faced this challenge many times. As he settled into the kayak, pushing away from the bank, the Green River was smooth, almost oily, reflecting the clear blue of the August sky, although just a short distance downstream it would break into the confused chaos of the rapids. Even now he could hear the dull featureless roar—white water, white noise. He handled the kayak easily, expertly, guiding it slightly to the left, taking advantage of the current.

One of the great rivers of the west, the Green is born near the continental divide in the Wind River Mountains, spends its youth in Wyoming, middle age in Utah and expires, pouring its energy into the muddy Colorado. Along the way it meanders through wide meadows and narrow rock canyons and tumbles through turbulent cataracts. Over the years Gavin Citalli had run most of these and today felt the usual mind-focusing intensity of anticipation as he braced for the struggle with the boiling waters called Three Fords. Skill honed by fifteen years running the rapids on western rivers had given him confidence, and he faced the challenge with exhilaration. He dipped the paddle in on the right to correct his approach slightly and set up the best line into the rapid.

Concentrating intensely, he hardly noticed the splatter of cold water as the kayak slipped into the first standing wave. The water was piling up against the rock dead ahead and cascading off to one side. Gavin thrust the broad paddle in the current to the left of the kayak and with a slight backward stroke checked his motion and let the flow pull him around. Immediately, the kayak slewed sideways needing a quick thrust forward to control the erratic movement in the churning white water. This was the challenge he relished, this mixture of physical strength and swift decision making. He'd been through these rapids several times before, and even though not particularly challenging, they were difficult enough to be interesting. Where the bigger waves pounded the rocks, they kicked up spray and the sunlight made shimmering bits of rainbows that played in the mist, showing brightly against the dark canyon walls. He loved it all.

A short, smooth section of the rapids led into a towering wall of water. When he dropped into the hole in front of it, aiming for a route between huge water-smoothed boulders, his kayak started to roll. Somehow that didn't seem too important. It was almost as though everything was happening in slow motion. Normally, he would gulp for air, quickly complete the roll, and be back in control. This time he made only a half-hearted attempt to right the capsizing boat, but failed. It hardly seemed worth the effort. As the kayak was swept upside-down, a large underwater rock knocked him out of the hull and he was carried down into the deeply scoured base of the channel. Here the fast moving current rolled him over and momentarily pinned him against a submerged granite slab. His mind screamed for him to strike out for the surface. Leaden limbs showed little sign of responding. A minute might have gone by, but it could have been ten. He didn't know. Time had lost any meaning, it seemed to be passing lethargically. The sharp thump as his shoulder hit another rock barely registered and he was hardly aware of the darkness in the deep water. The flowing water swept his compliant body through the chute and bounced him over more angular rocks. Eventually the eddying river floated him toward the surface and the sunlight, but even though the water got lighter, for Gavin it was getting steadily darker and finally it was black.

The unique genetic mix that was Professor Citalli, the respected teacher and researcher with curly hair and gray eyes, and a husband called Gavin, no longer existed.

T. Wrecks

Chapter 1

It's always difficult to accept a purely accidental death, to accept a world without design or logic. There has to be a reason; we need somewhere to lay blame. Candrew Nor, Professor of Geology, had spent his whole career in science. He'd learned how to look for inconsistencies and expose flaws in logic, and had developed an intuitive feel for when things weren't right. Now he felt uneasy.

For the past fifteen years Gavin Citalli had spent his summers researching fossils in the Four Corners area, where Arizona and New Mexico meet Colorado and Utah. And he'd taken every opportunity to float the western rivers. Candrew had been impressed by Gavin's strength and river skills—and by his caution. As close friends, they'd often run rapids together. With so much white-water experience, why hadn't he been able to control his kayak in a simple rapid? Could he really have been knocked unconscious when he wore the best protective headgear? No, accidental drowning seemed an unlikely explanation. It didn't have the ring of truth.

Now Candrew was seated at the end of a pew in the university chapel beside his close friend Renata Alcantara. He tried to focus his attention on the university chaplain who, although a respected theological scholar, droned on in a near monotone. Candrew squirmed on the hard wooden bench, feeling uncomfortable in his dark gray suit, one that was fashionable fifteen years earlier and now a little too tight. Like most geologists, he was more at ease in jeans and tee shirt than jacket and tie.

He glanced around at the congregation, and after twenty years on the faculty most were familiar. But not the heavy-set man with a shaggy moustache seated alone in the back row. He didn't give the impression of a typical staff member. Physical Plant maybe? While trying not to be too obvious, Candrew watched the stranger systematically scan the church goers. The man seemed a lot more interested in the people than the service itself.

Candrew rose with the rest of the mourners for the next hymn. Light from the arched, stained-glass windows filtered into the flower-filled church and somber voices joined the swelling organ music. He'd not been in a church since Penny's funeral over six years ago and now overwhelming memories came flooding back. While he'd learned to cope with his wife's absence in the things he did every day, it was the unusual that caught him off guard. Sometimes, letting enough time go by erases recollections— but those are only the shallow ones. Memories of Penny bubbled up into consciousness when he least expected them, triggered by an odd event, a phrase, even a smell. It had been wrenching to watch the wife he loved deteriorate over the months, fade and die as he stood by helplessly. At least Marge Citalli had not had to go through that. Now she stood half a dozen rows in front and seemed to be stoically making this difficult rite of passage. Beside her, a tall, auburn-haired woman, presumably her sister, appeared to be providing both the physical and psychological support she needed. Candrew had been surprised to see Marge wearing a hat, but was not at all surprised by the dark glasses.

Another hymn and a final prayer ended the service and the

mourners spilled out of the chapel, blinking in the bright summer light. Renata, herself a professor at the university, held Candrew's arm as they walked through the thick-walled doorway. Explaining she needed to get back to her office and finish a report, she gave him a peck on the cheek and left.

The heavily buttressed adobe Chapel of Saint Cecelia glowed in the early afternoon sun, sharply outlined against the intense cobalt sky with dark shadows from the protruding vigas etched diagonally across the ochre walls. Built seventy years earlier, the chapel was one of the oldest buildings at the University of Northern New Mexico. Originally it had stood in serene isolation on the southern edge of campus, but an expanding university had encroached on three sides. Even subjects like computer science that didn't exist when the chapel was constructed, now had new buildings that edged up to the low adobe wall surrounding the small cemetery. A broad flagstone plaza stretched out in front of the huge buttresses and heavy wooden chapel doors. Here, small scattered groups talked in subdued voices of the uncertainty of life and the unpredictability of death.

Marge struggled to keep back the tears as she faced—for the first time alone—old friends, colleagues and the merely dutiful. "I still can't believe it really happened. He had so much experience with kayaks; he was always so careful. The park ranger told me fifteen million people floated rivers last year—why was it Gavin who died?"

Candrew joined the group and struggled to find the right words, or any words, but all he could do was to take her hand and simply say, "I'm so sorry, Marge. If there's anything I can do, anything at all." Feeling he needed to say more, he added charitably, "I thought the chaplain did a nice job of the eulogy." Candrew agreed with all the chaplain had said, especially his remarks on life's major transitions. It was just that for Gavin they'd come too soon.

"This is my sister, Anne." Marge introduced the dark-haired woman who had stood beside her in the chapel. She had bright lively eyes and gave Candrew a friendly smile. He felt certain this was a younger sister. Marge turned and forced a smile as the university provost and the dean came over to offer their condolences while Anne stood quietly to the side, looking uneasy and very much an outsider. She was here to give her sister support, but in this group Marge didn't seem to need it and appeared relaxed, or perhaps *resigned* was the proper word.

"Would you want to meet some of Gavin's colleagues?" Candrew asked.

Anne turned and nodded. "Yes. I'd like that." She appeared to appreciate being rescued from an uncomfortable situation. "I'm surprised we haven't met before. Last time I came to see Gavin and Marge was in the summer and you were away."

"Yeah. I'm usually gone for most of June and July doing field work."

They strolled in silence for a moment. "It's strange to be here without Gavin," Anne said. "I feel numb. He was so outgoing and enthusiastic. And I worry about Marge coping without him. She's way too young to be a widow. I'm afraid she's in for a rough time."

Candrew knew that from personal experience. "Marge was so helpful and comforting when Penny, my wife, was ill. Don't know what I'd have done without her. I hope I can be just as comforting."

After walking a few steps, Anne abruptly stopped. "I've been concerned about Marge for several months now. You were a very close friend, I know I can confide in you." She grasped his arm and turned to face him. "Whenever I phoned, she sounded depressed, agitated. That wasn't like her." Anne took a deep breath and peered directly at Candrew. "She always said everything was okay, but clearly it wasn't. You knew them well, did you notice anything unusual, particularly in the last few months?"

"No. But then I've been away almost all summer." He pursed

4

his lips, hesitated and said, "Now that I think about it, so has Gavin. He seems to have been doing a lot more field work than usual."

Candrew tapped on his front teeth with his forefinger, a sure sign he was puzzled. "Let me ask around, talk to some of the grad students, see if they've noticed anything. I'll do it discretely."

Anne and Candrew sauntered over to a group of Gavin's faculty colleagues and graduate students from the geology department. A round of handshaking and a barrage of welcoming noises followed although the students stood in silence. Fully two-thirds of the geologists had beards and most sported rich suntans. Almost as a counterpoint, a few were clean-shaven and perhaps even a little pasty-faced. These were the computer jocks and laboratory analysts who spent their creative hours in front of humming equipment with flickering lights and multiple screens.

Wes Evans, rotund and full-bearded, clearly fell into the first group. He gave the impression of a prospector who should be off in the wilderness leading a loaded mule and panning for gold. When Anne said, "So, you're all geologists," he replied with a broad grin, "Yeah, that's true. We're all from the same species, although geologists come in lots of different flavors and study everything from volcanoes to oil. But Gavin and I were the only faculty who studied fossils." He squinted at her through wire-rimmed glasses that had such thick lenses they made his myopic eyes look distorted. "Gavin worked with the remains of vertebrates—big animals with backbones, things like early horses, crocodiles, even dinosaurs. Me, I work with microfossils that you need a microscope to see."

Candrew watched Anne as she listened politely and could almost see her wondering if too much peering though a microscope was the reason he needed those bottle-thick lenses. Wes finished by saying that his research didn't have much in common with Gavin's.

"So, Gavin worked alone?"

"Oh no, that's not at all what I meant. He had lots of

scientific collaborators at other universities and, of course, his grad students here on campus." Wes nodded toward the three students who smiled but said nothing. "For the last few months Gavin had been real busy working with an off-campus group on some new project, but I don't know much about that. He was tight-lipped — never told me what he was up to."

Or me, Candrew thought.

"I'm Kurt Tadheim." The intrusive speaker, tall and lean, had a round head, receding hairline and a face dominated by a craggy nose. He gave Anne a long, direct look. "And I don't work with fossils at all."

"You don't even work with rocks," Wes said.

Anne was puzzled. "So why're you in geology?"

"I'm a geophysicist. I make loud noises on the Earth's surface and listen to the echoes that bounce back." He paused to let that arcane piece of information have its full impact. "The sounds coming from the rocks underground let me figure out how deep they are. That sort of thing."

"Sounds complicated."

"Give me a big enough computer and I can handle it," he said with cockiness.

Although Candrew had little day-to-day contact with Kurt in the department, he always found him to be brusque and humorless. He didn't particularly like him. And his arrogant manner and intolerance for anyone with lesser mathematical skill didn't help. Candrew was surprised he'd even come to the church service. As far as he knew, Kurt and Gavin had nothing in common: geophysics and fossils rarely mix.

Thoughts of Gavin permeated the group and it was Mark Kernfeld who voiced them. "I just can't believe it was an accident. Are they sure he didn't have a heart attack or something?"

Anne, who knew Gavin best, told them, "There's no family history of heart problems. And he seemed to be in great shape"

"A stroke maybe? Or could he have deliberately . . ." Mark's voice trailed away.

"Suicide? Not Gavin. He was as well adjusted as anyone I know."

"Which isn't saying much on this campus" someone claimed. The attempt at levity was misplaced and the remark ignored.

"Gavin was always so positive. I never saw him depressed," Candrew said. "And he had everything to live for. He was passionate about his research and had no problems in his professional life, I'm sure of that."

"Still, it seems odd to me that someone in good physical shape like Gavin, with all his experience, could drown in a rapid he'd run a dozen times before—and Class IV a rapid at that."

They stood in silence, digesting the remark, but with nothing to add.

Gavin Citalli had been a long-time faculty member and it was entirely appropriate that he would be buried on campus in the small cemetery behind the college chapel. The crowd of friends and colleagues that had nearly filled the chapel, even though it was still summer vacation, were beginning to drift away with just a few isolated clusters left. Off to the side, Nicholas Rosenberg, chairman of the geology department, was still talking to Dean Hunter O'Neil and one of the vice presidents. O'Neil, standing with hands in pockets and only half paying attention to Rosenberg, slowly looked around at the few remaining people. Finally, he said, "I see our football coach is still here. Was he a friend of Citalli's?"

"Not as far as I know," Rosenberg said. "I heard his wife sat in on one of Citalli's dinosaur classes and they became friends. She probably dragged Coach to the service."

"Think he'll have a winning team again this year?" For the vice-president, who thought only in terms of success, this was a typical concern.

"Who knows? At this time of year every coach in the country is going to have a winning season," was Rosenberg's cynical reply.

Candrew walked with Anne back towards the small group still talking to Marge. Anne dabbed her eyes with a tissue. "I feel so sorry for her. Every time she runs into one of those other geologists, she'll see them getting on with their lives and wonder why Gavin's was cut short." They joined the group and Candrew put his arm around Marge, told her he'd drop by the house later and left. After her kindness when Penny was dying, now he'd do everything he could to help.

As Candrew cut across the plaza to the parking lot, a black diesel truck with jacked-up suspension pulled noisily out of visitor parking. From his brief glimpse of the driver, he was sure it was the stranger he'd seen sitting at the rear of the chapel. That lush moustache was unmistakable. He casually glanced at the departing pickup noting the saguaro cactus and purple mountains of an Arizona license plate.

Rosenberg hurried to catch up. He was clearly agitated, although that was nothing unusual. "What the hell is going on?" he said with intensity, but in a low conspiratorial voice. "Right after lunch, I got a call from some guy at the Bureau of Land Management, and then just before I left for the chapel service there was another call, this one from an agent with the FBI. They both wanted to know the same thing: what was Gavin doing out in the Four Corners?" He looked exasperated. "You knew him well, any idea what he was up to?"

"I haven't the foggiest," Candrew replied truthfully. "Digging fossils, I guess."

"Well, we need to find out what was going on, and soon." They strode towards the cars in silence. "If you find out anything let me know immediately, and I mean immediately." Rosenberg hurried away.

Candrew pulled off his tie, stuffed it in his jacket pocket and fumbled for the car keys, wondering what that was all about. He knew Marge was returning to a very different life—but thought life for him was going to go on as usual.

Chapter 2

It was mid-morning when Candrew crossed the bridge over the rocky arroyo and drove to the gravel parking lot behind Kinblade Hall, a three-story building that housed the geology department. Built in the thirties, it was one of the oldest on campus and he entered through the imposing neo-Georgian portal and hustled up the wide stone steps to the departmental office on the middle floor. Taking the stairs was a small gesture toward keeping fit and about the only exercise he got during the semester, in spite of repeated resolutions to do more. The corridor at the top of the stairs was lined with dark wood cases displaying rocks, fossils, and a few impressive crystal clusters. Maps and photos of erupting volcanoes hung above them. Even with its generous proportions, the hallway had a rather dismal feeling made worse by the small windows and dusty smell.

As Candrew went into the office to collect his mail, he was greeted by Maria, the geology secretary, who got up from her desk and handed him a note. "I was just going to put this in your box. The president's administrative assistant wants you to call her back as soon as you can."

"And what I'm expected to do for our illustrious leader?"

"She's just trying to set up a meeting with the president sometime this morning. Sounded urgent."

Absentmindedly he scanned the note, said, "Fine," and walked down the hall to the stairwell and up to his office on the top floor. The president rarely got involved in departmental affairs and spent most of his time politicking with the state legislature or schmoozing with wealthy alumni to raise the money that kept the wheels of academe well-oiled. So, why did the president need to see him?

Candrew called the president's office shortly after ten-thirty and was told that the president had no time before lunch." The pleasant and efficient voice asked, "Would two o'clock be okay?"

"Yes it would." So much for urgency.

For the rest of the morning Candrew sat at his desk lethargically moving paper from one pile to another without achieving much that was useful and finally gave up any attempt at serious work. Gavin's drowning had left him stunned and disoriented.

It was five minutes before two when he got to the president's suite. He waited, more or less patiently, for fifteen minutes until the administrative assistant shepherded him in.

This was one of Candrew's rare visits to the president and he felt the carpet thickness increase as he stepped in past the heavy mahogany door. The office was large enough to emphasize the president's status, but not so large that it invited criticism for conspicuous consumption. Full-length windows gave a sweeping view with the mountains providing a dramatic backdrop to the old engineering building and the new visual and performing arts complex. A substantial, leather-topped, wood desk hosted only a single sheaf of papers and a coffee cup. The president, overweight and balding, came out from behind its protective bulk and grasped

Candrew's hand in a large paw.

"Come in, come in. Dreadful business about Citalli." He ushered Candrew over to a chair at a conference table in front of the windows and sat on the same side. "I didn't know his wife very well. How's she coping? Is there anything we can do?"

The president was saying all the right things, although Candrew sensed a lack of sincerity. He was reminded of a water-worn pebble—smooth and polished, but hard and inflexible. After a series of probing questions, the president shifted in his chair, resting his arms on the table, his fingers tented. "I'm sorry to bring this up at such a sad time, but yesterday I received a phone call from an agent with the Bureau of Land Management in Farmington, and later a call from the FBI in Albuquerque. The BLM had been informed of Dr. Citalli's death and wanted to know more about his research. The agent in Farmington seemed especially anxious to get details of a fossil excavation they suspected he was carrying out in the Four Corners area. He implied—though I must admit he never actually said it—that the excavation site was on Indian land. Without a federal permit this would, of course, be illegal. He also had questions about where Citalli stored the fossils he dug up. In particular, he wanted information on collaborators and the names of graduate students."

So that was the reason for this royal summons. Candrew was surprised by the implied accusation. "Although I was a close friend, I don't know much about his field work. I'll help in any way I can." He paused, tapping his teeth, thinking. "My guess is, his graduate students would be the best source of information, especially Karen Seligman. But Rosenberg can get you a complete list."

"I understand the agent's already contacted Dr. Rosenberg and plans to visit campus in the next few days. The university's legal council is aware of this and I've asked Rosenberg to meet with her, but she may need your help as well."

"Of course. I'll get together with them any time that fits their schedule."

"Excellent. Provide whatever help you can. And please remember, we have a policy of full cooperation with law enforcement agencies." He fixed Candrew with a stern look. "I know you were a close friend of Gavin Citalli's, but this is not the time to protect him."

Candrew said nothing, although at this point he thought there was nothing to cover up.

The president shifted in his chair and glanced out of the window. "When I talked to Dr. Rosenberg he raised the issue of liability. Do you know if Citalli was on an official university field trip when the, uh, accident occurred? Or perhaps working on a sponsored research project?"

Candrew felt that raising this problem now was right in keeping with Rosenberg's generally insensitive nature. He explained that as far as he knew the float trip on the Green River had been purely personal. However, several students had gone along with him and they intended to collect fossils to add to the department's teaching collection.

The president sighed. "Another one of those gray areas. No wonder the world is full of attorneys." He smiled, and after a few pleasantries Candrew realized he was being politely dismissed.

The walk back across campus would have been pleasant in the early afternoon sunshine, but the shadow of Gavin's drowning loomed over him. Why hadn't Gavin told him about a major fossil excavation? And what made it important enough that the BLM and FBI needed to get involved? Reminded of his own mortality, he felt fragile and vulnerable. He wondered how Penny would have handled *his* sudden death.

In need of distraction, Candrew cut round behind the Business School and entered Kinblade Hall through a side door, taking the stairs down to the basement. Following the passage past laboratories and student offices, he detoured past a shiny metal tank full of liquid nitrogen and skirted a large, wooden packing crate. The door to the sedimentology laboratory—his lab.— had recently acquired a new sign with white letters cut into the dark blue plastic strip: *Dr. Judy Westerlund*. He went in without knocking.

Judy was seated at a long work bench. Tall for a woman, she was solidly built, though not fat, her chestnut hair cut short in keeping with her no-nonsense approach to life. She swiveled on her stool to greet Candrew. "Look at this." She picked up her glasses and slid off the stool to make way for him.

Candrew took the seat in front of her polarizing microscope and made a small focus adjustment. "Interesting." *Interesting* is one of those non-committal words scientists use when something is intriguing, but they don't fully understand it—yet. "We need to take a look at the deeper part of this sandstone unit, check the porosity there."

Candrew got up from the 'scope and stretched, putting his hands behind his head and meshing his fingers. "I just got back from the president's office."

"Really? It's good to know he actually exists," Judy said, grinning. "I've been here five months and have never seen him, but then I'm just a lowly research associate."

Judy's main job was to take care of the day-to-day running of Candrew's lab and she'd impressed him with her competence and enthusiasm. In the short time she'd worked with him, he'd gotten to like her a lot and appreciated her positive attitude, good sense of humor and straightforward manner—even if at times she could be disarmingly blunt.

"The president wanted to talk about Gavin's drowning and why the BLM and FBI guys are interested."

"They are? Whatever for?"

"Good question. I'm supposed to meet with some of the

agents in the next couple of days, so I'll probably find out then."
He pursed his lips and stared at the wooden shelves stacked with
core boxes. "It disturbs me that Gavin was keeping his activities a
secret. That's not like him. He was normally so open, so outgoing."

There was a moment of silence.

"Coffee?" Judy asked.

Candrew declined and as she got up to fill her mug he picked
up a small hand-lens and studied one of the rock cores laid out on
the bench. He could see individual sand grains. Concentrating on
the rock fabric isolated him—both in space and time. His mind
went back a hundred and fifty million years and saw the waves
breaking in endless rolls on a sunlit beach, sorting the sand grains,
rolling them around, building the layers, developing the sand
ripples that were part of the core in front of him.

"You know Karen Seligman?" Judy's question broke into his
reverie.

"Not well. Only that she was one of Gavin's grad students."

"Yeah. She's near the end of her Ph.D. and I'd helped her
with some samples a month or two ago. She came in yesterday."
There was a long pause. "She told me Gavin had her working on
fossil remains that were very different from those she's studying
for her dissertation. And he wouldn't tell her where they came
from. Now she's worried about finishing her Ph.D."

"Odd," he said, tapping his teeth. "Why would Gavin do
that?" But Candrew had nothing useful to add.

He was getting up to leave when Judy adjusted her glasses,
hesitated for a moment, then said, "I wanted to ask you if it'd be
okay for me to be gone on Friday? Dorian asked me to spend the
weekend with him."

Dorian, Judy's steady boyfriend, worked for the U.S.
Geological Survey in Las Vegas. Candrew had only met him once,
but approved, and was pleased they were getting on well together.
"Yeah, no problem," he said. "And good luck at the casinos."

Nicholas Rosenberg was relatively new to campus and had been chairman of the geology department for only two years. He'd not meshed well with the rest of the geology faculty, a situation created by his Ivy League education, east-coast background and attitudes, coupled with an abrasive personality. After his move from a small private school to a large rural state university, he was only slowly adjusting to life in northern New Mexico. The view from the large window of his corner office left no doubt about his western surroundings, with the long vista to the pine-covered mountain slopes, the high peaks thrust up above tree line, and the intense ultramarine sky.

The buzzer on the intercom interrupted his rambling thoughts. Maria's always cheerful voice told him that the graduate advisor from anthropology had called. "He's trying to set up a meeting about medical insurance for students doing field work."

"Call him back and tell him I'll be there. And tell him to stick to his schedule. I've got no more than an hour for his damn meeting."

"Also, Dr. Nor's here to see you."

"Oh, he is, is he? Send him in."

Rosenberg sat behind a large glass-topped desk with stacks of well-ordered papers and books. The sleeves of his blue Oxford-cloth shirt were rolled up and he was wearing a tie, although as a concession to summer the knot was hanging loose. Rosenberg's geologic specialty was volcanic andesites, very different from the sort of rocks that interested Candrew. Their research topics had little in common, and past interactions had dealt solely with the bureaucratic minutia of the department.

Pushing his high-backed chair away from the desk, Rosenberg leaned back, putting his hands behind his head. As Candrew laid a manila folder on his desk, he asked, "I don't suppose you've managed to find out anything about Gavin's activities?"

"No, not yet."

"Nothing at all?" He sounded peeved. "Pity. Makes my life difficult. I'm being hounded by the BLM. They phoned again this morning. I thought you'd be able to come up with something by now." He glared at Candrew. "So, when do you think you'll have any information?"

"I've no idea." He was just as keen to find out what Gavin had been doing, but resented being badgered by Rosenberg. "That's not the reason I'm here, although in a way it does concern Gavin. Semester starts in two weeks and someone will have to teach his paleontology class."

"Quite right. I've been thinking about that." Rosenberg tried to look sincere and give the impression he was in control and on top of every one of the department's problems. "Wes is our only other paleontologist and he's got a full load. It won't be easy to find a substitute at such short notice."

"Which is why I'd like to suggest Dr. Westerlund."

"Westerlund? I didn't know she had any background in paleo."

"Her Masters research on coral reefs at Florida State included a lot of fossil work. And she also got involved in fossil studies when she was doing her Ph.D. at Colorado." He started to flip through Judy's résumé. "Teaching would be valuable experience and could help her a lot in getting a faculty position."

"Well, I don't suppose I've got much choice at this late stage." Rosenberg seemed piqued that his hand was being forced and the decision not entirely his. He stroked his chin and glanced out of the window at the clouds building over the mountains. "Let me arrange a contract as an adjunct. I'm sure I can find a budget with a few thousand in it."

Candrew reminded him that he would not have to pay Gavin's salary and money shouldn't be a problem. "Would it be okay to issue Dr. Westerlund a key to Gavin's office? It'll be a big help if she can use his course notes and access his fossil collection. She's only got a couple of weeks to get ready."

"Yes. I suppose I can authorize that. Tell Maria to fill out a key request card." He paused, glancing around the office. "You'd better make sure all Gavin's personal things are out of the office. Get his wife to help you. I know you've got a lot to do right before semester, but you were a close friend and you'll be the best person to start sorting everything. We'll need to have the office completely emptied before any permanent replacement gets hired, though I'm sure that'll take at least six months. Anyway, start as soon as you can. Right away. Okay?"

The note of urgency gave Candrew the impression that there was a hidden agenda.

On the way back to his own office, Candrew walked up the broad stone stairwell, turned along the wide corridor and, without enthusiasm, used his faculty master key to let himself into Gavin's office. Late afternoon sun flooded in through half-closed blinds. Candrew wandered slowly across the silent room and stood in front of the swivel chair looking around the large, cluttered office. He felt like a ship's captain on the bridge surveying the horizon, a captain whose ship has just come to a dead stop, a moment frozen in time. On previous visits, Gavin's office had always been full of life—the phone ringing; students coming in for help; Gavin talking in his animated way. Now the empty coffee mug, a calendar with appointments he would never keep, and—most of all—the quiet stillness, produced an overwhelming sense of loss.

Gavin subscribed to the localized chaos school of organization, and even though tottering stacks of papers occupied every horizontal surface, each pile contained related materials. At the end of the side table a pile of memos had a large cluster of interlocking brachiopod fossils sitting on it, serving as a paperweight. Under the table were stacked cardboard boxes, each one labeled with a fossil name in black magic marker— *ammonites, cnidarians, crinoids.* Large pieces of rock and more boxes were stacked along the opposite wall. At the end furthest from the entrance stood a large white plaster cast, about twice the size of a football, but thinner and with flattened surfaces. Candrew had no idea what it was, but then his research didn't involve fossils. Hidden by the surrounding stack of boxes, the plaster object wasn't visible from the doorway.

Bookcases lined the opposite wall with photographs occupying niches among the books. While several were group shots of students, one showing Gavin had obviously been taken some years ago. Holding a broad-brimmed field hat in his left hand and a geologic pick in the other, he was perched on a rock outcrop, grinning for the camera. In the last few years he'd added a few pounds, but otherwise hadn't changed much. Even in the photo, his hair was already thinning down the center. The large tufts on each side and his pointed chin gave his impish face a distinctly triangular look.

Candrew was not yet ready to face all this. Carefully, he locked the office door and left.

Cumulus piled up behind Candrew as he turned his car east and drove down Juniper Road towards the edge of campus and home. Bright sun-splashed edges on the clouds contrasted with their dark, brooding interiors and the still-luminous, azure sky. Lightning flickered almost continuously, thunder rumbled, and the first fat raindrops splashed the car's windshield. An intense bright flash made him blink and instinctively he began to count: *one Mississippi, two Mississippi, three . . .* It was six seconds before the loud boom and reverberating echoes reached him. "A bit over a mile away," he thought. Candrew had counted like this since he was a kid. He was a compulsive problem solver and in a very real sense this was the appeal that science held for him. The trick was

19

to choose the important problems, to ask significant questions. But now was not the time.

The torrential downpour made driving difficult, and he was glad to pull into his driveway, although he got drenched even in the short dash to the side door. As he dried his glasses with a paper napkin, the drumming rain sent water cascading down the kitchen windows, distorting the view of a patio brightened by intermittent flashes. Chile, his beloved dog, watched, nose flat on the ground, only the eyes moving. Candrew knew that look and got a can of dog food. As he reached over to switch on the old television that shared the end of the kitchen counter with a stack of unread magazines, nothing happened. For a moment he thought the geriatric set had finally succumbed to old age, but quickly realized the electricity was out, a casualty of the thunderstorm.

His immediate problem was to open the dog food when the electric can opener wouldn't run. Chile sat patiently by his feet looking up, confident his master would figure it out. After scrabbling around in the kitchen drawers, Candrew eventually found an old manual opener. With the dog taken care of, he thought about his own meal. There was half a loaf of French bread and that, together with several types of cheese, meant food wasn't a problem. Neither was wine. Most of the merlot was left from last night—and for Candrew red wine and cheese were inseparable. When he ate an hour later, the light was fading although he could still see well enough without candles and almost didn't bother to light any. But they added a welcome pool of light in the darkening room and gave a flickering, romantic glow. Smiling to himself, he remembered a similar power outage many years ago when Penny had said, "Candy"—she often called him that when she was in a teasing mood—"You can't play your records, can't watch television, and can't use your typewriter. You may actually have to talk to me." Sadly, he wished they could talk now.

Chile's wet tongue licking his hand tugged him back from

the memories. Each evening Candrew took him for a walk, which seemed only fair since he was the one who provided Chile with too many treats, prompting the need for extra exercise. Tonight they took Martinez Road, following it past the end of the pavement and onto the graded gravel. The sweet, smoky aroma of barbecues from the widely scattered houses drifted through the evening air: it seemed everyone had the same solution to the problem of cooking without electricity.

The passing thunderstorm had wrung all moisture from the atmosphere and the stars looked close in the dry air. Twilight had almost deserted the western mountains, the moon hadn't risen, and without town lights the now cloudless sky was a dark mantle perforated by bright points of starlight. The Vikings thought stars were holes where dead heroes cut their way through to heaven. What came to Candrew's mind was Navajo myth and Coyote. The Navajo Black God used mica crystals from his fawn-skin pouch for the stars and carefully positioned each constellation with a star to ignite it. But then Coyote, the Trickster, grabbed the pouch and scattered the rest of the stars randomly across the sky—except for one, which he placed with care. Today, we know Coyote's Star as Antares in the constellation Scorpius, and Candrew looked for it low in the southern summer sky. The star twinkled, almost as if it winked at him.

Chapter 3

The Brazos Mountains to the east were dark and featureless, lit from behind by the rising sun, when Candrew pulled back the drapes and thought about breakfast. With the electricity back on, he toasted two slices of bread and ate them with scrambled eggs, cheese, and chile—more elaborate than his usual hurried breakfast of granola and skim milk. He read the morning paper at the kitchen table, not surprised that another local politician had been caught with his hand in the till. Chile lay stretched out licking his paws. Most days the breakfast dishes sat in the sink until evening; today they were washed, dried, and neatly stacked. There was no need to load the washing machine; Candrew did it anyway. Finally, he ran out of diversions.

With no more reasons to procrastinate, he was forced to confront the prospect of going to the university and sorting the contents of Gavin's office. Essentially a private person, Candrew loathed the idea of rummaging through the debris of a colleague's life and wished he could leave it to Marge, to someone closer to Gavin. As far as he knew, the contents of the office were only professional and technical, though he really wasn't sure. Maybe there were personal things as well. Still reluctant to accept accusations of Gavin's possibly illegal activities out in the Four Corners area, he was apprehensive about what he might find. But the Gavin he'd known was not someone who'd get caught up in an illegal fossil dig.

The void left by Gavin's unexpected death would be hard to fill and he drove to the campus remembering their friendship with pleasure and sadness. Once more, Candrew let himself into Gavin's office.

As a senior professor, Gavin had a large office, but had still managed to fill it with the accumulations of an active researcher. Candrew stood scanning these trappings of an academic's career, the remains of a life in science. Well, perhaps not all of what remained. There was a legacy of influential technical publications and, of course, a generation of well-trained students. But the little observations, the half-formed theories, and new fossil locations he planned to study—all those were lost.

Just like yesterday, Candrew scrutinized the room, trying to decide where to begin. The amount of stuff was daunting: rolled-up maps, piles of papers, books, boxes, and fossils. Incongruously, a rolled umbrella hung from the corner of a small blackboard covered with a jumble of half-erased drawings. Beside it on the wall, a two-foot square cork bulletin board was encrusted with out-of-date lists and pinned-up memos. Candrew was sure he'd filled it up and then never touched it—there was even a basketball schedule from four years ago. It appeared that Gavin used his computer monitor in the same way; it was festooned with hand-scrawled messages, reminders and phone numbers on fluorescent yellow Post-Its, many of them faded.

Although not aware of it at first, Candrew realized he was looking around the office for anything that might throw light on Gavin's suspicious fossil excavation. He saw nothing obvious. But even with the clutter, he became vaguely aware that something was different, not quite the way he'd left it. Tapping his teeth, he stood dredging his memory, trying to figure out what had changed. When he failed to pin anything down, he thought he'd been mistaken, but the idea hovered at the edge of consciousness.

As he started planning the tedious chore of getting library books boxed up, he suddenly knew—the large white, oval plaster package was gone. Since he'd no idea what it contained, it was hard to guess why anyone would take it. His gaze swept the office trying to establish whether anything else had been moved, although with so much confusion it was impossible to be certain. As far as he could recall from yesterday's brief visit, nothing else had been disturbed.

Candrew felt he could use help and called Judy, telling her he needed assistance, and asking her to bring up some cardboard boxes. Ten minutes later she peered round the half-open door, then struggled in and dumped five boxes on the floor.

"That's all I could rustle up at short notice. Physical Plant'll have more if we need 'em."

"At least there's a bit less to pack now." He told her about the disappearance of the enigmatic plaster cast. "I don't think anything else has been taken, though it's difficult to be sure."

Judy followed his look around the office. "Anyway, how would someone get in? I don't see any evidence they tampered with the lock or anything. So, who has keys?"

"The cleaners, I guess, senior faculty, possibly his teaching assistant."

Judy pushed the empty boxes away from the door and perched on the edge of a, stout wooden table. "But why wait 'til last night? That cast could've been stolen any time during the last week or so." She paused, thinking out loud. "Could be he's just heard of Gavin's death. Or maybe he's just got back into town."

"How can you be so sure it was a 'he'?" Candrew asked with mock seriousness, grinning. "Don't women steal?"

"Yeah, sure. Only the way you described that white thing made it sound so heavy. Of course, I immediately thought the thief had to be a big strong guy." She smiled condescendingly.

Candrew countered. "Unless more than one person was involved." He thought about that for a minute. "It would help if we knew exactly what it was."

"And why someone thinks it's important enough to steal." She scanned the office, but nothing seemed to offer clues. "Whoever took it knew exactly what they were after. That would suggest a colleague, wouldn't it?"

Candrew agreed. "Yeah, I'm sure you're right. One of the cleaners would probably have taken the stereo, or maybe some books, or even gambled on selling a couple of the big fossils."

The telephone answering machine light was blinking, demanding attention, and Judy pressed the replay button. There were a couple of clicks from callers needing to talk to a real human, one student stammering excuses for a late paper, and then, "Hi! Chuck Semley. Just touching base. Got Mishikubo on my tail—as usual. He called from L.A. to find out how things are going. We haven't heard from you in a while and he's his usual self, real impatient, wanting the latest info on how you're doin'. He's pushing me to keep the project moving, doesn't want it stalled. I'll call again when I've got details for the next stage all flanged up. Talk to you then." He left a number with the 602 area code, said "Good hunting" in a flat voice that made it sound more like an order than a casual remark, and hung up.

"Interesting. I wonder what that's all about? Where's 602?"

"I only know the symmetrical numbers, like 303 and 505. Oh, and 202!" She fumbled through the phone book on the desk. "Arizona."

Candrew reached around the silver frame with Marge's picture in it and tore a page off the pad beside the phone, jotted down Chuck Semley's number and tucked it into his shirt pocket.

Suddenly Patsy Cline loudly informed the world, "*I go out walking, after midnight, out in the moonlight . . .*" Judy had just dropped a CD into the stereo, and, flustered, she hurried to turn down the volume. The compact system of three black cubes nestled among books and binders on the bookcase's middle shelf. Candrew came over and glanced at the rack of CDs stacked beside it. "They're not all country and western," she said. "About half seem to be classical, and there's even some film scores. Quite a mix really." She paused, looking a bit guilty. "I hope you don't mind me playing one of the CDs."

"No, not at all," Candrew quickly replied and meant it. He was pleased to have a pulsing sense of life in Gavin's office and suggested she leave it on—but not quite so loud.

An hour later, four cardboard boxes held all the books destined for the library and they pushed them over by the door. Judy straightened up and stretched. "Now that's done, I'll have to hunt for Gavin's course notes. A lot of the stuff in the paleo course is new to me, particularly vertebrates."

"Okay. Let's see if we can find where he squirreled them away."

Against the short wall opposite the window were two gray, four-drawer filing cabinets and one rather battered, buff-colored, three-drawer unit. Books and papers were piled on top. Half the drawers were unlabelled, while others indicated their contents were *Correspondence, Reprints, Committees* and the inevitable *Misc.*

"I don't see anything labeled *Class Notes* or *Paleo*." She looked disappointed. "You think they're in the computer, or on his web site?"

"I very much doubt that. He was unenthusiastic about computers and never did take the time to set up a web site. I'll bet you a dollar, he was still using his old paper copies. You've got to remember, it's only an introductory class: the contents hardly change from one year to the next." Candrew cast his eye over the filing cabinets. "You'll have to hunt through the drawers and find the folders."

Judy started with the top drawer of the smaller cabinet. It was filled with student files. The middle drawer was packed with copies of old research proposals. Bottom drawers seem to accumulate ancient paper work that is too important to discard, but is never actually needed again. This one was two-thirds full. While several of the files had neatly printed labels, the attempt at a logical system had long since been overwhelmed by a host of additional folders. She scanned the handwritten tabs. Nothing seemed relevant, although one file, labeled *Wrecks*, did catch her attention.

Judy had spent many weeks diving off Miami and in Belize when she worked on coral reefs and had used the opportunity to explore more than half a dozen shipwrecks. Floating quietly through the shadowy, coral-encrusted remains of old ships had always given her an exciting feeling, a sort of affinity with the past, and she was curious to know where Gavin had dived. The folder was rather bulky. She pulled it out, dragged it over to a chair so she could sit and open it on her lap—and was completely unprepared for the photos that tumbled out.

"Candrew, what do you make of these?"

Before he had a chance to look, they were interrupted by a knock on the door and a short, slightly-built young woman asked in a hesitant voice, "Is Dr. Citalli here?"

"No. I'm afraid not. Did you need to see him?"

"I just wanted to give him this report. It's for my independent study. He said to get it in, like, before semester started. Can I leave it for him? I worked all night to finish it." She was holding it out nervously, as though she felt she'd done sufficient work and couldn't get rid of it fast enough.

The young student looked so fragile that Candrew hesitated to tell her about Gavin's death, half afraid she'd just break down, but he told her anyway.

"Dead? Really? That's awful." Her eyes moistened with tears. Visibly upset and confused, a range of emotions flickered across her face—self interest prevailed. "Will I still get a grade?"

"You'd better talk to Dr. Rosenberg. He's reassigning all Dr. Citalli's students."

The young woman left looking dazed. Judy wondered aloud whether that was due to the news of Gavin's death or to an all-night session writing the report.

They turned back to the *Wrecks* file. "What do you make of these skulls?" Judy held up three large photos of a fossil skull showing front, side, and top views, almost certainly a dinosaur. The front view glared directly at her with black, unblinking predator eye sockets. This must have been the last thing a lot of prey animals saw, and even now the malevolence of that sixty-five-million-year-old stare made Judy shudder.

Candrew was impressed. "Wow! Judging from the length of the scale bar that skull must be over five feet long. Something that big would have to be one of those huge, Late Cretaceous predators, maybe even a *Tyrannosaurus rex*."

She pulled out another large print. "This one's obviously a *T. rex* and it's mounted for display."

Over the next half hour, they examined several dozen more photographs of fossil bones. All the specimens had been carefully prepared and almost certainly came from museum collections.

"What I don't understand is why he would label a file about *Tyrannosaurus rex, Wrecks*." As soon as he heard himself say the words Candrew knew the answer, and burst out laughing.

"Now all we've got to figure out," Judy said, "is whether he was just having fun—or trying to hide something."

"Good question. Let's see what else is here." Candrew pulled out the two unlabelled folders that had been in the filing cabinet drawer behind *Wrecks*. One contained photocopies of articles from paleontological journals and he put that on the floor. The other one was full of loose pages, notes, receipts and more photos of fossil bones. But these photos showed unmounted bones with most still embedded in their rock matrix.

Judy peered at her watch, a little after twelve-thirty, and she was getting frustrated. "I still haven't found a copy of his paleo course notes. I'll come back and hunt for them later." She turned to leave. "I'm supposed to meet Mindi over at the astronomy building in fifteen minutes. We always play racquetball on Tuesday afternoons."

After Judy left, Candrew picked up the folder of dinosaur photographs and the files with loose pages and notes. About to leave himself, he took one last look around the office. Yesterday he'd been shocked when the President told him of the BLM's assertion that Gavin could be involved in illegal excavations on Indian land, now he wasn't so sure. The photos of well-preserved bones of big predators had taken him by surprise. And Gavin had never once said anything about a major project, or even that he was working with dinosaurs. Which raised the obvious questions— what had Gavin been hiding; who were his collaborators; where was the site? And, most significantly, who was putting up the money?

It was then that he remembered the telephone number jotted on the slip of paper in his pocket. Thinking he ought to tell the caller about Gavin's death, he picked up the phone and rang Arizona.

The call was answered with a curt, "Hello."

"Chuck Semley?"

"You got him."

"I'm calling from Professor Citalli's office."

"Yeah?" The reply was guarded. "How's Prof doing?"

"That's why I'm calling. I'm a friend and colleague and

wondered whether you'd heard he recently died in an accident."

"Jesus! Died? My God." There was a tone of genuine surprise. "What sort of accident?"

Candrew told him about the drowning.

Semley had a slew of questions. "When did it happen? Was he by himself?"

"Just over two weeks ago. With a group of students on a field trip. Did you know him well?"

There was a lengthy hesitation. "No, not really. Only met him a couple of times. Lots of e-mails. Chatted quite a bit on the phone."

"But you did have business dealings?"

"Yeah. In a manner of speaking." Semley offered nothing more.

"Anything his wife should know about in settling up his affairs?"

The question was left unanswered. Semley changed the subject. "How'd you get my name?"

"You left a message on Dr. Citalli's answering machine."

"Right. So I did." There was another pause, as though he was trying to remember what he'd said. "You know about his fossil work?"

"A bit." It was Candrew's turn to be cautious. "He was a professional paleontologist."

"You a paleontologist? You work with him?"

Increasingly intrigued by Semley and his relationship with Gavin, Candrew hedged. "I work with fossils in some of my research projects." He'd only taken one fossil course as an undergraduate and was stretching the truth a bit with this reply.

"Not a geophysicist then?"

The question almost seemed a non-sequitur and took Candrew by surprise. "No. Not at all." The message on the answering machine had mentioned "the project" and implied a "next stage" was being planned. Who was Mr. Mishikubo? He realized the cautious verbal sparring would go nowhere if he didn't take a few risks, so he said warily, "I worked closely enough to know he was excavating a big dinosaur out in the Four Corners area. You interested in dinosaur bones?"

"Could be." There was yet another long pause and Candrew let it drag out. Then abruptly, Semley said, "Well, thanks for phoning and letting me know what happened." There was a brief hesitation. "You better give me your phone number. May need to contact you." Candrew gave him the number, added his e-mail address and the call was over. He put the phone down and sat staring at it, trying to decide just what he'd learned. His face remained calm and showed no hint of the conflicting thoughts tumbling around in his head. Was Semley involved in Gavin's dinosaur excavation? Almost certainly. Was he a co-worker, the source of money, or a buyer for the fossils? Impossible to say. And Mishikubo? He'd learned nothing about him. Where did he fit in?

Candrew stood up slowly and gathered together Gavin's folders. He dropped them off in his own office before going to lunch in the Faculty Club where he often ate with a group of colleagues.

An hour later on his way back across campus his thoughts returned to Gavin's big dinosaur excavations. But where would he get more information? Gavin's computer was the obvious place to look, but Gavin had been a reluctant computer user and his aging PC was not much more than a glorified typewriter. Even so, Candrew wanted to check the files and e-mails, particularly after the enigmatic phone message from Semley. With a "next stage" being planned he should do that as quickly as possible. But without Gavin's password that could be a problem.

Back in the geology building, he took the stairs up to the second floor two at a time and strode swiftly down the passageway without actually breaking into a run. For the first time, he thought seriously about the problem he faced. Since he didn't have Gavin's password, getting into his files would be difficult. Maybe one of Gavin's students had it so he could access data, or perhaps Marge could find it. Both seemed unlikely. The system administrators in computer services, they could get in—but not without authorization. He didn't know who would have to approve such things. Certainly Rosenberg, probably the Dean, maybe even a VP. All that would take time. Perhaps the direct approach was best— just take the whole damn unit and let Judy's techie friends over in astronomy figure out how to access the files. Maybe it would be easier to remove the hard drive. He knew forensic information could be retrieved from the discs, the problem was, he didn't know how to get a hard drive out.

Still pondering the computer problem, he hustled round the corner, with the key to Gavin's office already in his hand, and saw Maria down the hallway bending over an irregular, bright yellow pile. She was outside Gavin's office and straightened up as he came rushing along. Sensing his urgent destination, she stepped over the yellow pile and stood with her back to Gavin's office door. This already had one yellow strip across it, attached to the wall on each side with duct tape. "Can't go in there."

"Why not? Who says so?"

"Rosenberg."

Rosenberg? But it was Rosenberg who'd told him to start sorting out the office. Confused, Candrew looked at the tape. It was fluorescent yellow with the word *CAUTION* printed every couple of feet.

Maria followed his glance. "We didn't have none that said *CRIME SCENE.*"

"Crime scene?"

"You got that right." The deep, male voice took him by surprise and he turned to see one of the university's security police in full uniform, including the cap. The pocket label read *Manny*

Garcia. "We've been given strict instructions not to let no one in. And those instructions came from the F.- B.- I." He pronounced the letters slowly and distinctly, obviously impressed by the law enforcement company he was keeping.

"I see." Thwarted, Candrew was furious with himself for not getting the information out of the computer when he'd had the chance earlier in the day. He smiled and tried a soft-sell. "Well, Manny, I only wanted to pick up some notes for a class. Can I just get those before you tape up the door?" It was a long shot and he wasn't sure he could get anything useful out of the computer in only a few minutes. He could certainly stuff his jacket pockets full of CDs.

The guard was adamant. "No way. I don't make the rules. This here is a crime scene being investigated by the F.B.I." Again, the letters were said with reverence.

An impasse. The only option seemed to be a tactical retreat.

Chapter 4

Frustrated, Candrew pushed open his office door, glanced at the two files from Gavin's office now on the desk, and sank into his chair. He refused to believe Gavin was illegally excavating fossils—there must be some other explanation. Candrew was certain that if he could get access to all Gavin's records they'd show he wasn't involved. And he was equally sure that the BLM, even the FBI, wouldn't have the experience to evaluate all the subtleties of the geological data. There was so much he wanted to see. Depressed that he had no direct way to prove his friend's innocence, he sat with his head in his hands.

The phone rang. It was Renata.

Renata Alcantara, a professor in anthropology, was a close friend and with many shared interests they frequently had dinner together or went to social events. He confided in her his suspicions of Gavin's illegal activities, all that happened in his friend's office, and how Security had shut him out.

"I'm just leaving the department," she said, "and was going to suggest we take in a movie tonight, but clearly you're not in a socializing mood."

Candrew grunted.

"Why don't I drop by and cheer you up?"

He thought that was a good idea and she promised to be there in five minutes.

Renata arrived on time, all smiles and with a positive attitude. Without enthusiasm, Candrew pushed the two bulky files across the desk to her and outlined what he'd seen. Together they flipped through the stack of photos showing huge fossil bones.

Renata looked at the back of one of the prints to see whether it was labeled and at the top were penciled letters: *YYC.* "Do you think that's someone's initials?"

"Could be. My guess is it's more likely some sort of filing system." Candrew sat tapping his teeth. "Anything on the back of that one?" He wrinkled his forehead and pointed to the photo she was holding.

She flipped it over. "Yeah. This one's got *SFO* written on it. Again, it's probably initials, or a filing system reference. Though I suppose it could be a code."

They looked through several dozen photographs of fossil bones and finally Renata neatened up the pile and put it on the desk. "None of this is really surprising," she said. "After all, Gavin was a paleontology professor."

But what they found next *was* surprising.

Several pages in the second folder had scrawled lists of numbers that were clearly budgets, but with few items identified, it wasn't possible to figure out what sort of project was being financed. A typed sheet, paper-clipped to half a dozen hand-written pages, had *$240,000* in large, bold font at the top, and beneath it, also in bold type, *J-D—$130,000.* Under a broad space, the next line was *JASOND—$130,000,* and this was followed by *POP $5000; CAT $25,000; SHIP $10,000; LOCK $10,000; ANTARES $40,000,* and *IRIDIUM $40,000.*

Puzzled, Renata shook her head from side to side. "That's a

weird list."

"Sure is," Candrew said.

Short, handwritten columns with four- or five-figure dollar amounts and subtotals were scattered across the page, as though Gavin had been trying to check expenses in various categories, or perhaps calculate an overall total. But a total for what?

Candrew sat tapping his teeth with his nails, his unconscious response to problems. "These are big numbers. Gavin never said anything about a research grant with that kind of money."

"Then where did it come from?" Renata asked.

"Damned if I know. But it must be one hell of a 'cat' for twenty-five thousand. And five thousand dollars buys a lot of 'pop'." He scanned the lists again. "Jason D matches with the J-D at the top. As far as I know, we don't have any grad students in geology called Jason. Could be he's in another department."

"There must be dozens of Jasons on campus."

"Ted Devereaux's son is the only one I've run across. Ted's the guy in the Business Office I have lunch with."

"That fits with the 'D'," Renata said.

"Right, it does. You've probably seen him around campus. He's got long, blond hair and usually wears a combat jacket. And drives a red Jeep Wrangler."

Although she hadn't known who owned it, she'd seen the jeep. It was hard to miss. The body was bright red, the roll bar striped blue and white, and its oversized tires stuck outside the line of the chassis giving it a chunky "can do" look. She wondered out loud, "It's a lot of money for an undergraduate. What was he doing to earn that?"

Candrew had to wonder too.

Back home a little after six, Candrew fed his dog and his aging cat 'Pixel', and was himself ready to eat right away, but didn't feel like preparing anything elaborate. A can of tomato soup went into the saucepan and he perked it up with a microwaved tomato and lemon grass. He'd just poured most of it into a ceramic bowl, picked up a spoon and a big chunk of fresh bread, when the phone rang. He muted the CD he was playing and grabbed the receiver.

Marge's clear voice greeted him. "Sorry I didn't get back to you earlier. Anne and I were out all afternoon and only got home half an hour ago." After a short pause, she said, "I'm not interrupting anything, am I?"

"No. Not at all. I called you earlier to ask about Gavin's office. Rosenberg, our chairman, wants me to sort out all the . . ."

"This soon?" He heard her suck in a deep breath. "I know it can't be kept as a shrine, but ten days seems a bit of a rush."

Candrew took a conciliatory tone. "It's mainly a case of getting materials so Judy Westerlund can prepare the paleo course. She's new to teaching and Gavin's notes would help her get off to a good start." He waited, but Marge didn't say anything. "I'd like your help while I sort through the office."

"I don't think I'd be any use at all; I'd just get in your way. You know a lot better than I do what ought to be done with his stuff. And all those fossils. The books should probably go to the library. And the ones they don't want, you can give to students. If you run across any photos of Gavin, I'd like to have them. You know, in the field or with students."

"No problem. I'll take care of that," Candrew said. "But it may take a while because the FBI want to go through his things first."

"The FBI? Why are they involved? You know what they want?"

"I'm not sure, but they've sealed off Gavin's office."

"I see," Marge said. There was a long silence. She changed the subject. "I'd got used to Gavin being away in the summers—you know, doing his field work—but his death is so final. I feel as though I've been set adrift in the universe." Candrew waited, letting her organize her thoughts. "I feel sorry for the new students: they're going to miss out on so much, all his experience. And they won't get his good-humored mentoring either. His enthusiasm was infectious."

"True. And it's not just students. Lots of people are going to miss him."

"I don't think he kept much departmental stuff at home," Marge said, taking a more practical tone. "You're welcome to come over and see what's here at the house, if you think it could be useful." She hesitated. "This isn't going to get any easier for me and probably the sooner I face all these things the better. I don't know what your schedule's like, but I'll be here all day tomorrow. Come over any time—in the morning if you want."

Candrew didn't think going to the house would be much use. He was, however, happy to do anything that would help Marge cope with this difficult transition and work towards some sort of closure. "Yeah, sure. I'll drop by late morning. Midday be okay?"

"That'll be fine. I'll look for you then."

Candrew drank the lukewarm soup and poured himself a mug of hot coffee.

Although one of the guest bedrooms in his home was fitted out as an office and accumulated books and papers, Candrew rarely used it, preferring to read in the living room or work at the university. After retrieving his briefcase from the hallway, he took it into the main room. Gavin's fat folders filled most of it and he tugged them out and spread them beside himself as he settled into the sofa. Pixel perched for a while at the far end of the sofa with her tail neatly covering extended paws, eyeing the world in a disinterested way, before giving a long, leisurely yawn and rolling into a comfortable ball. Chile was lying on the old Navajo rug beside Candrew's feet, his nose resting on outstretched paws.

The first folder had photographs he'd looked at with Judy

and Renata. Again, he scanned the stack of eight-by-ten prints. While most showed dinosaur bones still encased in rock matrix, others were of cleaned bones displayed in groups or assembled as skeletons. One set of photographs in an unlabeled, buff envelope left him completely mystified. The five prints, all black and white, were held together by a paper clip. Each showed patterns of small lumps arranged roughly in rows, and two of the photos included irregular, torn-looking edges that gave the impression of a damaged piece of coarse cloth. There were no labels or written comments to help and even after a thorough examination, he still had no idea what they were. He stuffed the photos back into their envelope and penciled a large question mark on the back.

The folder also had line drawings of dinosaur reconstructions, several photocopied technical papers, and at the back a bulky, creased geological map of the Four Corners. Although Candrew was familiar with much of the area, he spent considerable time examining the map in detail, including the back and margins, looking for any significant comments or notations that Gavin might have written. Failing to find any, he put the map back, being careful to keep it in its original sequence.

The second folder was not so bulky. In it Candrew found additional photographs of fossil bones and, more importantly, a hand-drawn map. But there were few clues to the map's location, just a single penciled road number—and was that a "3" or an "8"? He leaned over and pulled the large geological map out of the other folder and tried to establish the position of the sketched area. "Where's the damn road number?" he mumbled to himself, searching the faint printing for over five minutes. When he finally found the right number, it was in the middle of a broad area colored blue and the rocks there were identified as Cretaceous in age, a time when *T. rex* thrived.

Candrew also discovered a set of smaller, hand-sketched, maps on a much larger scale. These seemed to be rough working drawings of an excavation site, and if the numbers were in feet, then the area was roughly one hundred by two hundred. Outlines of bones had been sketched on one of the maps, though many lines were dotted, suggesting to Candrew that locations were tentative, probably because they were still buried. A skull was prominently outlined and when he checked it against the scale it had to be over five feet long. "Wow," he thought, "that's huge, almost certainly a big predator, could well be a *T. rex*."

Flopping back in the sofa, he tried to figure out how Gavin fitted in with all this—and why he hadn't told anyone. Tired from the long day, he took off his glasses and with his hands behind his head stared up at the big, square wooden beams of his living room ceiling. Ten years ago when he and Penny decided to buy the house, she especially liked these beams and the way they complemented the rusty-orange Saltillo tile floor. What appealed to Candrew were the big picture windows and the views—to the mountains on one side and across the plains on the other. The original owners had made no effort to landscape the patio areas leaving Penny with a free hand to design the layout. Although Candrew still spent an occasional weekend working in the garden, without Penny his enthusiasm for gardening had waned. About the only thing he did regularly was fill the birdfeeder.

Candrew pulled his drifting attention back to the last folder, the one that listed dollar amounts, presumably for an operating budget. He went through it all again, wondering what *Cat* and *Pop* and *Lock* were. And was Jason Devereaux, a teen-aged student, really getting a hundred and thirty thousand dollars? If so, for what?

Between two of the budget sheets was a page folded in half that he'd missed before. Part of the top had been ripped off, but the remaining area had *Polanca* and *KT* written across it. Candrew wondered if KT could be the symbol geologists use for "Cretaceous", but that was usually written with a small "t". The middle third of the page was covered with an elaborate doodle and below it, in underlined block capitals, were the words *Antares* and *Iridium*. That was interesting. Candrew recalled both those words—names?—being items on one of the budgets. He ferreted through the piles of paper and retrieved them—forty thousand dollars beside *Antares*; forty thousand beside *Iridium*. He put the pages back in the pile, again trying to maintain the original order.

The photographs and papers, particularly the budgets, had raised lots of questions. Questions were easy to come by, but where could he find answers? Convinced that a careful search of Gavin's office would have turned up additional information, he knew that wasn't an option any more since he no longer had access. He seethed, thinking of all the boxes he and Judy hadn't opened when they had the chance. And all those file cabinet drawers with folders that still needed searching.

Candrew relished the intellectual challenge of taking limited information and figuring out the overall pattern; and if you did it right, you won. It was just this sort of puzzle that got him interested in games and in geology. Even now, after more than fifty years, he could still recall as a child piling colored wooden blocks on top of one another until they collapsed in a heap. And he could still feel the anger and frustration at seeing all his efforts topple just when he thought the crowning piece was in place. Games of all sorts had been an important part of his young life and his mother had taught him checkers, and it was only a short move from that to chess, and he played with focused intensity all through high school. In college, it was his turn for bridge. At least in bridge the total number of cards and their denominations were fixed—and known. In geology you took scraps of evidence—chunks of rock, parts of fossils, deformation patterns, all spread over tens of square miles and millions of years—and tried to work out what had happened. The hunt, the chase, the need to solve the puzzle, was what got him hooked, and to solve it was to win. For most professional geologists the end product might be petroleum, metals, or gems, but for Candrew it was the academic challenge that drew him in and urged him on.

Later he lay in bed, wide awake, trying to solve the puzzle and understand the importance of everything he'd uncovered about Gavin and what was clearly a major dinosaur discovery. But why was Gavin keeping this a secret? Who were his collaborators? And who was funding the project? Most worrying of all was the possibility that the fossil site was on Indian or federal land, which would make excavation illegal. Would Gavin really get involved in something like this? It might explain why he was keeping everything secret, and it could certainly be the reason that the guys from the Bureau of Land Management were showing so much interest.

If Gavin was doing anything illegal, he'd be more likely to keep detailed records at home, rather than in his office at the university. When Candrew told Marge he'd come by the house in the morning, he was just being polite and trying to help her get through this difficult time in any way he could. Now, he was impatient to see Gavin's home office, eager to find out if it would throw any light on what could be a criminal excavation.

He looked at the clock—two forty-five a.m. and he was still awake. Coyotes were howling down by the arroyo and he could hear a more distant group respond. Normally, he liked to listen to their yipping calls, the sound of unfettered nature, but tonight it seemed to have a more ominous, predatory edge. He felt sure he wouldn't get back to sleep—a thought interrupted by the raucous noise of the alarm clock. It was seven fifteen.

Chapter 5

Judy had only been in the lab for ten minutes when Candrew came in around nine thirty. She looked comfortable in her loose khaki trousers and muted plaid shirt while at the same time her large glasses gave her a scholarly air. But Judy was doing a good job of covering up the headache that the painkillers wouldn't subdue. Usually she started work before eight, but today had been different and she'd needed extra sleep.

After yesterday's racquetball game with Mindi Allison, they'd gone back to her apartment to recuperate and chat. And Mindi really wanted to talk. Depressed about the chance of ever getting a permanent academic position, since her last three faculty applications hadn't even gotten her an interview, she'd complained to Judy, "I'm sure it's because I'm a woman. They just want to keep that all-male club intact."

Judy felt this was just an excuse, a way for Mindi to accept rejection without having to admit that it reflected on her marginal research record. However, she'd been skeptical enough to say, "I think it could actually help being female. There's lots of pressure these days to balance the quotas with women and minorities."

Mindy remained unconvinced. "Minorities maybe."

"Well, if you can fake it as a paleontologist, there's a position coming up in geology." Her attempt at levity showed no signs of reassuring Mindi.

They talked all evening—and drank all evening. Anyway, Judy really needed that coffee when she finally got out of bed this morning. Her coffee-maker was automatic only in the sense that if you plugged it in and turned it on it made coffee. She'd done both and headed for the shower. That helped. Finally, after a little foundation and some lipstick, she'd been ready to face the day and rode her bicycle into the geology department.

"Did you hear anything from the core storage people in Denver?" Candrew asked.

"No, not yet."

They talked about the research project for a while and Candrew tried to stay focused. But his thoughts kept wandering back to Gavin and after ten minutes he gave up and told Judy some of the things he'd discovered in going through the folders from Gavin's filing cabinet. He was particularly intrigued by the words *Iridium* and *Antares,* and wanted to know if she had any ideas. Apart from iridium being a metal and Antares being a star, they drew a blank.

Judy had been luckier checking up on the names that were listed with the budgets. "The campus phone book has three pages of names starting with *D.* Apart from Jason Devereaux, none of them has a *J* initial except for a *Jarvis Denley.* He's with the university's motor pool. The name Polanca was easy too. There's a single listing and that's for Teresa Polanca, an assistant professor in zoology."

"I suppose a biologist could have an interest in fossils," Candrew said.

"It's always possible, of course, that the names might be for people outside the university. Or even outside the state."

"Or outside the country. Let's just stick to the simplest explanation first."

"The other thing I did was talk to Maria about Jason Devereaux. She checked and found he's a junior majoring in communications. She also e-mailed a friend in the records office and got his grade point average: 2.4." Judy paused and then added, "I didn't think you'd mind, so I called the department and talked to one of his professors. He thought Jason was bright and did well when he applied himself. Too often, though, he didn't study consistently and easily got distracted."

"That's a good description of half the students in the university," Candrew said. "He seems pretty average. I don't suppose you asked if there had been any changes in behavior in the last few months?"

"No. But remember he didn't go to summer school and hasn't had any classes since May. That's more than three months."

"Yeah. Three months with nothing to do. I wonder what he's been up to?"

"If he's like most students, he got a summer job to help pay for school in the Fall. But I guess if he's really getting the money listed in that budget, he wouldn't need to do that."

Judy hesitated, looking a little guilty, and said, "There's one other thing I want to tell you. When we were sorting stuff in Gavin's office I played a few of his CDs."

"Yeah, I remember," Candrew said.

"Well, I borrowed several to take home. He had a lot of music I normally don't listen to and I thought it would be fun to hear something completely different for a change." After Candrew assured her it wasn't a problem, as long as they were returned, she continued, "When I tried to play them, all I got was a bunch of garbled noise or nothing at all."

"That's odd."

"I thought so too. Only one of the six CDs I tried had real

music on it. And that was the only one with a proper printed label. The others all had plain white Office Depot labels with handwritten titles. Things like *Beethoven Fifth Symphony. First Movement: 218.*"

"He probably copied someone else's discs and burnt his own CDs," Candrew said. But when he thought about that, it didn't make sense. "Why would he only put one movement on a disc? And the First Movement of Beethoven's Fifth lasts a lot longer than two minutes and eighteen seconds, or even 218 seconds."

"I told all this to Mindy—the woman I play racquetball with—and she had the idea that Gavin could be using the CDs for some sort of data storage, or maybe even custom software, that he wasn't really recording music."

Candrew's reaction to this idea was that Gavin wasn't a sophisticated enough computer user and wouldn't know how to do it. That was certainly the image he'd projected.

"I plan to give Mindi a couple of the discs—if that's okay—and she's going to see what's on them. She works with Professor Mackenzie-Burns in astronomy and they have all sorts of data evaluation equipment."

"No problem. It'll be interesting to see what shows up." He thought about the unfolding complexity of Gavin's activities. "We need to take a look at all his other CDs—and while we're at it, check out the rest of the files in his computer. Assuming we ever get access."

After talking for nearly an hour, Candrew left, took the stairs to the third floor, and made his way down the passage heading back to his office. He was ambushed by two students.

"Can you sign my enrollment card?"

"Not without reading it."

"Damn, and I was hoping to sneak into that course on Egyptian hieroglyphics."

"He thought it would help him read your handwriting," his

friend added impishly.

Candrew smiled—he always had a soft spot for the bright, mischievous students—and pushed open the door. "Come on in." He promptly took care of their needs, then sat at his desk checking e-mail, before hunting for his list. He was a compulsive list maker. The on-going struggle with too many obligations always seemed to leave him teetering on the edge of descent into chaos and lists provided an illusion of order, of control. Eventually he found it propped against the books in the shelf at the end of his desk. He wrote the lists on three-by-five cards and each item got deleted as he completed it, giving a sense of progress, although new additions always kept pace and his list never got any shorter. The unspoken goal, of course, was to get "caught up". He enthusiastically agreed with whoever it was that said, "There is really only one question—what to do next."

That question was answered when the phone rang and startled him. He grabbed it almost as a reflex.

"Professor Nor?"

"Yeah."

"Chuck Semley. We talked last week. You called to tell me about Gavin Citalli's unlucky accident—hey, I guess all accidents are unlucky, aren't they? Anyway, I need to talk to you some more. Now a good time?"

"Sure."

"I think you know Professor Citalli was doing field work out in northwestern New Mexico, right there in the Four Corners."

"Yes, but I don't know anything about the details. I've only got a vague idea of the location and I don't really know what he was digging up." Candrew decided not to say anything about the amounts of money that appeared to be involved, at least, not at the moment. And he didn't want to raise the possibility that the whole venture might be illegal. His main interest was to discover as much as he could about the other participants.

"The project's a bit, er, shall we say, sensitive. It's being done for a wealthy collector, but at the moment excavation isn't anywhere near complete. Without the professor we're looking for someone to take over the site and wrap things up."

"And you're hoping I can help you find someone? Anyway, who's the 'we'?"

"That's not what I meant. Look, Dr. Nor, you and I need to talk. I'm calling from Arizona, but next Friday I'll be in Santa Fe. It would be in your best interest to drive down so we can talk this over face to face. Also give us a chance to look at some maps and photos. And have a beer together."

Candrew hesitated a moment. He had no idea who Semley was. All he had to go on was just a rasping voice at the end of a phone line, but it was the voice of someone with the potential to fill a few of the gaps surrounding Gavin's death. This could be the break he needed, an opportunity to fit together more pieces of the developing puzzle. "Okay. But you've got to realize, I'm not making any commitments." Candrew quickly reviewed his options. "Why don't we get together over lunch?"

"You got yourself a deal—as long as it's not some fancy restaurant. No white table cloths, no waiters in penguin suits."

"Counter Culture would be good. It's real casual, low key. If you're heading out of town on Cerrillos Road, it's just a right turn onto Baca Street. There's a traffic light." He decided those were sufficient directions, but added, "Twelve-thirty would be good. And I should tell you how to recognize me, I'm . . ."

Semley interrupted. "Well, I assume you've got white hair, a goatee and wear thick glasses, a bow tie and a tweed jacket. Don't all profs look like that?" Now that their initial tense sparring had ended, he seemed more relaxed.

"Not this one. I don't even own a bow tie and . . ."

"You'll never make tenure. They won't let you into the club."

Candrew had been a tenured, full professor for nine years

but let the remark pass. "I'm five-eleven, glasses, no white-hair yet, and no beard. And you? How do I pick you out?"

"Don't worry, I'll spot you first." It was said with a certainty that was a little unsettling.

Suddenly, Candrew had a mental image of a long fiber optic cable linking him to Semley five hundred miles away—sort of like a spider and its prey. He wasn't sure which was which. "See you Friday." It came out a bit too curt and he put the phone down abruptly wondering whether he'd made the right decision.

One of the few perks of being on the faculty was that you could eat—and drink—in the faculty club lounge. While comfortably furnished and adequately decorated with polished wood and carpets, it certainly wasn't as opulent as the administrator's lounge—just good enough for those who actually did the work. The food was the same as that in the student cafeteria, meaning it was unimaginative—and you only had to pay a couple of dollars more for it. You did, however, get linen tablecloths and waitress service. The fifth floor view of the mountains to the east and north was impressive and a small group of regulars took advantage of it by occupying the corner table beside the floor-to-ceiling window. When Candrew ambled over, the sole member of the regular group was sitting with the morning paper opened wide and his chair rocked back on two legs. Candrew glanced over his shoulder at the editorial page.

"Well, Mr. Historian, are we repeating the mistakes of the past?"

"Hell no, we're making new and improved ones." He produced a deep, resonant laugh.

Anton Lubinski, universally known as "Lubie", was a history professor who'd come to the U.S. from Hungary in his mid-teens, and still retained traces of an eastern European accent. Now in his early sixties, there was hair on his chin but not much on his head, and his rotund frame gave a weighty resonance to his pronouncements. He looked up from his newspaper. "I was real sorry to hear about Gavin's drowning." He glanced down at the paper and then back at Candrew. "Geologists seem to be a long-lived bunch—if they avoid accidents. Great guy. Pity he died so young."

It certainly was. And Candrew still harbored a nagging concern about the drowning. While it might have been a freak accident, he still felt Gavin was too experienced a kayaker to have let that happen. If not an accident, then what?"

He'd just settled into the chair opposite Lubie and picked up the menu when two of the other lunchtime regulars joined them. The one waving his arms yelled, "Five purchase orders in one week! How can she screw up that many? We're not talking rocket science here."

Ted Devereaux worked in the business office and his tirades against incompetence were frequent and loud, with Hispanics the usual target. His disdain for all aspects of their language and culture was widely known. "Why won't they let me fire the bitch?"

His colleague leaned over and grabbed a menu. "No way you can do that, not in a state university. Have to keep all those quotas straight."

"How the hell can they expect you to run things efficiently if they force you to hire incompetents?"

"Come on, Ted. They're not all incompetent," Candrew said. "You always boast that Juan Chavez is a first rate accountant."

"Yeah, that's true, but he's just a coconut." He saw Lubie's eyebrows rise in a mute question. "Light brown on the outside, white on the inside." He paused with exasperation. "The least they could do is make them speak English in the office. And while they're at it, get all that Spanish off the signs."

Lubie quietly pointed out that the Spanish speakers were here first. "And if you want to be a purist about it, the Indians got here long before the Spanish. We should all be speaking Tano or Keresan."

"You're a historian; you know that history is written by the winners and in this country they wrote it in English," was Ted's tart response.

Out of deference to their waitress, Rosita, who was both Hispanic and efficient, the topic was dropped. They concentrated on ordering lunch and moved to marginally less divisive discussions of sport and politics.

Candrew looked at Ted with more than his usual interest. Did he know what his son Jason was involved in? But this didn't seem an appropriate time to raise that issue.

Chapter 6

Professionally, Gavin dealt with the fossilized remains of organisms long dead, but the garden in front of his house showed he hadn't neglected the living. As Candrew followed the flagstone path lined with boulders and chamisa, it curved through a swath of olive greens complemented with clumps of bright flowers. The lushly-bordered walkway contrasted with the dusty, sparse desert growth beyond, and for Candrew all gardening was an attempt to control nature. But he realized a benign effort to impose human will on the natural system had its flip side in the enormous dams of the west, where even the great floods of spring are channeled and controlled. Somehow gardening seemed fair, sort of one-on-one with Mother Nature, but armies of engineers with their earth-moving machines and concrete mixers, that was unfair: a one-sided contest, like fishing with dynamite.

Three broad flagstone steps led up to the heavy wooden front door, and Marge opened it before he could ring the bell, gave him a wordless hug and welcomed him in.

"You know Anne, my sister?"

"Yes. We met after the chapel service."

Anne had on a three-quarter length denim skirt and plain white tee shirt. Candrew smiled courteously and noticed she was not wearing shoes—or a wedding ring.

"Come on through to the dining room. Anne's helping me sort out all the paperwork. She's good at figures." Marge gestured to the piles of bills and receipts littered across the table. "There's such a lot to take care of. I'd no idea how much Gavin filed away, things I never even thought about, like all the insurance and medical records. It's going to take forever."

Marge seemed overanxious, eager to talk. Candrew thought that was a good sign, better than bottling everything up. He knew how hard it would be for her to adjust to a whole new way of looking at life. For a few weeks, there would be plenty of people around, lots of support, and then, one by one, they'd go back to their own lives, leaving her to cope alone.

"There, I'm being such a poor hostess—can I get you a drink or fix you some coffee?" Two in the afternoon was a bit early for a drink, even for Candrew, and when he opted for coffee she disappeared into the kitchen. There was an awkward moment of silence and then he quietly said to Anne, "How's Marge doing?"

"Seems to be coping well enough, though it's difficult to know how things are when she's alone. Even as a kid, I remember she was always good at covering up the way she really felt. Now her philosophy seems to be to keep busy so she doesn't have time to brood."

Candrew understood. He had published more scientific papers in the two years after Penny's death than at any other time in his career. Science provided a haven, a place to go where everything was still normal, where everything obeyed the rules. He wondered what haven Marge would be able to turn to. Time does not heal, it's just that grief bubbles up into consciousness less often.

Marge came back with coffee mugs, suggested they'd be more comfortable in the living room and led the way. They followed her into an almost square room with a far wall of french doors and flanking windows. Outside, the afternoon sun cast crisply-etched shadows across low walls and a flagstone patio. Marge waved towards a generous, wide-armed sofa, pulled a small side table out of a nest of three and put his coffee on it and sat in the adjacent arm chair. Anne settled into the wing-backed chair on the far side.

Gavin and Marge always had a party between Thanksgiving and Christmas, and Candrew's memories of the room were of being with Renata and a crowd of people joking and laughing, drinking a bit too much—and eating far too much. There was none of that spontaneous gaiety now. He sipped his coffee and glanced at Anne before giving attention to Marge. She was sitting on the very edge of the chair, like a bird on a twig, and seemed very rigid, as though making a determined effort to hold everything together.

Candrew was in no hurry to get on with business, mainly because he had no idea how he was going to go about it. He still hadn't made up his mind whether to tell her all the details of the dinosaur dig, at least as far as he knew them.

It was Marge who broke the silence. "I hope sorting out Gavin's office isn't going to take a lot of your time, be too much of a burden. I know how busy you professors are, especially right before semester starts."

"Well, I've taught the course for years, so I'm in pretty good shape. At least some things get easier with time." Candrew paused, wondering how he was going to make the transition from pleasantries to the questions he really wanted to ask. He took the direct approach. "Yesterday, I was in Gavin's office with Judy Westerlund, pulling out the notes and fossils she'll need for the sophomore paleo course. We found that Gavin was working on a major fossil excavation. One that involved some pretty substantial budgets. Did he say anything about his funding?"

"No. I don't know anything about that. But then, he didn't talk much about his research. I wouldn't have understood most of it anyway."

"What about changes in his work schedule?"

"He always did a fair amount of field work, of course. Maybe there was a bit more than usual this last summer. And he was down in Albuquerque several times, to the university. Really though, I'd got used to him being gone." She glanced away.

"Any big changes in the last eight months or so? I mean things like bank balances, or opening safe deposit boxes, or changing TIAA-CREF options. What about alterations to life insurance policies—especially new ones? Or recent big purchases? Did he talk about getting a new car or anything like that?"

The questions came tumbling out and Candrew felt like the police inspector in an English murder mystery where all the suspects are gathered for questioning in the squire's library. At least, they had facts, suspects and a genuine murder. Candrew wasn't even sure that Gavin had been murdered; it was just a gut feeling—and that was an uncomfortable position for a scientist who was used to documenting every step in an argument with unquestioned facts.

"What about unusual expenditures on credit cards?" Candrew asked.

Anne broke in. "We haven't finished going through all the statements, but the monthly totals seem about right." She paused and glanced at Marge who'd been sitting in silence. "The only unusual item we've found so far is a recent purchase of forty-five thousand dollar's worth of mutual funds."

"Wow, that's a lot." Candrew pushed back his hair and frowned. "How long ago?"

"I don't remember the exact date; maybe six weeks."

Marge looked uncomfortable. "I have no idea where he got all that money and I'm upset he didn't tell me." She spoke slowly and quietly. "We always do everything together—used to do everything together." Changing the tense seemed to bring home the finality of Gavin's death. Marge stared straight ahead saying nothing, her eyes filling with tears. She turned away, buried her face in her hands, and sobbed quietly, whispering almost inaudibly, "I'm so sorry." There were threads of silver in her dark hair and lines around the corners of her eyes and at the edges of her mouth that he'd not noticed before. Anne quietly moved towards her, but Marge got up and left without saying a word. Candrew knew all too well how she felt.

Anne smiled in a way that implied, *no big deal; this is to be expected.* And Candrew agreed. They talked more about the savings accounts, even though he felt this was really none of his business, and conversation then drifted to more general topics.

After five minutes, Marge came back, more composed. "Maybe we should take a look at Gavin's study." Anne and Candrew got up to follow her. "I rarely went in, but I'd be surprised if there's much research-related stuff. He didn't work at home very often."

A short passage decorated with framed photographs led back to the office which had probably been intended as a small guest bedroom. One of the longer walls was lined with bookshelves that were half-filled with journals, books and magazines, together with a few interspersed fossils, CDs, and photos. The opposite wall was mostly windows and gave a pleasant view across the corner of the patio to the mountains. A computer keyboard, monitor and printer sat on a large wooden desk that dominated the far wall and the only other pieces of furniture were a gray, two-drawer filing cabinet and a low-backed arm chair.

Two black and white photographs, both in shiny aluminum frames, hung on the wall behind the computer. Candrew casually glanced at them—and stopped: enthralled, fascinated and amused. On the left was the classic Ansel Adams image of *Moonrise over Hernandez* with the clear moon low over the parched headstones of a New Mexican cemetery. Beside it, a NASA photograph, taken from an almost identical low angle perspective, showed the cloud-shrouded Earth rising above a sterile, gray-cratered lunar foreground. Typical Gavin. Just like him to make an insightful comment with a touch of humor.

Marge watched for a moment, then returned to the business at hand. "Nothing's been touched, everything's the way he left it. Just go ahead and look at whatever you need to."

It was awkward being in Gavin's office while she watched, but in his methodical way Candrew started to check the bookshelves. All standard stuff until he got to the end of the second shelf where he was surprised to find a variety of computer manuals. They included *ArcView 3.1, Illustrator 10, Adobe Photoshop* and several sophisticated image-processing packages. Not the sort of thing he expected for a computer illiterate, which is what Gavin always claimed to be. Even in the department, he got grad students to load new software for him. Candrew thoroughly examined the computer tower that stood next to the desk—a top-of-the-line Dell. Although no computer geek himself, it seemed clear to Candrew that Gavin had been making a deliberate effort to mislead everyone about the level of his computer skills.

He turned to Marge. "Do you know his password?"

"No, I don't."

The bookshelves beside the computer had several piles of CDs in plastic boxes. After Judy's discovery that some of Gavin's discs were not what they were labeled, he searched through the stacks carefully. All but two of the discs had plain labels with hand-written titles like *Beethoven Symph No. 7 : 324.* The two exceptions had commercial labels, both Brahms symphonies.

"Can I take the CDs with me?"

"Yes, of course. I'll get you a bag."

Going through the drawers of the filing cabinet felt too much like prying for Candrew's comfort, but they housed nothing of interest. Gavin's desk, however, did produce one significant artifact in the form of a paperweight. While technically all the pieces of rock, fossils and clusters of minerals that perched on paper piles could be considered paper weights, they had obviously been selected for geologic or aesthetic reasons. On the end stack of paper was a fossil tooth about the size of a small banana. It had serrations down one side and even though Candrew was no fossil expert, he was almost certain it came from a big carnivore, maybe even a *T. rex*. As he was putting it back on the paper pile, he noticed that an adjacent piece of rock also had a large carnivore tooth embedded in it, this one only partially exposed. A detailed examination showed it to be similar in size to the first one with the same sort of serrations. For Candrew, this seemed to imply that Gavin was involved in excavating a large dinosaur.

The bottom drawer of the desk also held a surprise. At the front were half a dozen six-volt lantern batteries. Behind them, a grey plastic device, looking vaguely like some kind of flashlight, was lying on its side. Candrew didn't recognize it. When he lifted it out onto the desk, he could see that there were two narrow bulbs, each about a foot long. The manufacturer's label identified the device as an ultraviolet lamp—a *black light*. The unit was obviously portable with a carrying handle and compartment for batteries. Candrew had no idea why Gavin would need one and it seemed to be the only thing in the whole office that was out of context. He stood tapping his teeth, trying to figure out its significance.

As he turned to leave the office, he stopped in the doorway. "One last question. Did Gavin take any out-of-town trips? I mean, in addition to his usual research areas?"

Marge bit on her lower lip and gazed into the distance. "He made one quick trip to Denver and was also down in Houston for a couple of days. I think he was visiting one of the oil companies. That's all I can remember. Oh, yes, he did have a meeting with somebody in Edmonton, or was it Calgary?—I don't remember which. I always get those two mixed up."

"How long ago was that?"

"Let me see now . . . back in the spring. Must have been

April."

Candrew was surprised to find himself in the parking lot behind Kinblade Hall, remembering little of his trip back to the university. Fortunately, his subconscious seemed to be a competent driver and had got him there without incident. He parked beside Rosenberg's green BMW with the *GEO-CEO* plate.

During the drive over, he'd been preoccupied trying to establish some sort of pattern in everything he'd found out last night and today. One thing was clear—Gavin was involved in getting a big fossil skeleton exhumed. Since he was a paleontology professor, that wasn't out of line: he'd excavated a variety of sites during his career. It was the fact that he was keeping it secret from the faculty—and his wife—and obviously working with (or for?) people who were not his usual academic colleagues. Like most fossil research, Gavin's previous work had been done on a shoestring with graduate students providing slave labor. This project was well-funded. Who was putting up the money? And why—what did they expect to get for their money? And overriding it all was the fact that Gavin had died.

Apart from Jason's involvement with Gavin, he had no idea about the importance of "iridium" and "Antares". But at least he now knew Polanca was a zoology faculty member. He grabbed his office phone.

"Zoology department," answered the pleasant voice.

"Dr. Monica Henderson, please."

"I'm sorry she's not here at the moment. I don't expect her back until late this afternoon." The zoology secretary was straightforward and efficient. "Can I take a message?"

"Would you tell her I'd like to come by tomorrow morning."

"Yes, I'll certainly do that. And the name again?"

"Candrew Nor. I'm in Geology."

Chapter 7

The next morning Candrew drove to the department a little after ten-thirty, parked in his usual slot outside Kinblade Hall and from there walked to the north edge of campus where a new glass and concrete building housed agriculture and the biological sciences. Taking the elevator to the third floor, he followed the signs to the zoology main office.

"Is Dr. Henderson in?" Monica Henderson was Chair of the department and, although he didn't know her well, they had served together on a faculty affairs committee. The secretary dutifully escorted him into her office.

The large sunlit room was basically neat, but its occupant was clearly fighting a losing battle against the onslaught of paperwork. Monica greeted him with a smile and motioned him toward an empty chair. "Haven't seen you for a while. What brings you to this side of campus?"

"I'd like to get some information about Professor Teresa Polanca."

"What sort of information?" Her tone was guarded.

"Information I hope we can keep confidential. You probably

heard that one of the geology faculty, Gavin Citalli, drowned this summer. I'm sorting out his office and stumbled on some things that make me suspicious about the circumstances surrounding his death. One of his files had a list of people who appear to be cooperating on well-funded, joint research. Included on the list was Dr. Polanca."

"Really! That's intriguing. I haven't been told about any collaborative research between geology and zoology, and certainly none involving big bucks. Teresa isn't around right now; she's out doing field work."

"What exactly does she do in the field?"

"Studies scorpions. For several years she's specialized in *Centruroides sculpturatus*, especially in northern Arizona and around the Four Corners. It's one of the few species with a fatal sting, at least for young kids and small animals."

Candrew was wondering what studying scorpions had to do with fossils, particularly dinosaur fossils. "Sounds like a dangerous way to make a living."

"No, not really." She grinned. "Most scorpions aren't nearly as aggressive or poisonous as people think. The main problem is their nocturnal habits."

"You mean she's scrabbling around in the desert at night looking for scorpions?" Candrew's eyebrows rose in surprise.

Monica laughed. "It's actually quite easy. You only need a black light and the scorpions glow in the dark; they fluoresce in the ultraviolet. You can easily watch them hunt and mate."

"Has she always worked with scorpions?"

"No. Teresa's had quite a varied research career, mostly with small reptiles before she got involved with scorpions."

"Could I get a copy of her résumé?"

"I don't see why not." She paused, apparently reconsidering. "Maybe I should clear it with the dean just to be safe."

Candrew wondered about the sort of woman who'd be alone

in the desert at night peering at scorpions. "What's she like as a person?"

"Dr. Polanca's fairly new on the faculty, so I don't know her all that well. She's got an acid wit and a reputation for cynicism, but the students seem to like her classes. Which reminds me, on Thursday we have a welcoming pizza lunch for new students and several faculty are going to talk about their research. All quite low key, with the emphasis on entertainment. Teresa's giving a general talk about her scorpion work." Monica got up and consulted a typed list scotch-taped to the side of a filing cabinet. "It'll be in Room 310 at two o'clock. You could just sit in the back of the lecture hall and see what you think of her."

"That's a great idea." Candrew pushed up his slipping glasses. "One last thing, is she married? Have close friends?"

"As I said, I don't know her terribly well. I really can't answer that."

They chatted for another ten minutes about research in zoology and university matters in general and Candrew left.

It was close to lunchtime and Candrew headed for the faculty lounge. He cut across the main plaza where Russian olives shaded one side and Tenby library cast its shadow over much of the rest. Returning students walked with an easy, condescending confidence, while newcomers and their parents looked more like tourists as they tried to figure out how to get to the bookstore and where orientation was scheduled. For Candrew, it was the start of another semester, just like the last twenty. For the students, it was that time in life they would always remember, the time when they moved out into the world on their own, or at least into the halfway house between home and career.

Professor Teresa Polanca, scorpion woman. Why was her name in Gavin's file? And what was her role in the well-funded project? As far as Candrew knew, Gavin had no professional interest in scorpions. Maybe he was more interested in Teresa, an affair perhaps? Candrew had to admit that was completely out of character with the Gavin he knew. But then, human nature being what it is, anything was possible. So what was the relationship? And how was an expert on scorpions involved with a *T. rex* fossil? Good God—why hadn't he thought of it before? Polanca used a black light to track scorpions at night and Gavin had a black light in the desk drawer in his home office. No way that could be coincidence. He was snapped out of his reverie by a bright yellow Frisbee landing with a clatter a yard away and sliding almost to his foot. A student across the plaza yelled, "Sorry!" and one nearby retrieved it. Unsure what to make of the information about Teresa Polanca and her scorpions, he strolled slowly and pensively over to the faculty club and rode the elevator to the top floor.

Candrew settled into his usual chair in the corner of the faculty lounge. "Let me have the chile rellenos." He handed the lunch menu back to Rosita.

"So how's life with you?" asked the thin man to his right.

"Hectic." He didn't mention the time he'd spent sorting Gavin's office. "Pretty much on track for this time of year."

Further discussion ended when Charlie Lister, a short, tanned man with twinkling eyes and a shock of unruly hair, walked in.

He slumped into the last vacant chair and Arlan Dee passed him a menu. "Hi Charlie, haven't see you for a while."

"No. Since we got back from visiting the kids in Dallas, I've been out painting most of the time. Good to get up in the mountains again."

Charlie taught design and the freshman painting course. His fairly realistic landscapes, with the palette just a little exaggerated, showed lush sunsets and lots of trees reflected in lakes. They were despised by the art department's two abstractionist painters who dismissed them as "Chocolate Box art". The fact that he sold well in galleries in Scottsdale and Santa Fe may also have had something to do with their disdain.

"Apart from a couple of hikers the only people I saw up there yesterday were Jason Devereaux and his girlfriend. Cute girl. Hispanic."

Candrew put down his fork, anxious to hear more. Ever since he'd seen Jason's name on Gavin's budget he'd been eager to know about his role in the dinosaur project.

But Arlan broke in. "Hispanic girlfriend? Hey, that'll make Ted happy."

Ted Devereaux's intense dislike for the local Hispanics and all aspects of their culture had been a frequent subject of his many diatribes. Usually one of the lunchtime group, today Ted was missing. Candrew had looked forward to getting more information about his son, but now it seemed he'd have to wait to find out what Jason had been doing all summer.

Charlie laughed at Arlan's comment. "Yeah. I think I took them by surprise when I was fishing from the bank. Which reminds me, I've got four good-sized rainbow trout for you, Candrew. Didn't have time to drop them by last night. I'll get one of the grad students to bring them over after lunch."

"Ah, fresh food." The voice was Lubie's and the tone carried a somewhat critical edge. "Just what our far distant ancestors ate— before all those genetic modifiers gave us a loaf that stays fresh for a month and beer that's fizzy for a year. We can even look forward to square grapes that'll fit neatly in a box."

Before his family escaped from Hungary, Lubie had known real hunger. The intensity of that pre-teen experience remained etched in his mind and for many years he kept a can of tuna in his pocket or briefcase, a sort of insurance. Although over that now, the memories ran deep. His attitude to food remained purely practical. Candrew, on the other hand, had a reputation for liking good food, well prepared. Lubie turned to him. "If you were a cannibal you'd only eat free range missionaries."

Candrew smiled, assuming it was just another of Lubie's witticisms, not realizing the depth of feeling. Lubie let it pass.

Arlan Dee stood up. "Well, I have a one o'clock committee meeting."

The tubby prof seated beside him also rose. "And I need to get my class handouts duplicated at Kinkos." Lubie smiled and levered himself out of his chair.

A little after three, Candrew was interrupted by a loud pounding on his office door. The hand doing the pounding was attached to a large, tattooed arm that extended from a torn, black tank top. The tall, heavy-set student had shoulder-length, black crinkly hair and wore circular, wire-rimmed glasses. His jeans were almost completely covered with splashes of paint, looking like a Pollock drip painting, and Candrew wondered if this counted as wearable art.

"Charlie wanted me to bring these fish over before all the ice melted." He held out a Styrofoam carton with a red plastic handle. "Don't know how you can eat that stuff."

"Fish?"

"Any animal that had to be killed, you know."

"Oh, you don't eat meat?"

"It's proven; meat's bad for you, man. Grains and vegetables are, like, really really healthy."

Considering his huge bulk, Candrew thought he had the appearance of an archetypal meat eater, a *T. rex* of the student world. A practicing carnivore himself, he didn't want to get into this argument and said simply, "Well, thanks for the delivery anyway."

The student offered a half-smile, added slyly, "Watch out for the bones," and left.

Four fresh trout. He knew exactly how he'd cook them—and who he would eat them with. He picked up the phone and called Renata.

The card was addressed to *Dr. Candrew Nor or Current Wine Lover.* Held in place by a rubber band, it had been strapped to the visor of Candrew's Jeep Cherokee for a couple of weeks and he pulled into the parking lot of the liquor store hoping that the promised fifteen percent discount hadn't expired. It hadn't. He bought half a dozen bottles of his favorite Chardonnay and headed home.

In the kitchen, he grated radishes, adding grated lemon, lime and orange peel, some lemon juice, and a little sugar. He checked the Creole seasoning recipe: this was going to be a problem—he'd forgotten it needed cilantro. All his spices and herbs were piled on one pantry shelf and any attempt at organization had been abandoned long ago. Ferreting through the glass jars, plastic bags and odd-looking tins, he finally discovered some cilantro, not the freshest but it would have to do. He coated both sides of the cleaned trout with the seasoning ready for the oven.

Candrew liked to cook for Renata because she was an excellent cook herself and appreciated his culinary efforts. Although "just good friends" they frequently ate out together. Her point of view after a movie or faculty party was typically very different from his—which he found stimulating. He was thinking about the Santa Fe opera performance they'd been to when he heard her car pull into the driveway.

Renata carried in a large bunch of flowers and kissed Candrew on the cheek. "I know you wouldn't buy flowers for yourself, or even go out in the garden and pick some, so I brought you these. Have you got a tall vase?"

"That's thoughtful of you. Thanks." He was preparing carrots for the slaw and with the grater in hand waved vaguely in the appropriate direction. "Up above the cupboard."

They talked about the small inconsequential things that only close friends can without feeling awkward. Candrew took a serious sip of wine, turned his attention to the lemon butter sauce, and then slid the trout into the oven. "Fifteen minutes and they'll be ready." He reached for his wine glass. "I'm glad you're back on campus and could come to dinner at such short notice. The last couple of days have been draining and I needed distraction."

"So, the only reason for inviting me to dinner is to distract you?" Renata pushed back her long black hair and laughed, amused at Candrew's obvious discomfort. "I must admit you have good bait. The food looks fantastic." A rich aroma was permeating the kitchen.

Although not really necessary, Candrew tried to atone by asking how her week had gone.

"Well, I got some great news from the National Science Foundation. They're going to extend my funding, and I can continue the research for a couple more years." Excavating an early Mayan site in Guatemala had been the focus of Renata's life for almost three years. She'd grown up in Costa Rica and had been familiar with pre-Columbian pots and figurines since she was a young girl and that early interest blossomed into a career. "Two years support will distract me from all the mundane things I should be doing, like revising freshman course notes." She sipped her wine. "Okay, tell me, what do you need to be distracted from?"

Over dinner, Candrew outlined the circumstances of Gavin's death; what he'd found in the office; the major dinosaur dig involving large sums of money; and his general unease with the idea that drowning had been accidental. "I just have this gut feeling that Gavin was too experienced a kayaker to lose control in a simple rapid."

"You think it wasn't an accident? That it may have been done deliberately?" She shook her head slowly from side to side as

67

if to imply this couldn't possibly be the way it was. "Who'd want to kill Gavin? And why? And how would they get away with it in front of a bunch of students?"

"I've asked myself those questions a dozen times, and I have no idea."

"What about the *T. rex* excavation? Wasn't he a fossil expert? I would have thought that's the sort of thing he'd be doing anyway?"

"True. But I don't think he'd ever worked with dinosaurs before. His specialty was Tertiary mammals. What's unusual is the way he was keeping everything secret. That, and the size of the budgets."

"Which brings up the central question: where did all that money come from?"

Chile came quietly padding into the dining room and flopped down under the table with an audible sigh. In theory, Candrew didn't give him tidbits during meals, but he was a smart dog and had learned that by being cute and persistent the rules could be bent. It was always worth a try. This time it didn't work since Candrew was too involved telling Renata about his surprise phone contact. "The other odd incident was a phone conversation with a guy called Chuck Semley. He'd left his number on Gavin's answering machine. When I called, he was pretty guarded. He didn't sound like an academic, although he certainly seemed to be clued in on the dino dig."

"You think he's one of those commercial fossil dealers?"

"Possible, I guess. It might explain why Gavin hadn't told anyone. And it would also explain the money. Anyway, I've agreed to meet Semley in Santa Fe on Saturday, so we may get some answers then."

"Well keep me up to date on what you find out."

They cleared the table together and while Renata stacked plates in the dishwasher, Candrew went through the ritual of making coffee with a French press. They carried their mugs into the living room. "Speaking of unexpected phone calls," Renata said, "I got one from an old friend, well really only an acquaintance." She settled into the corner of the sofa and cradled the coffee mug in both hands. "It's odd because I don't know him very well and haven't even seen him since we were on a committee together over three years ago. He's an archaeology prof named Joel Iskander. Called out of the blue because he's going to be visiting the university in a week and wanted to see if he could come by the department." She took a long swig of coffee and thought about that. "As far as I know, he's never been here before."

"Which university is he at?" Candrew asked.

"Illinois."

"And he's interested in the Maya?"

"No. He's never worked in mesoAmerica. The decline of civilizations is his research specialty and he studies the Anasazi as an example. The most surprising thing was that he asked about you."

"Me?" Candrew raised his eyebrows. "I've never heard of him."

"Well, he's definitely heard of you. Said he'd seen your name on geological reports describing sandstones in southeast Utah."

"I guess that could be something of mutual interest. The whole area out there has hundreds of Anasazi ruins. When's he coming?"

Before she had a chance to reply, the phone rang. Candrew picked it up and Renata discretely retreated to the kitchen for a coffee refill. Apart from an occasional word, he said little, just listening. Eventually, he joined her in the kitchen where he stood unsmiling and visibly shaking, still gripping the phone, not noticing it was making a dial tone. Renata pried it out of his hand and replaced it in the holder.

Candrew steadied himself against the counter. "That was

Anne, Marge's sister. The Office of the Medical Examiner called this afternoon to tell them the pathologist's tests showed Gavin had been drugged. His blood had traces of carfentanil. Apparently that's very fast-acting."

"You mean someone deliberately drugged him."

"That's what it looks like. He would have lost consciousness and drowned."

"So he was murdered?" Renata said.

Distractedly, Candrew took off his glasses and ran his hand back through his hair. His breathing was fast and shallow. Renata put her arm around his shoulders. For a moment they stood in silence.

Tapping his teeth, Candrew stared into his coffee mug, unseeing. "And they must have drugged him right before he kayaked into the rapid."

"Could someone have spiked his Gatorade? Anyone notice him drinking anything before he started? One of the students, perhaps."

"I don't know. But the police are going to be talking to everyone who was on the trip."

"Then it's definitely murder."

"Certainly looks like it." Candrew stood shaking his head not wanting to believe what he'd been told. "Why would anyone kill Gavin? Marge is devastated."

Moving in a daze, he got glasses out of the cupboard and poured a couple of hefty shots of scotch.

Chapter 8

It was difficult to concentrate. Candrew had sat at his office desk for more than hour, achieving nothing, his thoughts constantly drifting back to Gavin. Such a senseless murder. Who would kill Gavin, and why? He had to find out. Bastards. Maybe students on the river trip would have insights, although he knew most weren't yet back for Fall semester. There was always a chance that Semley could be a possible source of information—if he was prepared to help. After all, he was the one who'd suggested they get together. What did he want to talk about? Candrew fussed for another hour and finally gave up, deciding he needed to do something physical.

As he stepped out into the hallway, locking the door behind him, Meredith Seligman shouted, "Dr. Nor." A graduate student, she'd been doing her research with Gavin Citalli. Now she hurried up to Candrew saying, "I need to talk to you. Do you have a minute?"

"Sure. What do you want?"

"It's so sad about Dr. Citalli." She paused and looked away for a moment. "I was working with him on a field project and he'd told me Dr. Tadheim was collaborating and would have important information for us. When I went to see him, he just brushed me off. He was pretty blunt, said it wasn't significant any more. And anyway, I wouldn't have any use for it now. But I've got to finish my research. I need to get everything together for my dissertation. He wouldn't even tell me what sort of data he had." She gushed on, close to tears, obviously worried and angry.

"You should talk to the department chairman."

"He's away right now, and since you were a close friend of Dr. Citalli's I thought you might be able to help."

"Well, I don't know any of the details of Citalli's project," Candrew said. But he realized he didn't even know whether Kurt Tadheim had been involved in research with Gavin, and if so, what role he'd play in a dinosaur excavation. "What did you expect to get from Tadheim?" he asked.

"He's a geophysicist and was supposed to put together an image of what was underground. He knows how to use seismic."

"I see." But Candrew had nothing to add and Seligman left unhappy.

Candrew headed down to his basement laboratory.

After telling Judy that Gavin's death was no accident, they sat subdued and talked for a while about the implications. Eventually focus returned to their current research project. Judy showed him the stack of newly delivered core boxes and Candrew suggested they start to put them in order.

Lifting cardboard boxes loaded with rock cores was hard work, and it was twelve-fifteen before they finished sorting them all.

"I think we've got everything in sequence," Judy said. "I can see where you want to take samples for thin sections." She wiped her forehead with the back of her hand and pushed up her slipping glasses.

Candrew dragged a stool out from under the bench and

flopped down. "We've made a lot of progress. How about a break for lunch? You want to go over to the cafeteria? I'll buy."

"Make it a salad, and I'm with you."

The cafeteria was on the far side of a small quadrangle, and the quickest route was through the campus store. They made their way past scattered students—the well-organized buying textbooks, the fashion-conscious buying tee shirts and the hungry buying candy bars. Candrew and Judy settled into a cafeteria table beside one of the large plate-glass windows and watched this interesting subgroup of humanity as it scurried across the quad with backpacks and bicycles. With the start of semester a week away students had time on their hands and were relaxed, noisy, and irreverent. The males seemed to be evenly divided between those with shoulder-length hair and those with shaved heads.

Candrew always drank coffee without cream or sugar, but he'd picked up a spoon and was slowly and absentmindedly stirring his drink, although ignoring the swirling liquid and rising steam. Grinning broadly, he was intently watching one particular group of students at a nearby table.

"What's so funny?"

"I was just thinking of Ted Devereaux with an Hispanic daughter-in-law." He explained for Judy. "Ted's one of the group I usually eat lunch with. He's as bigoted as anyone I've ever met in the South. Most of the time he's bitching about Hispanics in general and his staff in particular. Now, see that blond-haired kid two tables over?"

Judy looked in the direction Candrew nodded and inspected the student he was talking about. Sitting at the table beside him, very close beside him, was a strikingly attractive girl with olive complexion and long, wavy black hair.

"That's Jason Devereaux. And I'll bet you a dollar that's his current girlfriend. And obviously she's Hispanic." He recalled Charlie Lister's comments from yesterday's lunch.

Candrew had only met Jason once or twice when he was with his father at basketball games. Now he studied the young man intensely, his curiosity tweaked by the fact that his name was on Gavin's list—a list that had taken on added significance with the news that Gavin had been murdered.

He wasn't sure what he expected to see, but found himself looking for any signs of conspicuous consumption. There were none—unless you counted the Air Jordan shoes. Candrew never could understand why anyone, except maybe a professional basketball player, would pay several hundred dollars for a pair of sneakers. Faded jeans and a worn, green, short-sleeved tee shirt with no logo completed the outfit, and his long, sandy hair was held in place by a simple leather thong. If he really was getting the generous sums listed in Gavin's budget, he certainly wasn't spending the money on clothes. Or jewelry. Candrew couldn't see any rings, or even a watch.

As he scrutinized Jason and his girlfriend, two other Hispanic girls carrying large sodas joined the couple at the table. Obviously close friends, they greeted each other in Spanish and there was a lot of good-natured kidding around. Relaxed and comfortable in the group, Jason's Spanish seemed more than adequate to handle this social setting. One of the girls soon left to join other friends, and shortly afterwards the others got up and headed out.

Judy watched them go. "Show's over!" They hadn't spoken for the last five minutes.

"Sorry. It's just that I'm intrigued by Jason's role in this whole *T. rex* affair. And after last night's stunning news, it's taken on even more urgency. I keep trying to figure out what he's doing with a group of professionals, and where those Hispanic friends fit in—if they're involved at all. I suppose it's possible he could have discovered the dinosaur fossil and is being paid to keep quiet about it, or maybe he's demanding money, in which case it's blackmail."

"True. Also, he's young and fit . . ."

"You noticed."

". . . and may actually be helping with the logistics of the dig."

"He's a well-paid laborer if that's true. I just want to find out his role, and what he's doing to justify all the money."

"I can't help you with that. However, on a related topic, I did search the web to see what I could find out about the other names on Gavin's list. Remember, *Antares* and *iridium*?"

"You're turning into a real computer jock."

"Closer to a nerd than you know. I ate a microwaved pizza and a Twinkie sitting in front of the computer." The memory made her laugh. "Most of the information for iridium was about the satellite communication system. With that you can phone from anywhere on Earth, even the poles and the middle of the ocean. It would certainly work out in the Four Corners." She frowned, working through her mental list. "There's also, of course, the metal iridium. The name's from *Iris*, the Greek goddess of the rainbow." Judy smiled at the amount of arcane information the internet came up with. "It's the densest metal known, and you can get your very own sample for a thousand dollars an ounce."

Candrew was surprised—almost as expensive as gold.

"The other interesting thing about iridium is that it's found in high concentrations in rocks from the very end of the Cretaceous."

"Yeah. That's right." High iridium at the boundary between the Cretaceous and the Tertiary time periods had been well documented by geologists. Candrew knew it was this information that led Professor Alvarez and his Nobel–laureate father, to suggest that it arrived in a huge meteorite that hit the coast of Mexico with an impact big enough to cause a global catastrophe and wipe out dinosaurs everywhere.

"That's sort of relevant since *T. rex* lived right at the time of the extinctions."

"So there's a possible tie to Gavin," Candrew said. "But I

still don't see how this fits in with his fossil dig, or with the big budgets."

"Can't help you there." Judy took a big gulp of her lemonade. "I got a lot more variety for *Antares*, everything from house builders and poetry, to investment companies and data bases, even a beer. Most hits were the rocket that a commercial space outfit is developing for NASA. They had a couple of successful launches, and then recently one blew up." She drained the last of her soda. "Everything seemed to be named after the star Antares. That's in the constellation Scorpius. The web site said it's a bright supergiant and best seen in July, which, of course, is about when we think Gavin was at the fossil site."

"I guess it could all fit together, although I still don't see how. Anyway, I'm impressed you came up with so many possibilities." Candrew picked up his coffee cup, realized it was empty and put it back down. "I ran across one myself. Apparently there's a two-mile thick layer of salt deep below the surface in the Gulf of Mexico that's called the *antares salt*. Shell has a huge oil and gas field close to it, named "Mars". Marge told me she thought Gavin had been consulting with Shell in Houston. But there's still the problem of why this name would be in a file that only had information on dinosaurs."

Judy smiled. "That's interesting for a completely unrelated reason. Aries was the Greek name for Mars, so Antares means 'anti-Mars'—another gem I found on the web. I wonder if Shell knew that when they named their oilfield Mars?"

They sat in silence for several minutes trying to make sense of all the unrelated facts dumped out by the internet. This was no longer an academic exercise. Buried in all these bits of information must be clues leading to Gavin's killer—if only they were smart enough to figure them out.

After sleeping fitfully for a couple of hours, Marge had

got up and for the last three hours had been wide awake. Except for a small bedside lamp, the silent bedroom was dark, the only illumination coming from a square of bright stripes on the floor where the moon shone through the slats of half-closed blinds.

Gavin murdered. He'd been her whole world, and now she was cut off, left alone, isolated. She was not religious, in the sense of going to church regularly, but found herself praying to a God she didn't know. Praying for what? For solace, guidance, help moving into the future? She flipped through a couple of magazines, but nothing kept her interest, she even started one of the word puzzles, and quickly abandoned that. Distant coyotes had been calling intermittently for half an hour but then stopped abruptly, probably signaling death for some hapless prey. In the stillness, Marge felt the aching emptiness of her own loss and the uncertain future she faced without Gavin.

The long bedroom wall, opposite the windows, had doors to walk-in closets and she opened the left one: Gavin's. Inside, she reached up and took down from the top shelf a large cardboard box which she carried to the bed tipping out its contents. Photographs from the last twenty years spilled across the blanket. With tears in her eyes, she sifted through the piles, looking at shots of skiing in the winter, beaches in summer, camping in the mountains—all the things they'd shared. Sorrowfully, she realized there would be no more photographs of them together.

Murder. She couldn't conceive why anyone would want to kill Gavin. She thought back over their life together and found herself searching for recent changes, anything in his life she didn't know about. She'd always taken their togetherness for granted. The only difference she could think of was that he'd been away more than usual in the last year, apparently doing field work.

Gavin looked so young in those early photos. He was only twenty-seven when he joined the faculty in northern New Mexico, straight from UC Berkeley. Academic jobs studying vertebrate fossils were hard to come by, and he was pleased to move to an area he knew and liked, an area where he'd done field work in the past. He had settled easily into campus life and the academic routine. But preparing lectures and getting his research program up and running left little time for a social life, and it was pure chance that Gavin and Marge met.

Gavin had been collecting ammonite fossils on Vancouver Island and after several rainy days was hauling out his rock-filled pack. Earlier Marge had trailered horses up there with her friend Jane, but Jane's horse had thrown her and she was lying on the ground in obvious pain. Now as Marge sat on the edge of the bed in the dim light, she remembered Gavin taking charge and how he carefully organized getting Jane to the emergency room. While they waited, she'd chatted to Gavin—small-talk at first, but with an increasing awareness of how much they had in common. She liked his humor and his obvious intelligence. In the early fall, Gavin attended a technical conference in Los Angeles, close to where she worked as a real estate agent in Santa Monica. They had dinner together. Marge still recalled the warm feeling she'd had when Gavin invited her to visit New Mexico for Thanksgiving. The relationship grew and deepened and within the year Marge became Mrs. Citalli. She sorted through the pile and found their wedding photos.

One of her Santa Monica clients had been a wealthy Japanese-American who'd been looking for a house. He was charming, attractive, and good company and they'd had business lunches quite a few times as they checked out houses on the market. There'd been several social dinners as well. The relationship had gone no farther and Marge had almost forgotten about Mishikubo—that was his name—until a couple of years ago she'd got a phone call from her past client. She wondered why he was calling, but he had had a whole series of penetrating questions about Gavin and his research with fossils, especially dinosaurs, most of which she couldn't answer. When she told Gavin about this he didn't seem surprised and the issue never came up again. But a few weeks later Marge got a gorgeous bouquet of flowers and a string of Mikimoto pearls. She had never told Gavin and now felt a pervading sense of guilt. She wondered what relationship Mishikubo had with Gavin.

Wiping away a tear, Marge carefully replaced the photographs, her only tangible record of past memories, and took the box back to the closet. She stared at the rack of now purposeless clothes, including a couple of formal suits that Gavin rarely wore. Shoes were neatly lined up on the floor and against the wall was the box of clothes the police had brought to the house. Now there was a murder investigation, she wondered if they'd want to re-examine everything. But she decided that a quick look wouldn't do any harm, especially if she put everything back in its original place. She'd postponed opening the water-stained cardboard box for the last couple of days and peered at it for several minutes before slowly removing the lid. Tearfully, she lifted out the scuffed pair of field boots that he would never wear again, his sneakers and the small dark-blue day pack and put them all on the floor. Gavin's sleeveless khaki jacket, with lots of pockets, was in a creased pile. The police must have thrown it in while it was still wet and she shook it out and reached for a hanger. There were still things in the pockets and emptying them produced a pile containing his hand lens, notebook, two pencils, a folded hand-drawn map, sunscreen, and half a dozen candies. From an inside pocket, she pulled a key attached to an orange disk marked with letters and numbers. She added it to the pile, but as an afterthought picked it up again. She didn't recognize it. The key was certainly not for anything in the house and she'd never seen Gavin use one like that. There was no company name on the key itself, and the handwriting on the cardboard disc meant nothing to her. It seemed to be "*ACED16*". Maybe Anne, or more likely Candrew, would have some ideas.

*　　*　　*

Early the next morning Marge telephoned Candrew. He was in the shower and she left a message telling him about the map and key she'd found, and suggesting that he come over to the house and have a look.

Intrigued by her discoveries, Candrew stopped by on his way to the university. When Marge opened the door, wearing a terrycloth robe, she looked tired and drained.

"I hope I'm not too early?"

"No, not at all. I've been up for hours."

Candrew believed it. Marge's hair was tousled and her eyes dark-rimmed. He followed her into the breakfast area beside the kitchen where she had been reading the morning paper and drinking herbal tea. The nearly empty cup stood on a Formica-topped table next to a small vase of flowers and a plate with a half-eaten piece of toast.

"Coffee?" She'd been a friend long enough to know that he wasn't fond of herbal tea. When Candrew accepted, she poured him a mug full and they sat together at the table. "I realize you're trying to make sense of Gavin's research and last night I stumbled on a map in one of his jacket pockets." She got up and retrieved it from the kitchen counter. "It's hand-drawn and looks as though he was still working on it." Her eyes lingered a moment on Gavin's writing and she passed it to him.

As he took the map, he was disappointed to see it was only a field sketch. "My guess is that he was using it to record sample locations." He examined it more closely. "The numbers are sequential; see, here's *218*, then *219* and *220*. And over here a *D2-6*." He spent a few more minutes examining it. "I'll check it against the one Judy and I found in his office . . . but I can't recall seeing any 'D2' series." He refolded the map carefully along the original creases.

"I don't know if this is important." Marge handed him the

small key with the attached orange disc. "I found it in one of the inside jacket pockets. It's not for any of the locks in our house, I'm sure of that. Maybe it'll open something in his office at the university."

Anne came in and joined them, pouring herself a cup of coffee. She held up the pot. "Need a top-up?" There were no takers and she sat with them at the table.

Marge slid her chair along to provide more room. "We've just been looking at the map I found," she said.

"I'm pretty sure it's a sample location map, although it's not clear for which area," Candrew said. "I'll see if I can find it on the bigger maps when I get back to my office." He glanced at his watch. "I need to go. Sorry to rush off." Picking up the key with its attached disc, he glanced at Anne and smiled, then folded the map up and rose to leave. Almost as an afterthought he said to Marge, "One other thing I wanted to ask, did Gavin ever mention anyone called Chuck Semley?"

Chuck Semley. She said the name slowly and carefully, as though trying to jog her memory. "No. Or if he did, I don't remember."

Chapter 9

The fat folder with the large geological map was in Candrew's briefcase and he fished around and retrieved it. He had to shove several stacks of books and piles of papers to the end of his desk to excavate an area large enough to spread the sheets out. In contrast, Gavin's map wasn't large, about half the size of a legal pad, and there were only four pages, all water-crinkled but dried-out. Carefully he pried them apart. The writing was blurred in places after its immersion in the river, but fortunately most was in pencil and still legible. About a third of the locations marked on the moisture-soaked pages overlapped those on the big map, and there were also extra numbers that extended coverage to the north and east. Some dotted lines on the big map ran off the edge, but were continued on the water-stained pages where they appeared to outline the location of the fossil skeleton. Candrew thought he had the working plans for the excavation, and these suggested that well over half the bones had already been dug out. Where were they now? Since Gavin was keeping everything secret, obviously he wouldn't store them at home or at the university. In any case, they'd be far too large. He'd have been much more likely to ship them to the buyer, or maybe put them in temporary storage, probably in a rental unit—that would be the most anonymous way. Candrew had no idea how to set about tracking down such storage space. But in a flash of inspiration he realized the answer might be right under his nose. He picked up the key that Marge had found in Gavin's jacket. Was this the Rosetta stone? He dropped it in his shirt pocket.

The last of the small map's four pages showed a different area, one seemingly unconnected to the others. The numbers were all prefaced by *D2* and the coordinates showed an area several miles east-northeast of the main excavation. What was at this location that interested Gavin? Another puzzle.

After rolling the charts together, Candrew hustled along to the department office to make photocopies. As the copier disgorged the final pages, he turned to Maria. "Do you have the Albuquerque and Santa Fe phone books?"

"They should be on that end shelf—if someone hasn't walked off with them," she replied.

Candrew found both and looked up *Ace Storage. Ace* was the company name written on the disc attached to the key Marge had given him, and both Albuquerque and Santa Fe had some of their storage facilities. It was possible, of course, that there were others in Española or even Taos. After writing down the phone numbers he reshelved the directories under Maria's watchful eye. He couldn't imagine anything other than dinosaur bones that Gavin would want to store, and tracking down the rental storage was his best chance to get to them. But he'd need to do it fast, before Gavin's collaborators—his killers?—found out that he had the key and knew the location.

Candrew had forgotten about todays faculty meeting and it was lucky Maria reminded him. The meeting was scheduled for ten o'clock in the *Scholars' Library*, a pretentious name for the high-ceilinged, oak-beamed room that tried to look like medieval Oxford in spite of being built in Rio Arriba County less than thirty years ago. Dark, glass-fronted bookcases with crenellated tops were filled with leather-bound volumes and appropriate hardback books—no paperbacks here. Apart from a large, leather-covered oak table, a grand piano, and serried rows of chairs, the only other furnishings were two wing-backed chairs off to the side and several dark oil paintings—all portraits. Candrew was in a somber mood as he headed for a seat in the second row.

Susan, tall, elegant and the only woman professor present, gestured to the chair beside her. "With Rosenberg running this show, it could last all morning."

"Well, I'm not staying that long," Candrew snapped. "Scotty's going to beam me up in thirty minutes."

"Gentlemen—and lady—if I could have your attention." Nicholas Rosenberg stood behind the table looking out at the scattered group of a dozen or so geology professors. Dressed in his usual casual jacket and sober tie, he spoke in a clipped, near monotone, rarely gesticulated, and seemed fully in control, watching his words carefully so as not to offend anyone: a consummate politician. And like any successful politician, he chose to deliver good news in person. Today, he had assembled the faculty to announce that funds had been approved for a major piece of equipment.

"Carlos,"—he always used the familiar when talking about the Provost—"has just informed me that the Board of Trustees approved the purchase of a new electron microprobe for our microanalytical laboratory. I'm pleased to say that the full amount has been budgeted."

A tanned, slightly overweight, faculty member leaned forward in his chair and stabbed the air with his finger. "Value is what we should be talking about. Bang for the buck. I still question whether this is the best way to spend that much money." Harry

Denton wore an open-necked, checked shirt with a hand lens hanging from a leather cord round his neck. He'd spent his whole professional career mapping sedimentary rocks and resented the intrusion of the geochemists and geophysicists into "his" discipline. In particular, he resented the amount of money they spent—over a million for an electron microprobe. He always claimed he could fund a small army of students and do some real geology for that kind of money.

They'd all been through this before. The arguments played out like a chess game where everyone knew the moves and counter moves—and the outcome.

Rosenberg cut him off. "Harry, the decision was made months ago; we're talking implementation, as you well know."

"And I also know that all this money isn't the end of it. In a couple of years we'll be replacing the computers with the latest models, to keep the instrument 'state of the art'." He rocked his chair back on two legs and sat with arms crossed. He'd made his protest, salved his conscience and sat glowering but silent.

Candrew thought of his own four-year-old computer and how he needed to upgrade it. He wondered what would happen to Gavin's machine. After seeing his home office, he was almost certain Gavin was a more sophisticated computer user than anyone realized, which made his PC an obvious place to try to get information on what he'd been doing. But Candrew didn't have access. He squirmed in his seat, seething.

Rosenberg was irritated that the credit he expected for a significant acquisition had been compromised by Denton's attack, but he showed no sign of being flustered and smoothly continued. "The Deans' council will implement a new policy allowing students to take only one pass/fail class each semester." This prompted a heated discussion between a vocal minority who thought everything should be done to encourage students to take geology courses and those who thought university education needed to be a lot more rigorous. Kurt Tadheim was aggressively outspoken in support of more rigor. Although he almost never taught undergraduate courses, he argued that quality was an important issue for the department. "Our enrollment is fine and we sure as hell don't want to attract students who're here for an easy ride. Students should be in a course to learn, dammit. They're not there to squeeze by with minimum effort. This policy is only a small step, but at least it's in the right direction."

His brusque manner and the way he dismissed other people's views irritated Candrew, but although he didn't like Kurt personally, on this issue he agreed with his sentiments. After hearing the complaints from Seligman, Gavin's graduate student, Candrew paid more attention to Tadheim's views, still puzzled by his role in the dinosaur project.

Rosenberg eventually cut off further discussion. "I'm just passing on information. The decision's already been made." Harry Denton raised his eyebrows, but said nothing.

Rosenberg worked through the routine agenda, methodically ticking off each item, and finally told the faculty that he had asked Judy to teach paleo. There was a murmur of comments and he waited for it to subside. "I have one other announcement." He hesitated, obviously not sure how best to phrase it. "Apparently there were some suspicious circumstances with Gavin Citalli's drowning. Enough that the FBI is carrying out an investigation. Two of their agents will be visiting the department and I expect they'll want to ask all of you some questions. They're interested in Gavin's research projects and the people he's been collaborating with. They are planning to question his graduate students, particularly those who were with him on the float trip. At the moment, I don't know a lot about all this, but you need to be open and share any information you have."

The FBI. Serious stuff. Candrew wondered how many of his colleagues had heard that Gavin's death was murder. Marge had only been told late yesterday afternoon and it didn't seem to be common knowledge. However, it might explain why the FBI was involved.

There was an animated buzz of conversation and lots of questions Rosenberg couldn't answer. Finally, he held up his hands for quiet. "That's all I have for today. Is there any other business?"

There was none.

It wasn't long before Candrew got his chance to help the esteemed FBI with their inquiries. He was the first person scheduled for the afternoon interviews, and by two o'clock was in the seminar room settling himself onto the lone vacant chair. As he pulled it up to the middle of the conference table, the two FBI agents seated opposite nodded, silently acknowledging his arrival. The broad-shouldered one to the left had short-cropped, sandy hair and tinted glasses, dark but not quite sunglasses, and wore a navy-blue jacket with a garish orange and blue striped tie. He looked at Candrew over a large pile of papers, made a notation in his notebook and, unsmiling, said, "Good afternoon Professor . . ." and continued consulting several pages of notes in more detail before getting to ". . . Nor." The other agent was slimmer, like a marathon runner, did not wear a tie and had no papers or notebook, apparently satisfied to trust his memory. He looked directly at Candrew without actually making eye contact and said nothing. Their behavior irritated Candrew.

Striped Tie began. "How long did you know Professor Citalli?"

"Twelve years."

"Professor Nor, please tell us the nature of your relationship with him."

Candrew outlined both his professional and social interactions. Because of their curt, unfriendly attitudes he was not inclined to go into detail. They could probe if they wanted more.

"Dr. Rosenberg, the chairman of your department, says that on his instructions *you* were the person who searched Professor Citalli's office." There was an emphasis on the "*you*" that made it sound like an accusation.

This was not phrased in the form of a question, and Candrew was going to treat it as a statement that didn't need an answer. Let them work for their information. He sat tapping his teeth, but in the end said, "Your information's wrong."

"In what way would that be?"

"Rosenberg only asked me to start moving things out to make way ultimately for a new faculty member. There was no mention of searching for anything. I did suggest that the adjunct professor who'll teach Dr. Citalli's course this fall should be allowed to borrow his course notes."

"And who would that adjunct professor be?"

"Dr. Judith Westerlund."

The two men conferred in low voices, and Striped Tie jotted more comments on his pad. He looked up at Candrew. "Tell me, Professor Nor, what did you take out of the office before it was sealed off?"

Candrew told them about the library books that he and Judy had boxed up. He decided not to tell them about the files or the CDs. He wanted a chance to study them in more detail before turning them over. In a tone of mock cooperation, he added, "Perhaps if you could tell me what you're looking for, I could help. What sort of things do you need?"

"I'm not at liberty to say at this point in time." Striped Tie looked down at his notes. "I assume you kept a list of everything you moved."

"No." Candrew waited a moment, looking directly at both of them. "You can check with the library. Circulation should have a record of all returned books."

They were getting him rattled, probably standard FBI

procedure. He was a little unsure of himself. Why was the FBI here at all? FBI, that meant Federal. Why was the government probing Gavin's activities? Did this imply that the fossil dig was on Indian land? But wouldn't that involve the Bureau of Indian Affairs? Could he have been wrong about Gavin all these years?

The interrogation continued. "Would you explain to us just what research Professor Citalli was doing, what it involved and why it was important?"

"No. I don't know the details of his research."

"What do you mean: *You don't know what research he was doing*? You're telling me that as a distinguished geology professor, with three degrees from prestigious universities, you can't understand what another geologist is doing?"

Inside Candrew the tension rose. He wet his lips with his tongue and looked straight at Striped Tie. "Would you have open heart surgery from a proctologist rather than a cardiologist—they're both MDs and surgeons?"

There was a lengthy pause and Striped Tie's colleague finally said, sarcastically, "But you would recognize a fossil if you saw one?"

Candrew didn't dignify that with an answer.

Striped Tie resumed the questioning. "Did you take any fossils out of his office?"

"No. I told you the only things we moved from the office were library books."

"Do you know if anyone else took anything? His students perhaps, or your students?"

Candrew paused, trying to decide whether to tell them about the white cast he'd seen that first afternoon in the office. "Well, I did notice an irregular-shaped plaster cast the first time I went into his office and when I started sorting stuff the next day it was gone. But that's the only thing I recall."

"What sort of cast?"

"White, probably plaster of Paris, and roughly half as big again as a football. I have no idea what it was."

"But it had been removed from Professor Citalli's office."

"Yes."

"Any other items gone?"

"No. That was the only one."

"Are you sure? Sometimes memory deceives. Did your colleague remove anything, the lecture notes you mentioned, for example?"

"No. We couldn't find them."

The questioning continued in a similar vein, with lots of repetition, until they decided either that he had told them everything he could, or that he was such an accomplished liar they were not going to get any more information from him. Just when he thought the confrontation was over, the slim agent without a tie asked, "Did Professor Citalli collect anything other than fossils?" The question was posed in a quiet, casual tone.

"Collect things? You mean professionally, or as a hobby?"

"Either way."

"Like minerals?" Candrew answered his own question. "Not that I ever saw. He was only interested in fossils and then just for professional reasons. You'd hardly call it collecting, but he did buy a few antique maps. I can't think of anything else."

"Maps of the West?"

"Not that I saw. As far as I remember they were all from Europe. Italy, maybe." He recalled the pair of photographs in Gavin's study, but they didn't seem to be part of an extensive collection.

"Did he collect arrowheads or potsherds when he was working out in the desert? Remains of old pots, maybe?"

Candrew got the distinct impression that this line of questioning had arrived at its target. Did they suspect Gavin of digging for Anasazi pots and other artifacts? Was that why they were here? "I never saw any prehistoric pots, either in his office at the university or in his home. As far as I know, he wasn't interested in archaeology. You have to understand, he was very focused on fossil research."

"So you don't think he might have dug up a few pots while working out in the desert and sold them to one of the dealers in Santa Fe or Phoenix?"

"I suppose it's possible, although it doesn't sound like the Gavin I know . . . knew."

"Did Professor Citalli ever work as a geologist for any of the archeological excavations? Like providing information about rock types, or where the clay for pots came from? That sort of thing."

"Not to my knowledge. That's not his sort of geology. It's actually closer to what I do."

"One final thing." Striped Tie had resumed the questioning. "Professor Citalli scheduled an appointment with an FBI special agent in Albuquerque, but died three days before the meeting was to take place. You know of any reason why Professor Citalli might have wanted to meet with one of our agents?"

"I have no idea," Candrew said honestly.

After a long pause Striped Tie finally said something halfway pleasant. "Well, Professor Nor, we know you're a busy man and we appreciate your taking the time to cooperate in our ongoing investigations. If we have other questions we will contact you. I assume you're not going out of town any time soon?"

Candrew assured them that with the semester about to begin, apart from some local trips, he would be close to campus for the rest of the fall, and left.

Chapter 10

D-16 was the number on the cardboard disc attached to Gavin's key and, as well as the unit number, he'd written '*ACE*'. It had taken Candrew only half a dozen phone calls, and some bending of the truth, to confirm that it was one of the Santa Fe locations for the *Ace Secure Storage Company*. From then on it was easy. Early this morning he'd driven down to Santa Fe, followed Airport Road west, and located *Ace* on a short side street.

Now he was trying to humor the custodian in the office and pry from him as much information as he could. But all he got from the short, unshaven and tattooed man in a sleeveless Dallas Cowboys tee shirt was an account of his early life.

"Yes sir. Growed up on a farm down there south of Hatch. Town they call the chile capital of New Mexico—hell, maybe the world. Best bottom land in the whole goddamn state. Worst thing was them flash floods. Get a cloud burst come down one big arroyo and 'fore you could turn round the water'd be knee deep. Just open the front door and back door, let it pour through. All done in thirty minutes. Took the rest of the day to clean out the fucking mud. And hail like you never saw. Kill all the hens."

Candrew wondered what Chicken Little would have made of that, but didn't say anything. He just listened patiently, indulging the speaker, and then asked about storage unit D-16 and how long it had been rented.

"Don't know myself. Charlie does all them contracts—when he's not out screwing around or getting wasted." He wrinkled up his face with the effort of recollection. "D-16. That the sculptor?"

"Sculptor?"

"Yeah. Tall guy, real tall. Got a great big moustache. Don't got much hair on his head, though." He grinned. "Always hauling in them awkward white casts. Plaster of press. Usually I'm working evenings, seen him with his pickup. This week, I work mornings. You should've bin here yesterday."

"Why? What happened?"

"Your sculptor friend was over at the storage unit before sun-up, moving a lot of them casts. Could've used your help. Worked several hours. Hard work."

"Nobody was helping him?"

"I didn't see none. Struggled all by hisself." He paused to give the TV his undivided attention for a moment. "But a couple of different guys showed up this morning to load more stuff."

"They still here?" Candrew probed.

"Far as I know."

"Maybe I should take a look and see if there's anything I can do to help."

"No problem." He stepped out of the door of the small shack that served as an office and pointed off to the right. "Down there. Take the first right, third row."

Candrew drove slowly past the rows of roll-up storage-unit doors wondering whether he was doing the right thing. He had mixed feelings, and wasn't sure that confronting the two guys face to face was the right way to handle this. Before he had a chance to resolve his dilemma, a red truck came round the corner fast, braked hard. Candrew wasn't sure they had room to pass him and pulled tight to the wall to avoid getting scraped. As he turned and looked over his shoulder, he saw them ease past and accelerate away. The truck was loaded with large white casts roped together, but what stuck him was the New Mexico license plate—*007*PHD*. He smiled to himself: *Dr. James Bond*. But the two guys driving the truck had none of the sophistication of secret agents.

The D-16 storage unit was locked and he parked several units further along the row and waited. When nothing happened for fifteen minutes, he walked back to D-16 where the roll-up door was secured by a single padlock. At first, he couldn't make Gavin's key work, but after several attempts got just the right orientation and the padlock snapped open. The roll-up door was stiff and difficult to lift, but when it did start moving, it got away from him, shot up and slammed to a stop with a resounding clang.

The storage locker stood exposed like the shadowed mouth of a cave and he peered in, seeing little in the gloomy interior. Except for some piece of metal framework toward the back and a couple of boxes, there were only two large plaster casts off to one side, both with cryptic lettering in black magic marker. He fumbled for the light switch and moved in to take a closer look.

The equipment turned out to be a large chain hoist. All he found after examining it thoroughly was a small metal label with the name of the Royce Rental Co., and under it their identification number. He wrote that down. The hoist, like the floor, was dusted in white chips of plaster of Paris.

The storage unit was roughly ten feet wide and nearly twice as long. Starting at the back wall, Candrew methodically searched the entire floor, systematically moving from side to side and working his way towards the door moving some pieces of scattered cardboard. The sole reward for this effort was a broken utility knife, unless you counted a couple of cigarette butts and a piece of string. There was a slight chemical odor and dust hung in the air making Candrew cough.

One of two cardboard boxes near the back of the storage space was empty, but the box closest to the wall was half full of dark-colored rods, each about an inch in diameter. Candrew wondered if they were sticks of explosive, but wasn't sure. They could have been used for blasting rocks overlying the buried parts of the fossil *T. rex*. One of the rods was broken into several pieces and he picked out a short length with a metal cap attached. He dropped this into his jacket pocket, planning to take it to a friend in civil engineering who might be able to identify it.

He stood glaring at the empty space. Damn. He'd only missed "the sculptor" and his casts by less than a day and stood disappointed, reviewing what little he'd found. Candrew had read enough about excavating large fossils to know it was standard practice to wrap them in burlap and then encase them in a protective jacket of plaster of Paris. Plaster chips and white dust covered the floor and this had obviously been a temporary storage location for the bones of the big *T. rex*. Where were the guys in the pickup truck taking them? Probably on their way to some private collector willing to pay the price—unless they'd been moved to another temporary storage facility. Was this why Chuck Semley was in town, to supervise the transfer?

The Hatch-chile man was seated with his feet on the metal desk and his chair rocked back watching a game show on the small television when Candrew returned to the office.

"You a got a phone book I could use?"

"Sure." Without taking his eyes off the television, he pulled open the left-hand drawer and flipped a battered copy of Mountain Bell's opus onto the part of the desk not occupied by his feet.

Royce Rentals was off Siler Road and Candrew thought it should be easy enough to find. He pushed back the directory, "Thanks for your help." As he turned to leave, he hesitated. "Could you let me have the name of the guy who rented D-16?"

"'Fraid not. Against company policy. You know, confidentiality." He smirked at his chance to wield authority. "You want the manager to give you a call?"

"No. I don't think that'll do any good. I'll talk to him next time I come by." Candrew hesitated. "Why don't you give me one of his business cards. I'll call him."

Royce Rentals was set back from the road in a long, low brick building with a protruding office section at one end. Candrew pulled in beside two pickup trucks parked out front.

"I just rented a storage unit and whoever had it before me left one of your chain hoists," he explained to the attentive young Hispanic man wearing a Lakers baseball cap and a maroon tee shirt proclaiming, "*The Royce is Right!*"

"I'm surprised the storage company didn't tell us it was there when the lease ended. They're usually pretty good about things like that."

Candrew said nothing.

"Let me check the number you've got and I'll see what I can find." He pecked away at the computer keyboard, peered at the screen for several minutes, then stepped over to a metal rack and pulled down a bulky, three-ring binder. It produced the information he needed.

"Yeah, I remember this one. Usually it's a couple of teenagers wanting to pull the engine out of a low rider. And they just take the hoist for a couple of days, or over a weekend."

"They don't sound like the sort of people who'd rent a storage locker."

"No. That's right. The hoist you've got was rented to a woman and she took it for two months. It's not due back for another three weeks."

"Really. I wonder what a woman would be doing with a chain hoist," Candrew said, although he had a pretty shrewd idea what this one was being used for.

"Don't ask me, I just rent 'em." He hesitated. "Maybe she's into gardening or something. You know, needs to move big bushes or rocks."

Candrew took the opportunity to probe. "I guess that's right. Did she seem the gardening type?"

"To be honest, she was pretty cute, athletic, 'though not at all butch."

"So you remember all the cute blondes." Candrew smiled in a conspiratorial way, trying to egg him on.

"Not a blonde. This one had a big mass of real curly, dark hair. Didn't sound as though she was from around here. Back-east accent maybe. You know, like, New York."

"Sounds as if I need to get her address and phone number— so I can contact her about the hoist."

The young Royce Renter was suddenly all business. "I'm sorry sir, we don't give out names of customers. Try to keep their privacy."

That was the second time Candrew had heard that this morning. "Of course, I understand. I'm sure she'll be by to get it. If it's still there when the rental ends in three weeks, I'll give you a call."

It was a disappointed and puzzled Candrew that pulled out onto Siler and made a left turn onto Cerrillos Road. Some jockeying through traffic brought him to the Paseo and he was lucky to find a parking spot close to the farmers' market. Candrew had forty-five minutes to kill before he was due to meet Chuck Semley and he wandered past the row of vendors. Although late in the season for apricots, that's what he was hoping to find, since local apricots were one of his favorite fruits. Even though he had several pet recipes, he wasn't averse to eating them fresh with a little yogurt—and a dash of Cointreau helped. Fortunately, the

Gomez brothers from Chimayó still had several pounds left. He bought them all.

Candrew got himself a fresh coffee and sat at one of the outside tables watching humanity flow past. He tried one of the apricots: good, very good. As he ate several more, he thought of the big, gnarly old apricot tree planted years ago by Bishop Lamy at what is now *Bishop's Lodge Resort*, north of Santa Fe. He didn't know whether the bishop ever preached under it the way Confucius taught his philosophy under an apricot tree. What was it about apricots that attracted these men?

His rambling thoughts inevitably drifted back over the events of the morning. The dominant feeling was frustration: he'd only missed getting to the fossil bones by a few hours. *Hours!* He thought about the woman who'd rented the chain hoist: athletic with a shock of dark curly hair. That could describe thousands of women—but with an eastern accent and renting a hoist? And the balding man with a moustache who'd been at the storage locker, where did he fit in? Something vague stirred in the deep recesses of his mind about this pair, but he couldn't pull out any coherent memories and sat tapping his teeth. And who were the two guys in the red truck? Did any of these people have a role in Gavin's death? And if they did, how was he going to find out?

A sudden raucous blast from a locomotive's horn jumped him out of his reverie. The *Rail Runner* was pulling out, leaving for Albuquerque, and the track was the other side of the row of vendors, less than twenty yards from where he was sitting. Trains always made him think of timetables and schedules, and he checked his watch. Later than he thought. Time to keep his rendezvous with Mr. Semley.

Chapter 11

It was a few minutes after twelve when Candrew turned off Baca Street and into the parking area outside the *Counter Culture* restaurant. He pulled into a space beside an ancient Volvo, looked round and tried to guess which car might be Semley's. He picked the black Dodge Ram truck with a rack of lights on the cab roof as the one best conforming to his impression of the man. And it had Arizona plates.

The restaurant entrance led past an outside patio where half the tables were occupied by late brunchers and the vanguard of early lunchers. The day was bright, sunny and already warm, well on its way to the eighty-seven degrees promised by the weatherman. Inside, it was cooler and darker, and it took him a minute to adjust to the lower light. A fit, fiftyish man in khaki shorts and polo shirt, his graying hair pulled back into a neat pony tail, was in line at the order counter and Candrew stepped around him, casually surveying the spare, functional but adequate space. An industrial concrete floor did little to muffle the sound of clattering plates, conversation and cooking and there was a satisfying bustle of activity. He nervously scanned the tables where small groups were eating and chatting and was suddenly unsure of himself, apprehensive. He didn't know what he was getting into or where it might lead. Clandestine meetings with strangers were all well and good in the movies, but the real thing left him with a dry mouth and quickened pulse. As he looked around for someone fitting his mental image of Chuck Semley, he spotted the lone man seated at a table in the middle of the far wall with a hand raised to attract attention. Candrew threaded his way around the tables.

"Professor Nor?" It was more a statement than a question. The man had risen partway out of his chair and was leaning towards the spot where Candrew stood rooted, offering his hand. He shook it, the firm grip bordering on excessive.

"Yes. You must be Mr. Semley."

"I prefer 'Chuck'. Don't like to stand on ceremony."

Semley—Chuck—settled back into the chair, sitting with his back to the wall, and examined Candrew with a steady gaze. "Just like your photo."

"Photo?"

"Yeah. I pulled up the geology department's web page. It's got pictures of all you illustrious faculty. Even has secretaries and technicians. Quite egalitarian." His mouth smiled but the dominant, canine-brown eyes were unblinking, still coolly evaluating Candrew. Semley, bulky and probably in his forties, was dressed in jeans and a short-sleeved khaki shirt with a pair of sunglasses sticking out of one pocket. He had thick, hairy forearms and wore a large watch with a black face and multiple dials. Thin, receding sandy hair capped a large head with a creased, well-tanned face. His only scar was hidden under a lush moustache. Although in good physical condition, Semley gave the impression of an athlete starting to lose muscle tone.

To Candrew, he seemed vaguely familiar, although initially he couldn't place him. It was the moustache that finally triggered his memory—this was the stranger who'd sat at the back of the chapel for Gavin's memorial service. That, of course, meant he knew about Gavin's death. When they'd talked on the phone, Semley had acted surprised, as though he was hearing the news for the first time. If he could deceive so effectively, could Candrew believe anything he said? Could he trust this man at all?

Semley's brash, confident voice brought Candrew back to the present. "Let's get our order in. Not good to do business on an empty stomach." They went to the counter where Chuck ordered a steak sandwich and a beer. Candrew had eaten at *Counter Culture* before and was familiar with the menu. He opted for one of the Asian dishes and decided to stick with coffee.

They settled back at their table. "Okay, so where do we go from here?" Candrew asked.

Semley pushed his metal chair away from the table and crossed his legs, exposing expensive, but well-worn, tooled cowboy boots. "Let me start at the beginning. I'm here on behalf of a Los Angeles business man, Mr. Mishikubo."

Candrew was rather nervous and said, "Chinese?"

"No. Mishikubo is Japanese. Really Japanese-American, he grew up in LA." Semley stared at Candrew for a moment trying to see whether he found this information significant, then continued. "As I'm sure you know only too well, it's always been hell of a struggle for professors to persuade someone to give them the bucks they need to dig up all those fossils. About a year ago, Professor Citalli talked to Mishikubo and sounded out the possibility of getting some funding for his fossil research. They worked out a deal. Mishikubo was real generous in providing lots of cash to support the excavations as well as Professor Citalli's fossil research."

"That must have been a lot of money. I'm surprised I didn't hear about major funding like that—especially since Gavin Citalli was a close friend."

"Well, it's damned unusual. Mishikubo was shelling out big bucks so Citalli could dig out dinosaur bones and describe them with all those fancy scientific names. Then Mishikubo was going to wind up with the fossil to add to his collection."

"I take it your Mr. Mishikubo is an avid fossil collector, or is this an investment?"

"Avid collector. That's what drives him, though he's not shy about making a few bucks on a wise investment."

A *T. rex* skeleton had sold at auction for $8.6 million and it seemed unlikely that the mysterious Mr. Mishikubo was paying Gavin Citalli anything like that amount. And it was also obvious from the papers in Gavin's files that a *T. rex* was what he was excavating. Candrew was direct. "So, Professor Citalli is selling Mr. Mishikubo a *T. rex* that could be worth several million dollars."

"You've been doing your homework," Semley said without smiling. "But don't forget, Mishikubo is getting his *rex* raw. No preparation, no fancy mounting. Just the bones the way they come out of the ground, still embedded in rock."

Lying beside the wall next to Semley's feet was a stout cardboard tube, about three inches in diameter, capped at the ends with yellow plastic covers. He leaned down and grabbed it in his large left hand and used his other hand to uncap one end.

"Maps," he said in response to Candrew's quizzical look, ". . . and aerial photos."

He started to let the contents slide out onto the table, but stopped, poured himself some beer and then with one sweep of his forearm slid the pepper, salt and napkins to the side of the table to make more room. He detached one curled map from the rest and smoothed it with his hands, putting the salt shaker on the far corner to keep it flat. The map showed the working areas currently being excavated and dotted lines where buried parts were suspected. It was just like Gavin's map.

"This thing is big, damn big. Look at the scale here." Semley pointed to the scale bar at the bottom corner. "We're talking nearly fifty feet nose to tail."

"How do you know that if half of it's still buried?"

"Citalli figured it out. Claimed that by looking at the size of the skull, plus the other bones he'd dug out, you can make a pretty good estimate of just how big that thing is. They've also done some sort of fancy echo sounding, seismic. At fifty feet this baby would be the biggest *T. rex* ever found. And preservation is super good, too."

"Why are you telling me all this? Isn't everything confidential?"

Semley stroked his moustache and gazed directly at Candrew for a moment. "You don't really know anything. You haven't got the exact location and the information is only word-of-mouth. If I need to, I'll deny everything." He grinned. There was a long pause. "Okay, here's the deal. A lot's been done already and a whole bunch of money spent paying for the professor's, ah, research. Even though Citalli is sadly no longer with us, Mishikubo still wants to see the project finished. It'd be a damn shame to leave the excavation half done, especially after all the hard work of planning and logistics. And anyway, a few big thunderstorms in the spring, those bones would be washed away, gone for ever, lost to the world. Mr. Mishikubo is fussing to wrap up the excavation as soon as possible and he needs someone to take over the project. You."

Taken by surprise, Candrew took his time to let the significance of this sink in and his gaze drifted past the photographs and paintings decorating the walls. Most of the people at nearby tables appeared to be locals with not a single turquoise-encrusted tourist in sight.

"I'm not a paleontologist," he said. "I know hardly anything about fossils. What makes you think I could carry out a project like this?"

"You're an experienced field geologist, you know the rocks in the area. And you've already heard quite a bit about what's going on. Anyway, we need to keep the number of people involved to a minimum."

"As I told you before," Candrew said, "Citalli never mentioned any of this. He didn't say a word about being involved in a fossil dig on this scale and I don't know any of the details. What about co-workers? He couldn't have been doing all this by himself. He must have had help." Candrew was tempted to ask about Teresa Polanca, Jason Devereaux and the mysterious KT, but he was increasingly uneasy about this whole deal. Best to keep quiet, he thought, not volunteer anything at this point, and see what shakes out. But he was well aware that Gavin had worked on Mishikubo's project and he'd been murdered.

"True," Semley said. "Part of the money the prof got was earmarked for helpers. He told us he'd hired a bunch of Mexicans. Illegal aliens, I'll bet. They were supposed to help dig out the bones and cover them in plaster for transport. As part of the deal, Citalli was going to ship everything directly to Mishikubo in L.A. He never did that. We found out that just before he drowned, he'd moved a lot of material. We want to know where it is."

So, they don't have all the answers, Candrew thought, but what he said was, "I don't have the vaguest idea where it went. I didn't even know Gavin had taken bones off site." Strictly that was true, but this morning's visit to the storage locker suggested otherwise. "I still don't see a role for me in all this."

"We'd like you to visit the dig site, take a look-see and check out the current state. See how far they've got in digging out the *rex*, check logistics, let me know what you think of their progress, that sort of thing. I understand you were a friend of the professor and you're clearing out his office. And that you also knew his wife real well. Anything you find out could be important."

Candrew's unsaid reaction was, *I'm being hired as a spy.*

"Of course, you're not being asked to do this for nothing. No peanuts. You'll get paid well, damn well, for what you do."

With a little bribery thrown in.

The waiter hovered with the lunch plates while Semley hurriedly cleared the maps off the table and stuffed them back into the tube. They started to eat and now that there was some sort of understanding of what was involved, Candrew felt more relaxed. Chuck Semley seemed to loosen up as well. He emptied the last of his bottle into the glass and drained it. "You ready for a beer now?" he asked. When Candrew accepted, he got up to go to the counter—and abruptly turned in surprise. "I'm all in favor of casual dining, but that pushes the envelope."

Candrew swiveled round to look in the direction Chuck was nodding and saw a slim, dark-haired man with a neatly trimmed beard leaning on the counter dressed in a red and white striped robe. He understood the surprise and laughed. "He's probably from the yoga group. They often come and get a soda after class."

"How about that? I could use some yoga myself right now. Still have trouble with my left knee, even after all these years."

"Old sports injury?"

"Not unless you call shooting Ethiopians sport." He caught Candrew's shocked look and added, "Mercenary. Took a piece of shrapnel under the knee cap in a fire fight. Got infected, damn near lost my leg."

Semley went to get their beers and when he got back, Candrew asked, "How'd you end up in Ethiopia in the first place?"

"Long story." He pursed his lips and looked around at the other diners. There was a lengthy silence and just when Candrew decided he wasn't going to be told what happened, Chuck said, "As a kid I really liked weapons and the idea of warfare. I was too young for Viet Nam. My older brother, Tom, was there with the infantry right up to the end. Got all the stories of war from him. He had a good time with the drugs, the women and the general mayhem. Made it sound exciting. I was just nineteen—young, bulletproof and dangerous—when I ran into a little misunderstanding with our local sheriff. Nam was over and I headed for Ethiopia as a soldier of fortune. Just loved the idea of being a hired gun, going to the highest bidder." He paused, ran his hand over his moustache and stared, unseeing, across the room as the memories flooded back. "Things got steadily worse after they deposed Selassie and finally there was the war with Somalia. When that was all over, I bummed around black Africa for a couple of years. Finally came back home to try and make an honest living. Well, it wasn't so honest at first, but it is now."

"So what exactly do you do for Mishikubo?"

"Anything he wants. He's the eight hundred pound gorilla." Chuck pushed his chair back from the table and grinned. "Mostly do errand-boy stuff for his dinosaur collection—like meeting you today. He's always been fair, pays well—as long as you deliver and you play by his rules, don't whine when he changes every one of those goddamn rules, and don't bitch even if he changes the game itself."

"You got other fossil excavations as well?"

"Now Professor, you're going too far. Topic closed." It was said in a voice that left no possibility of reopening the subject.

"Okay."

"One final thing. Mishikubo wants to talk to you in person. In Los Angeles. He's suggesting Monday."

"Monday! Does he have any idea how hectic things get in the week before classes begin? I don't have time to spend a couple of days going to California."

"Not a couple of days—one day." Candrew raised his eyebrows in a mute question. "One day. Mishikubo will send his private plane. You'll be there and back in a day. And that day's Monday."

Driving away from the restaurant, Candrew wondered what he was getting himself into. Did it really make sense to fly to L.A. just to see Mishikubo? But the wealthy fossil collector seemed to have a critical role and could be at the heart of the whole project. Candrew quickly convinced himself that if he was going to find out more about Gavin's murder he needed to get every possible piece of information about the scheme to excavate the *T. rex*. He was going to have to find out how Gavin fitted into the project—and who had a motive to kill him, as well as the opportunity. Was Semley really only an "errand boy", as he put it, or did he have a more significant role? Thinking back over the lunch meeting, he realized Semley had said nothing about Gavin's death.

Candrew drove toward the center of town, cutting though the South Capital area on his way to a couple of used-book stores he often visited when he was in Santa Fe. As he cruised along a quiet, leafy back street, he had to stop to let a car pass in the opposite direction because a pickup truck was loading at the curb. A red pickup truck. One with the New Mexico license plate *007*PHD*—how could he forget that? And two guys were hauling up large plaster of Paris bundles. He pulled around them, didn't slow down, and kept on driving, but veered left at the next turning and parked. Casually he strolled back down the road. The two men were working hard, struggling to load additional plaster casts they were dragging out of the house, and Candrew noticed they all had black numbers written on them. The men talked to each other in Spanish as they worked, nodding to him as he walked past.

Candrew strolled around the block, got back in his car and headed for a favorite downtown bookstore. As he browsed the shelves of used books, he wasn't really concentrating. Focusing his thoughts on the house with the red truck, he planned to go back later in the evening and see if he could learn anything useful.

A little after eleven, Candrew drove back to the neighborhood, and again parked on the adjacent street. He made his way around the corner, casually strolling past the house. The fully loaded red truck was in the driveway and a mid-size sedan parked on the road. A man on the other side of the street was walking two dogs and

Candrew waited impatiently for him to turn the corner. Then he reversed his direction making his way back.

It was quite dark with a clouded half-moon and the only light showing in the house was a sliver between drawn drapes in a back room. Candrew looked around, didn't see anyone, and went through an open gate into the garden of the house next door. Inching his way closer, he peered over the low adobe wall, but nothing moved and there were only dim downstairs lights. A bright flash made him jump, but it was followed a moment later by a rumble of thunder. There was no rain although the sage smelled rich from an earlier shower. Climbing over the wall gave him a chance for a closer look in the window and he crouched as he moved forward.

The blow startled him. Staggering to the side, he struggled to keep his balance, failed, and collapsed across a chamisa bush. With the second blow to the back of his neck consciousness faded and his mind spiraling down into blackness.

Chapter 12

When consciousness finally seeped back, it came with a pounding headache. Candrew was sprawled on his back, shivering on a damp flagstone floor, his mind seeming to float outside his body. He forced his eyes open, but saw nothing. He was in darkness. Consciousness lapsed.

Eventually, he woke again, still aching, and rolled onto his side. The room was gloomy and dimly lit by low early morning sunlight that filtering in through a high, narrow window. Candrew dragged himself up onto his knees. It was a long time before he could stand and, fighting nausea that was not helped by the musty smell, he grabbed a vertical metal pipe for balance. He found he was holding onto an old water tank in what seemed to be some sort of basement lined with brick walls. The dawn light from the lone dusty window hurt his eyes. He sat down on the floor, rubbing his throbbing shoulder and the back of his neck where he'd been hit. At least he hadn't been tied up. His mind cleared only slowly and for a long time he sat dazed. Then he heard scraping noises, under what must have been the floor of the room above. At first he thought it might be mice. Or rats? He'd no idea what sort of place he was in. Perhaps some deserted house? But then on the floor above there was a shouted discussion in Spanish before an angry Anglo voice broke in and yelled, "For God's sake just get on with it. Quit the arguing."

Shortly afterwards Candrew heard a truck drive away and later what he assumed was a car. An early morning stillness settled. Were those his captors leaving? Had they left permanently? Was there a guard upstairs? He listened carefully for a long time, but heard nothing.

Candrew carefully surveyed his surroundings. Few houses in Santa Fe had basements, but then he'd been investigating a house in the South Capital area, one of the few parts of town where basements were not uncommon. So, who dumped him here? Was he still in the house he'd been checking out? That would certainly fit with a truck and a car driving away. He anxiously considered whether they were planning to come back for him. More importantly, how was he going to get out of this dank prison? He sat with his back to the old water heater evaluating options, but concentrating was difficult, his thoughts still only partly coherent. Finally, he struggled up and stumbled over to the rickety wood staircase in the corner. Dragging himself up to a wooden door at the top, he wasn't surprised to find that it was bolted on the outside. When he pushed with his shoulder it didn't budge. Then he tried kicking it, largely out of frustration, but since it was hinged to swing inwards, he had no success. And when he knelt and peered under the door, he couldn't see anything.

Candrew sat on the bottom step, breathing deeply, trying to focus. He turned his attention to the sole window that was about four feet above the floor and set in a cemented steel frame. It was a foot or so below ground level and when he lurched over to it he could see through the grimy glass that outside there was a concrete well around it that was thick with weeds. They blocked his view. And there was a big puddle of water, presumably from last night's thunder storm. He pulled on the window's metal surround but it was securely fixed. Maybe he could break the glass—but with what? His shoe, of course. With the glass in the window broken, he could yell for help. That, of course, might attract his assailants, but what choices did he have? There were precious few. Candrew eased himself down to the floor, his back against the boiler. As he leaned forward to unlace his shoe, he was distracted by feeling the pen in his jacket jab into him and that prompted him to sit up and made a quick search of his pockets. This produced a note pad, pens, hand lens, car keys, candies, and a compass. He unwrapped one of the candies and ate it.

There was also the chunk of dynamite—if that's what it was—which he'd picked up in the storage unit. Carefully he studied this piece of potential explosive. The metal cap had a short cord-like extension that appeared to be a fuse, although it was awfully short. If he could rig it properly, perhaps he could blast out the metal bars on the window and create an escape route. He thought about that for a while, and realized he'd have to make the fuse longer or he wouldn't have time to take cover. He needed something that would burn. He considered using his handkerchief or even one of his socks, but quickly realized the solution was right there—paper. There was plenty in his notebook.

But how was he going to light the extended fuse since he didn't have any matches? However, he did have a hand lens and the sun was shining, and he remembered as a boy, using a lens to focus sunlight and set paper on fire - as well as to terrorize ants. The immediate problem was that the early morning shaft of sunlight was shining high on the wall so he'd have to wait a while. He crammed the dynamite up against the metal frame in the corner of the window, then tore a page out of his notebook and rolled it up using it to lengthen the fuse on the piece of explosive so he could light it with his lens. He waited for the sunlight to creep lower.

Later, with the sun higher in the sky, he used his lens to focus a hot spot on the end of the paper. It smoldered, then caught, and burned slowly but steadily towards the blasting cap. Candrew scurried over to the boiler, which was barely big enough to shield him, and crouched behind it with his jacket over his head and his hands over his ears. This whole damned thing was a long shot and he'd no idea what the effect of the explosive would be—if it really was an explosive, and he wasn't even sure of that. He worried that the blast might not be powerful enough to take out the metal frame. On the other hand, if it was too big a piece it could do real damage to the wall, the house, and him. He waited. Nothing happened.

He was about to give up when there was a flash so bright he saw it through his closed eyelids and a hail of metal and brick shards pelted the walls and the water tank with staccato noise. The shock wave in the small space knocked the breath out of him, and the detonation left his ears ringing. He was covered in dust and tasting grit in his mouth. Stiffly, Candrew stood and slowly moved around the tank peering through the swirling haze of dust at the bright light beaming in through the hole where the window had been. Although the explosion had blown out two-thirds of the metal in the frame and collapsed several bricks above it, unfortunately the hole didn't look big enough to climb through.

As he stood peering at the damage, he felt a strange sensation, like some creature crawling down his back, inside his shirt. He tried to reach it by stretching his arm up his back, but couldn't. The feeling got colder and extended down below his belt and that's when he realized it was a stream of water. A metal fragment from one of the window bars must have punctured the tank and he was being squirted with water. He wheeled around and jumped away.

Candrew moved over to the hole in the wall, cupped his hands and yelled. But the noise of the explosion had been loud enough to bring the neighbors. The weeds outside parted and a woman on her knees peered in through the hole. "You hurt? You okay?" She told him that police and firefighters had been called. The dust made Candrew sneeze as he turned away.

Five minutes later he heard the bolts slide back on the door at the top of the wooden stairs and a voice yelled, "Police. You okay?"

Candrew learned from the two officers investigating the explosion, that according to the neighbors, the house had only been occupied for a couple of weeks. Also, that the old man two doors away was convinced the occupants had been illegal immigrants and was certain they were dealing drugs. Moot now since they'd disappeared.

The more senior officer interrogated Candrew at length and took his statement and contact information. It helped that he knew the license number of the truck, they could easily trace that. The officer wanted to know if he intended to press charges.

"Not at the moment, I'll have to think about that before I take any action." Candrew was well aware that technically he'd been trespassing.

The police had searched the house and found it deserted. Candrew asked if he could go through again, because they'd stolen his briefcase—which was a lie, but a convenient fiction. After some hesitation they agreed, but there was nothing to see, only a few white plaster of Paris flakes on the floor of the living room, cigarette butts, pizza boxes, and empty beer cans. Nothing else. He turned to the officer and thanked him. Then added, "You might want to turn the water off before the basement floods."

With the police questioning over, he was glad to drive back to the university, though the trip was unpleasant. His neck and shoulder still ached, in spite of the few painkillers he'd found in his glove box. And the dust in his hair, the powder that got sprayed with water, was starting to set into a solid layer. He was glad to get home and luxuriate in a hot shower.

He'd forgotten Renata was coming to dinner, and had nothing prepared. But Renata was always tolerant of such screw-ups, eager to console him, and happy to eat a microwaved dinner—and drink his wine. After he'd told her the details of his entrapment in the basement, they talked about the storage unit and the rental outfit. But mostly they talked about Chuck Semley. He told her that Semley worked for a wealthy collector on the west coast, but they didn't know where the fossil bones had been shipped. Then he recalled the American voice that had interrupted the two Spanish speakers loading the truck, could that have been Semley? He'd lied before, so could he be hiding the truth about what he knew? Or was it someone else?

"When I asked Semley at lunch if he knew Jason Devereaux, or anyone with the code name Antares or iridium all I got was a perfunctory denial." Candrew grinned and added, "Which was exactly what I expected." He drained his wine glass, refilled it, then reminded Renata that Semley's name wasn't on Gavin's budget list.

"Maybe," she said, "that's because he was the source of the money."

"Or it could be he's only the courier for Mishikubo, just like he claimed. The 'errand boy' as he put it." Candrew grinned. "I suppose . . . "

The phone rang in the living room and he got to it on the fourth ring.

A hesitant voice said, "Candrew Nor?"

"Yes."

"This is Anne, Marge's sister."

He stammered, "Oh. Hi. How're things working out?" A dumb question to ask.

"That's why I'm calling. Marge drove over to Taos today. Claimed she needs to see her dentist in the morning, although I'm sure she really just wants time alone. I can understand that." There was a long pause, Candrew said nothing. "I'm calling because there are some things I'd like to talk to you about. Do you have time soon? Perhaps over lunch tomorrow?" She hesitated. "This must sound awfully pushy; I hope you don't mind."

"No. Not at all." Candrew thought of the pile of papers waiting for him in his office. None of them had an actual deadline, and none promised to be as interesting as lunch with Anne. The draft of his unfinished research manuscript could wait a while longer. He thought for only a moment. "How about Chama? *Viva Vera's* has been there forever, and serves good home-made New Mexican food. It's only a fifteen minute drive."

"That sounds great. And I'd rather not meet on campus."

They agreed on twelve-thirty and he gave her directions. "Couldn't be simpler. Come across campus on Central 'til you hit 84, then turn north. It's on the right just before you get into Chama. Big blue roof, prominent sign, can't miss it. The parking lot's right in front."

He stood unmoving for a moment, thinking about the call. Clearly it wasn't social. Candrew couldn't help wondering why Anne needed to talk to him without Marge being there. But it seemed he would find out soon enough.

"Well, what was that all about?" Renata asked, not smiling, just slicing the pie she'd brought for dessert.

Candrew told her.

"Why do you have to go to lunch? All the way to Chama. couldn't you talk on the phone?" She seemed jealous of his planned lunch with Anne.

Chapter 13

Candrew was a couple of minutes late arriving at the restaurant and Anne had already picked a table.

"I hope I wasn't too melodramatic on the phone," she said, "but I really needed a chance to talk to you when Marge wasn't around."

That was just fine with Candrew, and he said, "I didn't have anything urgent scheduled today, so it worked out well." But what he thought was, *She's a damn good-looking woman, prettier than I remembered.* In a single glance he took in the sleek auburn hair, the elegant white neck and the ample bosom, wondering whether his hands would ever get to follow his eyes.

They sat facing each other in one of the half-dozen booths that overlooked a dry arroyo shaded by cottonwoods. A young Hispanic boy brought tortilla chips and salsa, and Anne took a large chip, absentmindedly broke it in half, ate one part and dipped the other in salsa. "I was sort of restless this morning and drove up an hour ago to see the sights of Chama."

"You should have called me, we could have taken the tour together." He smiled at the thought. "And it's too bad you've already missed the highlight of the year. If you'd been here last month, you could have savored all the joys of the Spam festival."

"A Spam festival? You're kidding me." Anne gave him a direct, penetrating look, clearly trying to establish whether he was joking.

"No, I'm serious. You could have eaten Spam barbequed, with honey and cinnamon, or even in jambalaya. If you were really adventurous, you could have had a 'spelk' lunch."

"What on earth is that?"

"Two parts elk, one part Spam. Of course, the cynics claim the best recipes are the ones with enough ingredients to disguise the Spam taste. Frankly, I'm sorry I missed it, particularly the Spam diorama with a dinosaur eating Spam fossils."

She grinned, obviously liking this man. "A wealth of unknown culinary creativity in northern New Mexico, and I thought their only claim to fame was the train."

"Ah, now that's a worthy claim. We really ought to take the ride over to Silverton if you've got time."

"I'd like that. I saw the locomotive and the conductor was effervescent with enthusiasm. He overwhelmed me describing the spectacular scenery and dramatic views. Still, I don't have to tell you that, do I?" She gave a warm, disarming smile. "I know you geologists spend all your time clambering around in the mountains, collecting rocks and things. All rugged, out-door types." Furtively, she ran appraising eyes over him.

"Well, that's the myth." Candrew took another chip and scooped up salsa. "Teaching, committee meetings, lab work, publications, research proposals, and on and on—that's the reality."

"You make it sound so dreary."

"Well, it's certainly not that." He laughed. "I know lots of geologists who thought they'd be doing field work in exotic places, but geology in universities is a lot less physical and a lot more intellectual than the myth."

"Anyway, I won't have a chance to take the train with you

this time." He caught the slight emphasis she gave to *this time* and picked up on the almost imperceptible tilt of her head to one side, as if she were asking mutely: *Would you like that?* "Now Marge is on her own, I'm sure I'll be visiting a lot more often. All her friends are here, she enjoys northern New Mexico, and has no plans to leave. I just hope she can handle life without Gavin."

Anne stared into the distance as though she was thinking over a problem. Candrew kept quiet. They weren't here to talk about Chama, the train, or the mountains and it seemed best to let things flow, not interrupt with questions, let her take her own time. He didn't wait long.

"You must be wondering why I'm so anxious to talk to you when Marge isn't around. Well, last Saturday night we sat out on the patio after dinner and had a couple of margaritas. Things got pretty relaxed and Marge started to talk to me about Gavin. I don't know how to put this . . ."

The waitress arrived with their food, warned them the plates were very hot, asked if they needed anything else, and left.

Anne hesitated, then picked up where she'd left off. "Marge started to cry and told me that Gavin had been having an affair. I was stunned. I didn't know what to say. He didn't seem the sort of man who'd do something like that."

He certainly didn't, and Candrew was astonished. "You're kidding?" He took an involuntary deep breath and ran his hands back through his hair. "Gavin? An affair? Good God! That's the last thing I'd expect."

"Me too. It's so out of character."

Nothing in his dealings with Gavin had prepared Candrew for this. He found himself mentally rerunning their recent conversations, but if there were clues he'd missed them. "Is Marge certain? How did she find out? She any idea who the woman was? Surely, not a student?"

"She didn't mention a name; it probably wouldn't have

meant anything to me anyway. The woman's in Albuquerque—on the faculty at the university there."

"UNM. Do you know what department?"

"Geology, I guess. Apparently, she was doing some sort of analyses for Gavin. Isotopes? Does that make sense?"

"It might. You remember anything else she said about her?"

"When I asked how long it had been going on, she said at least six months." Anne paused, her gaze sweeping the room. "I thought Marge was kidding me when she said the women's specialty was 'dating', but then I realized she meant dating rocks—finding out how old they are."

"That would fit with isotopes. Must be Ilya Redfern; she's the only one doing geochronology." He saw Anne's puzzled look. "Sorry, that's the jargon for dating rocks." Candrew sat in silence for a moment, glancing out at the cottonwoods, watching their leaves shimmer in the breeze. "How did Marge find out about all this?"

"I'm not sure. She never actually said. But she did tell me Gavin was visiting Albuquerque regularly, sometimes even staying overnight. In the last few months he'd been away a lot more than usual, especially on weekends." Anne looked away, apparently thinking over what she'd been told. She turned back to Candrew. "Marge seemed relieved that she'd confided in me, but then it was almost as if she thought she'd gone too far and clammed up. I wanted to ask her if she ever confronted Gavin, but the topic was closed. She didn't want to talk about it anymore."

Candrew sat tapping his teeth, mulling over the significance of this new information. They sat without talking for a few minutes before he leaned forward and said quietly, "Let me see what I can find out."

She offered an appreciative smile and laid her hand on his arm. "Be discreet, please. I'd hate Marge to find out we're checking up on Gavin." The shared secret seemed to strengthen the bond developing between them.

For the next half hour, Anne talked about the visit she was planning to make to the Anasazi ruins in Chaco Canyon and Candrew outlined his research project with Judy. Then, reluctantly, Candrew pushed back his chair. "I have to be on campus by two-thirty." He fumbled in his pocket for a tip. "I really enjoyed the lunch—although not the news that came with it." He pushed five singles under the side plate. "I'll let you know what I find out. Give me a call if Marge tells you any more, or if you think I can do anything else to help."

They strolled out to the parking lot together and as she said, "Thanks for lunch," he put his arm around her shoulders and gave her a peck on the cheek. She swung into him, put her arms around his neck, and kissed him full on the mouth—a surprise, a pleasant surprise, and one he hoped would be repeated soon, often, and in a more accommodating setting. He held the door as she got into her car, shut it, and watched her drive away.

When he got into his own car it had a rich, pleasant, fruity odor—apricots. He'd forgotten he'd bought several pounds at the Santa Fe farmers market on Saturday, and for the last two days they'd sat ripening in the sun on the back seat.

Candrew rolled down the window and headed south on Highway 84 thinking that, to his colleagues in the department, Gavin's life looked simple, organized, routine, even humdrum. They'd seen none of the entanglements Candrew was starting to unearth. At first, murder had appeared an unlikely possibility, but now that it was a fact, understanding the complications of his activities had become crucial. Who would want to kill Gavin, and for what reason? Candrew had read enough murder mysteries to know the usual motives—money, hatred, jealousy, revenge. Revenge seemed out of line. There was no evidence for it. Same with hatred. After the news of Gavin's affair at lunch, he'd have to consider jealousy more seriously, though he was hardly ready to admit that Marge could be involved in murder. A month ago he would have discounted money. Although Gavin was adequately paid as a senior professor, it was hardly enough to kill for. What he had learned in the last few days had changed all that. Gavin was clearly involved in some lucrative dinosaur project that might make money a possible motive. And if he could believe Semley, that was coming from Mishikubo. Then there was the question raised by the FBI about digging up Anasazi pots and selling them. Another possible source of money.

His rambling thoughts made him wonder whether Anne's tour of Chama had included the Foster Hotel. There were rumors it was haunted. One of the ghosts was supposed to be a man who'd had an affair with a married woman and been killed by the jealous husband—death by spouse. Was there a hint here? However jealous and upset Marge was, Candrew couldn't believe she would kill Gavin: out of the question. And anyway, how would she have done it? A contract murder? He thought, *this is getting way too bizarre.* Or was it?

Candrew hadn't been paying close attention to his driving and the flashing lights behind seeped slowly into his consciousness. Instinctively he eased off the gas pedal and checked the rearview mirror. It confirmed his fears. The State Police cruiser was right on his tail and there were no other cars on either side of the road. It had to be for him. He braked gently and signaled his right turn onto the shoulder, thinking to himself: *stay calm, do everything right.* Candrew pulled to a stop, fished around in the door pocket for his wallet and rolled down the window.

The officer seemed too young to be an authority figure. He asked for Candrew's driver's license, but before he even looked at it, half smiled. "Ah, Professor Nor. You gave me a D in physical geology." Candrew was at a loss for words. He couldn't place him as a student. "A 65 as I remember. Funny how things work out. I just clocked you at 65. Unfortunately, you were doing it in a 50 mile an hour zone." He stretched out his hand. "I also need your car insurance."

Irritated with himself, Candrew sat patiently while the police officer walked back to the cruiser and went through the routine of calling in the information and filling out forms. The officer had the stocky build and dark complexion of the local Hispanics, but the name tag on his pocket said, *O'Hara*. Odd that he had a name more appropriate for an Irish cop from New York. Officer O'Hara came back, handed the citation to Candrew and leaned with his arm resting on the car roof. "I'm giving you a warning. Think of it as an *Incomplete*. By the way, in spite of the outcome, I enjoyed your class. Even learned some stuff. Have a nice day."

Candrew was annoyed with himself for not paying more attention, but happy to get away without a fine. He headed down the highway at a circumspect 50 mph and watched in the rear-view mirror as the predator made a U-turn and settled in to hunt more prey.

As Candrew made his way down the corridor to the departmental office, he ran into Mark Kernfeld scurrying along with a pile of manila folders under one arm. "So how did your tête-à-tête with the investigators from the federal bureau go?"

Candrew gave a fake grimace and replied, "Like a visit to the dentist—unpleasant, but not unbearable, and thankfully over. And yours?"

"I had the privilege of cooperating with the FBI for an hour after lunch. As a tax payer I'm proud to have people like that looking after my security." He smiled ironically. "I know even less about Gavin's clandestine activities than you, which didn't stop them from probing. It ended up with more archaeology than paleontology."

Candrew raised his eyebrows quizzically. "You too?"

"They wanted to know if he was a pot hunter. I'm so naïve I

thought they meant searching for wild marijuana!"

Candrew didn't believe that for a moment. "Me too. I got the same questions. Think there's something to it?"

"Who knows where the truth lies. Frankly, I doubt it." He laughed. "Based on absolutely no evidence."

Back in his office, Candrew finally unearthed a dog-eared copy of the *Directory of Geosciences Departments* in a pile of catalogs. It was three years old, but academic institutions don't change that fast and he quickly found the listing for the University of New Mexico and Redfern's number. He was about to send an e-mail asking if he could visit the lab and then at the last minute decided he'd rather hear her voice, the better to gauge her reaction. Reaction to what? A simple request from a professional colleague at a nearby institution, or would she treat him as a friend of Gavin's? And what treatment would that be? He called her number. It rang half a dozen times and rolled over to an answering machine. Disappointed she wasn't there, he started dictating. "This is Dr. Nor in the geology department up at UNNM. I'd like to . . ."

"Hold on, I'll switch this damn thing off." Dr. Redfern's voice broke in. "Use it as a protection from students. They'll take every minute you've got."

"I hope I'm not catching you at a bad time."

"No worse than usual. Go ahead."

"I know you do isotope dating studies and I'm going to be on the UNM campus on Wednesday. Could I come by your office and talk about some research I'm planning?"

"Don't see why not. I should tell you we are not doing much neodymium work any more. Mainly back to dating with argon-39."

"That's exactly what I need to discuss."

"You got funding?"

"Some limited support. We can talk about that."

"What do you need to date?"

"Diagenetic clays in a sandstone matrix. Should be about 200 million years old, give or take."

"Okay. I plan to be here all morning. Come by the lab any time after eight."

The conversation had been brusque and to the point with Ilya Redfern appearing blunt and not someone with time to spend on trivia. Did he catch her at an awkward time? Or was she always like that? What he really wanted to know was what it was about her that attracted Gavin. With luck, he'd find out in a couple of days.

Redfern's role added a whole new dimension to an already messy problem. Was she also embroiled in the dinosaur project? Candrew put the phone down and stood beside his cluttered desk, gazing out the window. Looking into his office just reminded him of the many things he needed to do, and all the fast-approaching deadlines. With his back to the office, he could see the mountains in the distance and they grounded him in the real world—but were too far away to get tangled in details. This was his favorite location for thinking things over.

He knew so little about the people involved. Semley was just an "errand boy"—maybe, and who was the Mishikubo he worked for? Jason was the son of a casual friend he'd only seen a couple of times, and Teresa Polanca a faculty member he'd never met. And then there was "Antares" and "KT", if they were actual people. What did an expert on scorpions and an undergraduate student in communications have to do with a dinosaur excavation? And a murder? Why were their roles important enough to justify the amounts of money they were getting? The fact that Semley's name was not on the budgets was consistent with him, or more likely Mishikubo, being a possible source for the money. Was Marge involved in Gavin's death? And if so, how? It was always possible, of course, that Gavin's drowning and the dinosaur project were unrelated, the timing a mere coincidence. Even though this had to be a possibility, he didn't like the idea. It seemed too much as if he were ducking the real issues.

With the surprising news that Gavin might have been having an affair, he hadn't given much thought to his recent meeting with the two FBI agents. Their suspicions about Gavin's involvement with prehistoric Indian artifacts raised a completely new set of issues. Dinosaur bones sold for a lot of money, but Anasazi pots and other archaeological remains also commanded huge sums in the specialized galleries that treated them as rare art objects. There were always rumors of a thriving black market in these artifacts. While it was legal to dig on private land, by the time a pot ended up in a gallery there was usually no provenance, making it impossible to prove that it had actually come from federal land. The Bureau of Land Management and the FBI needed to catch thieves in the act, and this might explain their curiosity about Gavin's excavations. Could he really have been part of the illicit trade, and if so, was there enough money at stake to provide a motive for murder?

Windows provided a view from one world into another, a view limited by the obvious constraints of a frame. Know your constraints and the view was set—sort of. A change in viewing angle could present a whole new picture. Candrew knew the constraints, but was he looking at the picture from the right point of view? What else would he see if he changed his perspective? He was missing something.

Chapter 14

Candrew was at the wheel of a university minivan following a comfortable distance behind Mark Kernfeld in another one. Each year, a few weeks before Fall semester begins, the department arranges a field trip for new students. While they do actually visit some geologically significant areas, the purpose is mainly social and the trip provides a chance for them to get to know one another.

The pair of vans headed south toward Española, the road making a broad sweep to the left. At first, Candrew didn't pay much attention to the red jeep coming out of the back road that led west to the Christ in the Desert Monastery. Only when they were almost opposite the turnoff did he realize it was Jason Devereaux driving with the dark-haired Hispanic girl beside him. He wondered what brought Jason to this remote area, or was it something along the way that attracted him and his girlfriend. Maybe just the isolation.

Candrew was watching the jeep in the rearview mirror, and thinking about how well Jason knew the area's back country trails, when Mark's van slowed and turned into Ghost Ranch. The entrance, marked by a simple sign with a stylized white ox skull, led into a wide gravel road that twisted away through low bushes. Spectacular long mesas with prominent multicolored rock layers dominated the view to the north and on both sides. This eroded landscape of ochres, tans and yellows had been made familiar by the paintings of Georgia O'Keeffe, and she had drawn the design for the skull that graced the entrance sign.

O'Keeffe may have been attracted by the skulls of cows and horses, but it was the bones of much older animals, 225 million years older, that brought the first fossil hunters to the area. What they found were thousands of skeletons of an agile, eight-foot long dinosaur they called *Coelophysis*, and this was still the largest known group of carnivorous dinosaurs anywhere in the world. The site was the main reason that Candrew and Mark were bringing the geology students here.

They parked the vans on the gravel in front of a group of low adobe-style buildings that included both the anthropology and paleontology museums, and the students piled out.

"How did this place get a name like Ghost Ranch? Is it haunted or something? That why they have a skull as their sign?" one of the students asked.

Mark started to explain. "Well, now it belongs to the Presbyterian Church and . ."

"Couldn't they exorcise the ghost?"

Mark smiled, ignored the student's question, and continued telling them about the local history. "The ranch was given to the church by Arthur Pack and his wife. He was a wealthy publisher and had bought it in the thirties from a cowboy who'd won it in a poker game. Or so the story goes. Originally it was called *Rancho de los Brujos,* that's Spanish for witches, but nobody seems to know where the name came from."

The students ambled into the museums, making their way through the twelve thousand years of the area's history presented in the anthropology section. Candrew was always struck by the interesting juxtaposition of anthropology and paleontology—both displayed items of value that told us about our past, about mankind's place in the grand scheme of things. Unfortunately, both fossils and archaeological artifacts were now "collectable" and commanded high prices. It made him furious to think of an expensively mounted fossil or a well-displayed prehistoric bowl shown just to impress friends—or worse, acquired simply as an investment—when all the information about the broader location had been lost. He knew many people believed fossils and artifacts scattered across the landscape were there for the first person who took the trouble to pick them up. In reality, they belonged to everyone; they were part of humanity's heritage.

Inevitably the mix of fossils and prehistoric artifacts made him think of Gavin. Professionally, of course, he studied fossils, but most of those had little commercial value. Was he augmenting his geological studies by digging out a few Anasazi pots and other paleo-Indian artifacts when he got the chance? Conservatively, they could fetch in the tens of thousands of dollars. But the *T. rex* dig was different, and a well-preserved specimen could sell in the millions.

The students were gathering in the paleontology museum, milling around a large block of *Coelophysis* bones that were being painstakingly exposed from the enclosing rock.

"Next you'll get to see the quarry where these fossils were discovered and where this block came from," Candrew told them. "We're going to hike up the trail to Kitchen Mesa. There's no kitchen there, so if you want to eat, bring your lunch with you." The trail headed east and Mark and Candrew led.

Jeans and tee shirts were standard attire, and almost without exception the students' shirts proclaimed some sort of message. There was the usual *Stop Continental Drift* and *Geologists Make the Bed Rock*, and, interestingly, *Ranchers Should Fear Vegetarians More Than Wolves*. But Candrew preferred the one that neatly summed up the scientific method: *Find the Facts / Filter the Facts / Face the Facts / Follow the Facts*. As far as figuring out the reason for Gavin's murder he was still squarely at step one; he needed to find the facts. All he had was surmise and supposition, not the sort of thing that would stand scrutiny in a court of law—or with his scientific colleagues.

Mark resumed his role as professor. "This mesa is the location of the quarry where they've excavated the *Coelophysis* bones, including the ones you've just seen in the museum."

"*Coelophysis*? How did they come up with a name like that? Totally weird." The student struggled with the name: *seel-oh-fi-sis*. "Is it, like, Latin, or something?"

"Greek, not Latin. It means 'hollow form.' *Coelophysis* had hollow bones to save weight, so it could run faster and make a living as a predator. It seems to have been slender and graceful, an attractive animal—if you weren't the prey."

"Don't birds have hollow bones?" asked a girl with a swinging ponytail.

"Yeah, and a whole bunch of paleontologists think birds descended from dinosaurs." It was the long-haired student with the *Stop Continental Drift* tee-shirt and a baseball cap on backwards.

"*Coelophysis* got to evolve into a bird?" There was a note of genuine amazement in the student's voice. Most freshmen thought of dinosaurs as huge lumbering beasts. "You mean *T. rex* learned to fly? How could something really, really awesome end up like a sparrow?"

Candrew tried to explain. "Not all dinosaurs were huge. Some weren't much bigger than chickens." The student still looked puzzled. "That *Coelophysis* you saw back in the museum probably weighed no more than a hundred pounds, and it was only about three feet tall and eight feet long—and most of that tail." Candrew looked around. "But it did have lethal curved claws and sharp, serrated teeth. Quite a predator."

"Still, it's pretty amazing." The student shook his head. Candrew always liked to get students thinking about how things happened. He bent down and picked up a small piece of a fossil bone and posed the question, "How did this fossil die?"

"He stopped to eat the grass, and smell the roses, and got jumped by a *T. rex*," one grinning student volunteered.

"No way." It was *Stop Continental Drift* again. "*T. rex* was Late Cretaceous."

"So?"

"Well the rocks here are 140 million years older. *Coelophysis* was long gone before *T. rex* put in an appearance. He was, like, way too late for dinner."

Candrew enjoyed seeing students learning from each other, but this flash of insight wasn't going much further and there was a long pause. "Yes, and there were no roses to smell," he said. "Plants with flowers didn't become common until the end of the Cretaceous."

"It must have been a drab world without color. I guess there were no butterflies either."

"Probably not," Candrew said, then added, "And grasses didn't evolve until all the dinosaurs were extinct. I'm afraid you were wrong on all three counts."

The students spread out across the hillside with its sparse shrubs and scattered rocks, showing varying degrees of interest in the location of the old quarry. They were taking notes, taking photos, or taking it easy—most in the last category.

A pair of students wandered over to Candrew and Mark, one holding a chunk of rock about the size of his fist. "Is this, like, a fossil? Part of one of those seely..."

"*Coelophysis*. Let me look." Candrew took a hand lens from one of the pockets in his field jacket and studied the specimen. "Yeah, I think you've got a bit of bone here."

"Can you just go and dig up fossils anywhere you want?"

"Not without permission. If it's private land, like here at Ghost Ranch, you need to ask the owner. On federal land, the government can issue a permit to collect fossils, but you've got to be a genuine researcher."

"What about the guys selling fossils in the rock shops?"

"All commercial dealers have to get their fossils from private land."

"But the government owns way more land than it can look after. They can't watch it all, can they? How could they possibly know where people are digging up fossils?"

"Not easily—and that's a problem. There's almost certainly lots of illegal fossil excavating going on." As Candrew spoke he thought: *including Gavin's T. rex dig.*

Another student asked, "Didn't that professor who drowned used to lead this trip? I guess he studied the fossils here."

"You're partly right. He did study fossils, but not the ones here—and not dinosaurs." *Well, not until the last twelve months,* was Candrew's unspoken thought.

A small group had gathered, listening. "I did my senior research project with Gavin Citalli." Candrew recognized the speaker as one of the students just starting graduate work. "He was fun to work for, well, at first. But he wasn't available nearly as much in the last few months, and, like, more guarded about his office and things than he used to be, somehow a lot more secretive, less outgoing."

"Were you on the float trip with him?"

"Yeah." He looked off into the distance and there was a long silence. "I'll never understand that. He didn't seem to make any effort. He looked as though he was sleepy, you know, like not really trying." A couple of other students nodded in agreement. "When he came round the rocks he was only paddling half-heartedly and when the kayak flipped he didn't seem to make, like, much of an effort to get it upright, and then the boat popped up without him in it."

Candrew could see this all too clearly in his mind's eye. He'd imagined the capsizing kayak a dozen times—and the outcome was always the same and never what he wanted. "Was there anything unusual about Dr. Citalli's behavior before the accident?"

"No. Not really. Pretty much his usual self. You know, running around getting everybody psyched up and everything."

"He did keep borrowing my cell phone." The information was volunteered by a tall, blonde girl with holes in the knees of her jeans. She sported the tee shirt that warned farmers about vegetarians. "He must have used it at least half a dozen times."

This was surprising information. Gavin always said he hated the idea of phones in the wilderness, except possibly for emergencies. "Any idea who he was trying to call?" Candrew asked.

"No. He didn't say, and every time he used it he walked over to the cliffs before he called."

"Did he talk for a long time?"

"Not really. The calls were real short, like, maybe, two or three minutes. I sort of figured he couldn't get through. He promised to pay me for the minutes he used."

Candrew asked if her phone recorded the numbers he tried to reach. She said she'd check and let him know.

A day keeping pace with eighteen energetic students left Candrew with quite an appetite. The first thing he did when he got back to the house was thaw some of his home-made marinara sauce in the microwave and boil water for spaghetti—and open a bottle of wine. With that taken care of, he turned his attention to feeding the animals. He could hardly ignore them any longer since both Chile and Pixel were underfoot.

Candrew had just finished dinner on the patio, thrown away the olive pits and was putting the tomatoes, olives and remains of the wine in the refrigerator, when the phone rang.

"Hi. It's Renata. Thanks so much for dinner the other

evening. The way you prepared those trout was fabulous and I thoroughly enjoyed them—but then I always like your cooking."

"Coming from you, that's a real compliment."

"Now it's my turn. I'm calling to invite you to dinner." Renata usually made spicy, South American dishes and Candrew was fond of her strong but subtle flavors. He liked most good food, especially when he didn't have to cook it himself. Before his imitation of Pavlov's dogs got any further, she said, "This time I'm going to cheat and take you out to a restaurant. Remember I told you about Joel Iskander, an anthropologist friend, well, more of an acquaintance really? He just called to say he's planning to be on campus tomorrow, and Casa del Rio seemed like a good place to take him to dinner."

Second best to Renata's cooking, Candrew thought—but a close second. "I'd like that," he said, and meant it. But he wondered just why Iskander was visiting.

"While I think of it, could you e-mail me the times for the limo service from Albuquerque airport? I know you've got a schedule."

"No problem."

"I've been thinking about Gavin's murder—I can't get it off my mind. You were explaining the other evening how a complete *T. rex* skeleton weighs a lot, especially when it's still encased in the rock matrix. So he must have had lots of help."

"Either that or some heavy equipment," Candrew said. "Or both."

"Even when they've hauled the fossils out, it'll still take a lot of work to separate the bones from the rock and put a skeleton together," Renata said. "I wonder where they'll do all that?"

"And who's going to do it? It needs expertise and specialized facilities—and lots of time. There aren't many good preparators around."

*   *   *

It was eight o'clock before Chile got his evening walk. Candrew let the dog off the leash and strolled leisurely through the cool evening. With the information from the student who'd lent Gavin her cell phone on the float trip, he had one more piece of information to fit into the puzzle—Gavin's urgent, and obviously unsuccessful, phone calls. But who was he so anxious to contact while on a river trip? Did he want to tell them something, or did he need information? Did he know something ominous was pending?

After Renata's comments, Candrew thought about all the effort going into the *Coelophysis* reconstructions at Ghost Ranch—and compared with a *T. rex*, those dinosaurs were tiny. So, who was doing the tyrannosaur work? And where? He needed to form a clearer idea of what was going on and develop a realistic picture of the scope of the project. And soon. Candrew also wondered about Jason. He seemed very familiar with the back country. Was that his contribution to the project?

Candrew stopped at the end of their usual trail and as the sound of footsteps on the rubbly ground faded, only the buzzing of unseen insects broke the silence. The low, rich-red disk of the sun, perched on the horizon with its lower edge just touching the dark outline of the western hills, lit the bottom edges of the clouds scattered across the darkening sky. Unlike the searing intensity of midday, the muted glow of dusk made it possible to look directly at it, and Candrew was entranced by its serene beauty. D. H. Lawrence was wrong when he said, "Knowledge has killed the sun, making it a ball of gas with spots." Candrew knew how the sun worked; he understood the nuclear reactions that power our local star; he understood the adsorption of light by the atmosphere that made it look red; but all of this had no effect on his appreciation of another spectacular New Mexican sunset. It was very quiet as he turned and headed back to the house.

Out on the main highway west of campus, the university ran a small hotel for visitors. It served as the drop-off point for the commercial shuttle from Albuquerque airport, a good two hours drive away. It was just after 10:00 o'clock when Candrew got there to pick up Judy and he hustled into the lobby area where other scattered groups of people were standing around, clearly with similar intentions. Among them was a tall, lean man casually dressed in a fringed leather jacket, bolo tie and cowboy hat. He detached himself from the group, and with a slightly bow-legged, rolling gait strolled over to Candrew.

"Hi, Dr. Nor. How's the rock business?" He grabbed Candrew's hand in both of his and shook it vigorously. "Not hit rock bottom yet?"

David Willis, known to everyone as "Slim," was a dealer in Taos who owned a shop full of old cowboy equipment and leatherwork, as well as fossils and minerals, a sort of cross between an antique store and a trading post.

"How's your business? Still trying to cheat honest geologists out of their best specimens?"

"Sure. Like they don't know the value of things." Slim grinned broadly.

"You know much about dinosaurs in the Four Corners area?" Candrew asked.

"Just enough to figure out that a fella could go broke trying to deal in them. It's all damned federal land—and what isn't, is owned by the Indians. Not enough for the likes of me to make a buck. Not that the Feds would let me anyway. They watch like goddamned hawks."

"So you never get offered any good fossils?"

"Oh, maybe once in a while. All from private ranches, of course." He said it with a deadpan face. "Why? You need a hadrosaur or a nice triceratops for the department's collection?"

"We couldn't afford your sky high prices."

"Hey, you know me. I'd cut you guys a hell of a deal." He took off his hat, pushed his hair back and resettled the hat.

"Ever run into a guy by the name of Chuck Semley?" Candrew asked.

Slim stared steadily at Candrew for a moment before a slow smile spread across his weathered face. "Bit out of my league. Deals in real high end stuff." There was a long pause. "How'd you get tied up with someone like that?" He didn't give Candrew time to answer. "Has a reputation for being persistent, relentless. Doesn't seem to be, you know, a dealer. Buys, but doesn't sell." Slim stuck his hands in his belt and stood with his legs apart. "And what he buys is first class. Never questions where it comes from."

And was the next big dinosaur coming from Gavin, Candrew wondered. "Does he ever buy—or sell—Anasazi pots or artifacts?"

"Not as far as I know. That's a bit outside my range." He stood thinking for a moment then shook his head. "Anyway, anything I can do, you let me know." Slim ambled over to rejoin a couple of well-dressed men by the far wall.

Conversations among those waiting ended in a flurry of activity as the "orient express" of northern New Mexico pulled in and delivered its passengers, Judy among them.

"How was Vegas? Win enough to pay for the trip?"

"That's the trouble with visiting people who live there. They get on with their lives without even thinking about *The Strip*. But Dorian and I had a good time in spite of that." Judy picked up her pack, slung it over one shoulder as they walked around to Candrew's car, then dropped it on the back seat of the Cherokee. She clambered in beside him. "Solved one of your problems."

"Great. I need all the help I can get. Which one of my many puzzles did you figure out?" He turned in his seat and backed out carefully before heading around the edge of campus toward Judy's duplex.

"Remember when we were looking at the dinosaur photos in

Gavin's office, a lot of them had letters on the back? Things like *DEN*, and we thought it could have been a code or a filing system, maybe?"

"Yeah, I remember. Though I haven't given it much thought since then."

"Well, it's been intriguing me and I told Dorian about it. He took one glance at *YYC* and immediately said, *Calgary.*"

Candrew was puzzled. "I still don't see the connection."

"Neither did I. Apparently, *YYC* is the airport code."

"So what's that got to do with photos of dinosaurs?"

"Dorian had an answer for that too. Last summer he was at a meeting in Calgary and stayed on for a couple of days to visit Drumheller . . ."

"Of course!" Candrew immediately knew the connection. "The Royal Tyrrell Museum. That's one of the biggest collections of late-Cretaceous dinosaurs in the world." He glanced in the side-view mirror and turned onto the street leading to Judy's duplex. "So Gavin was using the three-letter codes for the nearest airports to identify museums with reconstructed dinosaurs. Probably the ones he visited."

"Right. And all the other codes make sense too. *DEN* is Denver, *OAK* is Oakland, which is close to the Berkeley collection. *BWI* puzzled us and we had to look that one up—it's Baltimore/Washington. I couldn't remember the others, but I bet New York, and Pittsburgh are there."

"We need to check those. But this all makes a lot of sense." Candrew pulled to a stop in Judy's driveway. "Gavin would have needed to see some fully-reconstructed skeletons as a guide to the layout of the bones he was excavating. Something more than just the diagrams in the reference books."

"And, of course, it also showed that he was deliberately covering his tracks, using code letters rather the museum names."

Chapter 15

Gerry Brunton and his wife had remodeled—more accurately, rebuilt—an old adobe. Long abandoned, it had been the main hacienda on a Spanish land grant before falling into disrepair. When Gerry failed to make tenure in civil engineering, he decided to stay in northern New Mexico. Gregarious and articulate, he was a natural for a restaurant owner and with his wife's culinary skills and kitchen supervision they had developed a loyal clientele. Gerry pushed open the heavy wooden door of the restaurant with a flourish and greeted Candrew.

"Renata Alcantara made reservations for three."

"That's right," Gerry agreed. "I put you over on the west side. Gave you a ring-side seat for the sunset." He guided Candrew to the table and pulled back the chair. "Would you like a drink while you're waiting?"

"Sure. A margarita." And would you make it with *reposado tequila*?"

"Happy to do it."

Candrew came to the *Casa del Rio Restaurante* infrequently, and while the *Casa* always impressed him, the *Rio* was disappointing. Little more than a shallow arroyo, it rarely hosted a flowing stream, although the huge, mature cottonwoods showed the small valley wasn't entirely without water. The main dining room was well-proportioned with thick, undulating adobe walls and deep window sills that produced a feeling of age and a real sense of continuity with northern New Mexico's history.

Cradling the icy drink in both hands, Candrew looked forward to a relaxed evening, though from Renata's comments, Joel seemed a little odd. Finding it difficult to relax, he caught himself working through yet another mental list, but a long, slow drink of margarita, savoring its aroma, helped him forget about his research, Judy, and the geology department.

Casa del Rio was a lot fancier than most places around the university, though he often went to one of the high end restaurants when he was down in Santa Fe. Candrew thought back to his last visit to the City Different and the meeting with Semley. The Los Angeles trip he'd agreed to make next Monday would take precious time, and he had very mixed feelings about going. He was unsure of Semley, and knew even less about Mishikubo. On one hand, if he was ever going to find out exactly what Gavin was involved in—and how he'd been murdered—he would need to grab every opportunity to get closer to the people involved. On the other hand, Semley was luring him into an illegal dinosaur excavation. And he still had no idea where Jason and the others fitted in.

"Sorry we're late." Renata brought Joel to the table and introduced him.

Candrew gave her a hug and a kiss on the cheek. "You look terrific." And she did. Her hair was piled up on top and she wore a simple, pale blue dress that complemented her dark complexion. He felt a slight twinge of envy. Had she made a special effort for Joel?

Slightly overweight with a large, fleshy face and thinning hair, Joel produced what seemed a forced smile and gave Candrew a penetrating look. Candrew disliked him instantly. He rarely felt that strongly about people, certainly not on a first meeting, and couldn't figure out what he was reacting against. Insincerity? Apparent lack of humor? This could be a long evening. Joel pulled back the chair for Renata and they settled in around the table.

After initial pleasantries, conversation sputtered and they struggled to find areas of common interest. Joel was an archaeologist working in the Four Corners area and specializing in the Anasazi. These ancestral puebloans built their multistoried buildings and ceremonial kivas long before the present day Indians moved into their pueblos, or before the Navajos and Apaches migrated down from western Canada. Field work provided a shared interest and they talked about the difficulties of doing careful research under adverse conditions.

"You guys have it easy, working in the desert." Renata laughed at the pair of them. "You should try the jungle: heat, humidity, not to mention every type of biting and stinging bug known to man— and woman." She glanced from one to the other. "All you need is a broad-brimmed hat and a gallon of water; you've got it made."

Joel leapt to the defense of males, but in a surprisingly humorless way. "Nearly true. We do have rattlesnakes and scorpions."

"I'd never given scorpions much thought until last week." Candrew told them what he'd heard about Teresa Polanca and how she worked in the desert at night with a black light. "Scorpions can be pretty nasty, though I'm told that around here their sting isn't often fatal."

Joel listened attentively, but seemed unconvinced. He shifted in his chair, leaning towards Candrew. "I guess the best advice is, *don't turn over any rocks.*"

Candrew laughed. "That's difficult advice for a geologist to follow."

"Field work's always a challenge; things always go wrong."

Joel kept his serious demeanor. "I heard one of your faculty just drowned on a float trip with his students. Where was Citalli working?"

Candrew picked up on the fact that he knew Gavin's name, but ducked the question. "It was planned as a recreational trip for the students, with some fossil collecting thrown in." There was a gap in the conversation and he filled it by adding, "I'd inherited the problem of sorting out his office, until the FBI stepped in."

"Really?" Joel tilted his head to one side.

"Yeah, but the sheer scale was daunting. There had to be at least a thousand books. And what an idiosyncratic mix. Marge, his wife, wants to donate them to the library."

"But only the last five years of scientific literature is still pertinent," Joel pointed out. "Just junk the rest."

"Well, you might be right for physics and chemistry, but geology seems to have a longer shelf life. You often find that the definitive mapping of an area, or the description of some type fossil, was done fifty years ago. Sometimes, even more."

"What about archaeology?" Renata asked Joel. "The early descriptions of Anasazi sites and all their pots and artifacts, they're still valid, aren't they?"

Before he had a chance to reply, the waiter interrupted by putting a basket of freshly-baked bread on the table. Renata took a piece and passed the basket around. As she reached for the butter, Joel turned to Candrew. "Did Gavin stumble on any Anasazi sites? There are thousands that aren't documented out in the Four Corners, and my guess is he must have run across quite a few."

Interesting question, Candrew thought, wondering why he asked. "Yeah, but most of the areas he worked are federal land."

"That hasn't stopped a horde of pot hunters from digging. And they've done pretty well selling to the high-end galleries."

"Until they got caught by the FBI," Renata said.

"You mean like the old-timers out in Utah?" Joel asked.

"They've been doing it all their life. Part of the culture."

"But a couple of them felt guilty enough to commit suicide," Renata snapped.

"Anyway, are you suggesting Gavin was illegally excavating pots?" Candrew seethed at the implication.

Joel raised both hands in an uncharacteristic defensive gesture. "No. Not at all. I just wondered whether he'd acquired any information that could help my research." He paused. "And talking of which, you could help me with some of the rock descriptions."

"Maybe." Candrew was non-committal.

There was a few moments silence, a truce, as they munched and drank. But Joel kept pursuing his questions about Gavin. "What's going to happen to all Gavin's fossils?"

Candrew downed the remains of his margarita. "I expect the best ones will end up in the department's display cases." He paused. This was not something he'd thought about. "Students will keep working on some, I suppose, and a lot will go to collaborators at other universities."

"But none will be sold?"

"Sold?" Candrew was taken aback by the question.

"Why not? Most of them are probably duplicates, or triplicates. And I'll bet most of them aren't unique or even rare." He seemed pleased with Candrew's surprise. "And there's quite a market. I'm sure the department could use the money."

"That's hardly the point."

"What is the point? Why do academics think they have the sole right to every fossil that comes out of the ground?"

"Well, in this case the collecting was paid for by the National Science Foundation. That's taxpayers' money."

Joel was combative. "So the average taxpayer who footed the bill never gets to see them because they're buried in the basement of some university museum?"

Renata adopted a conciliatory tone. "But they do get to share in the understanding of the past that comes from studying fossils. And studying them takes time."

"Museums already have more material than they have people to work on it," Joel shot back. "Look at the Smithsonian. Forty million fossils. *Forty million.* They can't possibly be doing research on all of them, not with the staff of only thirty-five who work in that department."

Candrew did a quick estimate: more than a million fossils each.

"And I can't believe that every one of those fossils is a critically important specimen," Joel said.

"But would amateurs be able to recognize everything important?" Candrew asked. "Even the professionals are fooled sometimes. Like those fakes from China, the ones made by splicing together a couple of different fossils to create something that appeared novel. That's the trouble when fossils have high commercial value—there's an incentive to be dishonest."

"Was that the one where the *National Geographic* had to apologize to all its readers," Renata asked.

"Yeah, that's right." Candrew stopped buttering his bread and waved the knife to underline his point. "It's a textbook example of the importance of peer review in science."

"Old fashioned!" Joel seemed to be on the opposite side of every issue. Warming to his argument, he leaned forward, his forefinger thrusting in the air. "Things move a lot faster today with e-mail, blogs and twitter. People only have a short attention span. We've got to get the message out quickly."

"True. But it's critical that the message we get out is the correct one," Candrew said. "You can't do science with a bumper-sticker and sound-bite mentality. Unfortunately, most of the problems in geology are too complicated to give an unambiguous answer in a hundred and forty characters or less."

"Same in archaeology. You never have all the facts," Renata

said. "It's always a work in progress."

Again, Joel took a different tack. "An individual can own a spectacular and unique diamond, why not a dinosaur fossil?"

"That's different. Studying diamonds isn't going to tell us much we don't already know. And since our information on how diamonds form comes from their imperfections and inclusions, the higher the quality of the diamond the less it can tell us." Candrew smiled, sure he'd made his point. "And remember, there are thousands of diamonds."

"Do you know how many *T. rexes* have been discovered?" Joel asked.

"About forty," Renata said, pleased with herself and glancing at Candrew with a smile.

"Very good." Joel used a condescending tone and then continued his impromptu quiz. "And do you know how many of those were discovered by professional paleontologists with the Ph.D. union card?" He paused for effect, and answered his own question. "Less than half of them. *Half!*" He was on a roll. It was obvious he felt strongly about fossils as commodities, not just protected material for paleontologists. "It's all in the timing. Erosion is the paleontologist's best friend and worst enemy. Fossils get uncovered, right?—but then they're quickly washed away. You've got to be lucky enough to be there at just the right moment. That's why the amateurs are so important because there are lots more of them, more eyes on the ground."

There was a sudden silence as the guitarist reached the end of his Spanish piece. A ripple of applause followed, and Joel swiveled in his chair to inspect the other diners.

Candrew was disturbed by Joel's equation of fossils with money. "I don't care who goes out looking for fossils, it's what happens when they find one. That's when it needs to be turned over to the professionals. Only an academic paleontologist is going to take the time to study the dirt under the toenails."

"Only an academic would want to!" Renata was struggling to keep a lighter tone to the discussion. "Anyway, what's the point in doing that?"

"The dirt's where you'll find pollen grains that show what type of trees were growing, what the climate was like, all of the context information. And that takes time. Einstein discovered that time is money," Candrew smiled, ". . . or was it Adam Smith? Whoever. The point is, the commercial dealers are selling fossils to earn a living, to make money. They aren't going to spend time to look at pollen or do the academic stuff. Papers in scientific journals won't make you rich. It's the bones that sell, and the bigger the better."

"Actually, the more unusual the better." Joel's viewpoint continued to be economic.

Renata was sitting facing down the room and saw them first. "Well, look who's here. That's my vet." She half rose out of her seat and nodded to him. "Good evening, Dr. Levorsen."

The tall, athletic man returned the smile and raised his right hand in a casual greeting. "Nice to see you." He paused and introduced his companion. "This is Teresa Polanca, but you probably know her from campus."

Candrew didn't know her, but he certainly knew about her. She was the "scorpion woman" and one of the people on Gavin's list. Did he imagine it, or did she do a quick double take when she saw Joel and then ignore him?

Gerry, ever the attentive host, ushered Teresa and her companion to their reserved table.

"So, you know the vet?" Candrew asked.

"Yeah, but not well," Renata answered. "And he obviously hasn't the foggiest idea who I am. He's new at the small animal clinic, and I was there last Friday taking my cat in for her annual shots."

"I'm surprised."

"That I was at the vet's?"

"No, that he didn't remember someone as stunning as you." Joel gave a rare laugh. "He must be really dedicated to animals. Anyway, I took you for a dog person."

"No. Two cats are all I can handle."

Joel rambled on about the relative merits of cats and dogs and by the time he got to fish and parrots Candrew was not even half-listening. He was more interested in watching Teresa now he knew who she was. She seemed very comfortable with the vet, and there was an easy camaraderie with none of the self-consciousness of a first date.

Their waiter returned, stood beside Renata's chair, and described with evident enthusiasm and in elaborate culinary detail the long list of specials. "I'll give you a few minutes to decide." He paused for effect and left with a flourish.

Candrew quickly made his selection, and as Renata and Joel scanned their menus he watched Teresa and her companion. He saw how the vet moved the candle to the edge of the table so he could lay his hand lightly on Teresa's.

A question about the quality of graduate students drew him back into the conversation. "On the whole they're okay," Candrew said, "but never as good as you want. I'd like them to be more independent, develop their own ideas aggressively. Yeah, I know we have to provide the basic ideas and a sense of direction—as my old prof used to say, a Ph.D. program is like giving a student a seed, but it's up to them to plant it, make it grow, and harvest the crop."

Joel gestured with drink in hand, making the ice cubes tinkle as the amber liquid sloshed in the glass, and commented on how important it was to get students out of the classroom and working at the excavations. "Did Gavin have a lot of student help? Did he like to use graduate students on his fossil digs?"

More questions about Gavin, Candrew thought. "Depended on the project," he said. "Sometimes he took several along."

"I guess it's the same in geology as archaeology," Renata said.

"Right. You have to take the students where the rocks are. Not much money for field assistants, though we use grad students when we can."

Discussion of students, faculty, and universities in general occupied them through the meal. Any consideration of the wider world outside academia was neglected. As their waiter picked up the empty plates, Joel pushed back his chair. "If you'll excuse me for a moment, I need a cigarette." He smirked. "I still have bad habits."

Renata and Candrew, left alone, had an opportunity to compare impressions of Joel. They agreed he was rather aggressive and at times unpleasant. Candrew admitted he felt uneasy about him—something didn't quite add up and he couldn't put his finger on it. He sat tapping his teeth with his forefinger. Renata knew him well enough to recognize this behavior, a sure sign he was perplexed. Both wondered why Joel was visiting the university.

"What's Joel been doing since you picked him up?" Candrew asked.

"I never did pick him up. He cancelled the shuttle from Albuquerque and rented a car. Which means, I don't know when he arrived, or when he plans to leave."

Further assessment of Joel was curtailed by his return. The waiter reappeared at the same time with another menu. "Leave room for dessert?"

As Joel settled back into the seat, he pushed a strand of his thinning hair back from his forehead and gave a doleful smile. "If you want your patrons to order desserts, you'd better start serving smaller portions. I'm stuffed."

"How about coffee, sir?"

"Yeah. Sounds good." The reply was unanimous.

Conversation drifted back to the field studies they all did. Joel was trying to convince them that he had the most difficult time. "At least the skeletons you dig up are complete," he said to Renata. "They don't have major bits missing and they're not all jumbled up. And in your case, there's probably even some writing on the tomb to tell you who's buried there, or at least give you a good idea of rank."

"Assuming that the grave robbers didn't get there first, and the forest roots haven't disturbed everything, and you can read the glyphs," Renata countered.

"Well, I'm not so lucky," Joel said. "The Anasazi didn't even have a written language."

Candrew couldn't help needling him. "You haven't deciphered all the petroglyphs yet?"

Joel ignored the jibe. "When you dig up fossils you don't have the problem of repatriating them to the nearest Indian tribe."

"Just to the nearest commercial dealer."

Thirty minutes later as they were leaving the restaurant, Renata asked, "How about a nightcap? Would you like to come back to the house?"

Candrew glanced at his watch. "No. I think I'll have to pass. I've got a few things to take care of early tomorrow morning before I leave.

Joel couldn't quite contain his interest. "Anywhere exciting?"

"No. Just some consulting." He was not sure why, but felt no need to give him any of the details of his impending visit to *McCullum Oil* in Carrizozo.

Chapter 16

Early on Thursday morning Michelle Ortiz swung her car into Candrew's rutted driveway with easy familiarity. An attractive girl, Michelle was one of the teaching assistants in the geology department. She went in through the side door, shouting, "Hi! It's 'Shell."

"Make yourself at home. I'll be right with you." Candrew's voice came from the back bedroom.

Chile's response was more immediate. He loped up to 'Shell, a familiar visitor, and she had to step around him to reach the cupboard where the dog treats were kept.

A few minutes later when Candrew came into the living room carrying a stack of folders and several long cardboard tubes, Chile was stretched out in front of the large stone fireplace distractedly chewing on a biscuit.

"I'm only out of town for one night," Candrew said, "but it'll probably be pretty late before I get back on Friday. Just feed Chile and Pixel as usual, and if you've got time, Chile needs to get out for a run."

"No problem. I'll take him down the arroyo and he'll get

plenty of exercise. He likes to chase the rabbits and there's lots along the banks."

"Thanks. It's really helpful to have someone who'll come at a moment's notice and take care of this wild animal." Smiling, he gently rubbed Chile's back with the toe of his shoe. The dog ignored him and kept chewing conscientiously on the dog biscuit.

"Well, this summer's been really, really dull. Apart from a few days with Mom and Dad in Albuquerque, my only time away from campus was on Dr. Citalli's float trip. That was so sad. Everybody liked him."

"So you saw the accident?" Candrew still couldn't bring himself to say *murder*.

"Yeah. The river bends a bit and there were some really big rocks up on the side. You couldn't see the top part of the rapid from where we all were. When he came into sight, it looked as though he wasn't trying. You know, sort of . . . as if he'd given up. Almost seemed he was falling asleep, and then he, like, disappeared." She was obviously upset by the memory and turned her head away, not able to continue.

Candrew didn't say anything, but was struck by the way she described Gavin's drowning—using nearly the same words as the students on the Ghost Ranch trip. They all agreed, Gavin had made no effort to save himself from drowning. He thought of the drugs that showed up in the medical exam. Obviously, this murder was set up to look like an accident.

After 'Shell got control of herself, Candrew asked if she'd seen Gavin using a cell phone.

Her brow furrowed. "No, but then he didn't like cell phones and never took one with him, even on field trips."

"Yeah, I know. But he borrowed one from that co-ed with the short, spiky hair—Patsy Groll. I wondered whether he'd borrowed anyone else's."

"Not that I know of."

Candrew hoped he might be able to find out what number Gavin called when Patsy checked her monthly cell phone bill. She'd told him her father paid for the phone and the bill went directly to him, but she promised to call and ask him to mail the August statement.

Candrew drove into the geology department to get a few things taken care of before he left for Albuquerque and on the way to his office picked up the previous day's mail. It included a buff-colored, university envelope nestled among the junk and he slit it open with his finger as he headed back along the passage. It disgorged a university format résumé—eight pages summarizing the entire academic career of Dr. Teresa Polanca. In his office, he threw the unsolicited catalogs into the recycle bin and slumped into his padded chair, propping his feet on a half-open desk drawer. He read the blunt, no-nonsense, fill-in-the-blank form and scanned through her academic training. She'd taken a random selection of courses at two New York community colleges before settling down and completing a life sciences degree at Brooklyn College. Ohio State followed and she had completed both her graduate degrees in zoology. The employment record showed that before going to graduate school she'd worked for a year with a vet in upstate New York, and in light of her dinner companion at *Casa del Rio*, he found that interesting. While a graduate student, Teresa worked as a summer seasonal for two years with the Park Service at Capital Reef National Park in southern Utah. He was scanning through the list of publications when the phone intruded. It was Monica Henderson, the chair of the zoology department.

"You must be psychic, I was just reading Teresa Polanca's résumé."

"In that case, I'm not a very good psychic because I didn't expect you to be in. Your secretary told me earlier that you'd gone out of town, and I was going to leave a message." She paused.

"Anyway, I'm glad you're there. I pulled Teresa's file to see if there's anything that might help you. It jogged my memory, and I recalled that when she was here to interview she was all business during the day, very professional, and the only topics were academic. But over dinner, she loosened up a bit—I guess a few glasses of wine will do that—and started talking about growing up in New York. Seems the family lived in a pretty rough neighborhood. Her older brother died after being stabbed in a gang fight, and less than a year later the father disappeared and she hasn't seen him since."

Candrew had grown up in rural Illinois with an older brother and a cohesive family and felt vaguely guilty that her life had been so tragic. "She must be pretty resilient to have pulled herself out from a background like that."

"Right. And as if that wasn't enough, her mother's now disabled and Teresa bears the brunt of the finances. All in all, a pretty tough life." There was a pause. "I asked a few of the faculty what they knew about her. None of them could add anything, but she doesn't seem to have much in the way of outside interests or hobbies. That's about it."

After thanking her for the information, Candrew sat trying to figure out just what sort of woman Teresa was. One item had caught his attention: her disabled mother. She had probably been the only point of stability in Teresa's young life, and if that was right Teresa would feel compassion, or at the very least a sense of duty, and would look after her mother even if only in absentia. Nursing care is expensive and Candrew wondered whether the need for money could have been a motivation that kept her in the project with Gavin. Another speculation to add to the pile.

Cinder cones from extinct volcanoes, dark and symmetrical, littered the landscape to the east, all sharply outlined against the irregular bulk of the Sangre de Cristo Mountains. Above them, scattered, flat-bottomed cumulus clouds with irregular hummocked tops cast patches of shadow, and Candrew and Judy drove in and out of bright sunlight as they headed south to Albuquerque.

Conversation with Judy lapsed and the hum of tires on tarmac had a relaxing effect, calming Candrew after his rush to get ready for the next day's petroleum exploration meeting in Carrizozo and the scheduled visit to Redfern's lab. He was still not sure whether that was a good idea.

Candrew turned east off Interstate I-25 and followed Central Avenue to the University of New Mexico's parking lot, just past the bookstore. After arranging to meet Judy back there at lunchtime, he set out across campus, threading his way between buildings to Northrup Hall, which housed the department of earth and planetary sciences.

He took the elevator to the top floor and the long, deserted passageway led him to the laboratory door marked *Geochronology*. Through its narrow, vertical glass window he could see a roomful of equipment and hesitated briefly before half-opening the door, peering round and enquiring: "Dr. Redfern?"

In his teens, deserted high mountain valleys, clear streams, and bright sunlit skies addicted Candrew to the great outdoors. Understanding what he saw—from the shapes of valleys, to minerals in rocks, and fossils in sediments—provoked his study of the way the natural world worked. He saw it as a series of puzzles that needed solving, and this early interest in geology ultimately drove him to a career as a field geologist. Although he now knew that many of the rocks he collected would end up in labs like this one, he had no urge at all to work with these complex instruments, in spite of the importance of the data they generated. He'd leave that to the Redferns of the world.

"Dr. Redfern?" This time he shouted it much louder and she appeared from behind a high metal rack covered with a complex maze of glass tubing, carrying a thermos of liquid nitrogen with white fumes swirling around her. His immediate impression was of a medieval sorceress, a female Merlin.

She gave a cursory nod. "You must be Candrew Nor. Surprising our paths haven't crossed before."

Ilya Redfern was medium height, stocky, perhaps a little overweight, with short, crinkled graying hair and no makeup. She moved through the familiar passages between banks of equipment with ease, like an animal in its den, and beckoned Candrew in. He began to replace his mental image of Merlin with the Minotaur.

"This is where we date rocks for fun and profit." She said it without smiling, giving the distinct impression that to her the profit was more important than the fun—an attitude opposite to that of most academics. "Come on into the office, it's not so noisy there."

He was ushered past several racks of electronic gear to a small, glass-walled area that served as the lab office. The cramped space was cluttered with computers, scanners and printers, the spaces between them stacked with papers and books. A curly-haired student working at one of the keyboards was the sole occupant, and Redfern introduced him as Don. "He'll be doing the analyses, but don't worry, he's had lots of experience. He's just finishing up his Ph.D."

Don smiled, murmured, "Nice to meet you," and tactfully left.

It was quieter away from the hum of laboratory equipment, and Redfern immediately got down to business, wanting to know about the type of rock Candrew wanted to date, the number of samples he had and, of course, the size of his budget.

He explained that the rocks were sandstones with small amounts of clay minerals, and he wanted to get some rubidium-strontium dates for those clays.

"No problem. The real hassle will be getting clays separated from the sand grains. Can you do that?"

"Sure. How much do you need?"

She told him and added, "A commercial outfit would charge you around five hundred dollars to date a sample. We can work out a much better deal than that."

As she continued talking through the research logistics, Candrew was coolly evaluating her—blunt; lacking in grace; rather unattractive. He tried to imagine her with Gavin, but failed. He couldn't understand how there'd been any romantic involvement. There must have been a side to Gavin he'd never known.

Glancing around the contents of the confined office, Candrew's gaze came to an abrupt halt at the calendar. The picture for August was one of the sites excavated at Mesa Verde National Park and there were two smaller inserts showing Anasazi pots. He was wondering about her interest in archaeology when she interrupted his thoughts.

"Best thing would be for me to give you one of our annual reports; it's a good summary of what we can do." She fumbled around in the desk drawer and came out empty handed. "None left. I've got some in my office." Straightening up, she headed out of the lab with Candrew trailing behind. Her office was halfway down the corridor. Although a typical academic's lair littered with piles of books and papers, she had no trouble finding a copy of the report. While Redfern flipped through the pages to locate a table of sample sizes, Candrew was staring at the top shelf of her bookcase. Between a horizontal pile of books and a framed photograph were two prehistoric pots. The larger one, about fourteen inches across, had a thin crack that ended where a small chip was missing from the rim. It's strongly geometric black and white pattern left no doubt which paleoIndian culture made it: Anasazi. The smaller bowl looked to be in perfect condition and was also Anasazi. Candrew's mind raced back to the FBI agents and their prying questions about whether Gavin was digging up pre-Columbian pots like this. Was he? And were some of these artifacts ending up as presents to his mistress, Ilya Redfern?

She had followed his look and gave an uncharacteristic smile. "They're nice, aren't they? I really like those shapes, especially their angular designs."

Candrew delicately pried further. "I've only seen pots like that in museums and in a few high-end galleries. You're lucky to have them."

"Certainly am. They were a present from my uncle. He's got a ranch up near the Colorado border with a couple of small Anasazi sites on it. Most of what's been excavated ended up here in the archaeology department."

Changing the subject, she turned back to the annual report, explaining the data in the table she'd been looking for. In less than ten minutes they were through with the technical aspects of the planned project and Candrew finally took the opportunity to get round to the topic of Gavin. "One of my colleagues, Gavin Citalli, said he'd collaborated with you on some dating and it was a real help."

"Yes, interesting research he's doing, or I should say *was* doing. Shame about the accident. How old was he?"

"Forty-eight."

"Too young."

It was said without emotion, almost as though she was commenting on an error in the age of a rock. Was he imagining it, or did her voice have a slight edge to it? Either way, it was a very unemotional response to the death of someone she seemed to be having an affair with.

Redfern had no more to add, and clearly this meeting was over. There was nothing else to discuss. Candrew fished around in his disorganized briefcase, retrieved a business card and gave it to her. "Here's my e-mail. Let me know what additional information you'll need."

She glanced at it before stuffing it in the top pocket of her white lab coat. They shook hands and he left.

*   *   *

The stairs were closer than the elevator and Candrew strolled down to the ground floor, wondering just what he'd achieved. Very little, or so it seemed. He'd got an impression of Redfern as cold and insular; that's all. And apart from her interest in Anasazi artifacts, there'd been nothing personal.

The lunchtime rendezvous with Judy was still thirty minutes away and he used the time to visit the meteorite museum on the ground floor of Northrup Hall. Part of the geology department's Institute of Meteoritics, it displayed an extensive collection with spectacular examples of both stony and iron meteorites. It was something he'd always intended to do, but on previous visits to campus he'd never found time.

The museum was deserted. He worked his way methodically around the dozen or so display cases, many of which included interesting information about how the samples had been acquired. Not surprisingly, pride of place went to a dramatic artist's impression of the impact that threw up enormous clouds of debris and dust as a huge meteorite ploughed into the Earth and caused a gigantic tsunami. This, of course, was the event widely believed to have ended the hundred and ninety million year reign of the dinosaurs. Beside the diorama was a small meteorite in a Plexiglas box. The caption explained: *This may have been the type of iron meteorite that led to the extinction of the dinosaurs at the end of the Cretaceous period sixty-six million years ago. It contains iridium, and this element is found in high relative abundance at many locations dating to the very end of the Cretaceous and the start of the Tertiary. In New Mexico, the Cretaceous/Tertiary boundary—called by geologists the 'KT boundary'—has a high iridium content. This has been well documented, for example, in the Raton area.*

Candrew was familiar with all this, but it was the *"KT"* that stood out, and in particular, its juxtaposition with *iridium* really set him wondering. KT. He was used to seeing that on departmental memos which listed all the faculty members alphabetically by their initials. And 'KT' was Kurt Tadheim. Here was the link. Iridium was high at the KT (Cretaceous/Tertiary) boundary where *T. rex* remains are found. So was this it? Was Gavin using *iridium* as a code name for Tadheim? It seemed reasonable, even if it raised the question of what his role was. He wasn't a fossil guy, a paleontologist, but Gavin's student Seligman, had said he'd been doing some seismic studies. Could that have been his contribution?

Judy was already in the coffee bar when he got there. "How was your visit with the femme fatale?"

Although Candrew hadn't told her everything about Redfern, he'd implied that her relationship with Gavin might have been more than purely professional. "She seems an unlikely candidate for a mistress, unless he was into something really kinky," he said.

"Do tell!"

"Not much to tell, really. She's all business. I got no inkling of her social life. We spent almost the whole time going through details of the research project I'm proposing, though I did get the standard tour of the lab. She's obviously very proud of her new isotope ratio mass spectrometer. You can see what turns her on."

"Did she say anything about Gavin?"

"Only in answer to my question, and then just to say how sorry she was to hear he'd died. Pretty cool response. The one thing that made her smile was her Anasazi pots. She seems to have an interest in archaeology." He paused and pondered that. "I always thought Gavin's only interest was fossils. Now, I'm beginning to wonder if he got caught up in the illicit trade in pre-Columbian artifacts. If he'd been involved in illegal digging for old pots, that opens up completely new possibilities and could put a very different spin on his death."

A tall, lanky student, a bit older than most, came to the next table and dropped down half a dozen paperbacks. He smiled at Candrew and said, "Hi."

At first Candrew didn't recognize him, then realized who he was. He introduced the student to Judy. "This is Don. He works with Dr. Redfern."

That produced a wry smile. "Works *with*? Works *for*! Actually, slaves for. I'm just a serf, a peon in her feudal system. And she drives her slaves hard: no time off for good behavior."

"That bad? Couldn't you change your supervisor?" Judy asked.

"Believe me, I've thought about that more than once. The thing is, she's a really great scientist. Got an awesome reputation, and anyway I'll be out of here in a couple of months." He grinned at the thought. "Maybe with all her contacts she'll help me get a faculty position somewhere."

"I wouldn't bet on it. You'll probably end up doing a post-doc first." Judy spoke from experience. "Anyway, good luck."

As Don turned toward his table, Candrew asked, "Is Redfern married?"

"Are you kidding? She doesn't have time for that. Apart from work, I'm not sure what she has time for. And she certainly doesn't confide in me." He pulled out his chair and sat down. "The only non-scientific interest she's ever mentioned is film. Foreign films, of course, none of that Hollywood crap. I'm sure she thinks it's the only fun you can have in the dark." He smirked and turned to peruse his pile of paperbacks.

"Let's go eat," Judy said. I got here early and if I drink one more cup of coffee I'll be pinging off the walls. I'm craving something solid."

Candrew's watch showed one-thirty and his stomach agreed that it was well past lunchtime. He retrieved the car from visitors' parking and they drove over to the Frontier Café. Candrew ordered a Frontier burrito and Judy finally made a decision to have the huevos rancheros. They slumped into a booth near the window and when their orders arrived promptly, ate hungrily and in silence.

Candrew wiped his mouth with a paper napkin. "One thing I don't understand about Redfern, she's listed in the *North American Directory* as just an associate professor. I would have thought that she would have made full professor long ago, with all her funded research and stacks of publications. She's even edited a couple of books."

"Sounds like another case of academic backbiting," Judy replied. "At least she's got tenure, but I'll bet the male faculty aren't about to make her a full prof without raising all sorts of hell. She's probably made enemies among her colleagues in the department; they've got to be jealous of her success."

"That wouldn't surprise me, I'd say it's quite likely. And she's not very sociable. You know, we always like to keep up the myth that science is a logical, cooperative, unemotional process. But anytime people are involved, there's always going to be personality clashes."

"And gender clashes," Judy added.

"Speaking of male faculty members up to no good, I had quite a revelation in the meteorite museum, an epiphany." Candrew laughed. "Under the obligatory artist's impression of a meteorite causing mayhem and wiping out the dinosaurs was a piece of an iridium-rich, iron meteorite and a brief description of high iridium in the rocks laid down at the time of the impact."

"We already knew about that."

"True, but as you're well aware, geologists refer to the Cretaceous-Tertiary boundary as the *KT boundary* and in a flash of inspiration I put KT and iridium together. *Iridium* is the code word Gavin used for Tadheim because his initials are KT."

Judy was impressed. "Wow! And it fits beautifully with *T. rex* being at the top of the Cretaceous, right up at the boundary where the iridium is."

"I hope we're not reading more into this than is really there. After all, he's a geophysicist, not an expert on fossils. What could he possibly be contributing to a dinosaur excavation?" Candrew paused, thinking again of Seligman's comments. "Unless, of course, he'd been pressed into service to run some geophysical view of what's underground."

"Well, in the best tradition of science, it's a good working hypothesis."

Albuquerque's airport, grandly named the *International Sunport*, is just a couple of miles south of the university campus. Candrew headed to the arrival gates, reading the signs with one eye and negotiated the multiple junctions with the other. Judy had taken the opportunity to get a ride down to the campus with him so she could do some research in Zimmerman Library, but now Candrew was going on to Carrizozo and she had a reservation on the shuttle bus back to UNNM. It left from the airport. She retrieved her folders, slammed the door and leant in through the open window to say, "Thanks for the ride. I'll see you in the lab on Monday. Drive safely."

Back on the interstate, Candrew turned south to Carrizozò, leaving his problems with Redfern behind and heading for new ones. He hoped Neville Chamberlin, the British prime minister, was right when he said, "A change of trouble is as good as a vacation."

Chapter 17

On the late August afternoon, white clouds piled up over the western hills as Candrew's world focused on the unwinding ribbon of Interstate 25. It led him south through Socorro and on to San Antonio where he turned east toward Carrizozo. Overhead a lone turkey vulture made an effortless half-turn, riding the air currents in search of an evening meal.

There was little traffic and Candrew thought over his visit to Redfern. He didn't know what to make of her, and couldn't understand how she might have been involved with Gavin, apart from age dating rocks. Anasazi pots, maybe? Was that also a common thread? Last night's dinner with Joel Iskander had also raised this topic—and so had the FBI. He wondered if Redfern knew Joel since he was an anthropologist researching the Anasazi and she was a collector of Anasazi pots. Neither Candrew nor Renata had figured out Joel's real reason for visiting campus, but he certainly seemed interested in Gavin, and already knew quite a lot about him. Joel had strong views on marketing fossils as well as artifacts in his own specialty of ancient Indian cultures. Had he somehow been involved in getting Gavin to excavate prehistoric pots?

The drive to Carrizozo from Albuquerque, at only a little over the speed limit, had taken almost two and a half hours, and it took another hour to check into the motel and eat dinner in a dingy café two blocks up the road. Back in his room, Candrew turned the window air conditioning unit up to maximum and cracked open the window six inches to get some air circulating in a futile attempt to rid the room of its pervasive, stale-smoke odor. Nothing in the room was real; everything was masquerading—the Formica window sills looked like marble; the artificial carpet was supposed to be wool; and the table was synthetic laminate chosen to resemble wood. Doing field work in remote areas across the west, he'd stayed in more than his fair share of cheap, generic motels—and without even checking, he knew the beds would have flimsy sheets that didn't reach the bottom of the mattress, the mirror would be cracked and dotted with brown stains, and there was better than a fifty-fifty chance the tap in the shower dripped continuously.

Candrew read through his working notes and the two reports with transparent covers and prominent *McCullum Oil* logos. An hour passed quickly as he reviewed material for the morning meeting. He needed to have his act together for this one.

The café that had provided Candrew's dreary dinner looked a lot more cheerful in the morning light and, as long as the choice was a breakfast burrito, the food was fine. Coffee was good, too. Four blocks further up the road was the two-story, brick building that served as headquarters for *McCullum Oil*. A couple of pickups were nosed into the struggling bushes and Candrew pulled his Jeep Cherokee in beside them, parking on the packed dirt.

Wrestling with two rolled-up maps in one hand and his briefcase in the other, it was difficult to push the door open and Candrew used his foot.

"Here, let me help you." Although hampered by a coffee cup, the tall, thin, gray-haired man held back the door with his free hand.

Candrew dropped everything on a low table off to the side and turned to shake hands. "Allen! Good to see you again. It's been quite a while."

"Yeah. You're looking great. Life in the Outback agrees with you."

Allen, a geology professor at the State University of New York, refilled his Styrofoam cup and poured coffee for Candrew. Chatting, they walked together to the conference room at the far end of the corridor.

Brody McCullum drove his black Mercedes with the window rolled down and his left arm draped across the side. Steering with one hand, he pulled into the parking lot in a tight, screeching turn. Leaving the window open—nobody in their right mind would steal from a McCullum in this town—he swaggered into the petroleum building, letting the front door slam behind him. Brody strode rapidly down the wood-planked narrow passageway and flung open the conference room door. "You guys figured out why it's a dry hole yet? Seven-thousand foot holes don't come cheap."

"Good morning to you, too." It was Gary Petersen, the exploration manager, who spoke. In the circumstances this was the best way to respond, and McCullum stood momentarily silent. Candrew never knew how to handle situations like this and usually reacted by being excessively polite.

McCullum nodded to Allen and Candrew. "Good to have you guys down here. Hope you can help."

Before Candrew had a chance to say, *I hope so too*, Allen quickly replied, "We're making progress, but . . ."

Brody cut him off and bluntly summed up the situation. "I've got 5000 acres leased. This is the second dry hole. We going to relinquish acreage? Or maybe farm it out?"

The map Brody unrolled across the conference table showed the large and irregular area that *McCullum Oil* had under lease. He weighted down the far end with a chunk of rock core to stop it curling up, and the four of them leaned over, discussing the location of the recent dry hole, comparing it with their previous, mostly successful, wells.

"We need more seismic," Petersen said.

"I can never see anything in all that geophysics—and the damn surveys cost the earth," Brody complained. "How you can make loud noises on the ground and figure out what the rocks look like thousands of feet under the surface, beats me. But then, that's why I pay you all the big bucks." For the first time, he smiled.

The arguments pro and con went on for the rest of the morning with Allen and Candrew explaining the geology, Petersen the seismic and Brody the economics. They finally finished just before one o'clock with a decision to go ahead and drill.

"How about a couple of enchiladas to fortify you for the long journey north?" Allen asked.

"Sounds good." Candrew was ready to be fortified.

"There's a Mexican restaurant out south of town. Nothing fancy, but the food's great."

Allen drove his rented Buick and Candrew followed. The low-slung, rounded body of the pale-blue Buick looked impractical and out of place among the dusty, heavily-used pickups and sport utilities. A mile down the road, Allen pulled off and parked. Candrew maneuvered into a vacant space beside a pickup truck with a cracked windshield and a large black mutt curled up in back. A couple of tractor-trailer rigs were parked off to the side of the single story, wooden building, and with a portale running along the front it looked more appropriate for horses than cars. Inside, a row of chromed bar stools with scuffed red vinyl seats stretched in front of the counter, the sole occupant waving his fork in mid-air to make an important point to the barman about last night's football game.

The two geologists settled into one of the booths and the

gum-chewing, unsmiling waitress, wearing an incongruous pink floral apron over her jeans, dropped two menus on the table. "Coffee?" she asked in a rasping voice.

"I need a beer. Two *Dos Equis*?" It was half a question to Candrew and half an order for the waitress.

She nodded and left without a word. "Remember, I only claimed the food was good; I didn't say anything about the service," Allen said, grinning.

Conversation lapsed while they contemplated the single-sheet menu entombed in plastic. The busboy delivered their beers.

Allen made his decision. "Tell her I'll have the beef enchilada plate. I'll be right back." He levered himself out of the tight space and headed for the door marked *Hombres*.

Candrew sipped his *Dos Equis*, looking around at the dark, scuffed wood-paneled walls, mostly covered with posters advertising Mexican beers. He thought over the discussions from the morning meeting and was comfortable with the decision to drill the next well, but his thoughts were soon interrupted by two truck drivers in the next booth, both talking loudly, oblivious to people around them.

Candrew heard the tall one with the brown, sleeveless tee shirt say, "Remember Randy? Bert told me he keeps his empty Big Mac containers. Then goes up to the gal at the counter and says, 'Hey, I paid for a Big Mac and there's nothing in the box.' That way he gets a free burger."

"That right?"

"Yeah, crafty bastard. Always pulling some stunt."

His friend paused, wiped his mouth with the back of his hand and smirked. "You can't never depend on nothing."

Candrew smiled at the double negative, or was it a triple negative? He was no snob and well knew that if professors and truckers went on strike, long before lack of education became a problem people would miss all the trucked supplies. This made him wonder how Gavin had transported the tons of rock and bones out of the remote *T. rex* site. If it was all going to be delivered to Mishikubo in L.A., how was he going to get it there? This was an aspect of the project he hadn't considered before. Main roads wouldn't be a problem, but Gavin would have needed heavy equipment, and that raised the question of access to the excavation site. Did it imply the location was close to a back road? Another addition to his lengthening mental list of unanswered questions.

Allen came back and slid into the cracked, plastic-covered bench seat on the opposite side of the table. "Well, what did you think of our Mr. Brody McCullum?"

"He's obviously got the money and personality to do whatever he damn well pleases. Or is there a heart of gold buried under that abrasive exterior?"

"More like a heart of black gold! He's making a ton of money in the oil business—enough to pay the exorbitant consulting fees you and I get."

"Yeah, sure." Candrew laughed. "How'd he get started?"

"Petersen told me that Brody's father just quit the ranch near here and started acquiring leases and drilling holes down in Lea County in the twenties. Did pretty well. Brody grew up around the rigs and was aggressive enough to build up the company and eventually take it over. Made piles of money and used some of it to buy back the old family ranch, which is why he keeps the head office here in Carrizozo."

"I noticed he'd lost a finger. How'd he manage that?"

"Now there's an interesting story. The version I heard was that Brody had an older brother who was engaged to the local beauty. Then Brody moved in, romanced her and ended up marrying her. The brother was mad as hell and in a fight one night cut off the wedding ring with Brody's finger still in it."

"Charming family."

"The brother left town. Hasn't been seen since." He took a

serious gulp of his beer. "Changing to another unpleasant subject," Allen said, "how are the faculty taking Citalli's murder?"

"Shock, of course, for those who knew him well. And there's still all the practical problems of reassigning grad students and covering his courses." Candrew paused, wondering how much to tell Allen.

But Allen spoke first. "I hadn't seen him for years. We were students together, in Berkeley, back in the sixties."

"Really? I didn't know that."

"Yes. He was quite a guy."

Candrew was curious about what that meant, especially in the context of California in the sixties. "In what way?"

"Had an eye for the girls. He'd worked with Texaco out in Bakersfield for a couple of years after he got his master's. So he was a bit older and a lot more self-assured than most of us other grad students. Drove a red British sports car—always envied him that! Just before he graduated there was a messy affair with the wife of one of the young assistant professors."

This was an aspect of Gavin that Candrew knew nothing about. "Well, he seems to have calmed down a lot since he joined our faculty." But in light of what he'd recently learned about a possible affair with Redfern, this was interesting news. Just on the off-chance, he asked, "Do you know Ilya Redfern at the University of New Mexico?" He tried to make it sound casual and hoped it didn't seem too much out of context. "I dropped in to see her on my way down here. She'd measured some rock ages for Gavin and agreed to do some for me."

"She's back then?"

"Back?"

"Redfern's been working in our department for the last year. On sabbatical. Wow! Is she intense. Worked like hell. I don't think she took a day off the whole year. At least, she was in the lab every time I went by. Early morning, late at night, made no difference.

She even came to faculty meetings—that's dedication."

"I spent several hours talking to her yesterday and she never once mentioned a sabbatical."

"Typical Redfern. All business. Why waste time on the peripheral stuff?"

Candrew digested this. Gavin had been having an affair for a year with a woman who never left up-state New York? Hard to believe, actually impossible to believe. There must be some other explanation. Could Marge have been wrong? And if she was, what led her to the wrong conclusion?

As Candrew retraced his route up I-25, the clear blue sky had no real clouds, only the long tendrils of airplane contrails, a fleeting record of passing travelers. Not like the ruts made by travelers on the Camino Real, the old Spanish Royal Road, that after two hundred years still scored the plains to the east. The contrails slowly faded in the high, dry air and Candrew figured they were up at least thirty thousand feet. Thirty thousand feet. About the same as the deepest wildcat well ever drilled. He tried to imagine a pipe less than a foot in diameter stretching from the ground to the contrails, but the petroleum engineers had to put that pipe through rock, not air, and sustain the high pressures and temperatures six miles below the surface of western Oklahoma. He remembered reading somewhere that molten sulfur flowed into the bottom of the well. Like putting a hole into Hell.

The deserted highway needed little attention and his thoughts drifted back to Marge and Gavin. Having met Redfern and talked to Allen, it seemed unlikely Gavin had really been having an affair. Clearly Marge had misjudged his behavior. As far as he could tell, her only evidence was Gavin's increasingly frequent absences, and a wife's intuition. Why had she thought the woman involved was Redfern? Candrew recalled the old joke that a successful scientist needs a wife and a mistress. The wife suspects he's with the mistress. The mistress thinks he's with his wife. And he's really in his laboratory working until the early hours of the morning. Could Gavin have just been working out at the dinosaur site? Or digging up Anasazi pots? Was that why he was gone so many weekends?

Candrew liked maps. He had a reverence for them that went beyond their role in his profession, although the reverence was entirely practical. Unlike Penny, who picked the area that mattered and scrunched all the rest back behind, he was pragmatic and carefully refolded maps along their original creases. He knew that they foretold the future. His horoscope in the newspaper (which he would never admit reading) might tell him something vague like, *How you deal with stress could make all the difference in the outcome.* But the map beside him in the car was more precise and told him that in twenty miles he would be at the exit to Highway 285, and that in another thirty-five miles he could take the left turn that leads to Tierra Amarillo and Chama. Twenty miles, fifteen minutes, an exit: knowledge of the future.

He was almost alone on the highway. The sun was low in the west and the bushes were brightly lit on one side and trailed long, dark tails to the east. He started to slow as he neared the exit and a tractor-trailer rig that didn't slow at all passed him, its wake rocking the car as he turned off. Candrew followed the road north and as he crested a ridge five miles further on, there they were, hundreds of them: striped orange barrels. The orange rows illustrated the laws of perspective down through the broad valley and up over the rise, and flicked by in his peripheral vision . . . flick . . . flick . . . flick. The rhythm was hypnotic. His thoughts began to wander. Flick . . . flick . . .

The wheel in his hands suddenly made a bid for independence, turning violently clockwise. He was instantly alert, instinctively trying to haul the wheel back, but it fought him. He clipped one barrel sending it spinning away and then hit the next one full on, shattering it into plastic shards as he ran over it and swerved into the closed lane. He struggled to keep the car straight as he braked hard, finally wrestling it to a stop, crunching on the gravel. His hands were tightly gripping the wheel. He was breathing fast and deep. And sweating. There was silence.

After a minute or two he opened the door and started to get out, but his legs were wobbling. Using the car for support, he walked around it. There was little damage and the culprit was obvious—a punctured front tire with a sharp metal spike sticking out, probably from the road construction. He felt both annoyed and relieved. Annoyed for the obvious reason and relieved that it would be a simple matter to change the wheel. He stood for a moment to take a few deep breaths, letting his adrenaline subside. The low sun was partly obscured by clouds with dark centers and glowing white edges and the eastern hills had a rosy glow contrasting with the dark blue sky. Candrew worried about it getting dark. Knowing he didn't have a flashlight in the car, he hurried to put on the parking brake and kick a few large cobbles up against the tires for insurance. He took the wheel off the jacked up car while there was still light.

As he was lifting the spare out of the trunk, he saw a pickup truck, with no lights, speeding up the deserted highway. At first it was partly obscured by the chamisa along the roadside, but as it sped closer he could see two people in the cab and noted a GMC emblem on the grill. He took a step away from the car towards the road, expecting the truck to stop. In this part of the world people were generally neighborly and pulled over when someone had a problem. But not this time. The truck didn't slow at all; the occupants never acknowledged that they'd even seen him. There was no hand raised in a friendly gesture. Almost before he realized they were not going to stop, they were gone. What made this so remarkable was that he thought he recognized the driver and saw on the truck's back window the bright orange triangle of a university parking sticker. Although he couldn't be absolutely sure in the fading light, he was almost certain the driver was Kurt Tadheim. He didn't recognize the woman and only got a glimpse of a shock of dark hair, but somehow she appeared vaguely familiar. Why didn't they stop? That question acquired added significance in the light of his new knowledge that Tadheim was probably the "KT"—iridium—involved in Gavin's dinosaur project.

It took him another ten minutes to mount the spare wheel and get the tools stashed. Carefully he pulled back into the open lane and headed north. The subsiding adrenaline rush left him tired and he turned on the "golden oldies" of KPEK in Albuquerque to keep himself awake. The Beach Boys obliged — *She'll have fun, fun, fun, . . . 'til her daddy takes the T-bird away . . .*

Chapter 18

Candrew was drained, tired, and glad to be home. He swung the car into the driveway too quickly and slid to an abrupt stop in front of the garage. The motion detector triggered the lights.

Disgruntled and weary, he let himself in through the side door and was greeted by an enthusiastic dog. "Okay, okay. I'm glad to see you, too." He'd been around Chile long enough to know that love was spelled *f-o-o-d*. He filled the empty dog bowl and opened a can of cat food for Pixel, who just happened to be sauntering by.

Without Penny, the aroma of good food never greeted him when he arrived home, and this evening the house had a slight musty odor after being closed up for two days. On the kitchen counter, beside the pile of mail, was a note from 'Shell with the big pepper grinder perched on top to make sure he didn't miss it. In barely legible writing, it said that Patsy Groll had phoned and wanted him to call her back.

Patsy was the student who'd lent Gavin her cell phone on the float trip. Although rather late in the evening, Candrew was eager to know if she'd found the number Gavin had dialed. He phoned her.

"I just got last month's bill from my dad," she told him. "I went through all the calls, I was real thorough, but I didn't see any listed for that day on the river. I guess he, like, never got through."

"Well, I appreciate you trying." As Candrew was thanking her, he wondered about the number. Did Gavin know it so well he had it committed to memory? Or was it written down somewhere? And if so, where? He didn't recall seeing any phone numbers in the notebooks Marge had retrieved from his water-soaked jacket. Who was he calling? Chuck Semley, maybe? Or the agent in Albuquerque the FBI guys had mentioned?

He put the phone down and it immediately rang. It was Anne.

"Sorry to call so late, but you'd better come over to the house in the morning as early as you can." When she explained what had happened, Candrew promised he'd be there first thing.

Candrew arrived at the house a little after eight o'clock and Marge hustled him into Gavin's home office. It was a shambles. Papers and books littered the floor, the contents of overturned desk drawers were strewn everywhere, and the texts from folders in the filing cabinet had been dumped out.

Marge turned to Candrew with tears in her eyes. "Why would anyone do this?"

"Exactly what I thought when Anne phoned and told me someone had broken in. You've called the police?"

"That's the first thing we did," Anne answered. "They said they'd send someone out early this morning, but nobody's come yet. We were told not to move anything. On the other hand, they wanted a list of what had been stolen." She gave a rueful smile and stood shaking her head in disbelief at the chaotic office.

"You any idea what's missing, what was taken?" The intruder seemed to have made a careful search, and Candrew was eager to find out what he was looking for.

"I didn't know what Gavin kept in here, and now it's such a mess." Anne let Marge do the talking and stood beside her saying nothing, her eyes downcast.

"My guess is the thief was looking for something very specific," Candrew said. "How did he get in?"

"Well, the window in the utility room door is smashed. It must have happened while we were out last night," Marge said. "But we were only gone a couple of hours." She glanced at Anne and across the littered floor. "It's scary to think someone's been watching us."

The phone rang in the living room and Marge left to answer it.

On his previous visit, Candrew had been impressed by Gavin's sophisticated computer system and now could see the monitor and printer, but not the processor tower—that was gone. He remembered borrowing some of Gavin's CDs, and realized none of those he'd left behind was on the shelves or in the debris scattered across the floor. Scanning the chaos, he tried to recall everything he'd seen in the office on his last visit. One thing that had surprised him then was the lime-green folder full of X-rays. At the time, he thought it odd Gavin would mix medical records with technical materials. Now he couldn't find the folder anywhere in the desk drawers or the disorganized piles. He stood tapping his teeth. Why was this particular folder something so important that the thief would want to steal it?

Anne broke into his train of thought. "The rest of the house hasn't been disturbed at all. We didn't even realize there'd been a break-in until late last night. That's when I called you." She looked around the devastated office. "Poor Marge, as if she doesn't have enough to cope with."

At that moment, Marge came back and told them, "The call was from the police. They're on their way and'll be here in fifteen minutes."

"I'm supposed to be on campus for yet another committee meeting at nine-thirty," Candrew said. "Sorry, but I've got to leave. I'll call as soon as I get through and see if there's anything I can do to help."

Anne walked out to the car with him.

Candrew, thinking aloud, said, "Whoever broke in knew exactly what they were looking for. The computer hard drive would have been the main target since it probably had all Gavin's files. And they took the CDs in case he'd used them for data storage."

"Wouldn't they need a password to get the information from the PC?"

"Yeah, but there's tons of software out there that can easily get around that problem."

Anne turned to Candrew. "The people Gavin was working with would know all about the dinosaur site. Why would they want his files?" Obviously puzzled, her brow furrowed. "Do you think there's a rival group?"

Candrew cocked his head to one side, frowning. "Possible, I suppose. It could explain the break-in." He hadn't considered this possibility before. "Gavin may have unearthed a second *T. rex.* and if they knew that, they could be trying to figure out where it is. Maybe that's the information being targeted."

They walked in silence for a while, Anne staring down at the gravel path. "I'm worried about Marge. She's not sleeping well."

"I could see that. Can the doctor give her some pills?"

"She's got sedatives, but won't take them. However bad it gets, she wants to be in the real world, not half-drugged. And so she spends most of the night wandering around the house and half the day asleep on the sofa. The map and locker key she gave you turned up in one of her nighttime forays."

"Do you know if she's found any of Gavin's field notebooks?" Candrew was thinking about the number Gavin dialed from Patsy Groll's cell phone. It might have been jotted down in his notes.

176

"I'll ask her."

He opened the car door and slid into the seat, leaving the door ajar and keeping one foot on the ground. "Did Marge say any more about Redfern?"

"No. After that initial revelation, she's said nothing. It's been a closed topic."

"I went to see her," Candrew said.

"You did! Was she suspicious? What's she like?"

"Not suspicious at all. I set up the visit to be purely professional and we just talked about dating—rocks that is."

She laughed. "I remember that from lunch in Chama."

"Redfern is an intense workaholic. And not a very attractive personality. I got the impression there's no way she'd find time for an affair."

"But if you believe Marge, somehow she did."

"It's more complicated than that. While I was down in Carrizozo, an old friend told me Redfern had been working the whole of last year in his department. And that's in upstate New York. She hasn't spent any time at all in Albuquerque. Only got back in July."

"So how could Gavin have been seeing her?"

"Exactly. I wonder what evidence Marge really has. You said she claimed he'd been away at weekends a lot more than usual. Was that all?"

"As far as I recall." Anne looked off into the distance, thinking. "I just can't face bringing up the topic again. You know, it's difficult to ask her outright."

"Yeah. I understand." Candrew smiled at her. "Look, I'm sorry to rush off, but I have to get to that nine-thirty meeting. Call me if anything develops."

Anne promised she would.

Candrew drove to the north side of campus in a philosophical mood. He was thinking about tires. This was not something he did regularly and most days he wouldn't have given them a second thought. But because of last night's flat, he'd detoured around to the Texaco garage on his way to the university and left the tire to be repaired. Like so much in life, tires were one of those things that aren't noticed until they go wrong. We just accept all the services and gadgets that make civilization work—until something like a thunderstorm knocks out the power and underlines just how dependent, and vulnerable, we are. It was exactly the same with long-time friends, and Candrew had never stopped to consider how important they were. Until now. Gavin had been part of his life for more than two decades and in an instant a callous murder had ended it all. He hadn't really given their relationship much thought, always assuming Gavin would be there forever. Friendships look back over shared experiences and forward to expected new ones. He'd taken for granted all their past lunchtime meetings, their animated discussions of sports and politics, their ideas about science, as well as Gavin's sense of humor. With his death, a part of the well-ordered, accepted and expected nature of life was gone.

The mechanic had promised Candrew the tire would be ready by noon and, true to his word, it was waiting when he went to collect it after lunch. Rusty loaded the wheel into the Cherokee and as Candrew started to pull away he lowered the window and leaned out. "Thanks a lot, Rusty. I appreciate you fixing it so quickly."

"No problem." He took off his Dallas Cowboys cap, holding it by the peak, and pushed back his greasy, shoulder-length blond hair. "Man, there was a humongous chunk of real jagged metal right there in the tread. Had to patch the inside. Tough dude. Anyway, she'll be, like, good as new. Get you another thirty thousand."

The short drive took him from the Texaco station onto Main

and back toward campus. As he got closer, driving demanded more vigilance. He wasn't sure of the best way to get to the parking lot behind the zoology building, but fortunately, he had plenty of time before Teresa Polanca's two o'clock lecture and eventually he found the one-way alley that led to the faculty/student lot.

When Candrew drove in, half-expecting it to be full, there were still three empty spaces. The choice was obvious and he didn't hesitate for a moment before pulling in beside the red Jeep with the multicolored roll bar. Jason's Jeep was unmistakable.

Candrew glanced around to be sure nobody was watching and opened the back door of his own car so that it would look as if he was involved with something inside. With this admittedly weak cover, he took his time to amble around the Jeep and look it over. The left part of the rear panel was covered with bumper stickers and a moderate sized dent decorated the Jeep's front fender. Inside, the driver's floor was dirty with dried mud and there were a couple of empty soda cans under the seat. The passenger side had a short length of rope and a crumpled baseball cap. Candrew peered in the back seat where there were only an old newspaper and a folded map on the floor. As he reached for the map, intrigued to find out what area it covered, he was jolted by an aggressive voice.

"You need something?"

Candrew wheeled around, startled. "Well, . . I, . . no." Jason stood with legs apart, facing him in silence—his body language said it all.

Candrew searched for something convincing to say, finally stammering, "I like your Jeep. I was just wondering how much room there is for passengers in the back."

Jason added a look that implied: *You're, like, way too old to be driving a Jeep Wrangler.* There was an awkward silence.

"Good time of year to have the top down. I wish I could do that." Candrew nodded towards his Cherokee.

Still looking suspicious, the pony-tailed teenager glanced at the car with the door open; then back at Candrew. He noticed the faculty parking sticker and frowned. "You a professor?"

"Yes. Candrew Nor in . . . "

"Oh, yeah, one of the guys dad eats lunch with. You teach rocks, right?"

"Close enough."

"And fossils too?"

"No. That's not my field. You interested in fossils?"

"Sort of. All those dead animals from millions of years ago. Kinda cool." He threw his small olive-green backpack onto the passenger seat. "Well, gotta go. See ya."

Leveraging himself in behind the wheel, he fired up the Jeep. Candrew stepped back and shut his car door to make space for him to back out. Jason gave a curt nod and accelerated away.

Candrew turned back to his own car, tapping his teeth, mulling over his brush with Jason. And that's when he saw the dark green GMC pickup at the end of the line. Looking as casual as he could, he sauntered over immediately noticing the faculty parking sticker on the back window. He became convinced this was the truck that passed him on the highway last night with Kurt Tadheim driving. Trying to appear inconspicuous, he didn't want to be caught a second time, he peered into the truck bed: lots of white plaster flakes, exactly what he'd expected. Now he was getting more certain that it was Tadheim who'd hauled at least some of the fossil bones out of storage. But where had he taken them?

Chapter 19

Candrew was five minutes late getting to the lecture room and Dr. Polanca had just been introduced. Hopefully, he'd discover more about her, more that he'd learned from her resume and the fleeting encounter at the Casa del Rio restaurant. Since her name was on Gavin's list he was desperate to find out everything he could.

Quietly making his way into the back row of the auditorium, he watched as she stepped up onto the low stage and asked, "Did you ever stop to think how much biology there is in the sky?" Polanca paused, pleased with the students' puzzled faces. "I don't mean birds and bugs. I mean the night sky. Think about the zodiac, we should probably call it the zoo-diac!—a crab, a scorpion, a fish, some mammals. My birthday is November 5th. Anyone know what that makes my sign?" A confident voice from the back and a more hesitant one from the side both said *Scorpio.* "Right. So maybe it's no accident that I work with scorpions, and maybe it's no accident I work mostly at night."

She flipped on the PowerPoint projector and a student at the back plunged the room into darkness before finding the switch that put the rear lights back on. It only took him three tries. The screen showed a scene from an old sci-fi movie with two huge scorpions, about the size of eighteen-wheelers, attacking an army tank and truck-loads of soldiers.

"Most of what people think they know about scorpions is pure fiction. Here in the southwest the largest is *Hadrurus arizonensis*, better known as the Giant Desert Hairy Scorpion. And it's a mere fourteen centimeters long." She emphasized the word *mere* and smiled. The next slide showed the large, hairy scorpion with yellow-rimmed, black body segments. "One of the commonest scorpions, *Centruroides,* is only six centimeters long." The slide presented an example.

Dr. Polanca paused, giving her audience time to absorb the information, and glanced around the auditorium. Everyone seemed interested in her topic.

"All scorpions are poisonous. The raised stinger, the telson, is like a couple of hypodermic needles that inject venom. Scorpions do this to kill their prey and also for defense. In some species the male stings the female during mating—and it seems to make her more receptive."

This piece of information produced titters from the audience. Candrew looked around and guessed there were maybe fifty to sixty students and perhaps half a dozen faculty and researchers. Medium height and rather stocky, Teresa Polanca was dressed in jeans and a tee-shirt with the university logo on it. She looked well-muscled and fit. Clearly, she was comfortable in front of an audience and gave the impression of someone who liked to be in control.

When he returned his attention to the screen, it was showing a ghostly phosphorescent green scorpion with dark, indistinct surroundings. Dr. Polanca was explaining that one of the biggest problems in studying scorpions is their nocturnal habits.

"During the day they hide under rocks and in crevices.

They're hard to find. But at night they're easy to spot. All you need is an ultraviolet light, a *black light*, and they glow in the dark." She showed several slides of eerily fluorescing scorpions. "Rockhounds have known for years that some minerals fluoresce under a black light. They would go out at night to look for fluorescing minerals and much to their surprise found scorpions." She paused again, letting this new information sink in.

"Even some fossil bones glow under ultraviolet." Another slide came up, although this one was difficult to see and showed only vague, faintly-luminescent outlines. "This is actually part of a dinosaur fossil. Sorry the exposure's not the best, but it's difficult to get everything exactly right out in the field at night." She clicked up the next slide. "Here's a better one. I borrowed this fossil from the geology department and took photos in the lab." She had images contrasting natural light and ultraviolet. They clearly showed that the bones were difficult to distinguish from the surrounding rock under ordinary light, while they stood out in sharp contrast with ultraviolet.

"Could I have the lights, please." She picked up a marker pen. "If we plot the wavelength of the fluorescent light against intensity and show the adsorption bands for different species . . ." She started to draw the graph on the white blackboard. When she turned her back to the audience, Candrew immediately recognized that large mass of curly, dark-brown hair. He knew exactly where he'd seen her before. While she was still writing on the board, he quietly slipped out of the darkened lecture room.

The bright passageway made him blink. Through the large windows he could see a few high clouds moving in from the west. But as he hurried along past the offices and labs, his mind was focused on Teresa Polanca, convinced that she had been the woman in the truck with Kurt Tadheim last night. That unruly mass of dark hair was unmistakable. It would explain why they hadn't stopped to see if he needed help. Obviously, they didn't want him to realize they knew each other, and that they were cooperating in some way. That had to be the explanation. And it might also explain why the green GMC truck was parked in the zoology lot, not geology.

He followed the corridor to the elevator and while he waited recalled Teresa's comments about being a *Scorpio*. That, and her work with scorpions, would have given Gavin a good reason to assign her the codename *Antares*, since it's the brightest star in the constellation *Scorpius*. It all fitted together beautifully. Or was he forcing it together; reading in things that weren't really there; finding patterns where none existed?

Teresa was a zoologist. *How*, Candrew thought, *was she involved with dinosaurs*? But he'd just been given the answer to that question—she had experience with ultraviolet lamps that could play a critical role in locating a dinosaur skeleton. She'd even used dinosaur bones as illustrations in a couple of her slides. But who in geology had lent her the fossil? Gavin? Something about ultraviolet lamps triggered a half-remembered thought—of course! Gavin had a uv lamp in his desk drawer. He could have been using it to explore for fossil bones. That's probably how he found the second *T. rex*. It would also mean that he'd have to be out in the canyons at night. A good reason to be away from home more often, and overnight.

Okay. If all of this implicated Teresa, what was Tadheim's relationship? And that still left Chuck Semley and Jason Devereaux. His brief encounter with Jason in the parking lot seemed normal enough given the circumstances, and Jason had reacted in exactly the way he would have expected. The only point of interest was his remark that fossils were "kinda cool". Candrew regretted not having had just a couple more minutes to check out the map in the back of the Jeep. Pity. So, he'd made little progress in figuring out Jason's role. Then there was Semley. And, of course, enigmatic Mr. Mishikubo, the wealthy fossil collector who was very likely the money behind the operation. But how did he fit in with Gavin's death? Maybe he'd find out on Monday's visit to California. Again, he was irked that he'd not got to the bones in the storage locker before they were taken out and shipped off, presumably to Mishikubo.

He thought back to the Hatch-chile man's description of the person loading "sculpture" from the storage locker: *real tall; great big moustache; not much hair on his head.* That was a good characterization of Kurt Tadheim and Candrew had no doubt he'd rented the storage unit, or at least stored the bones there. Had he hired the Spanish-speakers with the red '007PHD' truck? And was Kurt also the one who'd rented the house where Candrew had too close an encounter with the dank basement? If Kurt was the *"KT"* codenamed *iridium*—and after seeing the display in the meteorite museum he was convinced that he was—then it confirmed his collaboration with Gavin and Teresa on the *T. rex* project. But Kurt was a seismic geophysicist and they don't normally get involved with dinosaurs: at least not until they are dead, buried and turned into oil. It also seemed likely that Teresa had got the chain hoist for the storage locker, though this was a bit tentative and perhaps he'd been influenced by hearing her lecture.

When Candrew drove home, the setting sun was flaming the high peaks with deep orange, but the valley and foothills were already in the creeping indigo shadows of early evening. As he negotiated the deserted road through the scattered cedars and chamisa, he thought about Anne's phone call. She'd called mid-afternoon to tell him the police had made a thorough investigation and asked a lot of questions about Gavin's office. They did find a footprint. With gravel paths and a flagstone patio, that was sheer luck. They also dusted a lot for fingerprints.

Candrew was certain that whoever broke in wanted the CDs and computer files. But the discs he thought might have been used for data storage he'd taken himself, and they were all currently over in the astronomy department being processed by one of the technicians. Obviously, the intruder didn't know that. How long would it take him to figure out what had happened? It would depend on how well he knew Gavin and Marge, Candrew thought. And was it possible the thief might think Candrew had them at home or in his office? Could that make him the next target? The thought produced a strange feeling which crept up his spine and made his neck hairs tingle.

It was dark when Candrew pulled into the shadowed driveway at home. And this time he was pleased when the motion detector flooded the driveway with light. He approached the house cautiously. Inside it was dark and he switched on the kitchen lights. Feeling a little foolish, he worked his way through the living room, master bedroom, bathroom and guest bedroom flicking on the lights and leaving them on. Chile followed him suspiciously. The room he used as an occasional office was left until last and as he made his way down the hallway, a sudden noise made him jump. It was only the phone. Backtracking to the living room, he grabbed the receiver.

"Dr. Nor?"

"Yes, that's me," he said cautiously, not recognizing the deep male voice.

"I regret having to call you in the evening." There was a pause. "I tried to reach you earlier today."

The voice was slow and deliberate and Candrew felt like yelling: *Get on with it. What do you want?*

The voice on the phone continued, "I was informed that you'd been in Dr. Citalli's office at his home. Did you take anything away with you, or move any of the stuff?" Candrew said nothing. "I'm Inspector Montoya with the police department."

Beginning to doubt whether this really was a police officer, Candrew rather hoarsely said, "No."

"As part of our ongoing investigation, we would like to have your fingerprints on record. We need to be able to eliminate them in attempting to identify prints from the intruder."

That explanation eased the tension and Candrew took in a deep breath. "Yes. I can see that."

"Would you come to the police department on Monday morning? It shouldn't take more than fifteen minutes."

"I'll be pleased to do anything to help." He thought for a moment. "But I'll be out of town on Monday. Will Wednesday be okay?"

"No problem."

When he eventually made his way through to the office, it was undisturbed, just the normal disorganized stacks of books and papers. Most had been pushed to the side to make way for piles of tax receipts he'd reluctantly started to sort. Back in the living room he poured himself a generous scotch, glanced through the newspaper and casually watched television before going to bed. He slept fitfully through an uneventful night.

Chapter 20

The highway was deserted. Early morning mist veiled the low bushes and a dark line of trees to the west showed where the river meandered through the fields. Above them dark, fast-moving clouds were piling up.

Not a good day to fly, Candrew thought. *Especially in a small plane.* But no one had told him it was going to be small. He just assumed that a private plane, even if it was owned by a wealthy Californian industrialist, would be a lot smaller than any of the commercial jets.

Candrew got to the airport a few minutes before eight, but he'd not flown out of Santa Fe before and wasn't familiar with the layout. He drove past the main terminal with its squat control tower and pulled to a stop in the parking area outside the general aviation lounge.

Since the trip was just one day, the only thing he had with him was his well-worn briefcase. Candrew hadn't been sure what to wear. At times like this, he missed Penney's sensible advice. She would have known exactly how he should be dressed and without her help he always felt he was muddling through. A big city meeting with an influential company president seemed to call for a suit, but after all, LA was southern California. Anyway, he felt uncomfortable in formal clothes and settled for a compromise: navy blazer, slacks and, reluctantly, a tie.

Chuck Semley was waiting for him in the lounge. He appeared marginally neater than at last week's lunch and slapped his large hand on Candrew's shoulder, nodded to the girl behind the desk, and ushered him out through the glass doors.

"Grumman Gulfstream V," Semley informed him with a broad grin. "Twin Rolls Royce turbofan jet engines that'll push us up to nearly 600 miles an hour. Mishikubo's flying you in style!" The sleek white aircraft, with a single, broad green stripe, had no corporate logo. "Time to ship out." He guided Candrew across the windy expanse of tarmac and waved him up the steps, following him into the plane.

An efficient uniformed blonde woman greeted them and introduced the lean, fortyish pilot. Standing in the cockpit doorway, he gave a mock salute and said, "Nice to have you with us today. Probably be a little turbulence after takeoff, but should have a pleasant flight once we reach altitude. If you need anything, just check with Fran."

The captain rejoined his copilot in the cockpit, and Fran punched the button that retracted the aircraft steps, following her two passengers into the cabin. "Make yourselves comfortable."

Candrew thought that shouldn't be too difficult. The cabin had thick, taupe-colored carpets, a large sofa on one side and generously proportioned arm chairs on the other, all covered in softly tailored, cream leather. Farther back was a working area with dark leather desks and communications equipment. Candrew settled into one of the arm chairs. Coffee and danish were served shortly after takeoff.

Candrew was uneasy. He took out the manuscript he'd been working on, but found it difficult to concentrate on the technical details and his thoughts drifted ahead to the impending conference. Why would Mishikubo send a plane just to fly him to LA for a one-day meeting? With so many ways to communicate, was a meeting in person even necessary? What was so important that they had to talk face to face? Hopefully, he'd soon have answers.

Chuck, slumped in his seat, was uncharacteristically subdued, reading *Sports Illustrated* and saying little. Candrew asked, "So what can I expect from this visit? Why does your Mr. Mishikubo want to see me?"

"'Fraid I can't answer that. You'll just have to wait and see." He went back to reading his sports magazine.

After two hours the plane crossed the San Gabriel Mountains and Candrew could see sunlight sparkling on the distant Pacific. They landed at Van Nuys airport and the Gulfstream maneuvered into the general aviation lot. Semley shepherded Candrew through the security barriers and escorted him over to a large, black Mercedes limousine. The driver nodded a silent greeting. turned and opened the rear door.

"Hope your one-on-one works out real well." Chuck moved to shut the door.

"You're not coming?" Candrew was surprised.

"No. You're on your own for this one."

The driver turned, said, "Welcome to L.A., sir," then the glass partition behind him slid smoothly shut leaving Candrew cocooned in the ample rear seat. As the Mercedes pulled out of the airport, he drifted into sleep.

After hazy recollections of traffic, a parking lot, and being escorted up an elevator, his first clear memory was an offer of coffee by an attractive and efficient young woman. Helped by the strong brew, Candrew was soon fully awake. He found himself in a comfortable lounge tastefully decorated with modern furniture. A large black and white contemporary painting—Franz Kline?—graced the far wall. The only window showed a tree-covered hillside that could have been almost anywhere in the Los Angeles foothills.

Candrew yawned and the tall, fashionably-dressed woman, presumably an administrative assistant, replenished his coffee. "Mr. Mishikubo sends his apologies for inducing a little sleepiness on the drive over, but he strives to keep the location of this facility confidential. He will be here shortly."

Candrew was not kept waiting. His host materialized beside him and introduced himself without shaking hands. Tall and balding, the elegant, gray-suited Mishikubo spoke impeccable English with a delivery that was slow and precise, the unhurried manner accentuated with a slight pause at the end of each sentence. "I'm pleased you were able to come out to the West Coast and hope you had a pleasant flight. I'm sure you will find your visit worth the time. Please come with me." Turning toward a short passage, he indicated an elevator with a sweep of his hand. Inside, he took a small plastic card from his pocket and used it to access an unnumbered floor. They rode down in silence.

When the doors soundlessly parted they stepped out into a cavernous room that must have been at least twenty-five feet high. Candrew was overwhelmed; he stood amazed, staring and open-mouthed. In front of him was the most spectacular array of dinosaur skeletons he'd ever seen, anywhere. All were mounted in life-like positions. Incredible.

"Please, Professor Nor, take your time and savor the finest collection of dinosaur remains ever assembled." He paused and added, " . . by anyone in the world."

A sinuous walkway snaked past the skeletons that were arranged roughly in order of geologic age, but with a keen eye for aesthetics. None was labeled; this was clearly a collection for someone who knew what he was looking at. Many of the dinosaurs were unfamiliar to Candrew, but he recognized a group of *Coelophysis* like those being quarried at Ghost Ranch. The sheer number and variety of specimens was astounding, as was the quality. All he could do was mutter, "This is amazing, fantastic."

Mishikubo, obviously pleased by the visual impact of his fossils, let a flicker of a smile cross his face. "Some of my earliest memories were of so-called *dragon bones.* As a small boy growing up in Tokyo, I would visit my father's study where he kept pieces from his extensive fossil collection. My favorites were always the dinosaurs and I still remember one huge femur that stood in the corner and was a foot taller than I was. I'd try to imagine what that animal would be like, towering above me. Dinosaurs have remained a lifelong obsession."

"There haven't been many dinosaur finds in Japan."

"You are perfectly correct, Professor," Mishikubo replied in his clipped, precise English. "My father shipped many of the bones back from China. As a high-ranking, military official, he served with Japanese forces during the occupation of Shanghai in the early thirties."

This had been a sensitive time in Sino-Japanese relations and Mishikubo chose not to pursue it, though Candrew did wonder when and why Mishikubo had made the move from Tokyo to Los Angeles.

Candrew's first reaction to the collection had been as a scientist, impressed by its scope and quality. Now, as he ambled down the rows, taking in the astonishing range of specimens, he became increasingly angry. *Why should this superb collection be hidden away for the private pleasure of one man? What right did he have to keep all this to himself?* Normally tolerant of the way other people chose to spend their money, he was outraged at the arrogance of the money and power displayed here. For the moment, Candrew wrestled to keep these feelings to himself.

Mishikubo strolled along the path, shepherding him among the mounted dinosaur skeletons. "Much of my life has gone into accumulating this collection. And like my father, I have been fortunate in obtaining some superb examples from China. But I am no longer a young man and my sole remaining intention is to acquire a *Tyrannosaurus rex*." He paused and added, "Whatever it takes." His gaze slowly moved along the rows of skeletons. "It seems fitting to leave one of the last dinosaurs to evolve, and the greatest predator of all time, to the end. Chuck Semley was instructed to explain to you that Professor Citalli had an agreement to excavate a superb recent find in the Four Corners area. One that is almost complete and exceptionally well-preserved."

"Yes, but as I understand it, that's on Indian land and taking vertebrate fossils is a federal offense."

"Quite. I am well aware of the problems and the need for caution. Which brings me to your role in this matter."

"And if I decide not to get involved?" Candrew was struggling to appear calm, to conceal his anger. He had no intention of becoming an accomplice.

Mishikubo offered the merest hint of a smile. "Professor Nor," he paused for emphasis, "you are already involved."

"I may choose to opt out."

"You may, although I think that would be a most unwise decision. One of your colleagues has already come to an untimely end."

Shocked by the implication, Candrew opened his mouth to speak. "You . . ."

Before he had time to frame the question, Mishikubo cut him off. "I did not mean to imply that I had any role whatsoever in the . . ." he searched for the appropriate words ". . unfortunate accident."

Accident? Murder, Candrew thought. Someone had drugged Gavin and he'd drowned. Of course, if Mishikubo had been involved he was going to deny any role. Stunned and taken off guard, Candrew didn't know what to say. He felt apprehensive, even a little scared.

"I would very much like to know more about it, just what happened on the river. His death came at a particularly critical time." Mishikubo did not elaborate. "Coincidence is the explanation of last resort."

Mishikubo continued the leisurely tour, leading Candrew through the steadily evolving sequence of fossils. Finally, near the end, he stopped in front of a large skeleton with huge teeth, clearly a ferocious predator. Like the others, it was unlabeled. "This is *Herrerosaurus*, a *T. rex* precursor."

Controlling his anger, Candrew said in what he hoped was an even voice, "Why do you keep the collection all to yourself?"

"I see no difference between collecting exceptional fossils and collecting outstanding, and unique, works of art. And it's been quite acceptable for the wealthy to do that over the years."

Slowly, in silence, they continued walking among the fossils. Candrew paused and tapped on one of the mounted skeletons with the nail of his forefinger. It had a reassuringly solid feel. Mishikubo watched the action with mild amusement. "That bone, like most of the others, is real. Except where they are needed for missing pieces, I do not believe in using casts, mere fakes. Would you go to see a reproduction of the Mona Lisa, even if superbly done?" The question went unanswered.

The quality of preparation impressed Candrew. "You must have a skilled team of experienced preparators to mount a display like this."

"It's adequate. More than adequate." He paused. "Perhaps you would be interested to see my facilities?"

Candrew was taken down a short passage and through a half-glass door into an expansive workshop area. Two white-coated women were occupied chipping away at an irregular block of stone, while at the far end a lone figure hunched over a stainless steel table. Stocky and dark-haired, the man immediately stood and hurried towards them. As he made his way past the benches, boxes and equipment, Candrew glanced around the laboratory. Several large pieces of rock matrix, with partially exposed fossil bones, were laid out; hammers, chisels, and scrapers scattered around them. Other benches had more delicate instruments and he noted dental drills and brushes, as well as air jet abraders and tools he didn't recognize. Plaster of Paris casts were stacked along the far wall, most identified by cryptic numbers inked on the white plaster.

"This is Chen, our senior preparator," Mishikubo said as the stocky man approached them. Candrew shook his hand. "He's responsible for extracting the fossil bones and getting them ready for mounting. After twenty years experience, he is very good at it."

Chen smiled at the compliment and asked Candrew if he would like to see how they worked. Candrew's knowledge of the way dinosaur bones were prepared for display was sketchy and he willingly accepted the offer.

"Bones arrive from the excavation site encased in burlap with a protective plaster of Paris jacket. Fragile bones may need a coat of lacquer to hold them together," Chen explained as he led them into a glass-walled, side room. "We use picks and dental drills to remove the enclosing rock, often one grain at a time, very time-consuming."

Chen led Candrew into an alcove with three large computer monitors. "Commonly, fossil remains are incomplete. Then we are forced to make replicas of missing parts." Sitting at one of the keyboards, he typed a few commands that produced an image of a single bone, and additional typed instructions shaded the bone so it appeared three-dimensional.

"Sometimes it can be helpful to use a hologram," Chen said moving to an adjacent area with a large clear plastic box. Inside, a green-tinted image of the bone hovered in space. "You can view it from any angle." The bone eerily floated around to a new orientation. "This is especially useful prior to making a replacement with the 3-D printer."

Mishikubo had remained silent, but now turned to Candrew. "As you can see, Professor, this is a world-class facility. However, we are limited, of course, by the range of dinosaur remains that have been discovered. I am particularly concerned about getting the most realistic skin texture and color on my reconstructions, but well-preserved skin impressions are quite rare." He paused and looked around the workshop. "Professor Citalli reported finding some superb fragments of *T. rex* skin at the site he was excavating for me. Even some evidence for feathers. Color, unfortunately, seems to be beyond the capabilities of paleontologists—at least at present." That flicker of a smile again crossed his face.

Could he have a research team working on a project with dinosaur pigments? Candrew wondered. That would be exciting, to know whether they were all dull green or really sported the bright reds, yellows, and tans used in many of the newer reconstructions. Mishikubo interrupted Candrew's thoughts. "My computer tomography facilities let us image the interiors of dinosaurs." He gave Chen a code number and told him to get the file. A few minutes later Chen handed him a lime-green folder. Mishikubo carefully removed the X-ray photos and gave Candrew a set of computer-reconstructed, three-dimensional images. "We're still in the process of interpreting these. They seem to show the heart and, off to the side, the stomach. You can still see what appear to be remains of this dinosaur's last supper."

Impressive. But the lime-green folder, more than its contents, shocked Candrew. It was identical to the one stolen from Gavin's office. Could Mishikubo have arranged for that theft? Unlikely, since he certainly had his own copies of the originals. Maybe he wanted to prevent them getting into the wrong hands. But if Gavin had duplicates, they were already too late. This could be more evidence for a rival group.

Candrew began reconsidering his own role. He turned to

Mishikubo. "What exactly do you want me to do?"

"Clearly, you are aware of the excavation begun by Professor Citalli. I would like you to organize completion of that project. I believe Chuck Semley has already raised this possibility with you."

"I have no experience as a paleontologist. I've never worked with dinosaurs."

"I am well aware of your limitations. What I need is someone with extensive field experience who can supervise the retrieval of the remaining fossil bones. My staff has been very impressed with the detail and care shown in your published papers. Your peers around the country speak highly of you. I want you to see that the fossil material is adequately documented, properly protected for transportation, and safely removed. Identification, cleaning, or assembly is not necessary. You have seen the excellent capabilities I have in that area."

"There is still the matter of the site being on Indian land."

"Professor Nor, I can assure you that I am cooperating with the relevant federal officials to resolve that inconvenience." He was quick to change the subject. "Our first step should be for you to visit the site, familiarize yourself with the setting and evaluate its present status. Chuck Semley is available to help with logistics. He works with my full authority. I would, of course, be prepared to cover all your expenses and provide a suitable consulting fee."

He mentioned a daily rate four times what Candrew normally earned consulting for McCullum Oil, and he guessed that Mishikubo was more accustomed to dealing with corporate lawyers than geologists. But the thought was quickly followed by the realization that his host was a practical businessman who understood value for money. What did he expect for his money? And could Candrew, in all good conscience, help someone whose aim was to put some of the best preserved dinosaur bones in the world in a private collection no one would ever see—to dig them up on the Colorado Plateau and bury them again in Los Angeles?

Candrew heard himself saying, "I'll certainly consider your offer." He justified the response with the conviction that he must take every chance to find out how the operation was run, and to learn what he could about Gavin's role and the circumstances of his murder. And, of course, he really shouldn't pass up an opportunity to see the *T. rex* site, especially at someone else's expense.

The view across the city through the smoky glass windows was dramatic. Candrew was sure the elevator had brought them down into a basement, and anyway he didn't remember such an amazing vista from the office upstairs. He also noticed an occasional odd parallax as he walked past some of the dinosaurs.

Mishikubo had been carefully watching his response to the display. "You're most observant, Professor Nor. Your suspicions are indeed correct. The walls are not windows; they are telemetry from an array of remote cameras. It's one of the advantages of owning the world's premier imaging laboratory."

"I'm impressed."

"Many views are possible. I like this one." He didn't volunteer to show any of the other pseudo-landscapes.

The main display room was L-shaped and they turned the corner to the shorter segment. Here the dinosaur reconstructions had been fleshed out with muscle and skin. Back projection of trees together with holographic images of other trees gave a startlingly realistic impression of dinosaurs grazing in a forest. Candrew was awed by the scope of the collection and the level of technical skill that had gone into its presentation.

Mishikubo escorted him back up to the entrance lounge, and they sat together drinking tea. "One more thing, Professor Nor. My secretary told me that Dr. Citalli called several times in the couple of days before his accident. At first he insisted on waiting until he could talk to me personally. Later, he reluctantly left a message. He stressed that it was extremely important. Do you know what he wanted to tell me?"

Candrew took another sip of tea. "I have no idea."

"Unfortunately, he was calling from a remote river area and reception was poor. My secretary could not understand the message, so he carefully spelled out the key item. It was *s-e-c-r-e-x-e-n-e*. Does that mean anything to you?"

"No. I've never heard that word before. *Secrexene*. It sounds like some chemical, or a type of plastic."

"Could the first part have been 'secret'?" Mishikubo asked. "But then 'xene' doesn't mean anything to me."

Candrew remembered nothing of his return ride to the airport until the car door was being opened by Chuck. Grinning, he asked, "Well, did his beasties knock your socks off?"

"Impressive." Candrew slurred the word a bit and was still groggy as Semley helped him up the steps into the Gulfstream. The coffee served by Fran was welcome, and the sandwiches that came later seemed to help. She also provided two little yellow pills for him to take.

On the flight back to Santa Fe, Candrew was in no mood to do anything productive, certainly not work on his manuscript. He was furious at Mishikubo's attitude, accumulating whatever he wanted, anything his money could purchase. He thought about the future. Mishikubo was not a young man. What would ultimately happen to that incredible dinosaur collection? Many major, fine-art museums had started with bequeathed collections, and Candrew thought of the Frick, the Huntington, and the Gardner. And also how Mellon's collection formed the basis for the National Gallery of Art. He would have felt much better if he'd known that Mishikubo's fossil collection was destined for a public museum.

"You ready to go see a dino in the raw?" Chuck eased himself into the seat across from Candrew. "We need to take a look-see. And the sooner the better. Here's the deal." He outlined the schedule for a trip into the canyons and gave precise instructions on how to get to the site and where to meet him. Candrew jotted the details in his notebook. "Day after tomorrow will work just fine." Reluctantly Candrew agreed, thinking it would be good to get it over with before semester began.

As they lost altitude on the approach to Santa Fe, Candrew watched the plane's shadow moving over the ground. Eventually the shadow and the Gulfstream merged as it touched down in a remarkably smooth landing. Mishikubo chose his pilots well, the best that money could buy.

Candrew left the airport in something of a daze and joined the stream of traffic jockeying for position along rush-hour Cerrillos Road. A late-afternoon thunderstorm had drenched the area an hour earlier, leaving the ground mottled where it was still drying in patches. The clear air was cool and refreshing.

Heading north, he was well past Pojoaque before he felt fully recovered and wide awake. At Española he was feeling hungry, but he drove the extra fifteen miles to Abiquiu and pulled in beside a huge pickup truck in Bode's gravel parking area.

Sitting in the back of Bode's General Store, wolfing down a bowl of green chile stew, he thought over the day's events. It seemed a lot more than twelve hours since he'd driven through Abiquiu that morning. He'd acquired a whole new perspective on Gavin's role in the *Tyrannosaur* dig. It seemed unlikely Mishikubo was involved in Gavin's murder, since if he was, why would he have him killed when he played such a key role in excavating the *T. rex*? And at such a "critical time", whatever that implied. Why did Mishikubo show him the collection? Vanity? Hardly, or he would have it in a major museum with his name all over it. Perhaps to make the point that he was a serious—dead serious—collector with enormous resources. A collector who was used to getting his own way. Candrew anticipated his visit to the dinosaur site with mixed feelings.

Chapter 21

When Candrew eased his Jeep Cherokee to a stop outside Judy's rented duplex, the eastern sky was already a light, luminous blue, even though the sun wouldn't rise for another half hour. She opened the door at once and came struggling out with a large navy-blue backpack and a thermos of coffee. "Be right with you." She turned, picked up her camera, and got into the car, yawning and rubbing her eyes.

He greeted her cheerfully:

"Awake! for morning in the bowl of night
Has flung the stone that puts the stars to flight!"

"You're very erudite this early in the morning."

"Ah, the chore of the academic." Candrew was always in a good mood when he set out to do field work, even if today the euphoria was tempered with apprehension. This time he didn't know just what he was getting into.

Heading west on State Highway 64, there was little traffic, and by 6:30 a.m. they'd cleared Aztec. Their route took them from Rio Arriba into San Juan County, but as they crossed the imaginary line on the map, the scenery didn't change much.

Candrew fished around in the car door pocket, producing a geological map that he handed to Judy. It took her a couple of minutes to figure out where they were since geologists give mere man-made structures, like roads, minor billing. The rocks, on the other hand, were brightly colored in oranges, muted blues and greens—one color for each age unit. The sequence of near north-south bands showed they were driving across rocks getting steadily younger as they headed west. That would change later and the rocks would get older again, a pattern typical for a sedimentary basin. Judy glanced up from the map. "Classic. It's simple enough you could give it to a freshman class."

"They certainly need all the help they can get. I'm always surprised how many students have real trouble imagining things in three dimensions."

They drove in silence for the next ten minutes as Judy sipped her coffee and scrutinized the map. "So, the site we're headed for is in the Cretaceous?"

"Right. We'll be at the very top part, the youngest section, just 65 million years old. Those are the rocks that have the last dinosaur fossils."

"Just before they all went extinct," Judy added.

After several hours driving, Candrew followed a minor gravel road that Chuck Semley had marked on his hand-drawn map. Distances through the monotonous scrub were deceptive, and although Candrew was watching the odometer and counting the miles from the last intersection he didn't see the dirt track until the last minute and overshot, braking hard. A U-turn brought them back to the junction. He pulled off onto the dirt and turned to Judy. "Here's our route to dinosaur heaven."

"That's it?"

The road was little more than two deeply-grooved, parallel tracks curving away into the distance, disappearing around a clump of stunted piñons. Candrew drove slowly, carefully negotiating the pock-marked dry wash, trying to avoid the deepest holes. Everything loose in the Jeep was bouncing around as they lurched through the irregular ruts, and even with seatbelts cinched tight, they were bucking as well. After three and a half miles that seemed like ten, they found the arroyo that cut in from the side, right between the bare rocky outcrops. A pair of large, dark junipers grew on one side, just the way Semley described it. Candrew noted there weren't any tire tracks or footprints in the dirt. No-one had been through here recently.

Pulling off to the side on a flat area among the drab rabbit brush, he set the hand brake, jumped out, and opened the back of the dusty Cherokee. A much used and abused wide-brimmed field hat rested on a pile of rope and Candrew grabbed it, jamming it firmly on his head. And he picked up his well-worn geologist's hammer. Judy got her backpack.

They left two of the full, plastic water containers in the car and took a gallon each. In this hot dry atmosphere, that much was mandatory. Shouldering their backpacks, heavy with the water, they set off across the slickrock towards the canyon entrance.

With the sun up, the sky was the intense blue that comes with high altitude and low humidity. And the intense sunlight burnt out the colors, leaving the sun-bleached, water-smoothed cobbles only slightly off-white, the color of desiccated bones.

They followed the dusty arroyo. Cut by flash floods from the infrequent but torrential rains of summer thunderstorms, it had a flat bottom and chest high sides exposing an irregular mix of sand, pebbles and larger boulders. Occasional old, tangled root systems showed in the banks, but on the floor of the channel only a few small bushes had managed a foothold since the last downpour had swept the arroyo clean. A large black beetle was slowly trying to climb the sandy bank, but for every two lengths forward it slipped back one. *A metaphor for life*, Candrew thought, but Judy, younger and less cynical, probably only saw that God had an inordinate fondness for beetles.

The arroyo curved to the left, leading across a stony area that Chuck Semley had labelled "Dead Mule Wash" on his sketch map. It led them into a high-walled canyon where fractured and precariously-balanced rocks threatened imminent collapse. It was very still and getting hotter.

If Candrew hadn't pointed them out, she would never have seen them. Thirty feet above the arroyo floor, along a horizontal break in the almost-vertical sandstone cliff face, were small stone buildings. They looked as if they were part of the rock. Only the angular doorways and a few window openings showed they were man-made.

"Who built houses up there?" Judy asked.

"Anasazi. They lived all through the Four Corners area."

She stopped, staring up at the dwellings, seeing more of them the longer she looked.

"They made the spectacular structures at Mesa Verde and Chaco Canyon, then disappeared," Candrew said. "Some probably ended up in the pueblos along the Rio Grande or on the Hopi mesas, though nobody knows for sure."

"Why would they have left?"

Candrew was no expert, but he'd read quite a bit about these early inhabitants. "Drought, war, internal political friction, cannibalism, social implosion—take your pick. Lots of theories, not much confirmation." He was sure Joel Iskander would have a novel explanation. And with his cynicism, he'd probably invoke cannibalism.

"Were these the same people as the *ancestral puebloans*?" Judy asked.

"Yeah. That's the politically correct name. *Anasazi* is a Navajo word. It's usually translated as *enemy ancestor*, which isn't very flattering for the Indians in the pueblos."

Judy suddenly pointed. "Look at that, rows of handprints."

Pecked into the cliff's blackened surface were dozens of petroglyphs, images made by chipping through the veneer of dark desert varnish to expose the lighter rock underneath. Judy had seen few petroglyphs and was fascinated by the stylized figures on the rock-art panels. Working her way along the base of the cliff, she peered up at the strange patterns.

A few hundred yards farther into the canyon they got a chance for a closer look at of one of the ruins. A rubble slope provided access to a broad stone ridge that ran along under an overhanging part of the rock face and ended at the remains of three stone and adobe buildings. Judy, full of enthusiasm, quickly slipped out of her backpack, and clambered up. One ruined building still held remnants of a beamed roof and a window opening, but the others were just remains of collapsed walls a couple of feet high. Even where the overhang was highest, she had barely enough room to stand and found the inside of the recess cool and silent with the subdued lighting of a church. She'd never been in a space like this before and her quizzical expression showed that she didn't know what to expect, but the last thing would have been corn on the cob. Judy bent down and picked a brittle corn cob off the dusty floor just as Candrew stepped in over the wall.

"Look at this; it's tiny. Only a couple of inches long."

"Yeah, before selective breeding. And it's had eight hundred years to dry out," Candrew said.

"I suppose that's right. How come it survived this long?"

"Don't forget you're under an overhang and protected from the weather. This place is desolate and remote, not high on any tourist's route, so no one's been here taking souvenirs—except possibly locals looking for artifacts.

And the ruin at the end of the group showed signs of recent activity.

"Talking of pottery hunters, see these holes?" Candrew asked. He pushed the dirt in one pile aside with the toe of his boot and a couple of bones lay exposed. Beside them a large shard looked as though it was part of a pot rim.

Judy stepped over the low wall and joined him, looking at the half-dozen pits with piles of earth and rubble beside them. "You think Gavin could have been here?" she asked.

Although he'd not said anything, Candrew had been wondering about that. In a protected ruin like this nothing changes very fast and it would be difficult to know how long ago the sandy floor had been dug up. It could have been years ago—or last week. Candrew thought back to the FBI agents and their questions about looted pots. Gavin must have followed this route through the arroyo on his way to the dinosaur site. "I suppose he could easily have spent half a day digging; it would have been simple. And with prehistoric pots selling for thousands of dollars, even tens of thousands, it could have been very tempting."

"And pots don't weigh much," Judy said.

"No, although they're bulky."

However, Candrew couldn't believe that Gavin would plunder Anasazi pots. It was out of character. He had fond memories of his friend and didn't need a revisionist view. But he realized the inconsistency of this argument, and smiled to himself. After all, there was increasing evidence that Gavin was illegally removing—stealing—a large dinosaur fossil from Indian land. Why not some Anasazi pots as well?

Judy picked up a small piece of a broken ceramic and looked out across the arid landscape, all ochres and browns. The parched beauty was a world away from the wet green lawns and turquoise ocean of southern Florida where she grew up. Down on the floor of the arroyo a small dust devil whirled across the stark land blowing sand over the scattered sage.

Candrew was considering whether the spirals and other abstract shapes in the petroglyphs were Anasazi attempts to describe their world view as they were struggling to make sense of nature, to know about the moving stars and static mountains, the violent thunderstorms and bright, silent rainbows. He couldn't help wondering what an Anasazi shaman would think of our myths, like the *Big Bang* or replicating DNA.

Candrew and Judy clambered back down the steep slope to the arroyo floor, hot and panting, sliding on loose rocks and grabbing at the stunted bushes for support. They stopped in the shadows at the foot of the cliff to take a rest and drink. A pair of suspicious crows cruised overhead making rasping calls that sounded like unoiled machinery.

"Still no sign of Chuck Semley. Maybe he's up ahead, waiting for us at the site," Candrew said. He estimated there was about a mile left to go and they shouldered their packs and followed the arroyo another hundred yards before seeing the route angling off northwards.

Judy was leading up the gently sloping trail when she stopped abruptly and pointed. "Look!" Candrew wasn't sure what to expect, but her urgent tone made him uneasy and he stopped to peer in the direction she pointed. "Over there, see him?"

"No."

"On the rock, about fifteen feet away."

He'd been holding his breath and now let it out and laughed with relief. Standing on the rock was a nine-inch long, collared lizard watching them warily. "A not so-*dinosaur*," he quipped, a joking reference to the Latin name for the not-so *terrible lizard*.

The red and brown lizard did an impression of a push-up and was gone, the movement so quick Candrew couldn't follow it.

Another hundred yards and they made the final turn to the west, past the small rock slide they'd been told to expect. They had arrived. With his wide-brimmed hat tipped down against the sun's glare, Candrew picked his way through the sand and scattered boulders. The first impression was of a canyon just like the one they'd been hiking through for the last hour: a few hardy bushes, ominous piles of broken rocks at the base of almost-vertical sandstone cliffs, and not much else.

Judy took a long draft of water while Candrew, his eyes squinting in the bright light, searched for signs of the excavation. There was nothing obvious. He trudged from side to side in the loose gravel and then, about twenty yards off to his left, realized that half a dozen rocks, all roughly the same size, were neatly lined up. As he got closer, he could see they were holding down one edge of a tan-colored tarpaulin, almost the same shade as the sandy ground. He rolled off several rocks and pulled back the corner. Under it, in a shallow depression, were pry-bars, rock hammers, brushes and a pile of other tools. His yell brought Judy over and together they hauled more of the tarp away exposing other tools and a couple of plastic containers, but no sign of any fossil bones.

Candrew pushed one of the long-handled shovels with the toe of his boot. "Still using the same old tools they had back in the eighteen hundreds. Looks like the techniques haven't changed," he said. "Even with all Mishikubo's resources the process is the same."

"Well not quite." Judy had pulled the tarp all the way back and uncovered a gas-powered diamond-bladed rock saw. "At least we're in the right place," she said.

"Or close to it—even if we haven't found an actual *T. rex* skeleton."

They searched outwards from the tarp, discovering other evidence of recent activity. Although not obvious at first, because the overhead sun cast little shadow, there were lots of tracks and tire marks in the packed sand and gravel.

Candrew knelt down to get a better view from an oblique angle. "They haven't been washed out by the recent thunderstorms. Someone's been working here in the last few weeks, certainly after Gavin left."

"Good point. You don't suppose they've removed the whole skeleton, do you?"

"Well, that's got to be a possibility. Although it would have left a big hole in the ground." He looked around. "Where the hell is Semley? He's supposed to be our guide, tell us where things are."

They widened the hunt to improve their chances of finding the actual dinosaur excavation, or, at the very worst, where the fossil had been dug out. Candrew searched the area to the south and Judy worked her way over toward the cliffs and it was there she made the next discovery. "Here's another tarp. Whatever it's covering is huge." She struggled to dislodge some of the rocks as Candrew hurried over to help, and together they dragged off the cover. Shocked, they stood in surprised silence looking at the row of huge teeth—all were worn, one was badly chipped and a central one missing.

"Wow! Not what I expected."

More tugging exposed the rest of the metal bucket which was bright yellow, in contrast to the abraded steel teeth that had lost most of their paint. The Bobcat was about fifteen feet long, with a backhoe on one end and a front-end loader at the other.

Candrew hadn't given much thought to the practical aspects of digging out fossil remains. "I guess a block of rock with bones and matrix could easily weigh a couple of tons. You're not going to move that with a wheelbarrow."

"True," Judy said.

Together they searched the BobCat and found only an empty plastic water bottle, a couple of cigarette butts and a faded John Deere cap. They continued hunting around the area as the sun moved imperceptibly west, leveraging the dark shadows across the arroyo floor.

Twenty minutes later, Judy retrieved her pack and dragged it into the shade. "You ready for lunch? We need a break."

"Not nearly as much as we need a *lucky* break. Where the hell are the *T. rex* bones? No dino, no Semley, just some equipment. One out of three isn't going to make it."

They sat in the shade under the cliffs on the west side of the canyon, eating lunch in silence. Judy had a sandwich, but Candrew's lack of planning meant that before he'd left home he'd just grabbed a plastic container with some leftover lasagna.

"That big Cat gives some idea of the scale of this operation," Judy said. "Presumably Mishikubo is footing the bill,"

"Yeah. And that just leaves us to figure out how a rich Japanese guy in Los Angeles fits in with a scorpion woman, a student in communications, and a seismic expert—as well as a murderer."

"Not to mention the absent Mr. Semley."

Candrew had no answers. "However, we've been missing one obvious thing."

"What's that?" Judy asked.

"There's no way you'd get a piece of equipment like that Bobcat along the trail we followed. And there were other tracks around here as well. So, there's got to be another, easier way in. That's something we'll have to check out."

"Would it show on aerial photos."

"Possibly."

Judy ate the last of a raisin granola bar, stuffed the wrapper into her pack and took another long swig from the water jar. "It's difficult to imagine this as a wet, lush green coastal plain with *T. rex* chasing hapless herbivores through the trees."

"Maybe they were really scavengers, just lurking around waiting for an easy meal." Candrew took off his hat and raked his hair back with his fingers.

"Everyone wants to make *rex* the king of the predators. I would have thought paleontologists would be more sympathetic to the scavengers 'cause that's the way they operate—just grabbing whatever fossil remains they're lucky enough to stumble on. Letting the eroding water and wind do all the work for them." Judy glanced at their present surroundings which showed no trace of water. "But I can't help wondering how a huge carcass like a *T.*

rex gets preserved in the first place. You'd have to do something real unusual to protect the dead body right away, or the predators would spread the bones all over the landscape."

"You're right. Most people in the business seem to think that something like a river setting is the best bet. Then when the dino drowns, it gets covered with sediment so fast it has a good chance of being preserved."

Attracted by its raucous call, Candrew glanced up and idly watched the raven as it flew through the blue shadow of the bluff to reemerge into the sunlight. When he looked back, Judy had taken out a small matt-black box not much bigger than a cigarette carton and was holding it out in front of her. "My new toy—I treated myself to a GPS. If I can get enough satellites lined up from down here in the canyon, it'll figure out where we are to better than five feet. I took my first reading where we left the car and now it shows the direction we've come and the total distance we've hiked. And, of course, it gives the distance as the crow flies." She handed it to Candrew and the dimly lit green screen showed: *1.86 miles: WNW.*

"So we know where we are. Now all we have to do is find where the bones are."

"Which is where Semley could help a lot."

Candrew pulled out his cell phone and tried calling him, but out here in the canyons there was no reception. He took another long drink. "I'm surprised he never showed up. He gave us such precise directions for finding this site, almost as if he expected us to get here on our own."

Judy looked up at the surrounding cliffs. "I wonder if he's hiding, watching us?"

Chapter 22

Chuck Semley sat concealed in the shadows between two junipers high on the cliff face, his back to the smooth, warm rock. Adjacent parts of the north side of the canyon were near-vertical where large slabs of thick, yellow-ochre sandstone had sheared off. Narrow, irregular ledges, almost horizontal and strewn with boulders, threaded among the precariously-poised blocks of rock. Here, a few dark, gray-green junipers had established a foothold and grew in locally thick clusters among the rocks, their roots searching the narrow crevices for the patchy soil.

Chuck's knees were drawn up tight supporting his elbows and steadying the high-powered binoculars trained on the valley below. He wore faded jeans, a multi-pocketed sleeveless jacket with mottled camouflage, and sunglasses. A wide-brimmed hat lay on the ground nearby. Beside him, propped against a boulder, his well-worn backpack contained a half-full water bottle, four granola bars, a sophisticated GPS, maps, compass—and a hundred rounds of ammunition for the rifle leaning against the adjacent rock face. The high powered, bolt action Remington 700, fitted with Leupold telescopic sights, was already loaded.

This was the hottest part of the day and Semley eased himself up, moving slowly and deliberately as he drank from the plastic container. Keeping in the cover of the trees, he turned his head first left and then right to extend the muscles cramped by the last hour's inactivity and followed this by stretching his legs and upper body, all the while keeping an eye on the two figures down in the arroyo. When he resumed his position against the rock face, the woman was working her way across the sandy wash and her companion was bent over, carefully examining a dark object beside his foot.

On the floor of the canyon, the intense heat made rocks and bushes shimmer and look insubstantial, adding an air of unreality. The dry wash meandered past piles of tumbled rubble at the base of the cliffs, and Candrew hiked several hundred yards upstream through the loose sand and pebbles before seeing anything unusual. Since all the tools and equipment they'd found so far had been carefully hidden under tarps, he expected the excavation itself to be well disguised. But it was the stark white lumps that caught his attention, and then only because they formed a line crossing from full sunshine into deep shade. He scrambled over the rocks towards the limey material, pushed through a clump of low bushes, tripped and almost fell into a broad ditch. Four feet deep, it curved away to his left, getting shallower along its length. Picking his path with care, and avoiding the deeper pits, he followed for nearly thirty feet. Several side areas had been dug out, although a couple were only partially excavated leaving obvious outlines of fossil bones.

"Here's what we came for," he yelled to Judy. Grinning broadly, he waved her over. "Come look at this. We've found our *T. rex.*"

Judy hurried breathlessly across the gravelly arroyo and helped him move rocks and roll back yet another dun-colored tarp. This one had covered the shallow end of the trench and its color blended well with the surroundings.

Neither of them was prepared for the sheer size and malice of the skull they exposed. With a half-revealed, empty eye socket staring blindly back, it was more awesome than Candrew expected from a fossil still encased in its enclosing rock.

"Good God. Look at this." He pointed to the long row of teeth. The largest ones were the size of bananas, but smoother and darker than the surrounding sandstone. There were no gaps, and Candrew realized immediately that the teeth in Gavin's office couldn't have come from this dino, he'd got them somewhere else.

"Preservation's incredible," Judy said. "Look, you can see every detail."

"Yeah. And as far as I can figure out, the bones haven't been disturbed since the dinosaur met his end." He straightened up, shaded his eyes and peered along the curving trench. "Just some bending when the tendons contracted during *rigor mortis.*"

Dotting the surfaces of the exposed bones were patches covered with dimpled, knobbly plates, each roughly three or four inches across. Candrew knelt and studied these fossilized imprints thoroughly. Details were amazing and even in museums he'd never seen anything like it, yet there was a vague familiarity about the texture. Somewhere, he'd seen this particular pattern before. The flask on his belt was still two-thirds full of water and he sloshed some over the rock surface, washing away the dust, then carefully examined the shiny, wet surfaces with his hand lens. Preservation was good enough to show even minor details. Of course! Gavin's photos—that's where he'd seen patterns like this before. At the time, he hadn't been able to make much sense of them. Now, he realized they were close-up shots of dinosaur skin. This was what Mishikubo was enthused about. *I can see why he was determined to have Gavin excavate such a fantastic specimen*, Candrew thought.

Impressions of dinosaur skin had been found before, but Candrew knew that such finds were rare and usually quite small.

As far as he could remember, there were no skin impressions from a *T. rex*, certainly none as extensive as the ones he was looking at.

He sat on the edge of the trench staring at the partially excavated skeleton. The skull rested on a narrow column of rock where it had been undercut and was isolated from the rock around it by a trench several feet deep. "Looks like we got here with little time to spare." Candrew said to Judy, pointing to the pile of burlap cloth and sacks of plaster of Paris stacked at the end of the trench. "They were just about to wrap the remaining bones and coat them with plaster."

"From the size of the dug-out areas it looks as though they've already hauled away most of the skeleton."

"Yeah. Those bones were probably the ones in the storage unit. And in the truck at the rented house."

"So how come Semley didn't know where they were?"

Candrew leaned over the pits tapping his teeth. "Good question. Maybe there really is a rival group and they shipped them out." He stood up, took off his hat and used it to fan himself, then stared with awe at the huge skull that appeared to be a good five feet long. "At least they haven't got the skull."

They stood in silence for several minutes before Candrew mused, "We're looking at the end result of a hundred and seventy-five million years of dinosaur evolution—the ultimate killing machine. This beast could dispatch any animal in its ecosystem with one bite."

"Typical male perspective. Some paleontologists think they groomed and fed their young. Evidence of a caring parent." Judy chuckled at Candrew's slight loss of composure. "I wonder if other family members perished here as well. And anyway, how did this one die?" She turned to Candrew. "What do you think: drowned, or just died of old age?"

"Not many animals in nature die of senility. And I don't think this one drowned."

Candrew's geological specialty was river deposits, and even after the short time they'd been examining the fossils, he was convinced these sediments hadn't been laid down in water. "This looks like eolian—wind-blown—sand," he said. "You know, like sand dunes. My guess is that a small landslide buried the dinosaur. Then it asphyxiated and just slowly dried out."

"You mean, sort of mummified?"

"Exactly right. It would explain the fantastic preservation and the clear skin impressions. Quick burial would have made it hard for predators to get at the remains. And with porous sand there wouldn't have been much crushing."

He stood, tapping his teeth and pondering the implications of what he'd said. "If that's what really happened, then all the internal organs should have been preserved as well, which would make this one hell of an important find. A unique, world-class discovery." He recalled Mishikubo's CT-scans with the outline of the heart and other internal organs. The same images were almost certainly in the lime-green folder that had been stolen from Gavin's office. Anger welled up and he felt his face reddening.

Judy could see it too. "What's the matter?"

"I'm mad as hell that this tyrannosaur is going into a private collection where nobody'll get to see it. Superb specimens like this shouldn't go to some acquisitive jerk, just because he's got a lot of money. They should *not* go to someone pursuing a private hobby or feeding their ego."

Candrew stared down at the fossil bones. "Mishikubo's collection is amazing, but he doesn't have a single specimen in the same league as this one. He shouldn't have it. We've got to stop him."

Judy let him rant on for a while and finally said, "And just how do you propose to do that?"

"Call in the BLM. And the FBI." He paused, thinking of his recent brush with the pair of agents on campus. "I wonder how much they already know." His opinion of the FBI interviewers mellowed somewhat as he considered the possibility that the authorities might be ahead of him, and in a position to recover the excavated bones. That helped calm him down. He took a couple of deep breaths, pushed up his slipping glasses and stared out across the excavation trench.

The exceptional remains drew Candrew irresistibly back.

As he was poring over the remaining parts of the skeleton, Judy called to him. "Look at these." She pointed to a peculiar series of regularly-spaced holes, each about eighteen inches deep. They formed a straight line running across the canyon floor at an angle to the excavation. Candrew walked to the far end of the row and bent over to get a better look at one of the artificial, perfectly round holes.

"These seem to have been drilled recently," Judy said. Delving into her backpack, she pulled out her camera, wanting to record the way most had been blackened and broken at the top. "You think they were part of a seismic survey?"

"I'm sure that's what they were for. By setting off small explosive charges the echoes could be interpreted to show what's underground."

"And then they could figure out where to search for the buried parts of the dinosaur?" she asked as she leaned over to take another photo.

The whine, shower of rock fragments and distant report took her completely by surprise. She wasn't quite sure what caused it. A second bullet ripping through the air and smashing into a rock just a couple of feet to the side, left her in no doubt.

Candrew was yelling. "Get under cover. Some idiot's shooting at us."

There wasn't much cover to get under. Forty feet away, low bushes offered the best chance. Judy made a run for them, but was an easy target on the exposed arroyo floor and instinctively started zigzagging, dodging from side to side, until she could fling herself behind the shrubs. They were smaller than they looked—she was hardly hidden, and not protected at all. Panting hard with fear and exertion, she had to get out of there, and fast. She glanced around but couldn't see Candrew. Ahead and to the left, a short scree slope led up to the rock face where bigger blocks of sandstone formed vertical fissures large enough to hide in. That's where she had to get.

Judy hesitated to run into the open, but another bullet ricocheting off the rock face behind her forced a decision. She scrambled forward. It was difficult to get a firm footing. Loosely stacked pebbles and small rocks covered the slope and rolled away as she tried to get moving and several times she stumbled and fell forward onto all fours. Halfway up, two large boulders blocked her progress, but adrenaline provided the energy that lack of fitness could not. Grabbing at every crack and small bush, she clawed her way over them. Only twenty feet now. As she pushed forward, a loose rock rolled from under her foot. She fell, sliding with the rock debris, losing finger nails and cutting both knees. Dazed, she lay long enough to suck in one deep breath, got to her feet and stumbled upwards again. Another gunshot echoed around the cliffs.

With leaden legs, she seemed to be running in slow motion. Even in the dry mountain air she was perspiring profusely. Sweat ran into her eyes and made her blink, and she was gasping for breath. Ten more feet. The welcoming protection of the rock fracture was right in front. She squeezed in. But it didn't penetrate far into the cliff and, worse, was partly open to the opposite side of the valley where the shots seemed to be coming from. Protection was minimal. Judy flattened herself tightly against the rock wall and tried to catch her breath. Both hands, both knees and her right elbow were cut and oozing blood. Her left calf was torn and also bleeding badly. And still she didn't have good cover. As if to underline the point, a bullet impacted the opposite side of the fissure, spraying her with rock chips. She ducked back.

Judy was not the type to indulge in self pity and quickly evaluated her situation. Balling her fists with determination, she told herself out loud, "Keep calm. Think logically. Try to work it out." Breathing deeply and slowly, she forced herself to relax and carefully turned her head to look at the crack she was in. Not much encouragement. She was wedged in as far as she could get and there was no way up. The sound of another rifle shot reverberated through the canyon and as a reflex she flattened herself against the rock wall. Where was Candrew? Were those gunshots targeting him?

Not moving, Judy waited for what seemed like an hour, but was probably only ten minutes. There were no more shots. Cautiously and slowly, she peered around the edge. At the top of the scree slope, where it reached the base of the sandstone wall, was a flat strip, maybe eighteen inches wide. To her right, it dead-ended in a tilted stone slab. To the left, it reached a large rock pinnacle that was leaning forward, leaving a gap behind it: there was the haven she needed. The canyon was quiet with no sign of Candrew or the gunman. She took two deep breaths and dashed out along the narrow path, pushing aside small cedars, expecting to feel the impact of a bullet at any moment. In high school, sprinting down a track to shave a few tenths of a second off the time it took to get from A to B seemed pointless and she could never summon up much enthusiasm and run with real conviction. Now she was running for her life, running as she had never run before, straining every muscle, heart pounding, driving for maximum effort—and then some. Twenty feet from the rock pillar her foot caught in a root, pitching her forward. She rolled and fell. And then she was falling freely into darkness.

In an instant, her mind working fast and with amazing clarity, demanded answers: about the present—"Where am I falling?";

the future—"Will I ever see Paul again?"; the past—"Why did I ever leave the ocean for this goddamned desert?" Questions, but no answers. And then it ended. Ended surprisingly gently as she landed in a pile of loose sand. The fall had been no more than six feet.

Judy lay winded, flat on her back, stunned and panting in the cool half-light. It was like being underwater. Memories of diving off Miami flooded in: floating through clear waters, looking up at the undersides of boats and down at multicolored fish effortlessly cruising by. Even her labored breathing sounded like scuba gear. But it was a throbbing left leg that pulled her back to reality. A ragged gash in the calf was bleeding profusely: she had to stop it. Cut and bruised fingers made it difficult, but she unbuttoned and took off her workshirt, ripped out the sleeves, and wrapped them around the oozing leg. Her crude bandage was only marginally effective.

Candrew! She'd completely lost track of him in the frantic scramble for her own safety and immediately felt guilty—and worried. There was a flash of panic: what if Candrew had been shot. Could she find him in this rugged terrain? And what if she wasn't able to, could she make her way back out of the canyons. Her GPS might help, but she wasn't certain. Sucking in a deep breath she steadied herself, although getting up wasn't easy and she had to lean against the rocks for support. From her high perch, she had an uninterrupted view down the hillside to the dinosaur excavation site. Nothing moved. She had no idea how long it had been since the shooting and paused, wondering whether the gunman was waiting. Warily, she studied the far hillside searching for a figure, or at least some movement. There was no sign of either. She felt alone, isolated. Finally, taking a risk, she yelled, "Candrew!" the name echoing around the cliffs.

There was silence, only a slight breeze rustling the bushes. Judy cupped her hands and shouted again.

"Up here." Candrew's voice was off to the left and higher up the slope than where she was crouching. "Thank God I've found you. You okay? What happened?"

Only as he was scrambling down the hillside over the loose rocks, did she start to examine her surroundings. She was boxed in by walls of well-shaped stones fitted together with adobe that defined a space about ten feet long and half as wide. She had fallen through the remains of a wood-beamed roof that covered one end. The opposite end was missing and there the crumbling walls were only a few blocks high. Judy realized she'd landed in an Anasazi ruin, like the one they'd explored earlier that morning.

Candrew jumped down beside the broken wall. "Thank God you survived." He stepped over the adobe blocks and saw her clearly. "Jesus, what happened? You're all beat up, you look awful." Blood had seeped through the hastily-applied bandages. Congealed blood covered the scratches on her arms and legs, and a large blue-black welt was developing over her left eye.

"Here, I've got some water." He sat beside her on the remnant of the low adobe wall, handing her his plastic water bottle. She took a long drink and was using some of the water to wash the dirt off her face when a shadow fell across the opening, startling them both.

Chuck Semley was standing, legs apart, peering down at them, his rifle with the telescopic sights grasped in one hand. The moment was etched in Candrew's mind—the burnt sienna rocks and the contrasting ultramarine sky; the bright sun casting dark shadows under the rabbit brush; the whirring sound of a jumping cricket; and Semley hovering like Charles Bronson at his most menacing.

Chapter 23

"You guys okay?"

It was not what Candrew expected to hear and he was taken aback. "What?"

"Are you all right?" Chuck Semley took one glace at Judy. "Obviously not. You take a hit?"

"No, I just fell a couple of times running for cover." She stared up at him suspiciously.

"You two made easy targets. My gut feeling is they were trying to scare the shit out of you. I pumped a few rounds into the bushes over there to keep 'em off balance. Couldn't see where they went." He shook his head. "Not even sure how many there were. A couple, maybe."

"You weren't the one firing at us?" Candrew asked dubiously.

"Hell no. I'll do a lot of things for money, but murder's not one of them. Well, not anymore."

"So why didn't you meet us like we arranged? You were here with a loaded rifle when we were supposed to be checking out the dinosaur excavation, not fighting a range war."

"Protecting you, that's why." Semley shook his head. "Man,

you were bait."

"What d'you mean?"

"Give you all the details later." He turned toward Judy. "Right now we need to get this young lady taken care of."

Judy leaned back against the wall and winced. "Let me catch my breath for a few minutes. I'll be fine."

"Doubt that," Semley said swinging off his back pack. He fished around in it and grabbed a small medical kit with antiseptics, bandages and tape.

Candrew stood watching as Semley cleaned and covered the wounds on Judy's arms. As Semley turned to pull out another Band-Aid, Judy gave Candrew a scared look, almost as if she was questioning whether they could believe Semley. Candrew was also worried, his thoughts drifting away, searching for reasons why Semley, or anyone else, fired at them. And if it wasn't Semley, were the others still out there. At least neither of them had been hit.

He probed, asking Semley, "Any idea who the guys shooting at us were?"

Chuck Semley used a Band-Aid to hold the end of a bandage in place, then looked up. "My guess is that some other people found out about the dino and want to cash in on it. You know, scare us off."

"Mishikubo's got the resources to deal with any threat like that, hasn't he?" Candrew asked. But he immediately realized it was Mishikubo who'd sent them out here. Was that timing a coincidence? "What's Mishikubo planning?"

Chuck didn't comment. He turned to Judy. "Now, rest a bit young lady and we'll scope out the trail." He turned to Candrew. "I take it you're all right. No injuries?"

"No. I managed to find cover quickly and just stayed there until the shooting stopped. I wish Judy had been that lucky."

Semley beckoned to him and they walked out of Judy's earshot. Candrew asked, "Think we can get her down to the truck?"

Chuck was confident. "Don't see why not." Quickly and expertly he scanned the rock-strewn hillside, picking a route that would take them up a short distance so they could get onto a ledge that sloped more gently, leading all the way down to the arroyo floor.

Although Judy was no featherweight, Chuck, athletically built and fit, easily supported her, helping her along the path. Candrew, loaded down with packs and rifle, made slow progress across the hillside. Nervously glancing around, he kept looking for possible gunmen, but saw none. After more than an hour's trek they reached the sandy floor of the canyon, and from there the path back to the car was flatter and easier, even if a bit steep in places. As they made the final turn on the trail, they could see the Jeep Cherokee in the distance, off to their left. It didn't look quite right, and as they hiked up to it Candrew realized why—the front tire was flat.

"Dammit, some jerk's let all the air out."

"He did more than that." Semley pointed with the toe of his boot to a large gash in the tire. They walked around the Jeep. The other front tire was also slashed.

"I've got just the one spare, and no air pump. Jesus, we're not going to be driving anywhere anytime soon."

The sand near the driver's side rear wheel was damp. Chuck scooped up a handful of the moist soil and sniffed it. "Doesn't smell like gasoline or power steering fluid. My guess is, just plain old water."

"From where? We're in the middle of a desert." But Candrew's mind was running ahead of him and he hustled round and pulled up the back hatch of the Jeep. Both water jugs were lying on their sides empty, their caps missing.

Chuck peered over his shoulder. "No transport, no water. Somebody was out to crush your grapes."

"I guess you're right. Look, Judy's in no state to walk far, and we're a long way from the road. One of us has to hike out and get help."

Semley was remarkably calm and let Candrew finish. He said, smiling, "How do you think I got here? On a broomstick? My truck's hidden over the ridge in the next arroyo." He propped the rifle against the hood, ferreted around in his pack for the GPS and slipped it into one of his many jacket pockets. "Give me an hour and I'll be back. That's if my tires haven't suffered the same fate as yours." He grinned and set off up the dry wash at a brisk pace.

Candrew opened the Cherokee doors and Judy sat in the shade on the passenger side seat with her legs out, looking shell-shocked. At least the pain-killer Semley had given her appeared to be working. "Should we have gone with him? Think he'll come back?" she asked. "Can we really believe what he says?"

That thought worried Candrew. He didn't trust Chuck, even though he'd passed himself off as their savior. And he was well aware that since Semley joined them no more shots had been fired—which would be consistent with him being the gunman. "Well, he's giving the impression that he's on our side," Candrew said, trying to reassure Judy. "Anyway, you're in no shape to hike very far. And he did leave his pack and half his water. That's a good sign."

"Yeah, but he took his rifle."

An hour dragged by and there was no sign of Chuck. After the copious quantity of sedatives Judy had swallowed, she was sound asleep, and Candrew had plenty of time to worry. What if Chuck didn't come back? Then he'd have to hike out to the highway. But that would mean leaving Judy, and neither of them would have much water. He checked their backpacks and found there was less than half-a-gallon between them. Not a lot in this arid place.

Anxious, he walked around scoping out the area, but keeping alert for any movement in the hills. There was none. He sat on a rock in the shade idly watching scampering lizards and a couple of crows riding the breeze.

Was that a sound he heard, sort of like a far away cough? Looking around, he saw nothing. But then he heard the noise again, recognizing it as a truck engine. And at that moment he saw a cloud of dust way off in the distance. So Chuck had come back— if this was Chuck, not the assailants.

Five minutes later Chuck drove up, jumped out of his truck and joked, "Four tires with no holes." He hauled out his water container.

Judy was only partly awake and still groggy. After she'd drunk some water, they helped her into the back seat of the truck's king cab and she slept fitfully the whole way to the emergency room in Farmington.

Candrew and Chuck sat in the entrance lounge drinking overbrewed coffee from the vending machine and waiting for the medics to deal with Judy. It took them nearly two hours.

When she finally emerged, supported by a helpful nurse, Chuck asked "You're all patched up, how about you check into a motel for the night, little lady?"

Even in her medicated state Judy glared at him for his condescending attitude. "No. Thanks. This 'little lady' would rather get home."

Chuck drove them the entire trip back to campus in the dark.

Chapter 24

Pam Harrington greeted Candrew at the door of the duplex she shared with Judy. She ushered him through to the living room where Judy was stretched out on the sofa reading a magazine, her bandaged leg propped up on the ottoman.

Although he'd talked to her briefly on the phone, this was the first chance he'd had to visit since they got back from the canyon. "How're you feeling?"

"Fine—as long as the painkillers keep working." Judy extended her index finger and jabbed it towards her leg, mimicking a hypodermic. "The ER guys in Farmington did a great job patching me up. But I'm still blaming you for dragging me into that whole mess. You knew what Mishikubo and Semley were up to."

While that wasn't quite true, Candrew did feel guilty that Judy had been hurt when she was only along as a helper.

Pam broke in to ask, "You want coffee or a coke?"

When he opted for coffee, she headed off to the small kitchen.

"The worst part of the whole damn thing was the ride out of the canyon in Semley's truck," Judy said. "I wish he'd been a bit less macho and driven through the desert, on those so-called 'roads', a little slower."

"Not much chance of that." Candrew grinned. "Fortunately, after the medics got finished, you slept nearly all the way back to campus—even with Semley's aggressive driving."

"Mother Nature's defense mechanism," she quipped.

Candrew was pleased to find she'd kept a sense of humor, even with the lacerations on her arms and the big bruise decorating her forehead.

"But the good news is: nobody got killed," Judy said, levering herself up on one elbow and adjusting the position of her injured leg in a futile attempt to get comfortable. "And the really good news is that *I* didn't get killed!"

"Well, if you can believe Chuck Semley, that wasn't the intent. As he elegantly phrased it, 'a blind drunk with his pants over his head could have snuffed you'. He thinks they were only trying to scare us off."

"And they succeeded, at least as far as I'm concerned." Judy frowned. "Although I can't help worrying that whoever shot at me won't give up, that they'll follow us here." She glared at Candrew. "Assuming, of course, it wasn't Chuck."

"Interesting you should say that." There was silence for a moment. "It turned out to be an informative ride back, and Chuck was more talkative than usual. He gave me his version of what happened yesterday. In a nutshell, they think they've got competition."

"Really? You mean, someone's trying to steal the *T. rex* that Mishikubo's trying to steal?"

"Right." Candrew smiled at her playful way of summing up the situation. "Gavin was the lone geologist working on the dinosaur dig for Mishikubo, so when he died everything should have stopped. But apparently it didn't. Someone dug up more of the fossil bones and hauled them away."

"How did they figure that out?"

"It seems they've been monitoring the site."

"Who's they?" she asked.

"Mishikubo's outfit. Could have been Chuck himself, though he's never admitted it, but perhaps he sneaks out there once in a while to keep an eye on things. He's certainly real familiar with that whole area." Candrew paused considering other options. "Maybe Mishikubo has his pilots fly over the arroyo and take photos. It's just the sort of thing he'd do. Remember, he owns a major imaging company."

"So what was the point of having us visit the site?"

"Ah, yes. Semley summed that up in one word: *bait.* My guess is that Mishikubo was trying to see what reaction there'd be if some new people showed up and started poking around the remains of the *T. rex* skeleton. They didn't expect the response to be gunfire."

"So why was Chuck carrying a rifle?"

"Good question. He claims he's always armed when he's out in the wilderness. Feels naked without a weapon. I guess that reflects his background as a mercenary."

Pam came in, quietly put two mugs of coffee and some cookies on the table and discreetly left.

Candrew took one of the cookies in an unthinking reflex and said, "I've been wondering about this whole incident. We retreated in such disarray, I'm sure we missed a lot of crucial information."

"Like what?" Judy asked.

"The Bobcat, for a start. A license number, even a serial number, might help track down who rented it."

"But Candrew, I thought Misikubo was putting up the money for that."

"Could be. I'll ask Chuck. There was a lot of other equipment lying round, some of that ought to be traceable."

Candrew took a second cookie and sipped his coffee. "In spite of all Mishikubo's vast resources, I'm almost certain they don't know where most of the excavated bones are. I got a sense of this when I first met Chuck down in Santa Fe. He admitted they hadn't any idea where Gavin was storing them. It was pure luck I stumbled on the storage locker, and then only because Marge found the key in Gavin's jacket. Pity I didn't get there a day earlier." Candrew shook his head. "At the time, I thought Chuck was in town to oversee the move. Obviously, not the case."

"Any ideas on the roles of our other suspects?" Judy asked. "We still don't know much about Kurt Tadheim, Teresa Polanca, or Jason." With difficulty, she again adjusted her position on the sofa. "Could Gavin have been a sort of double agent? You know, like giving the appearance of working for Mishikubo and all the time double-crossing him?"

"Fascinating idea." Candrew paused, looking round the room for a moment, organizing his thoughts. "Now that I think back, I can't remember Chuck ever mentioning co-workers. But then, he's rarely talked about collaborators, and never by name." Candrew wondered where they all were at the time Gavin drowned, and what they'd been doing for the last few weeks. He had no doubt about what he should do next: check their summer schedules. He needed some idea of how everything—everyone—fitted together.

Still mulling over all the unknowns, and tapping his teeth, his distracted gaze finally focused back on Judy. "There's another twist to this. I think Gavin knew the location of a second *T. rex* site."

"Really?" She looked surprised. "How did you figure that out?"

"Remember, the skull we saw at the excavation site had all its teeth?"

"Yeah, but is that significant?" Judy asked.

"Yes it is, because in Gavin's office at the house there were two, full-sized *T. rex* teeth. They couldn't have been taken from the skull we saw. Although one was in excellent condition, the other one was still unprepared and embedded in matrix. It didn't look like a commercial specimen and I'm assuming he took the teeth from another skeleton."

Candrew told Judy about the black light in Gavin's office and how that could have been used to locate other fossil bones.

"All pretty tenuous," she said, frowning.

"Agreed. But the critical evidence is the map that Marge found. He'd drawn in a second site, and it's pretty close to the other one, probably in one of the nearby canyons. There might be more information on the CDs. Has your friend in astronomy been able to process them?"

"That I don't know, but then I haven't talked to her since we got back from the dino site. Pam said she called earlier this morning, while I was asleep. When she comes by later, I'll ask."

"We ought to go and take a look at the new site."

"We?" Judy said, tilting her head to one side.

He laughed. "No, not you this time. I'll go with Chuck."

Judy and Candrew chatted for another half hour. Then he asked if she needed anything, said he'd drop by later and left, heading for Kinblade Hall.

Candrew went directly to the department office where, as usual, the efficient Maria was at her desk. "Do you have a copy of Kurt Tadheim's summer schedule?"

"Dr. Tadheim's already back on campus. He got here a week or so ago."

"Yeah, but I haven't been able to track him down. I need to know what he'd been planning to do this summer, particularly the conferences he was going to."

Maria was used to strange questions from faculty. She gave him a quizzical look. "Hang on a minute, I'll check and see what he gave me before he left in May. I don't think I've deleted it." She turned to the computer and typed in a few commands, her long, orange-painted nails clicking across the keyboard, waited, then typed a couple more. "Okay. He went to a conference at Colorado School of Mines and from there to visit a friend at the University of Illinois. After that he was going to spend a week driving to California and was scheduled to be at Menlo Park with the U. S. Geological Survey for five weeks."

Candrew mumbled, "Thanks," and left.

Back in his office, he jotted Tadheim's summer dates on the calendar. Why did the University of Illinois seem familiar? Candrew didn't have any friends there, no one he was collaborating with. He studied the schedule again. Last Wednesday he was driving back from Carrizozo, so it was quite possible that Kurt could have passed him while he was fixing his flat. The thought immediately brought up the question of Teresa Polanca since she was in the truck with him. Where was *she* all summer?

He reached for the phone and called Monica Henderson in zoology, got her answering machine and recorded a short message. That left Jason, and he had no information on where he'd been all summer and no easy way of finding out. Perhaps Ted Devereaux, his father, might have a general idea, but Candrew was not optimistic—teenage boys weren't noted for keeping their parents informed about the details of their social lives.

With only limited success in piecing together the critical summer schedules, Candrew gave up and headed to the faculty club and lunch.

"Did you see this morning's *New Mexican*?" someone asked.

The usual group was gathered in the faculty dining room, eating lunch and airing their views on a variety of topics, mostly outside their areas of expertise.

"Why, what happened?" Candrew asked.

"Some wealthy alum, with more money than sense, is giving the university a Georgia O'Keeffe painting. Supposed to be worth

1.2 million."

"What are they going to do, hang her giant flower in the botany department?" Arlen Dee asked.

"Not this one—it's a landscape." The prof who provided the information turned to Candrew. "It ought to go in the geology department."

"At least a lot more people would see it there than hanging over the fireplace in some wealthy guy's home," Candrew shot back. He felt the same way about outstanding pieces of art as he did about rare fossils: exceptional works of man or nature should be accessible to everyone, not just the privileged. Candrew had seen O'Keeffe's western landscapes in museums, and those images reminded him of the canyons he and Judy had been working in. But just the thought of those arid canyons evoked the fear he'd felt yesterday. In spite of that, he laughed. "The department budget isn't big enough to pay the insurance premiums."

A rambling discussion followed with everyone chipping in. "Well, it's nice to know our alumni have that sort of wealth lying around."

"Shows a UNNM education is good for something."

"Damn right. But he'd have a lot more impact on student education if he'd endowed a chair. We could have brought in some respected academic and paid a decent salary."

"You guys see the flaw in the system?" The chatter subsided, they all stared at Lubie, the history professor. "We rely on philanthropy. Our rich alums are expected to give out of pure generosity. We need to make it contractual."

"How the hell are you going to do that?" someone asked.

Lubie had his solution. "Simple. When a student enrolls, he agrees to give one percent of his future income to the department where he gets his major."

This produced a babble of comments, usually with several people talking at once.

"That's the best argument I've ever heard for having a medical school."

"Think the philosophy profs would go for it?"

"Maybe we could prorate it over the courses they took and even things out a bit."

"Anyway, students are making easier grades than ever. Did you see the editorial on grade inflation in today's paper? Says the average grade is getting closer to B than C, and some of the top schools give mostly A's."

"Gentlemen, gentlemen." It was Lubie again. They all stopped talking. "Tuition's going up, but so is the grade point average. The kids are still paying the same *dollars-per-GPA*. Don't you see, the value of education hasn't changed." His booming laugh left them wondering just how serious he was, but then with Lubie they were never quite sure.

Attempts at solving the world's problems, at least the academic world's problems, were interrupted when Ted Devereaux arrived and pulled another chair up to the table. Conversation broke into smaller groups and Candrew took the opportunity to ask him about Jason and what he'd been doing for the summer, trying to sound as casual as possible.

"No, he didn't take any courses. The poor boy's been slaving away for one of the biology profs. He spent most of the time out looking for aliens," Ted laughed. "Non-native plants, not the extraterrestrial variety."

"Here in New Mexico?"

"Mostly, but they did run a few surveys further west, one out toward Farmington and another in Utah, a few miles south of Blanding."

Well, well, well. Jason had been out in the Four Corners area for part of the summer. Candrew made a mental note—and probed. "I parked beside his Jeep a couple of days ago. I guess he's back for the fall semester."

"Right. He only worked for two and a half months. The project ran through the middle of July, but at least, it gave him some cash. His mother's been pleased to have him around for part of the summer."

Candrew tried to put it all together, but the timing for Jason didn't quite fit. Nothing about Jason ever seemed to fit. His role in excavating and removing *T. rex* bones was still no clearer. Just what was he contributing to the project?

Chapter 25

Dr. Calder P. Calloway, assistant professor of anthropology, swung open his office door. Tall, lean and fit, his long black hair was pulled into a pony tail. He wore a fringed leather jacket that hung half-open, partly covering a chunky silver and turquoise buckle on a wide leather belt holding up too-tight jeans that were tucked into cowboy boots. He had circular, wire-rimmed glasses and an orange band around his forehead. It was difficult to decide whether he was trying to be a cowboy or an Indian.

"Hi. I'm Pug Calloway." He extended a surprisingly chubby hand. Candrew shook it. "Come on in. Here, let me move some of that crap." He scooped up an armful of technical reprints to make room on the only chair that wasn't piled high with books and boxes. Three stacks of papers had to be condensed into one to clear a big enough space for him to sit on the table. "You said you need some anthropological help. Happy to do what I can."

"Well . . ," Candrew hesitated, "as I said in my e-mail, I'm hoping to get some background information on a faculty member at the University of Illinois. An anthropologist. A guy called Joel Iskander."

"I recognize the name, but can't say I'm a close buddy. Don't know him at all well." He paused for a moment, apparently searching his memory. "What're you trying to find out?"

"Nothing specific. I'm just trying to get a feel for what he does professionally. You know, some idea of his ongoing research. What his colleagues think of him. That sort of thing." Even as he was saying it, Candrew realized how lame it sounded. The truth was, he had no idea what he was trying to find out. It was just a fishing expedition to see if he could hook anything interesting. "Renata and I had dinner with Iskander the other evening and she thought he wasn't being completely open," Candrew said, and hesitated, but Calloway appeared interested. "I had to agree with her. I can't quite put my finger on it, but there's something a bit strange about him."

Calloway pursed his lips, glanced round the cluttered office and seemed unsure where to start. "I know about him because, like me, he works on the Anasazi. He's not published much, most of it coauthored papers with the Southern Illinois group working on Black Mesa."

"That's out near the Four Corners, isn't it? On the Hopi reservation?"

"Yeah, though a lot of it's actually part of the Navajo Nation. I've run into Joel a couple of times at conventions, had a few beers with mutual friends, things like that. Pleasant enough, but too cynical for my taste. I have to admit, I'm not overly impressed with him as a scientist."

"Renata told me he didn't come to see you when he was on campus last week," Candrew said. "Isn't that a bit odd, since you're both doing research on the same sorts of things?"

"Yeah, sure is, but then I work with stuff that's a lot older, pushing back into Basketmaker. I'm less concerned with pottery than he is. Still, you can always learn something new by talking to guys excavating sites in the same general area. It all makes me think Joel's not a serious researcher. Maybe he's more interested in teaching. Or becoming an administrator." Calloway smiled and jerked his head slightly, implying, but not saying: . . . *and who in their right mind would want to do that?*

"So you don't excavate pots?"

"You mean dig out the ones the pot hunters missed?" He smiled ruefully. "No, I've got more involved in pit house design and village layout." He paused and glanced away for a moment. "I was sorry to hear about that prof in your department who drowned. Borelli?"

"Citalli."

"Yeah. I only met him once at a faculty party. Said he ran into lots of Anasazi sites in the area where he's working. Wanted to know if they were all mapped. And was I interested. Said he often found some that seemed to be intact, not looted, still had artifacts."

"That's not something he talked to me about," Candrew said, and wondered whether he'd taken a few of those artifacts. "But talking of Anasazi artifacts, does anything else about Iskander come to mind?" Candrew asked, thinking back to their dinner conversation.

"Not right off the bat." Calloway started to slide down from his perch on the table and Candrew took the hint and stood up. As Calloway headed for the door, picking his way through the piles of books and papers, he said, "I probably shouldn't mention this because I haven't got any hard facts and it's all gossip, but there was an odd incident a couple of years ago." He paused, clearly considering the best way to phrase it. "What I heard through the grapevine was that Joel misappropriated funds. Took the grant money, then never did the site evaluation. Luckily, it wasn't National Science Foundation money and the feds didn't get involved. Some private group ponied up the cash and the university had to pay it back. I'm surprised Joel didn't get fired. I guess that's the tenure system for you. Anyway, the university hushed it up and I never did hear any more details, only rumors." Calloway couldn't recall the name of the sponsors and had nothing else to add.

They talked briefly about doing research in the desert southwest and Candrew asked where he was working. When Calloway told him he said, "That's close to some areas where I've done field work," but what Candrew was thinking was that it was quite a long way from the canyon that housed the *T. rex* remains. After a few pleasantries he left, convinced that the visit was worth it after all.

He climbed the stairs to the floor above, and as he walked to where Renata had her office, thought about how hallways in different academic departments develop their own style. Anthropology was like geology in many ways, with prime specimens displayed in glass-fronted cabinets that served as a mini-museum for visitors and a teaching aid for students. But some things are common to all departments—bulletin boards shingled with notices, both professional and social.

When he rounded the corner, two wooden crates stood in an alcove where the passage widened, one with a hand-written label in blue magic marker: *Fed Ex to Temple of Doom.* Candrew had seen *Raiders of the Lost Ark,* and all the other Indiana Jones movies, and thought about the popularity of archaeology. Last time he was in one of the few remaining chain bookstores, he'd found to his surprise that there were five archaeology magazines but only one for geology. Even in *Jurassic Park,* it was the DNA juggling that took the lead with paleontology merely a supporting role. He couldn't think of a geological equivalent of Indiana Jones.

The door to the end office was cracked open a couple of inches, and when he rapped on it, Renata called out, "Come on in; it's open."

Her office was at the opposite end of the neatness spectrum

from Pug Calloway's. She sat at an uncluttered desk in a tall modern chair with her back to the window, facing the door. One wall was covered with bookcases, half of them filled with precisely arranged journals and the other half with textbooks and binders. The side wall had wooden cupboards below a broad shelf, and above that were framed photographs and posters of contemporary paintings. A small stereo system was quietly playing Copland's clarinet concerto.

"I came over to the department to talk to Calloway. So, thought I'd pay you a visit."

"That's nice, I'm glad you came by." She pushed her loose dark hair back off her shoulders. "Want some coffee?" Candrew declined. "Did Pug have startling revelations about Iskander? Does he know where the skeletons are buried?"

That sounded like an archaeological insider joke. Candrew smiled. "He didn't know him well, but had one interesting piece of information." He told her about the misused funds. Surprised, she was about to make a comment when the phone rang.

"Excuse me a moment." Renata rocked back in her chair, picking up the phone from the side table. "Yes . . . he's right here . . . no . . . I see." She turned back to Candrew. "That was Maria, the geology department secretary. She wanted you to know that your assistant Judy has been taken to the hospital."

"Really?" Candrew looked shocked. "In Santa Fe?"

"No, she's been admitted to the infirmary here on campus."

"What's she gone in for? Is it related to the shooting?"

"Maria didn't say."

The small hospital at the northwest corner of campus served the university and the surrounding area. It was diagonally across from the anthropology department and Candrew and Renata hurried over together, getting there in less than fifteen minutes.

He led the way up the broad flight of stairs to the second

floor. "Here's 209, Room 227 should be down this way."

They stepped back to let two blue-garbed attendants wheel a gurney past, and negotiated groups of visiting friends and relatives talking in subdued voices. Judy's room was at the end of a short passage and Renata knocked gently on the half-open door. There was no reply.

Maria had said that Pam Harrington, Judy's housemate, had taken her to hospital early that morning. Pam explained she'd got out of bed and gone into the kitchen to make coffee, when Judy stumbled in, complaining of dizziness and a pounding headache, then collapsed in a heap on the floor. Candrew knew she been badly shaken by events at the canyon excavation site, but when he visited her yesterday, she seemed to be in good spirits. What caused this relapse?

Renata knocked again and pushed the door all the way open, peering in.

"Oh. Hi, Renata. I must have dozed off." Judy was making an effort to pull herself up into a sitting position.

"Here, let me help you." Renata hurried over. Moving easily into the role of mother, she fluffed up the pillow and adjusted the blanket. "How're you feeling?"

"Pretty good. At least I'm a lot better now that damn headache's eased up a bit and I can focus again. Last night I couldn't even stand up. The doctor who examined me was worried about concussion, so I'm being kept here for observation." She squirmed in the bed, trying to get more comfortable. "Anyway, enough bitching. I'm in sufficiently good shape to be complaining about the food here." In spite of the serious risk of concussion, Judy seemed to be quite perky. "But I'm already getting bored," she said.

"You got stuff to read?" Candrew asked. "We brought a couple of magazines to relieve the boredom."

"Just what I need. I started reading a paleontology book after lunch, but soon gave that up and switched to a McGarrity novel and finally turned on the TV. So, if you've brought me a *National Enquirer*, I'll complete my slide down the intellectual scale."

"Sorry to disappoint you," Renata said. "The best I could do when we rushed over was to grab last month's *Smithsonian* and the current *Science:* should be enough to stop the slide."

"You didn't bring me any grapes?" She laughed, took the magazines, dropping them on the bedside table. "Didn't do too well in my first encounter with a *T. rex*, did I? I'm just lucky they're extinct."

A broad grin spread across Candrew's face. "Don't feel too bad—that was a huge specimen judging from the size of the skull." And for Renata's benefit, he added, "They've certainly hauled a lot of rock out already, and it looked as though they've got most of the body and all his tail."

"*His?*" Judy grinned mischievously. "What makes you think it's male? Could just as well be a female. I agree it's probably one of the biggest *T. rexes* ever found, but assuming that the boys are always bigger than the girls, well, that's just male chauvinism."

Judy warmed to her argument. She was never shy about challenging assumptions of male superiority, even if it was only in size and even if it was only for an extinct dinosaur. She took every opportunity to chasten her men friends—and got particular pleasure from teasing Candrew. "There really is no good way to tell the sex of a *T. rex*. Some fossils are solidly built, but others are quite gracile. Is that male and female? And if so, which is which? Maybe they're two slightly different species?"

Candrew didn't say anything, merely nodding his head in general agreement. He knew that male mammals are usually bigger than females, but that's not true in a lot of birds—and most paleontologists think birds evolved from dinosaurs.

"Did you see that news report about egg-laying females?" Renata asked. She knew very little biology. "Involved some sort of special bone."

For an instant Judy looked puzzled, then said, "You mean the medullary bone?"

"Yeah. I think that's what they called it."

"It only develops in ovulating females, so if you find it in a fossil, you're sure you've got a female. But they've just found even more direct evidence—a pregnant *T. rex*. So the issue should get cleared up."

Impressed by the information Judy had acquired in the short time she'd been preparing to teach Gavin's class, Candrew asked, "What about the dinosaur that Sotheby's auctioned off? The one McDonalds and Disney paid over eight million dollars for. Boy or girl?"

"Well, they called it *Sue,* although it doesn't seem to be a case of a *Boy Named Sue.* They think that particular, solidly-built dino is female. And I've a gut feeling the heavy one Gavin was excavating up in the canyons is also a girl."

"Yeah, from what I've seen you could be right," Candrew said. "Sort of a "Queen tyrant lizard—*Tyrannosaurus regina*."

Judy smiled. "*T. regina*. I rather like that."

The discussion of *rexes'* sexes was interrupted by a heavy-set, dark-haired nurse who handed Judy a paper cup with two small grey pills in it and poured her some water. Judy dutifully swallowed her medication.

"There, that didn't hurt none."

"Right," Judy said, "and it's a lot better than having another needle stuck in me."

"You'll soon be out of here and good as new." The nurse picked up the remains of lunch and left.

Renata brought the conversation back to fossils. "I read somewhere they'd just found a mummified dinosaur."

"Yeah. That was a duck-billed hadrosaur. Common enough,

they call them the *cows of the Cretaceous*." Renata smiled at Judy's description.

"But no one's ever found a mummified *T. rex*," Candrew said. "That's what makes Mishikubo's dino unique. Preservation's superb." *And it's going to disappear into a private collection unless I can do something to stop it,* he thought.

There was silence for a moment, then Candrew said, "I'm really sorry to have got you mixed up in all this." Although relieved to find Judy in good spirits, he blamed himself for getting her involved with the dino-site shooting and felt personally responsible for her injuries.

"Hey, no problem. It was fascinating to see a big *T. rex* being excavated. They have quite an operation going on out there"

"Yeah, they're obviously well funded by Mishikubo and aren't lacking for equipment. That was a pretty impressive back hoe. And don't forget, they needed to haul out the plaster-coated bones as well as cart in all that plaster of Paris, and the water to mix it."

"Pop!" Judy punched the air with her fist, grinning.

"What?"

"POP. P - O - P. That's *Plaster of Paris*. Remember the budget we found in Gavin's file when we were sorting his office? It had $5,000 for 'pop'? It just popped into my mind—no pun intended." Judy smirked. "All I needed was a big bang on the head to figure it out."

Candrew hadn't thought much about the items on Gavin's list. He tried to recall the others. "I guess CAT is the Bobcat, the backhoe. At $25,000, that makes sense."

"Okay, so there's two items from the list. What about the others?"

"Well,..." Candrew thought back to what he'd read. "There's SHIP—but in a desert?" After a moment he admitted, "I just can't remember any of the others."

With no further insights, conversation for the next half hour rambled widely, ranging over topics both on and off campus. Judy got around to bemoaning the fact that she wouldn't be playing racquetball for a while and began explaining the finer points of the game to Renata who rarely indulged in sports.

The television was on but the sound muted, and Candrew idly watched the silent picture, only half listening to Judy and Renata. The National Geographic program showed an Australian crew in a *Land Rover* chasing a rhino. He watched as they careered through the brush and finally shot a tranquilizer dart that hit it in the rump. A few minutes later, the rhino slowed and looked as though it was trying to plod through molasses before finally staggering to a standstill and collapsing. Candrew focused his attention, mental wheels whirling. This seemed significant—and in an instant he knew exactly how Gavin had been killed. Mumbling excuses to Judy and Renata, he hurried out into the hall.

He wasn't sure why he'd left so abruptly. It just seemed that with the realization of how the murder was committed he needed to take action, immediately. But he had no idea what action. He followed the almost deserted corridor that led past the nurses' station and down the stairs towards the parking lot. Even before he made it all the way to the end, the antiseptic smell was replaced by the enticing aroma of grilled meat and coffee. He turned the corner and spotted the cafeteria. Suddenly, he felt hungry—he'd missed lunch—and on impulse headed to the counter and ordered a hamburger and fries, and as an afterthought, cherry pie.

While he sat waiting for his food at the table by the window, he thought over the consequences of his sudden insight into Gavin's murder. But who was implicated in firing a dart at Gavin? Semley? Kurt? Surely not Jason? Possibly Marge, if she had strong enough feelings about what she thought was Gavin's affair with Redfern. Confused, Candrew sat tapping his teeth.

Where would the killer get a tranquilizer? Kurt's friend Teresa was a biologist, and they were always using chemicals like that. And, of course, she was close friends with the new vet— what was his name? Livingston? He'd forgotten. The motive was obvious enough: money. What about opportunity? That was a good question. How did they get to the river bank with all those students around?

It was clear to Candrew that he needed to visit the part of the river where Gavin drowned. That was the only way he'd be able to figure out where someone could have hidden and fired the dart at Gavin, probably just before he entered the rapid. And he realized that it would be important to make a more serious attempt to pin down everyone's schedule, so he'd know where they all were when the murder was committed. With luck, he might be able to eliminate some suspects and narrow the field.

Chapter 26

Candrew worked his way along the stacks in an unfamiliar section of the university library. After several false leads, he eventually tracked down the reference books he wanted and hauled the heavy tomes over to one of the central wooden tables. Dropping them down beside his leather briefcase, he pulled out a notepad and mechanical pencil.

When the police contacted Marge, they'd said the toxicologist had identified an opiate in Gavin's blood, and this was what made him lose consciousness. The drug was carfentanil. Candrew searched the Internet for information, and found it was used by veterinarians. Now he'd got one of the standard books referenced by vets and had also pulled out a massive biochemistry textbook. He discovered carfentanil to be ten thousand times more potent than morphine, and just a millionth of a gram is active in humans: 20 millionths is fatal. Wow, Candrew thought—the murderer really went for over-kill. The drug, used mainly by vets to tranquilize large animals, has been effective for elephants, bison and elk—and even dinosaurs in the film *Jurassic Park II*. The text claimed it was "suitable for projectile dart administration," and this, of course, was the way Gavin had been drugged. A consistent picture was emerging.

After sitting and digesting the information for a while, Candrew reluctantly got back to working on the draft of his sandstone manuscript. He was able to quickly locate the journal he needed, and as usual, was impressed with a retrieval system that could unerringly lead him to what he wanted; in this case an obscure article on sandstones written by a scientist in Bulgaria half a century earlier. He wouldn't find that on Google. Looking around, Candrew wasn't surprised by the absence of students since they all relied on the Internet, books were passé. He tried to make himself comfortable in the unpadded wooden library chair, though he knew from previous experience he wouldn't succeed. Anyway, lack of comfort would help him stay awake.

Tired after the long day—it was already past eleven o'clock—he found it difficult to concentrate on the scientific article even though the library would close in less than an hour. His attention kept drifting away, rehashing the events of the last few weeks and especially this afternoon's insight into the way Gavin was probably murdered, and the information he'd just gleaned from the veterinary handbook. But he still had to figure out who fired the dart, and where they could have hidden.

As he mulled things over, he rocked back in his chair, hands behind his head, eyes roving casually across the shelves that towered above him. They seemed like a tsunami of books about to break and drown him in information. All that knowledge was intimidating, and once again it depressed him to realize how little of it he would ever have time to read, much less understand and remember. Sitting drained and discouraged, he stared at the wall of books.

Forcing his attention back to the technical publication, Candrew studied the pages of detailed text with equations, schematic diagrams, and rock sections. In a little over half an hour, he'd extracted what he needed, checked out of the library, and was on the way to his car. It was parked in the usual space behind Kinblade Hall and now he hurried through the deserted, poorly-lit plaza, his footsteps echoing under a clear, starry sky with a thin crescent moon.

Halfway across the open space, he was surprised to see a figure emerging from the shadows under the trees. He felt apprehensive when the man, head down, came purposefully towards him. As he got closer, even in the pale light, he could make out an unruly mass of white hair and deliberate gait that marked him as one of the profs, a caricature of a faculty member in music, or maybe particle physics. Relieved, and with a sense of late-night camaraderie, Candrew said amiably, "Good evening."

The white-haired professor stopped, looked puzzled, and uttered an enigmatic, "Ah, yes." No conscious thought seemed to be involved. After a moment's consideration the prof recalled where he'd been headed and resolutely set off again.

Candrew, smiling to himself at how apprehensive he'd been, continued in the general direction of his car and the dark shape of the geology building. The silhouette was broken by a few lights in top floor, student offices. A couple of labs were still lit and so was the computer room. The other offices were dark.

At first Candrew thought he imagined it—a slight flicker of light in one of the darkened windows. He stopped walking and stood in the suddenly quiet plaza, staring steadily at the window. Flames? No, it wasn't the random flickering of a fire, more like a flashlight. Yes, there it was again. Third window in from the end on the second floor. Good God, that was Gavin's office!

His first thought was to call Campus Security. His second thought was that they would probably take forever and eventually arrive with flashing lights and all their bells and whistles blaring. By then the intruder would be long gone. Although he never made a deliberate decision to check it out himself, he began walking steadily toward the building and unlocked the ground floor door. Inside, the gloomy passages were deserted and in semidarkness, only "Exit" signs illuminated. Candrew climbed the familiar stairs from the entrance lobby and stalked quietly along the dimly lit hallway heading for Gavin's office. Planning to catch the intruder red-handed, he hoped to find out what he was searching for, what he was trying to steal.

Ten feet from the office, it suddenly occurred to Candrew that the door might well be locked. He stopped, carefully propped his briefcase against the wall and fished the key ring from his jacket pocket as quietly as he could. He still had the sub-master key to Gavin's office and there was just enough light in the dim passageway to sort through and find it. Furtively, he crept toward the door, his heart thumping, his breathing heavy. The duct tape had been peeled back from three of the FBI's yellow *Caution* tapes and they dangled loosely at one side of the door. He carefully lined the key up with the lock, then with a quick, smooth action pushed in the key, turned the handle, opened the door and reached round to flick up the light switch.

The bright glare dazzled him and in that blinded instant he realized he hadn't thought this through carefully enough. What if the person in the office was armed? What if there was more than one intruder? Nobody knew he was there; maybe he should have told Security after all.

His sight rapidly adjusted. As he grew used to the light, he glanced around for the intruder. No one was there, at least not anyone he could see. Carefully, he peered behind the door and then over at the filing cabinets. Picking his way carefully through the office, shaking with tension, he didn't seem able to breathe fast enough to get all the oxygen his lungs demanded. And then, rounding Gavin's huge desk, he saw the toe of a shoe jutting out; someone was hiding.

He needed a weapon and grabbed the only thing within reach, a large, ammonite fossil. Disc-shaped, the rock was over a foot in diameter and must have weighed at least ten pounds. This was getting way too dramatic. He shouted in a voice that came out squeakier than he intended, "Who's there? Come out," and stepped up to the desk, peering over.

Sitting on the floor behind the desk was Kurt Tadheim.

"Kurt!"

"Who were you expecting, the Easter Bunny?"

"What the hell are you doing here?"

"I could ask you the same question?" Kurt shot back.

"Rosenberg told me to take care of sorting out Gavin's office, and when I saw the lights I . . ." Candrew stopped. Why should he be on the defensive, making excuses when he was here for a perfectly legitimate reason? "You're sure acting guilty, hiding behind the desk like that."

"Just taking precautions. I had no idea who'd come bursting in here at midnight, threatening me with a big ammonite."

Candrew had forgotten he was holding the fossil and pushed it onto a nearby bookshelf. "So why are you here? Nobody's supposed to be in Gavin's office." He glared at Kurt and demanded, "What're you doing? And why are you searching by flashlight in the early hours of the morning?"

"Since when have you been the university's secret police? The university president make you a deputy, give you a star?" Up to this point Kurt had remained seated on the floor. Now he hauled himself up and plopped down in the old leather, swivel desk chair. It irked Candrew to see him sitting there in Gavin's place.

"Look, let's quit the verbal sparring." Candrew felt he had nothing to lose. "I know you were conniving with Gavin—and Teresa Polanca as well—in getting the bones of a big *T. rex* dug out. You're not a paleontologist. So why are you involved?"

"Simple really. I was invited."

Candrew waited; nothing more was volunteered. "Invited to do what, dig?"

"Actually, to tell them where to dig." There was another long pause.

"And get paid for it?"

He pursed his lips and stared across at Candrew. "You're a persistent bastard."

"Yeah, you got that right," Candrew snapped, pushing a pile of papers off an adjacent chair and slumping down.

Kurt gave a cynical smile. "Let me make life easy for you and tell you what happened, since you're in no position to do anything about it." He pulled the chair up to the desk and picked up a paper clip.

Candrew glanced around the office. The computer monitor was on; several cardboard boxes were partially filled with folders; drawers were pulled out and their contents dumped; filing cabinets open. Had Kurt done this, or was it the result of an FBI ransacking?

Kurt started to slowly untwist the paper clip. "The bones were found by Teresa."

"She doesn't work with fossils, she's not a paleontologist."

"No, but she's out in the desert at night with her black light ogling the sex life of scorpions. Some dinosaur bones glow under ultraviolet light and she had the dubious privilege of stumbling across a *T. rex*. As you said, fossils are not her specialty, that's why she told Gavin about it."

"When was that?"

"Oh, I don't know. Maybe a year ago." He paused and idly examined the mutilated paper clip. "Must have been in mid-June."

"What happened after that?"

"Gavin worked out a lucrative deal with some wealthy fossil collector in California. Never did find out who he was. Anyway, we were going to split the proceeds three ways and the guy in California would get the bones."

"You still haven't explained your role in all this." Candrew was aggressively pointing with his finger. "If you were getting a third of the take, it must have been major."

"Quite the detective." He paused, apparently unwilling to add anything else, but then suddenly said, "You know how big a *T. rex* is? That damn thing was over forty-five feet long—and thirty of those feet were embedded in sandstone, hidden underground. Gavin wanted to know if I could figure out a way to locate the buried part of the skeleton. He thought perhaps we could use one of my geophysical methods." Fiddling with the paper clip, Kurt added, "There's no point in digging out more rock than you have to."

"And did you come up with a method?"

"You doubt my professional skill? Of course I did. It turned out to be quite straightforward. Basically seismic, you know, make a noise at the surface with explosives and listen to the echo. Do some sophisticated computer processing and, bingo!, there's your image. Worked real well."

Candrew was familiar with the principle of seismic and knew how slightly different rocks, like sandstone and dinosaur bone, would reflect sound differently. What Kurt was claiming seemed reasonable. And Judy had found the row of holes that were presumably drilled for the small explosive charges.

Kurt seemed eager to flaunt the success of his seismic skills. "I got a good image and it showed the buried skeleton curving off to one side. Gavin brought in a back hoe from God-knows-where and started to dig it out." He grinned. "And of course it confirmed my predictions."

"So how come the job didn't get finished?"

"Professional pride." Kurt sneered and slowly shook his head as if that was something hard to believe. "Gavin just had to tell all his fossil buddies about this great new beast—'had to do the right thing,' was the way he put it. Wanted to have a big team of experts crawling over everything. We couldn't let him do that. Remember, the site's on Indian land, so everything done up to now was secret—and illegal. Things got out of hand when he told us he was determined to go to the authorities. He claimed the excavation should be done carefully by experts. Wanted to maximize information on taphonomy, and on environment, and on conditions where the dinosaur died and got buried, and all that garbage fossil guys get excited about."

Looking slowly around the office, Kurt paused, apparently unsure whether to continue, but then decided to. "Teresa seemed to have a proprietary interest in the fossil, since she'd found it in the first place. Thought of it as 'her' *T. rex*—*Teresa rex!* She was mad as hell that Gavin was backing out, thought we'd be losing control. She even said to me, '*There are lots of ways to have an accident in the Wild West*'. I couldn't believe she was serious. When I said, half joking, '*You going to let one of your scorpions sting him?*' she replied, '*I've got a bigger sting than any scorpion,*' and she said it with an intensity that surprised me."

"Are you saying Teresa killed Gavin?"

"Of course not. Gavin drowned accidentally: we all know that." He was smirking broadly as he said it.

He may have died from drowning, Candrew thought, but the question was, *who made him drown?* Now convinced the murderer used a tranquilizer dart to drug Gavin, he knew why he'd lost control of the kayak. But was it really Teresa who fired that dart? A biologist herself, and dating a vet, he knew she could certainly get access to carfentanil. It all fitted neatly.

"The cause of death was drowning," Candrew said, "but what was the cause of drowning?"

"Elegantly put," Kurt said sarcastically. "Perhaps you should ask Professor Polanca herself. If you do, do it tactfully. She's one tough cookie." From what Candrew had learned about her background and remembered from her résumé, that seemed a fair evaluation.

Kurt elaborated. "You got a taste of things when you were out in the canyon." That seemed to amuse him. "I saw her yesterday. Let's see if I can remember her words exactly, yes: 'Those nosey bastards were up there poking around, so I fired a few warning shots.' She's pretty good with a rifle and those bullets went precisely where she wanted them to go. Her intent was only to scare you off."

"She want to scare Jason off as well?"

Kurt stared straight at Candrew, looking puzzled. If he was acting perplexed, he was giving a good performance. "Jason? I don't know any Jason. Don't know what you're talking about."

"Really?"

"Look, I'm just being swept along in this whole thing. It's getting out of hand."

"I'd certainly call murder *out of hand.*"

"Enough!" Clearly angry, Kurt rose and stood glowering.

Candrew was not intimidated. "Did you take the white plaster cast from over there?" He nodded towards the back corner of the office.

Kurt took a step to the side of the desk and glanced over toward the corner. "Very observant. I'm going to have to elevate you to Sherlock Holmes' class, but *he* would have figured out what was in it, and you don't have a fucking clue. And I'm sure as hell not going to tell you." He started to edge around the desk.

Candrew persisted. "What happened to it?"

Smiling, Kurt gave a sweeping hand gesture. "I conscientiously stored it with all the other bones."

"You stored it? So you know where all the excavated bones are?"

The question was ignored.

"The Bureau of Indian Affairs keeps a close watch on what goes on out in that area." snapped Candrew, then regretted mentioning the BIA, though he couldn't quite put his finger on why he thought that was not a good idea.

"You know how many guys they have and how many square miles are out there?"

"It's not just the BIA; the FBI's also been helping, and here asking questions," Candrew said.

"You don't have to tell me that. I had to move all their silly yellow tape. They're the ones who ransacked the file cabinets and all our eminent professor's boxes of stuff." He waved his arm, gesturing around the office.

At that moment the computer screen flicked over to the screen saver, a dramatic view of Delicate Arch in the Utah National Park.

"What were you trying to find in the computer?"

With a broad grin, Kurt looked straight at him. "Me? I was just playing a few video games to break the monotony 'til the secret police turned up."

"You were searching his computer? What did you expect to find?"

Obviously, he had told Candrew as much as he was going to. Moving purposefully towards the door, Kurt said, "Don't forget to put the cat out and lock up." He left, striding off down the hallway. Candrew noticed he didn't seem to be carrying anything conspicuous.

Alone in Gavin's office, Candrew was unsure what to do and looked around at the disorganized piles of books, boxes and papers. He knew he should report the break-in to Security, but now he had the opportunity to do a little searching of his own. Perhaps he should go through the filing cabinets, or try to access the files in the computer. It was a tempting situation. He sat on Gavin's desk and pushed the computer mouse to clear the screen saver, but the dialog box came up, requesting user name and password. There was no way Kurt would have had time to log-off when Candrew burst into the office, which meant he hadn't been able to access Gavin's computer. Without the password, Candrew wouldn't be able to get into the files either, and again he considered pulling out the hard drive. The computer tower at the side of the desk had been dragged around and showed obvious signs of tampering. It looked as though several components had been removed, probably the hard drive had already gone. Was that Kurt's doing, or the FBI's?

Candrew stood pondering the evening's strange events. Why had Kurt told him so much? There was nothing stopping him from just getting up and walking out. The version he'd been given clearly implicated Teresa as the prime murder suspect. And she would have had no trouble getting tranquilizing drugs. She might even have had some experience darting bears since she'd been a summer seasonal with the Park Service. He thought about motive, and decided it was probably anticipated money from the sale of the dinosaur skeleton. She could certainly have used extra cash to help support her ailing mother. Candrew also thought it likely that growing up in a rough New York neighborhood had taught her to settle arguments with violence. But why had Chuck Semley never mentioned her? Everything would add up if she were part of a rival group, competition for Mishikubo. It would only have needed minor bending of the truth to make it all sound feasible. But then Candrew recalled she was listed on Gavin's budget, so he certainly knew her role. Could Gavin himself have had some sort of dual role, playing one side against the other? Was that what got him into trouble?

All Kurt's explanations seemed perfectly logical. But Candrew wasn't sure he could believe what he'd been told. And anyway, why was Kurt in Gavin's office? Candrew still had no idea what he was doing there, and why he was using a flashlight, instead of simply turning on the office lights. He didn't know if Kurt got what he was after before being interrupted. As Candrew locked the door and stuck the yellow tape back in place, he wondered whether the story had been carefully concocted to mislead him and obscure the real truths.

Chapter 27

Candrew leaned against the kitchen counter, reading the comics in the morning paper, while the microwave pumped its energy into yesterday's cold coffee. He had not slept well. Both his conscious and unconscious mind had been working over the significance of last night's bizarre encounter with Kurt Tadheim. On one hand, the account Tadheim gave was a little too glib and offered too easily, sort of like a well-rehearsed lie. On the other hand, everything seemed to fit. Candrew had no reason to question any of Kurt's assertions. They all added up; they were all consistent. Even specifics, like using seismic or taking the plaster cast from Gavin's office, matched the facts. But most important, he'd implied—though never actually said—that it was Teresa Polanca who fired the dart that led to Gavin's death, and he'd also claimed she was the one who'd shot at Judy and himself in the dinosaur canyon. Could he really believe one of the university's professors had murdered Gavin? Anyway, why would Tadheim tell him all this? Was this confession setting him up for something? And there was still the question, of course, of what he was doing in the locked office late at night.

*   *   *

The car in Candrew's driveway beeped its horn twice. He never knew when Renata would show up, but ten minutes after the promised nine o'clock seemed pretty good. She'd inherited a laid-back, *mañana* attitude from her Costa Rican mother and conducted her social life at a casual tempo. An invitation to lunch at noon was taken as a rough guide rather than a precise appointment and she could be there at twelve-thirty, but then again it might be one o'clock. In contrast, her professional life reflected the exacting and organized ways of a German father, and she was never late for class or a technical meeting. Candrew wasn't sure whether Renata considered taking him to collect his repaired Jeep Cherokee as professional or social. Either way, he was glad to get a ride. Grabbing his jacket and briefcase, he joined her in the car.

Renata negotiated a tortuous path through students on bicycles and haphazardly parked cars as she drove around to the auto mechanic north of campus. On the way, she listened enthralled as he described last night's encounter with Tadheim. Like Candrew, she was intrigued by the amount of information he'd volunteered, but had no penetrating insights.

"You think maybe Tadheim and his cohorts have got everything they want," Renata said, "and now they're sure it's too late for anyone to stop them, so they don't give a damn who knows."

"Possible, I suppose," Candrew said, "but there's still a lot of the skeleton left. The skull hasn't been excavated yet, and that's a major prize." He paused while she steered through an especially busy intersection. "There's also the little question of murder. They've got a long way to go before the statute of limitations runs out."

Speculation ended, at least for the time being, when Renata dropped him at the dealership where he regularly took his

Cherokee for oil changes and minor maintenance.

"Morning, Doctor. She's, like, ready to roll. Hang on, I'll get the keys." Rusty, a tall, thin youth with long, stringy hair spilling out from under a stained baseball cap, disappeared into the office and returned with the key ring. "The guy with the flat-bed truck, the one that hauled your car out of the canyon, cursed you every inch of the way. Said that track wasn't fit for goats." Rusty found that amusing. "You're lucky Dave was headed back this way. He drove it over for you. The mechanic at the Farmington dealership said both front tires was slashed real bad. The guy who done it didn't want you driving nowhere. He musta known you only had the one spare. All worked out, like, real well for you though— replaced that tire we patched for you last week, got yourself nice new Michelins." He winked at Candrew. "You're going to have to get the Jeep dealer in Santa Fe to fix your lock. Got messed up pretty bad when they broke in. Don't lock at all now."

That was news to Candrew. "There's not much worth stealing. Only some empty water containers," he added ruefully. "I'll take care of it. Anyway, thanks for getting everything done."

Candrew usually drove either deep in thought or with the radio on, paying no attention to the car itself. This morning he listened intently for any new squeaks or rattles and was sensitive to the way the car handled. Fortunately, it seemed just fine and no worse for its abuse. He parked in his usual spot and rifled through the old maps in the door pocket, the accumulated papers, and the other bits and pieces in the glove compartment: nothing of value. It didn't matter that he couldn't lock it.

Back in his office, Candrew pulled the desk chair up to the computer and logged on. His screensaver—a false-color, topographic map of North America—came up, but he flicked his mouse, maximized the e-mails, and started to work down the list, all eighteen items. A few, like the offer of cheap *Viagra* and the

Revised Price List for Maps, were deleted without being opened. Once again he made a mental note to unsubscribe.

Most of the routine messages received a superficial glance before being consigned to the trash. Candrew smiled as he read the one from Ray Connolly. Ray had prepared his taxes for at least ten years and in the process had evolved into his IRS conscience. Once more, he was gently needling Candrew to get together all the missing numbers needed to complete last year's return. Ray reminded him that back in April he'd filed for an automatic extension: *Perhaps between your forays into the field and the start of a new semester you could find an hour or two to get me the information on your consulting income for last year.*

Right, thought Candrew, so I can turn round and give a big chunk of it to the federal government. He picked up his list of things to do and added: *taxing assignment.*

The last e-mail turned out to be the most intriguing. It had no identifying subject. "*Dear Candrew Nor,*" it started, a bit formal for an e-mail. "*I knew Gavin Citalli. He was sort of a colleague. His death was unforgivable . . .*"

Unforgivable? Candrew thought that an odd word to use.

"*. . . and I need to talk to you about it as soon as we can. I heard you wer a friend and got th job clearing out his office. We have to talk immedaitely. It would be best if we meet off CAmpus. Can you come bymy house as sson as youc an? I'lll be there after*" Lots of mistakes and obviously unfinished, the message gave no address and no name. Someone was in a real hurry to get it sent.

He looked again at that ominous word: *unforgivable.* But who was in such haste to provide him with extra information? And why did the message end abruptly? With so many errors, and lack of a signature, Candrew was sure the writer was rushing to send the e-mail but got interrupted before finishing. He checked the e-mail address at the top of the screen: *tpol-zoo@unnm.edu.* Not much doubt about that, but just to be sure he rifled through one of the piles on his desk and retrieved her resume. This confirmed *tpol-zoo* was, in fact, Teresa Polanca in zoology. After Kurt Tadheim's insinuations about her role in Gavin's drowning, this message took on marked significance. What was so pressing that she needed to talk to him about Gavin's "unforgivable" death?

The short, dead-end road with widely scattered houses was deserted in the middle of the afternoon. Candrew parked outside Teresa's home, a small, single-storied house of no architectural merit, though it did have a well-tended, xeriscaped front yard carefully laid out with rocks, desert grasses and cacti. He followed the gravel path, unconsciously trying to make as little noise as possible, climbed three brick steps and rang the bell beside the heavy wooden front door. While waiting for someone to answer, he once again thought about the unfinished message with its implied need for secrecy, and wondered whether he should have parked in some less obvious place around the corner. Too late for that now.

No one came to the door. He rang again, and listened to the bell jingling in a distant part of the quiet house. Still no reply. The e-mail message that brought him here had ended, "I'll be there after . . " and, although it had a strong sense of urgency, it could just as well have meant "after nine o'clock" as "after noon" or "after dinner." He'd phoned her at the university, hadn't got a reply and assumed she'd be home. Now, he stood for a moment thinking that this had been a waste of time and was turning to leave when he noticed the front door was very slightly ajar. That didn't seem right, for the door not to be locked, even closed, when there was nobody in the house. Tentatively he pushed it open further and shouted, "Dr. Polanca?" The call went unanswered and he hesitated a moment before stepping inside, into the shadowed stillness.

The room was cheerless with little light penetrating through the draped windows. It was cooler than he expected. Although neatly arranged, the space had a lived-in look with newspapers,

DVDs and piles of books scattered on the sofa and coffee table. In the middle of the far wall was a curved, half-oval kiva fireplace that looked out of place in the conventional room; beside it a large cat lay curled up. Something about the way the cat was laying seemed odd to Candrew and glancing round he stepped over for a closer look. Actually, it was a small, black and white dog, its head twisted around at right angles to the body, dead. He took a step back and glanced quickly over his shoulder. He knew Teresa was a zoologist interested in small mammals as well as scorpions, although keeping dead animals in the living room was eccentric by any standards. The cool quietness of the room, with a dead dog against one wall, was unnerving, sinister. It sent a cold shiver through Candrew and the short hairs at the base of his neck stood erect. His instinct was to back out and leave. But curiosity prevailed, and he couldn't resist the temptation to find out what lurked in the rest of the house.

The kitchen was tidy enough with just a small stack of unwashed cups and bowls. In the middle of the wood-topped counter stood a large blender with the lid off, beside it an uneaten slice of pizza on an earthenware plate and a half-empty Chinese take-away box. A wall clock ticked off the seconds.

Next to the kitchen, a half-open door led into a large bedroom. The unmade double bed in the center was scattered with underwear and a nightdress. Apart from a comfortable chair and a small chest of drawers, there was little else except for a nightstand with a cell-phone charger, clock, and heap of cascading books. A reproduction of a Georgia O'Keeffe iris, framed in brushed aluminum, hung on the wall opposite a large window with half-drawn drapes. It all seemed normal enough to Candrew, but in the cool, quiet house he still felt apprehensive.

He called out once more: "Dr. Polanca?" Again, no reply.

At the end of a short passage were two more doors, the open one leading into a small bathroom. The door opposite was closed and he figured it must be a second bedroom. He knocked, heard nothing and entered cautiously. The small, almost square, room had been converted into an office. Down one wall, a computer, printer and scanner occupied a long table built over two small filing cabinets. Books crowded the bottom shelves on the wall beside the window, and there the upper shelves held a large number of small, creamy-white skulls.

Stacks of books and piles of papers were scattered over a desk in the center of the room. When Candrew stepped around it. Sprawled across the floor was the body of a woman.

Candrew stood immobile, horrified. Her tee-shirt was stained red and one leg was still draped across the overturned desk chair. "Good God," he said out loud. The woman needed help— and fast. She looked in bad shape: a pool of blood had seeped out from under her head and congealed in her dark hair. There was no sign of breathing. Stepping across, he felt for a pulse in her wrist, then tried her neck, but neither gave any hint of life. And the body was already quite cold. It looked as though she had been shot in the back of the head and the bullet had ripped a huge exit wound, tearing up most of the left side of her face. Nauseated, he rocked back on his heels and it was then that he saw the gun lying close to her right hand. Suicide? Without thinking, he picked up the gun, wondering if it was still warm.

"Don't move." It was said loudly and with authority. "Hold it right there, buddy." Before Candrew could turn round or do anything, the voice ordered, "Stand up slowly, get your hands over your head." He dropped the gun and did as he was told. "Don't try any funny business." Candrew was not planning anything humorous and was in fact shaking visibly, scared by the thought that if Teresa had been murdered the killer might want to eliminate him. From behind, hands patted him down thoroughly, though with a Polo shirt and slacks there weren't many places to hide a weapon.

"Okay. Turn around." He did and was immensely relieved to

be facing two policemen, even if one of them was braced with legs apart, holding a gun in both hands and aiming it at him. "You have the right to remain silent, . . ."

Candrew sat hand-cuffed in the back of the police cruiser watching the uniformed cops string yellow crime-scene tape round the house and listened as the officer in the front seat called for the ambulance, homicide squad and medical technician. He felt drained and his body was limp, like a balloon with the air let out. He tried shutting his eyes, but all he saw was a lifeless body with a shattered face in a pool of blood.

"Tell me, how did you come to be holding a gun and standing over the body of a dead woman?"

This was the third time Candrew had been asked that question, twice by a sour-faced, overweight detective called Gomez who grilled him for an hour and then left, and now by Detective Overhalten. They sat on opposite sides of a steel table in a windowless room at police headquarters with a young police officer standing silently in the corner. A tape recorder whirred quietly. Patiently, Candrew started his explanation one more time. "I got an unsigned e-mail . . ."

"What time would that be?"

"Well, I read it late morning, about eleven, maybe eleven fifteen."

"What time was it sent?"

"I didn't notice."

"You got a copy?"

"No. Anyway, it's still in the computer."

"You said it was unsigned. That strike you as strange."

"Yes it did. Most people put their name at the end of e-mails." Candrew adjusted his position in the metal chair, but got no more comfortable.

"So how did you find out who sent this one?"

"I looked at the top where it gives the sender's e-mail address. I recognized the name."

"And whose name was that?"

"Dr. Teresa Polanca."

"How well did you know her?"

"Not at all. I'd heard her give a lecture once, but never met her."

Detective Overhalten raised his eyebrows in a look of disbelief. Candrew ignored him. He thought about the zoology chair's comments on the tough life Teresa had endured growing up. It seemed sad that it had ended in suicide, or maybe murder, just like her brother.

Overhalten persisted. "But you didn't check the time she sent the e-mail?"

"I've told you that once. And I've already answered all these damn questions at least twice. Do we have to go through it all over again?"

"Professor, you're an intelligent man. The way this works is, I ask the questions and you answer them. Understand?"

"As I understand it, I'm entitled to a lawyer. I don't intend to answer another of your fucking questions until I get one." Candrew was exasperated by the drawn-out interrogation. He'd started by being cooperative and providing all the information he could, but the barrage of questions was getting to him, and it was slowly dawning on him that he was being treated as a suspect in a homicide, not as someone who was trying to help.

"I see." Overhalten stared straight at him with his lips pursed as though thinking, then he pulled a cell phone out of his pocket, turned away and mumbled something Candrew didn't catch. There was an extended silence before he clicked the phone off, picked up his brown manila folder, nodded to the police officer standing in the corner, and left.

The officer stood stiffly, unsmiling, his hands behind his back. Candrew swiveled in the uncomfortable chair. "There's been a terrible mistake." The policeman didn't answer, but the look in his eyes said it all: *Sure, they all say that*. Candrew continued to sit in silence, his elbows on the table.

In less than five minutes Overhalten was back, made a sweeping gesture with his hand and intoned, quite casually, "You're free to go. But don't leave town."

Dazed, Candrew mumbled "Okay," and made his way back along the passage toward the front of the building. He didn't pay much attention to the uniformed police officer coming the opposite way until Officer O'Hara greeted him cheerfully. "It starts with a speeding ticket and before you know, it's a murder charge. I just hate to see a professor turn to a life of crime." After the lengthy interrogation, Candrew was in no mood for jokes and could only manage a wan smile. "Looks like you need a chance to recover. Want some coffee?" O'Hara led him into a cramped room with vending machines down one wall and they sat at an orange Formica table with cigarette burns around its edges.

"I heard you found a corpse. Apparent homicide victim. Some woman professor at the university." In a small office, news travels fast and O'Hara already had most of the details.

"Yeah. But the gun was right there. Could have been a suicide. Why would a killer leave the murder weapon?" He thought back to the pool of blood and the shattered head. "Anyway, I'm glad they've let me go. I'd had enough of that relentless badgering. Do you guys always treat witnesses like that?"

"Only when they don't have their attorney with them." He smiled a broad, toothy grin and took a swig from his Coke can. "Don't be too hard on them, just doing their job—and they did let you go."

"True. I didn't understand that. Why would they suddenly change their minds. They convinced it was a suicide? Surely it wasn't just the threat of a lawyer?"

"I'll let you in on a secret. It wasn't an attorney that got you out; it was a medical examiner. The doc was certain the victim had been dead for at least four hours, maybe as many as six; that would seem to let you off the hook. Unless, of course, you were revisiting the scene of the crime." He tipped his head to one side, making the statement into a question, but not a serious one. Candrew stared straight ahead in silence. "And I'll tell you another secret—you were set up. Just about the time you went into the house the police got an anonymous call. I think someone was watching, waiting for you to arrive."

"That so? Did they trace the number?"

"Not yet. Whoever called was using one of those prepaid cell phones."

Candrew sat silently wondering what it all meant.

O'Hara stabbed the air with his forefinger and said, "The guys in forensics are real pissed off with you for picking up the gun and leaving prints all over it."

"Yeah, sorry about that. It just never occurred to me."

"You need to read a few more murder mysteries and a few less of those science books." He smiled at Candrew, who took a long drink of his coffee.

"What about the dog?" He was almost embarrassed to ask when the life of a human had been snuffed out.

"What I heard was that it had probably been kicked up against the wall. Probably died instantly."

What sort of person could be that cruel to a pet animal? But Candrew immediately realized that anyone who would kill another human in cold blood was not going to worry overmuch about a dog.

O'Hara downed more Coke. "Your college is providing us with lots of business right now."

"Why? What else has happened?"

"I'm surprised you haven't heard. One of your undergraduate students is missing up in the hills."

Candrew had a very uneasy feeling in the pit of his stomach. He found it difficult to frame the question, afraid of what the answer might be. "You have his name?"

"Jason Deverell. You know him?"

"Devereaux. Sure, I know him. I eat lunch with his father most days." So it was him. "How long's he been gone?"

"Coming up on three days, as far as we can tell. Nobody's seen him since Wednesday. His Jeep's gone too."

This information, with all its ramifications, jarred Candrew's weary brain into action. Gavin had been murdered, Teresa was dead, possibly murdered, and now Jason had disappeared. What were the chances he'd be found alive? Ted Devereaux and his wife must be frantic.

"Have you checked with his roommates?"

"The State Search and Rescue Team is doing all the usual things. That includes interviewing his compadres. No luck so far. Odd thing is, he had a date with a whole bunch of friends to go to a dance in Española that night. They say he never showed up. Didn't tell anybody he was going someplace else."

"Where are they searching? Was he by himself?"

"They think his girlfriend was with him, though that's not certain. We're looking for her as well. Anyway, they're sure the Jeep's gone. Hopefully, they'll see it from the air. I heard it's bright red, which should help the 'copter crew spot it."

"Helicopter?"

"Yeah. Those Search and Rescue guys are real pros. There isn't much to go on, though. Only information they've come up with so far is from an old Hispanic who lives out in the foothills. As far as he can remember, the Jeep went past his place in the early evening going towards the mountains. He thinks there could have been two people in it. But he don't see none too well. Can't rely on what he says: too many years, too many tequilas."

Chapter 28

Sunday morning was blustery with fast-moving clouds driving east, dragging their shadows across scrubby foothills and over the mountains. Candrew, blissfully unaware of all this, slept until mid-morning. He would probably have slept well into the afternoon if Chile hadn't put two large paws on the bed and licked his nose in a silent demand for food and attention. Candrew rolled onto his back, scratched his beloved dog behind the ears and laid contemplating cracks in the ceiling, slowly easing back into consciousness. Events of the previous day had left him drained and worn.

Memories of Teresa came flooding back: the lifeless body, the thick, curly black hair matted with congealed blood, the pistol. He thought of the last time he'd seen her when she was with the vet at the Casa del Rio restaurant. And he recalled her enthusiastic zoology lecture on the sex lives of scorpions, remembering how she sketched a graph on the blackboard. But in the instant of that clear mental image, he realized she was drawing *with her left hand*. Abruptly he sat up in bed, excited by this insight. Slowly the pieces were coming together, or rather, not fitting together. Teresa was left-handed and the gun had been lying by her right hand. She'd been shot from the right side producing that ragged exit wound on the left. If she'd fired the pistol herself, it would have been the other way around. This was no suicide. This had to be murder. Did the police know she was left-handed? He needed to tell them, soon.

Chile was persistent and eventually Candrew caved in to the dog's demands. Donning his robe, he let him out while he hustled down the driveway to fetch the fat Sunday newspaper in its yellow plastic sleeve.

Back in the kitchen, still mulling over the killing, he stood with the refrigerator door open, scanning the half-empty shelves trying to decide what to eat. Before he reached a decision, the cell phone ringtone intruded and he scurried around, finally tracking it down to his jacket pocket.

The caller ID showed it was Judy. "Good morning. How're you feeling?" Candrew asked.

"Glad to be out of that damned hospital and almost back to normal. But I'll tell you one thing, it's going to be a while before I'm playing any racquetball. And if I quit exercising, I'll have to eat a lot less or my weight'll shoot up. Anyway, I didn't phone to talk about diet; I called to tell you I have some exciting information."

"About the *T. rex* site?"

"How did you guess?" He heard her chuckle. "Mindi Allison, the woman I play racquetball with—when I'm able to—called to say she'd used some of the fancy equipment over in astronomy to check out Gavin's CDs."

"You mean the ones you borrowed from his office? Or the ones I took from the house?"

"Both. Remember they didn't do anything on the CD player or the computer, we thought they might be used for data storage? That's exactly what they were. Mindi set up my laptop so it'll display all the images and I've got a set of printouts as well."

"Great! I'm eager to see them. What do they show?"

"You'll see. I could bring them over right away. You going to be there for the next hour or so?"

"Yeah. I'll be here working on my taxes all afternoon. Come on over anytime." He paused, thinking about logistics. "Are you mobile?"

"It's a bit tricky with my bandaged leg, but nothing I can't handle. I shouldn't have any trouble driving to your place."

"Good. And I've also got some interesting news for you," Candrew said. "I think I've finally figured out where Jason Devereaux fits in. I'll explain all that when you get here."

Candrew slumped onto the wood chair at the kitchen table, excited by the prospect of seeing Gavin's data storage, hoping it would help clarify the scraps of information he'd been piecing together.

After a hurried brunch, Candrew dialed the police office. The phone rang several times before clicking over to a secretary. "I'm calling for Officer O'Hara."

"I'm sorry, sir, he's not in today," the woman replied in a flat, official tone. "He'll be back first thing in the morning. Can I take a message?"

"I'm Candrew Nor. I just wanted to give him some new information about the death of the university professor, Dr. Polanca. Is there a cell phone where I could reach him? Or a home phone?"

"I'm not supposed to give out personal information, but . . . can you hold a minute?" He heard her talk quietly to someone in the office. "You're Professor Nor, correct?"

"Yes."

"Okay. It'll be alright to give you his cell phone number."

Candrew wrote it down and immediately called O'Hara. "Hi. This is Candrew Nor. Hope I'm not disturbing you, but I've just stumbled on a piece of information that might be helpful in your investigation of professor Polanca's death."

"That so?" He seemed dubious.

"Yeah. Polanca was left handed, but the pistol was lying by her right hand, and she was shot from the right." Candrew was talking fast, gushing. "If she'd shot herself, it would have been from the left."

There was a moment's silence while O'Hara digested what he'd heard. "Fascinating. You might be interested to know that we'd already decided the wound wasn't self inflicted so your ideas fit right in. We're treating this as homicide."

"That makes sense," Candrew said. "It's hardly likely someone would shoot themselves behind the ear. That's real awkward."

"Right. Anyway, she was shot with a different gun."

"How d'you know that?"

"The caliber of the bullet we recovered was smaller," O'Hara said. "And the gun probably had a silencer—none of the neighbors heard a shot."

"The murderer must have been pretty dumb to use a gun with a different caliber if he was trying to set it up to look like suicide. That hardly fits, does it?"

"No, it doesn't." There was a long pause. "Here's what we think happened. The assailant came into the house, and since there's no evidence of a break-in, we assume he was known to the victim. He shot her. One of the graduate students told us the professor had several guns and always carried one when she was doing her field research, since she was alone out in the wilderness at night. The perp sees one of her guns on the shelf in her office and gets the idea of making it look like she shot herself. So he takes it down, wipes off his fingerprints, and throws it on the floor beside her. Probably did it on impulse, never considered the different firing characteristics of the two weapons." O'Hara paused to let his ideas sink in. "There was none of Dr. Polanca's prints on the gun — and the deceased don't usually wipe off their fingerprints. The only prints we lifted were yours. Luckily, we had them on file from the investigation of the break-in at the Citalli house."

"Impressive sleuthing," Candrew said, delighted to hear that the police were making progress. "You have a suspect?" he asked.

"You mean, apart from you?" O'Hara let the silence run on. "You're still only an outside possibility."

Candrew was glad to hear that. He took a deep breath and changed the subject. "You have any information on Jason Devereaux?"

"As a matter of fact, I do. But right now it's confidential. Anyway there'll be a press release in an hour, so I'll tell you, but keep it under your hat 'til then. One of the search teams found the Jeep abandoned on a Forest Service logging road. The young guy who owned it, and the girl who was with him, are both fine. They've been located over in Española."

"Thanks for telling me that. I really appreciate it, and I'm glad to hear they're safe." He put the phone down with an audible sigh of relief.

Keeping books was just fine with Candrew. Bookkeeping was not. One of his few indulgences was paying someone else to complete the tax forms that were needed to provide the IRS with an acceptable, and hopefully legal, tax return. Trying to compile the receipts and forms required for all the allowable expenses, different sources of income, and deductible items was a miserable chore. He'd already spent several evenings trying to organize his poorly-filed paperwork.

The ringing doorbell broke his concentration, but, after several tedious hours of hunting through credit card records, bank statements, and service receipts, any distraction was welcome. Candrew went to the front door, let Judy in, and guided her down the passageway to his office.

Limping along, Judy followed Candrew. "I heard about Teresa Polanca's death," she said. "It was on television last night. They didn't seem to know whether it was suicide or homicide. But either way, coming so soon after Gavin's murder, that's real scary. Two faculty deaths in a matter of weeks."

Apparently, the local television channel hadn't mentioned it was Candrew who'd found the body. After he told her, and explained why he didn't think it was suicide, they shuffled into his office in a subdued mood.

Judy dropped her satchel down beside the chair. "It raises lots of new questions about Teresa's relationship with Gavin."

Candrew agreed. "I'd just about convinced myself she was the person who darted Gavin. It's still possible, I suppose, but I'm beginning to have doubts. If there really are two rival groups, as Anne suggested, that would put a whole new perspective on this affair."

"Could Gavin and Teresa have been, like, on the same side?" Judy asked.

"Well, it's starting to look that way. I guess it would have teamed them up with Mishikubo and Semley. But who's the competition? Kurt Tadheim? He's certainly shaping up as a prime suspect."

For a moment, both considered the implications and stood quietly with their own thoughts.

Candrew pulled up a stool for Judy and said, "Death and taxes. Life's certainties." Eager to move on to his information about Jason, he explained, "We've had our death, actually two deaths, and ironically I've spent most of today working on taxes." He grimaced at the thought of both unpleasant businesses. "I want you to take a look at one of these pieces of paper."

"You're kidding. You got me here to help with taxes?" She shook her head. "Wrong person. This is my first year in a real job and with the pittance I got as a graduate student, I never had to worry about handing money over to the IRS."

"I don't need help with taxes. You're off the hook." Candrew laughed. "No, that's not why I wanted you here. It's that I think life's two certainties might be linked."

"How so?"

Candrew pushed his chair back from a desk covered in irregular piles of receipts and IRS forms that were avalanching into one another. "As you know, I do consulting work for oil companies and in the eyes of the IRS that makes me partly self-employed. I get to deduct business expenses which include my office bills for electricity and gas. Here, take a look at the bills for the past twelve months."

Judy, clearly puzzled, was obviously wondering where all this was leading, but she scrambled off her perch and hobbled up to the desk.

Each month's utility costs were lined up in a neat column of twelve numbers. Candrew laid his open hand across the top half of the page covering the first six months of the year. "Okay. See the first column."

Judy did. It read: *July, August, September, October, November, December*, except that Candrew had only used the capital letter for each month: J, A, S, O, N, D — Jason D! Judy whistled softly and smiled—the sort of smile that comes with pleasure, the pleasure of a problem solved, an unknown made known.

"Jason D. Then that note in Gavin's file wasn't a name, and certainly not about Devereaux's kid. Probably, a schedule, or maybe a budget."

"Exactly. And remember, we never had anything that actually said *Devereaux*, only *JASOND*. I went back and checked the papers we took from Gavin's file and every time he wrote it, he used all capitals."

"That means we can eliminate Jason being one of the people involved with the *T. rex* dig," Judy said, nodding her head. "That's quite a big step forward."

Candrew pushed his slipping glasses back up the bridge of his nose. "And it explains why I could never figure out where he fitted in. Nothing he did ever seemed relevant to the project. And if you can believe Kurt Tadheim, he flatly denied knowing anything about Jason."

"But it doesn't alter the fact that he's still missing," Judy said.

"How did you know that?" He raised his eyebrows and tilted his head to one side, questioning.

She shook her head. "Bad news always travels fast. I heard it from Mindi. I don't know where she got it."

"Well, it isn't true any more. I talked to the police just before you came and they've found him—unharmed. He was out in the hills in a Jeep with his girlfriend and had an accident. I don't have all the info yet. I'll call O'Hara later and see if he can fill me in."

"Let me know what you hear. I'm just glad he's alive." She leaned back on her stool, relieved that the complications involving Jason were getting resolved.

Chapter 29

Judy twisted around and settled on to the stool in Candrew's office. "Right. Now it's my turn," she said, obviously impatient to show Candrew the results of Mindi's data processing with Gavin's discs. Bending over, she hauled her laptop out of its carrying case and also pulled five large manila envelopes from the back pocket and laid them on the table.

Candrew glanced around for an uncluttered surface for the computer. Failing to find one, he carefully merged several piles of tax receipts to create enough space. While Judy booted up the laptop, he flipped through the pile of oversized envelopes.

The label on the top one was *CD 1–Beethoven 216*. Judy had already told him that the CDs contained data not music, so he wasn't surprised to find several photographs showing the CD contents. All were of the *T. rex* excavation site. Although most gave detailed, close-up images of individual bones or small clusters still encased in their host rock, a few showed the hummocky surface textures that Candrew had seen himself. Now he knew what they were—imprints of superbly preserved dinosaur skin, but the photos showed a greater variety than those exposed at the site, and a few were clearly feathers.

Awed that this *T. rex* was unique in so many fascinating ways, Candrew quickly scanned the prints in envelopes two and four. Both contained photographs of mounted *T. rex* skeletons from various museums as well as prints and line drawings of bones taken from books and monographs. The third envelope produced a variety of shots illustrating different stages of the work, and although they clearly showed the area on the canyon floor, unfortunately none included people. This set also had maps at various scales and these appeared to be detailed working plans where periodic updates had been sketched in. At the end was logistical information and several pages of budgets. Candrew smiled when he saw "JASOND: $130,000."

The contents of the last envelope, number five, were the most dramatic. As Candrew eagerly studied the prints, Judy leaned over and tapped on her computer. "I've got the full set of images up and running."

"Just give me a minute to finish going through these." He peered intently at each of the prints. They were aerial photos of the dinosaur excavation pits and even minor details were clear because they'd been shot at low altitude, or high magnification. But what excited him most was the way they vividly showed the relationship of the site to the arroyo and adjacent areas. Where had Gavin got these? They must have come from Mishikubo's surveillance.

The tire tracks and the Bobcat Candrew had seen when he was in the canyon convinced him there must be another, easier, access to the site. Chuck had confirmed this on the drive back from their last visit when he'd told Candrew about an alternative route from the north which, although more winding, was generally flatter and wider. This meandering access, with its northerly route showing up clearly in the photos, eventually led to a gravel county road. It was considerably longer than the path he'd taken with Judy, but this wouldn't have been a problem for the fossil thieves if trucks could have been used to haul in the Bobcat, water, plaster of Paris and tools—and to cart out the bones embedded in rock matrix. From the photos, it looked as though the route had recently been widened at a couple of points.

"It's important to see where this other route goes." Candrew said to Judy, flipping through the prints a second time, and noting again the excellent skin impressions. Thinking aloud, he mumbled, "Skin preservation on that *rex* is so amazing. I wonder how much there is?" He answered his own question. "They won't know that until they've finished the preparation and got it all out of the rock. And I'd really like to see what internal organs they find." He thought back to the X-ray images in the lime-green folder stolen from Gavin's office, ones similar to those Mishikubo had shown him.

As Candrew muttered to himself, Judy stood waiting patiently until finally, he remembered she was there. "Apart from the route information, I don't think the photos add much to what we already know," he said. "Except to underline what a superb specimen this is—and the fact that it's about to disappear into some private collection."

Judy sensed his anger. She was well aware this had become a major issue for Candrew.

Together they spent the next half hour working through the images brought up on the computer screen. They'd seen most of them already, but there were interesting new ones, although not much extra data. However, near the end were six detailed maps, one covering the canyon and the excavation site. It was hard to flip from one screen image to the next and figure out how these additional maps related to the location of the main site. Candrew was especially intrigued by the third map since it had a location marked with a prominent star, and he remembered Gavin had used a similar icon on his map showing the second dinosaur site.

Turning to Judy, he asked, "Can we print these?"

"Sure. Should be easy enough to hook up your printer." She fumbled with the cable and its USB connector and in ten minutes they had hard copy of all six maps.

The floor offered the only large, uncluttered surface and they spread them out, kneeling, trying to match edges and combine the overall layout. Candrew lined up the starred location with the excavation site and for reference jotted down the direction: east-north-east—*ENE*. He was convinced the star identified a second dinosaur site on Gavin's hand-drawn map and penciled in '*T. rex*', which gave *T. rex ENE*. That had a vaguely familiar look—and then he knew what Gavin's phone message to Mishikubo meant. *SECREXENE* was *2nd rex, east-north-east*. Obviously, he'd been trying to get these details to Mishikubo. Intently Candrew examined the map again.

As he wrote down the coordinates for the new dinosaur location, he commented to Judy, "You know, if Gavin really was double-crossing Mishikubo with another group he'd hardly be handing over this new information."

Judy wasn't so sure. "Yeah, but we don't know if this new location is real. Or even if there's anything there."

"Only way to find out is to go there."

After Judy left, Candrew poured himself a scotch, but before he got back to doing taxes he e-mailed Chuck Semley suggesting that they revisit the dinosaur dig on Tuesday. Candrew was eager to make a more detailed examination of the excavation equipment, especially the back hoe. It could give crucial insights. And the other piles of tools scattered around could well provide additional information.

He also wanted to follow the northerly route out from the site to see if there was anything pertinent, especially tools or tracks that would provide clues about the rival group's attempt to collect the fossil bones. And, of course, the new dinosaur site, SECREXENE, was less than a mile away and he was anxious to hike over and see if excavation had been started there. Also, at the back of his mind, was the idea that a second site visit might provide information that could help identify Gavin's murderer—or Teresa's.

Chuck's reply came later that evening. *"Tuesday no can do. Push back a day to Wednesday and you got yourself a deal. Let me know ASAP if that works for you. If yes, will meet you in Farmington at McDonalds' parking lot, under the Golden Breasts ;-)."*

Candrew knew that people who have never taught in a university think a schedule with only three hours of lectures a week leaves a lot of leisure time. It doesn't. Candrew wasn't sure that the following Wednesday would work and checked his monthly scheduler. Missing the first meeting of the university senate wouldn't be a problem, he was only an alternate anyway. And the meeting with two new graduate students could wait one more day. Everything else was flexible. He sent a reply saying he'd be there and added, "Make sure nobody gets shot at this time."

It was early evening before Candrew finished his taxes and got all the details about Jason in a phone call from Officer O'Hara. It seemed that he'd been with his girlfriend driving a dirt road through the National Forest when he took a bend too fast, slid on the poorly-maintained gravel and rolled. The Jeep hit a massive ponderosa pine, ending up on its side, jammed against the tree. Elena, the girlfriend, had her left leg broken in the crash, but Jason, although badly shaken, didn't suffer major injuries. The Jeep was too heavy to move and, with its front wheels pointing in different directions, was clearly undriveable. Jason improvised a crutch for Elena and it took them most of the next day to struggle down to the main road and hitch a ride into Española. O'Hara ended the brief account by saying, "It seems Jason didn't want his father to know he was up in the hills with his Hispanic girlfriend."

Candrew smiled to himself. "I'm not surprised. Well, thanks

for bringing me up-to-date." He was about to put down the phone, but hesitated. "Anything new in the Polanca murder investigation?"

O'Hara took a moment to reply. "They're still collecting evidence. It's early stages. As far as I know, there's no suspect and they don't have a motive. Nothing seems to have been stolen from the house, so it wasn't a robbery gone bad." There was another pause. "They'll want to interview you some more later."

After talking to O'Hara, Candrew mixed himself a margarita, dropped a disc in the CD player and sat at the shaded end of the patio listening to the Mendelssohn violin concerto. His attention soon slipped away from the music as he tried to make sense of everything that had happened in the last couple of weeks. What started out looking like a sad, accidental drowning of a close friend ended up being a homicide. And if that wasn't upsetting enough, it had been followed by a second one. These two deaths were almost certainly linked to the illegal *T. rex* excavation. But what exactly was the connection? At least he now knew Jason had nothing to do with it.

Obviously, the wealthy Mr. Mishikubo desperately wanted a *Tyrannosaurus rex* skeleton for his collection. Semley was organizing the acquisition for him with Gavin as the geologist and Teresa and Kurt helping. Everything about the illegal dig appeared to have gone okay until some sort of feud developed. Puzzled, he sat tapping his teeth. What had provoked that? And had Teresa sided with Gavin. Was that why she suffered the same fate? Or could he believe Kurt's claim that she was the one who darted Gavin and shot at Judy out at the fossil site? If not, who murdered Gavin? And did the same person kill Teresa? Still lots of questions. Candrew was glad he and Chuck were going back to take a more detailed look at the site. Last time they'd left so quickly, they must have overlooked all sorts of things, and the canyon needed a much more thorough search. The wide range of equipment being used in the excavation had the potential to provide lots of information. Also, he thought it important for them to follow the alternative, northern route and see if anything was hidden there. And deep down, he had to admit to himself that he really wanted another look at that fantastically preserved dinosaur skeleton, even if it was only the skull. But his overriding concern was to get to the site of the second *T. rex* fossil. What would he find there?

Chapter 30

Chuck drove his Dodge Ram too fast for the tortuous, rutted track that twisted between drab gray bushes and isolated clumps of grasses. With no early-morning breeze, the dust kicked up by the truck hung in the air behind them. Bouncing through potholes and sliding across sandy patches on their way toward the site of the dinosaur excavation, they were following the same route that Candrew and Judy had taken the previous week. Although more challenging than the alternative way into the canyon that had shown up on the aerial photos, it was considerably shorter; however, the final section could only be negotiated on foot. Conversation was sporadic in the noisy, lurching vehicle and Candrew was forced to grip the hand-holds tightly. He passed the time scanning the subtle variations in the sedimentary layers of the eroded sandstone cliffs they were passing. And he saw occasional Anasazi remains, like the one Judy had fallen into and the ruin they'd both climbed up to.

Candrew's drive over from the university had been uneventful. The surprise had come when he reached Farmington and met Chuck in the McDonalds' parking lot—with him was Kurt Tadheim. Chuck casually introduced Kurt as one of Mishikubo's team, assumed they knew each other, and left it at that. Now Kurt sat in the rear seat saying little. Silent and unsociable, but nervous and attentive, he was scanning the road ahead. Why had Chuck brought him, Candrew wondered? Were they planning more seismic or just picking up equipment? Or did they know about the second dino site and plan to visit that?

Forty minutes later Chuck reached the end of the poorly marked track and pulled onto a flat sandy area, killing the engine. The air conditioning died and the outside roasting air poured over them. All three shouldered their packs and set out in single file up the narrow trail, following it over the ridge and down to where it widened onto the flat wash. This time, there was no doubt about the location of the *T. rex* excavation and nothing had been done to camouflaged it with tarps. The trenched area that had held the animal's skull was hardly recognizable, and the skull itself was gone. Several tracts on the arroyo floor had been scooped clean, leaving no remaining evidence of the fossil dinosaur, and only white plaster of Paris flakes and the many tire marks showed recent activity.

Chuck stopped abruptly. "Well I'm damned. They didn't waste any time looting mother nature."

Candrew thought that was ironic. What Chuck really meant was: *someone else looted it before we got a chance to do it.* Surveying the area more carefully, Candrew tried to make sense of the confused tire ruts interlaced over the sandy floor of the wash, especially near the sandstone cliffs. Distinct tracks led toward the north end of the arroyo where they disappeared around a low bluff and he realized they must lead to the longer, but flatter, way out.

The three of them had been scouring the canyon floor for half an hour, searching the remains of the excavation site for information, when a lone figure came quietly out from under the dark overhang of rocks on the east side of the canyon. Most of his face was shadowed under a large, wide-brimmed hat and, although vaguely familiar, it took Candrew a moment to sort through confused memories and identify the figure out of context: Joel Iskander. What was he doing here? The last time he'd seen Joel was at dinner with Renata.

"Stick 'em up!" He'd stopped about thirty feet away and stood with legs apart, holding a large pistol with both hands. "I've wanted to say that for real ever since I watched cowboy movies as a kid."

Candrew and the others weren't sure if he was serious.

"Do it!"

He was serious.

"You," he pointed the gun at Kurt Tadheim, "pick up the packs. Put them in a pile over there." He indicated a spot by a large boulder, roughly twenty feet away. Sullenly, Kurt took their three packs and dumped them in a heap, a heap that now had all the precious water they'd packed in.

With a wave of the gun, Iskander motioned Kurt back to the group. He addressed the three of them. "Empty your pockets. One at a time."

Chuck threw down a small pistol—"I keep it as protection against rattlesnakes"—a compass, folded aerial photos, GPS, cell phone and half a dozen packets of gum.

Kurt emptied his pockets with a casual, resigned look. There was little in them, just a notebook and maps. But Joel didn't seem to notice he'd ignored the fanny-pack pocket.

Candrew had a hand lens, penknife, Brunton compass, notebook with pencils and a digital camera. Hoping for charity, he asked, "Okay if I keep the Brunton? Just sentimental value. I've had it ever since I was a freshman."

"Don't worry, you aren't going to need it much longer. You're close, very close, to the end of your illustrious career."

"And just what the hell does that mean?" Candrew demanded.

"*Sad, very sad.*" Iskander started talking like a newscaster giving the latest update on a developing story. "*Today the bodies of a geologist and his assistant were found in a remote canyon. The pair was reported missing three weeks ago, but an intensive search failed to find them. They had gone to the deserted area to study the rocks as part of a research project sponsored by the University of Northern New Mexico and apparently got lost . . .*"

Chuck broke in. "No dice. I know this whole area, better than a flea knows a dog. I could get us out of anywhere."

"If you were alive," Iskander said in a patronizing tone.

"So, the cops'll find bodies riddled with bullet holes?"

Iskander grinned. "Nothing so crude. You'll get a big shot of sedative," he patted his back pack, "and then just lie there in the desert sun and dehydrate. You'll die of thirst. And it'll look as if you got lost out in the canyons hunting those special rocks." Like so many things Iskander said, *special* carried a hint of sarcasm. "The search and rescue boys will probably find your bodies long after the coyotes and buzzards. One more unfortunate desert accident." And with his arrogance, he couldn't help adding, "Exactly the way I made Gavin Citalli's death look accidental."

Candrew stared, shocked, anger welling up. He took a step towards Iskander who retreated a yard but kept the gun pointing directly at him.

"*You* killed Gavin!"

"Gavin drowned; we all know that." Again, it was said with dripping sarcasm.

Candrew had heard similar words before—from Kurt Tadheim. Just where did he fit in? Right now Kurt seemed to be on the wrong end of Iskander's gun. But he was the sole survivor of Gavin's original team, now that Teresa was dead. Scowling, Candrew stared at Iskander. "And you killed Teresa as well? What happened, didn't she want to be part of your happy family?"

"Ah yes, our scorpion lady. She should have stayed away from fossils and stuck with living things. Maybe she'd still be one. But no, like Citalli, she wanted to have everything done by the experts. You know, people in universities are worse than the unions—can't cross the boundaries into someone else's academic turf. Though why they worry about job security when they've all got tenure beats me."

There was a faint smile on his face the whole time he was talking. He seemed to be enjoying this. Candrew could understand murdering someone in a blind rage, or even for revenge. What he could not understand was killing someone for convenience or money. He glanced at Chuck who gave an almost imperceptible nod. He seemed more optimistic than Candrew felt.

Iskander was getting impatient. "Okay, start walking up the trail that skirts those cedars." Kurt took the lead with Candrew behind him and Semley last. Joel, gun in hand, followed. As he watched Chuck's slightly irregular walk, he took a perverse delight in saying, "Limping already? Doesn't bode well."

"Old war wound. Not something I did on this trip." Chuck slowed as he talked and the gap between him and Joel closed a little. "Got it in a fire fight in east Africa. Spent four years there with special forces and saw a lot of places they show on *National Geographic* specials." Chuck kept talking, hoping he might be able to distract Iskander, or at least lure him into making a mistake, but he wasn't optimistic.

On the far side of the ridge, the descending trail steepened and narrowed and they stumbled on loose rocks and gravel down towards the floor of the next canyon.

Candrew's thoughts drifted back over his life, now about to end so abruptly. Centered around science, it had been fulfilling and productive. But there was a lot left unfinished. Was this how his wife Penny felt when she faced the end of her life, when she knew there was no cure for the cancer and death was inevitable? Candrew wished that somehow he'd been a lot more attentive, though there was nothing he could have done. Now he realized that somehow it was the little things that were depressing him: advice he'd not yet given to a graduate student, ideas for Judy that he hadn't got round to, the uncompleted manuscript, and all the other unpublished research. How would Renata take his death? And what would happen to Chile and Pixel?

He struggled down the trail, exhausted, his throat parched. Sliding into melancholy, he told himself to snap out of it. Candrew thought of himself as an intellectual, not a man of action, at least not in the James Bond mold. But even he had to admit that he wasn't likely to be able to think his way out of this mess. Their predicament demanded action—and soon. His thoughts ran ahead to options, of which there were precious few. Was it better to be shot now, rather than slowly dehydrate in the arid desert? The situation was grim, but Candrew was not the sort to wallow for long in self pity. He could only think of one possible ploy and . . .

Suddenly, Chuck slipped on a patch of loose pebbles and fell sideways, twisting as he went down and ending on his knees, facing up the trail. Iskander instinctively took a step toward him, but immediately checked himself keeping the gun leveled. Candrew, about twenty feet ahead, heard the clattering stones and Chuck cursing. Turning, he shouted, "You okay? Need help?" Iskander glanced at Candrew for an instant. It was all the time Chuck needed. He had both hands on a roughly rectangular rock about the size of two house bricks. In one fluid motion he swept it up and hefted it straight at Iskander. The gunman saw it coming and angled away, but not fast enough, and the rock slammed into him, striking his elbow and ribs. His arm jolted up and the shot he fired was too late, the bullet whining off high into the brush, the sound reverberating around the canyon.

Chuck followed the rock, springing forward, head down. Though built like a bear, he moved with the lithe grace of a big cat and hit Joel full in the stomach, knocking him off balance and landing with his full weight on top. He brought his knee sharply into Iskander's crotch, making him grunt in pain. The gun clattered onto the gravel and Chuck grabbed it. Iskander lay on the ground in a fetal position, groaning and whimpering. Semley looked down at him with contempt—he'd seen mutilated men die making less fuss.

Chuck aimed the gun at the prone figure and checked that the safety wasn't on. "Give me half an excuse and I'll blow your fucking head off." Keeping the weapon pointed at Iskander, he reached round to the back pocket of his pants and with his left hand pulled out a short length of cord. He tossed it to Candrew. "Here, tie his hands behind his back."

"Drop the gun! Now!" Kurt had moved so that he was protected behind one of the big sandstone blocks. The pistol in his hand was aimed at Chuck.

For an instant, Chuck wondered if he could fire fast enough and accurately enough. Not much of Kurt was exposed and he decided he couldn't. Reluctantly he let go of the gun and it rattled onto the dry pebbles.

"Move away from it. Well away."

As Chuck shuffled a few more yards up the trail, Iskander was on his knees, and with obvious pain stood and hobbled over to retrieve the weapon.

"Kurt, what the hell is going on?" Candrew was dumbfounded.

Kurt stepped out from behind the protective rock. "Get over there with Semley." He waited while Candrew complied. "You misjudged your alliances—fatally. Joel Iskander and I go way back. We're old friends. Now you could say we're sort of business partners." He didn't elaborate.

It took Iskander several minutes to recover and then Chuck and Candrew were marched down the trail at gunpoint. The sun had moved well into the cloudless western sky and it was still baking hot, making the rocks shimmer in the early evening heat haze. The dry air sucked moisture out of their bodies and no breeze shook the stunted junipers while they made their way across the bottom of a narrow, steep-sided arroyo.

As they started up the far side, a single-engine plane, flying low, cruised over the canyon rim scaring up a flock of turkey vultures. Iskander responded immediately. "Stop. Don't move." He was yelling loudly over the aircraft engine noise. "And don't try anything." With two pistols aimed at them, Candrew and Chuck had no choice but to obey. All four stood motionless among the rocks and bushes as the plane made a course adjustment before heading over the cliffs. The aircraft engine noise faded into the distance, somehow leaving the desert quieter than before. For the first time Iskander looked a little unsettled and he stared after the plane until it was completely out of sight. He took a long drink of water from his flask and then made them start moving along the trail again.

"Where the hell are you marching us?" Chuck wanted to know.

"No point in letting you die near the *T. rex* site. Nobody would believe you got lost that close in. So, you have the misfortune of hiking a few miles before you meet your maker."

Candrew tried to use the one piece of information he thought they could bargain for their lives. "You won't be able to sell the dinosaur because you don't know where the money is coming from." A slim chance, but their only chance. He was gambling that Gavin and Chuck had been the sole contacts with Mishikubo.

"You're quite right." It was Kurt who answered.

Iskander broke in. "We'll just beat the crap out of you 'til you tell us." He paused, then laughed. He took his hat off, pushed back his hair and resettled his hat. "You'll be relieved to know, we won't have to do that. What you don't seem to realize is that it doesn't matter where Citalli and his paleo-pals were getting their dollars. We've got our own buyer. This dino is on its way to Denmark and he—or is it a she?—isn't going to be lonely because it'll be part of a large, very large, private collection."

Candrew had trouble covering up his disappointment.

Iskander noticed. "And we're both going to Denmark with it. When the *rex* gets mounted in Copenhagen, maybe we'll add a brass plaque dedicating it to you. Homage from one set of bones to another." Iskander grinned at his version of humor.

The tiring trek through the canyons continued for another forty-five minutes before they stopped for more water—at least Iskander and Kurt did. They made the two captives sit on a rock and wait.

One question had been bugging Candrew and, even now that his personal situation was dire, he had to ask. "What was so important about the white cast that you took out of Gavin's office?"

"You've got to love academics!" It was Iskander. "Just a few more hours to live and he's got to get all the details sewed up. Dot all the *i*'s, cross all the *t*'s. No stones left unturned—appropriate for a geologist."

"And it was only the tip of the iceberg." This time it was Kurt talking.

Iskander grinned. Chuck and Candrew saw nothing funny.

"In that plaster cast was the tip of our *T. rex*'s tail," Kurt explained. Unique. This is the only time that the small fragile bones from the very end of the tail have ever been found. Is this a great dino, or what?"

Damn, *damn*, DAMN, Candrew thought. Yet one more reason why such an amazing *tyrannosaur* should not be disappearing into a personal collection. In spite of his own desperate and precarious state, he was bitter about the theft of this unique fossil, but resigned.

"Okay, let's move." Iskander waved the pistol and again they continued their odyssey, walking in silence, the only sounds made by their boots crunching on the loose gravel and the occasional pebble rolling ahead of them. A lone raven, appropriately black, gave a mournful cry as it soared past the canyon wall.

The setting sun had become partially obscured by irregular, low clouds and the light was fading. Furtive figures moved quietly among the high rocks and scattered brush, communicating through hand signals. The group leader glanced at his folded map, checked a small GPS, and consulted a text message. He indicated a possible pathway through the boulders and bushes with his outstretched arm and then with his hand motioned downwards and to the left. The others understood that they were to follow the path for a while then work their way down to the canyon floor. With quick and precise athletic execution, they moved silently and cautiously forward. They could hear Iskander's voice carrying in the dry desert air.

"Sorry your last night won't be a comfortable one—the Hilton was fully booked." Although he couldn't see Iskander's face in the gloom, Candrew knew he was grinning. "Still, I'll do the best I can. And just think, you'll both get a full night's sleep. Kurt and I are going to be up half the night guarding the pair of you."

Parched, Candrew found it difficult to be sympathetic.

"How much farther we going?" Chuck asked.

"I'm sure you'll have enough energy left to make it the half mile up and around the next bluff. A small arroyo comes in from the side and you can sack out in the sand. Call me soft hearted."

They trudged forward and rounded the rock outcrop.

"Freeze!" It seemed an unlikely demand when the temperature was in the high nineties. Candrew was tired, thirsty and emotionally exhausted. It took a minute for him to register the significance of the five men facing them with leveled rifles. But Iskander was sharper, more alert. He squeezed off a quick shot, crouched and rolled to his right, trying to scramble up behind the rocks, hoping to escape in the twilight. The rifleman at the end of the line was fast and accurate. Iskander yelped in pain as the bullet tore into his thigh. Outnumbered and outmaneuvered, he sat dejected, both hands grabbing his leg to staunch the bleeding.

"Nobody move," the leader ordered. All five of the team wore bulky camouflaged jackets that Chuck recognized as bullet-proof vests, but that information was lost on Candrew. The armed men flashed badges, identifying themselves as FBI agents.

"Mike," the leader shouted, "get me the medical supplies." The tallest of the five agents swung off his pack and pulled out a kit with the prominent red cross.

While two of them attended to Iskander, the others took Kurt's gun and searched him. Although the agents knew Candrew and Chuck were prisoners they were still uncertain about allegiances. Both were pushed up against the sheer canyon rock face and patted down for weapons. Finally, satisfied that none of their captives was armed, they set off down the trail. Iskander needed help walking, and in the fading light progress to the waiting trucks was sluggish.

The tortuous, slow hike, illuminated by the agents' flashlights, took several hours—but at least Candrew and Chuck now had some water, food, and a guarantee of safety. And the emotionally-draining threat of imminent death had been lifted. They were, of course, still suspects in an illegal dinosaur excavation.

Chapter 31

The FBI agents demanded all the details and their thorough, and frequently aggressive, debriefing lasted several hours. Only then were Candrew and Chuck driven to the Holiday Inn Express on the main road through Farmington, but by the time they checked in it was nearly two in the morning. Exhausted, they agreed to get together for a late breakfast.

Next morning they walked over to McDonalds and, after wolfing down a couple of Egg McMuffins each, got Candrew's car from the parking lot. Reinvigorated, they set off back to the canyon to retrieve Chuck's truck, and as they drove the deserted road through scattered shrubs of the western landscape, Candrew called Renata. No reply. He left a short summary of all that had happened and asked her to drop by his house and feed Chile and Pixel.

When he flipped shut the cell phone cover, Chuck quipped, "You were a bit cavalier. Made it sound like a casual Sunday school outing."

"Well, I didn't want to worry her. And anyway we're survivors — the action's all over."

"I just hope you're right. And I hope Mishikubo sees it that simply." Chuck grinned.

They recovered Chuck's truck without incident; it was just as they'd left it. On the drive back Chuck followed Candrew as far as Farmington, then turned south onto Highway 550, beeped his horn, waved, and headed to Albuquerque.

Still disoriented by everything that had happened, especially the prospect of premature death, Candrew drove at a leisurely pace arriving home late in the evening. On the way Renata called to tell him his animals had been taken care of and to ask if he'd like her to come to the house and cook dinner for him. He'd tactfully declined her offer.

Candrew slept late, partly because he actually needed extra sleep, but mainly because he was putting off facing all the particulars that would have to be wrapped up. It was just before lunch when he eventually made it into his office at the university. He knew there would be more grueling interviews with the FBI, the police, and the lawyers. And, of course, the television and newspaper reporters were enthusiastically tracking the story, each one wanting an exclusive with complete details. As if to underline that point, Maria, the secretary, called to say the university TV station was asking for an interview. "They suggested some time around four o'clock."

"Yeah, I guess that's okay," Candrew said reluctantly.

The phone continued to ring every few minutes. Finally— after being soundly criticized by an aggrieved caller for disturbing a dinosaur that was part of the earth and should have been left alone to preserve the balance of nature—he decided it was time to head for the dubious haven of lunch in the faculty lounge. All those e-mails could wait until he got back. As he locked his office door the phone was ringing again.

"Here's our local hero!"

The group of regulars, seated around their usual corner table, greeted Candrew with humor, but also with relief that he'd survived his ordeal in the canyons.

Arlan Dee pulled back a chair for Candrew. "Can't say I liked Tadheim. He was an arrogant bastard. Though I never thought he'd get involved in murder. What's happened to him?"

"He's in police custody waiting to be formally charged. And, of course, so is his accomplice Joel Iskander, the archaeologist. He seems to have been the master mind."

There was a barrage of questions from around the table, everyone wanting to hear the inside story.

Candrew told them about Mishikubo and his determination to get a *T. rex* as the culmination of a lifetime of collecting dinosaurs. "But none of the bones ever got shipped to him, even though he was providing all the money for the excavation. Gavin had been the only recipient of any cash, and the only direct evidence of wrongdoing, so the case against Mishikubo himself is circumstantial."

"What about that mercenary guy who was working for him?"

"Chuck Semley? He's free at the moment. But with Mishikubo's money and high-powered attorneys, I'm sure he'll never be found guilty of anything."

"So this wealthy Japanese tycoon won't get his *T. rex*? So who ends up with it?"

"My guess is, it'll become the star attraction at some lucky public institution, probably the National Museum of Natural History." He smiled at the thought that Tadheim and Iskander were also going to end up in public institutions—but not on display. "It's probably the best preserved *tyrannosaur* ever found, a fantastic mummified fossil with its internal organs still intact. Really rare. And such incredible detail, even showing it had feathers. Now it'll get carefully studied by professionals, which is what it deserves."

There was silence for a moment. Candrew sat sipping his coffee, thinking that if a rival group hadn't got involved, Mishikubo might have acquired a superb *T. rex* for his collection. And perhaps even gotten a second one if the new site to the north-east proved to be a productive dinosaur location. Then he'd have rounded out his collection with a pair of *T. rexes*—male and female? Candrew was delighted that the new location would get the expert attention of paleontologists, and that any fossils would eventually be mounted and displayed. Unless, of course, the dino on Indian land was put up for auction and Mishikubo bought it.

Candrew strolled back to Kinblade Hall after lunch, thinking about his own role in the whole affair. Was he technically an accomplice? Although he'd visited Mishikubo in Los Angeles and had been to the site twice, he'd not been involved in any of the illegal excavations and didn't stand to profit from them. But he was aware of them. He had only told the BLM and the FBI what he knew of the dinosaur excavation after his first visit to the canyon and the unprovoked shooting. Thank God he had. Ultimately, it was this information that had gotten the FBI monitoring the site, accumulating evidence to build a case and document criminal activity. For Candrew and Chuck Semley that had been a matter of life and death.

He'd been back in his office less than a minute, summoning up the courage to see how many e-mails were waiting, when the phone rang once again. His impulse was to let it ring, but he answered and was glad he did. It was Anne.

"Are you alright?" she asked. "I've been e-mailing you and tried calling several times. I saw the report about the arrests on the TV morning show. That was a close call."

"Right. I'm glad to have gotten out of it alive. But I'm fine now, although I've got to admit I was pretty scared a lot of the time. For a while there, things looked really grim." He felt no need to adopt a macho stance with Anne. "I'm just glad it's over."

She hesitated. "I've been helping Marge for nearly a month now and I'm sure she can get on well enough by herself. It's time to get back to my own life and I've decided to fly home on Saturday."

"I'll be sorry to see you go." Without pausing, he added, "Would you like to have dinner tomorrow?"

"Yes, I would, but I really feel I should spend that last evening with Marge."

He hesitated, disappointed. "How about lunch?"

"Sorry, but I'm going to be busy packing and everything."

There was a pause and, hunting for an excuse to see her one more time, Candrew asked, "You need a ride down to the airport?"

"Yeah, but you'll have to get up before dawn, it's an early flight."

"No problem. I'm happy to do it."

They talked for a while about how Marge was coping without Gavin before Anne hung up.

Even though physically revived, Candrew was still emotionally drained. Being so close to death had exacted a toll. From now on, he'd look at life in a very different way and begin to think about what mattered, although after losing Penny he knew what was really important to him. The things he valued most needed to be stressed more; so much of life was taken up with trivia. He had to get back to a life that was less fractured, put on an even keel, and he resolved to spend more time with friends, with Renata, and the people who meant most to him. He needed to quickly establish a routine for the new semester and catch up on everything he'd let slide during the past frenzied weeks. Now he'd have time for the research he thrived on, be able to contribute more to the project with Judy, and finally complete that unfinished manuscript on the Utah sandstones.

His thoughts rambled back over the events of the last two

weeks and he felt lucky to have survived. Odd how a death sixty-five million years ago could echo down through time and lead to more deaths. An historic find like this should have been celebrated not the reason for a painful sense of loss. He still felt pangs of guilt about Judy's injuries, even though they were minor and she was sure to recover completely. Anyway, they were mere trifles compared with the tragic deaths of two faculty members.

Candrew sat thinking about Anne and how much he'd enjoyed her company. He was sorry she was leaving. Staring blankly across his office, he glanced at the clock, a few minutes to three—and it's Thursday afternoon. "Good God! My graduate seminar starts in two minutes." He grabbed a couple of textbooks, and the three-ring binder with his lecture notes from last year, and hurried down the hall to the lecture room.

THE END

T. WRECKS

Glossary

This murder mystery is set in the southwest where some of the words are of Spanish origin and may be unfamiliar or pronounced differently. So, here's a very short Glossary:

Arroyo: a natural stream channel. Typically dry most of the year, except for flash floods.

Banco: a solid bench built as part of a wall. Usually made from adobe.

Canales: drainspouts extending out from a parapet of a flat roof and designed to protect adobe walls from falling rainwater.

Chile: the usual New Mexican spelling for "chili".

Duke City: Albuquerque (named for the Spanish "Duke of Alburquerque").

Huevos rancheros: (literally, "ranchers eggs"). Fried eggs served with lightly-fried corn tortillas and refried beans topped with tomato-chile sauce.

Katchina Doll: doll carved in the likeness of a spiritual katchina figure and given to children.

Kiva: a partly buried, roofed circular religious ceremonial chamber. Can sometimes be rectangular.

Latillas: (pronounced with the Hispanic 'y' for the 'll') Juniper or alder branches installed between vigas on ceilings.

Mesa: (Spanish for "table"). A flat-topped hill.

Petroglyphs: rock art made by chipping away the surface layer to expose different colored rock underneath.

Piñon: the piñon pine is a small to medium-sized tree that grows above about 5000 ft in the U.S. southwest and Mexico. It produces edible nuts.

Portál [or Portale]: quite different from a portal, this is a covered porch that has a beamed roof over an outside patio and usually runs along the side of a house.

Posole: corn and meat stew, traditionally with pork, spiced with red or green chile.

Vigas: beams made from debarked tree trunks that are exposed in a ceiling where they hold up the roof.

OTHER CANDREW NOR MURDER MYSTERIES

FALSE PERSPECTIVE. Murder in the Art Department

ICY MOON. Murder in the Astronomy Department

*   *   *

PRAISE FOR *FALSE PERSPECTIVE*

"Well written, exquisitely structured mystery that kept me guessing till the end. Introduces us to a score of well-developed characters, all participating in some way in art, its collection, and its provenance."

Bruce Merchant. Author of "Moonkind"

"The book is beautifully written, and informative about stolen art, which makes the book a fascinating read. Barker (a professor like his protagonist) is an excellent writer and takes us on a ride through academia at a small New Mexico university."

M. B. Grana. Author and winner of the
2000 Willa Cather Award for 'Begoso Cabin.'

"The mystery's characters are vividly portrayed. I am a fan of mysteries (and) look forward to Candrew Nor's next mystery."

Stephen Jones, poet, author and Amazon reviewer.

"A hidden gem. A great "who dunnit" that will keep you guessing to the end. I loved some of the characters."
Hopeyouhavebetterluck. Amazon reviewer.

"Captures the northern New Mexico landscape and culture . . . while giving the reader a glimpse into the Santa Fe art scene"
Susan Cummins Miller, author of the
Frankie MacFarlane mysteries.

PRAISE FOR *ICY MOON*

"A jolly good read." Judge Stephen Weiss, Santa Barbara.

"I like this book. In 'Icy Moon' [Barker] mastered his prose—streamlining it to where nothing's wasted. The story tells itself, as it should—and well. This time around Mr. Barker weaves an unusual story, blending alleged alien signals from Europa, a moon of Jupiter, with down-to-earth murder."
Stephen Jones, poet, author and Amazon reviewer.

"I found 'Icy Moon' enjoyable and the science plausible. It came up with an interesting and novel twist on the idea of an intelligent extraterrestrial signal, and I thought that the aftermath of discovery, and the murder here on earth, well thought out."
Dr. Cynthia Phillips, NASA Jet Propulsion Lab

67201127R00176

Made in the USA
Charleston, SC
06 February 2017